# BuZz RIFF

## Also by Sam Hill

*Buzz Monkey*

# BuZz RIfF

## SAM HILL

An Otto Penzler Book

———

CARROLL & GRAF PUBLISHERS
NEW YORK

BUZZ RIFF

Carroll & Graf Publishers
An Imprint of Avalon Publishing Group Inc.
245 West 17th Street
New York, NY 10011

AVALON
publishing group incorporated

Library of Congress Cataloging-in-Publication Data is available.

ISBN: 0-7867-1390-9

Printed in the United States of America
Distributed by Publishers Group West

*For Liz*

# BuZz RIFF

# CHAPTER 1

*I* *didn't much like my new client, and I wasn't* particularly upset when someone shot him. I didn't like him for the same reason no one else liked him—he's an embarrassment. But he is also a tenured professor at the university, occupying the Latham Chair of Southern Studies. And he was my client because I needed the twenty thousand dollars.

He'd become my client on Thursday at 8 A.M. at his office in the Institute of Southern Studies, located in a restored antebellum on Lumpkin Street. Significantly, the smallish mansion was situated across the street from the university proper, and marked only by a tiny sign tucked under a small round boxwood shrub. If the university had its way, I am sure they would have exiled him even further away, say to the campus of Georgia Tech.

I drove by twice before I found the sign, and saw the small, discrete, crushed-marble driveway that led beside the white mansion and around to a lot. In back were four parking spaces, two with small white-on-brown university-issue "Visitor" signs. Both of the other spaces were unlabelled. In one sat a new, silver Mini Cooper, and beside it sat an older maroon Jag XKE, the one with the long phallic hood. A small chrome badge for the Bonnie Blues, a Confederate version of the DAR, was bolted to its license plate.

I stepped out of the truck, drained the last of my extra large White Hen coffee-of-day and tossed the empty disposable foam cup in the pickup, where it joined three empty Heineken beer bottles, an old rusty jack handle I'd picked up from the middle of the highway, and a crumpled up Dunkin' Donuts bag. If every pickup in America cleaned the trash out of the back bed simultaneously, landfills would overflow like a shaken-up Coca Cola soda can.

I wore a black T-shirt, black jeans, and hiking boots—a little more somber than my normal attire, but I'd learned a long time ago that things went smoother if you fit the client's stereotype. My girlfriend Amanda had told Pope-Scott I was a mercenary, and so he'd be expecting a mercenary. I dressed to expectations.

*Girlfriend.* There's a word that seems like it belongs in the sixties. But all the alternatives—lover, significant other, seem too clinical for me. So I'm stuck with girlfriend. The word, that is. I'm not stuck with Amanda. Not that I'm saying I'd mind being stuck with Amanda.

In April in Athens you can sometimes feel the heat before it starts to register on the thermometer. This morning was cool, but the air held an implication of the warmth to come. In the distance, I could hear a faint chant, most likely football players over on the new Astroturf practice field, readying themselves to improve on last year's number three national ranking. (I had my doubts, since they'd graduated the entire offensive line and lost three underclassmen to the NFL. But in Athens in the spring, anyone with doubts about the Dawgs is best served keeping those to his or herself.)

There was a brick walk that led from the lot to a back door. The back door, though, was heavy gray steel spotted with a line of shiny brushed-steel and brass locks. On the door a square sign in italics read, "*Please Use the Front Door, y'all.*" Someone had scrawled a Nazi swastika in bright red marker across the face of the sign.

I made my way noisily along the loose driveway. Despite my misgivings about the new client and working this close to home, I was delighted to be working. This day a familiar riff of adrenaline rippled up my spine. I tasted the acrid dryness of excitement in my mouth, and knew I was fighting a grin. I was buzzing, and to quote REM, "I feel fine."

In the front another small brick pathway wound from the driveway to a set of broad stone steps leading up to a massive wooden porch. The wide porch was painted gray, and was home to six white columns and a dozen or so large green wicker rocking chairs. At the top of each corner of the ceiling a security camera swiveled and blinked. I noticed there was the faintest trace of mildew on the wall where the porch connected to the face of the house. Other than that, the place was immaculate.

I stood quietly on the porch, then closed my eyes and rotated my neck in one direction, then reversed it, hearing the soft pops of my stretched tendons. I hung my arms loosely down by my side, and shook them out. I raised one hand to eye-level. It still trembled noticeably as I rang the bell. There was a soft muffled ding dong somewhere deep in the house.

Answering the door, to my mild surprise, was not an ancient Bill Robinson-style butler, but a pretty blond woman in her midtwenties. She wore a red linen sheath dress, so simple it must be very expensive, a single gold strand necklace, and diamond earrings of noticeable size and clarity.

"Mr. Keirnan?" she lisped softly. "Mr. Keirnan" came out as a lazy, seductive roller coaster of a dozen or so syllables, all lovely. There are two primary Southern accents, mine, a flat nasal cracker drawl, and hers, the soft, refined accent of people from Virginia and the Atlantic coastal cities. Or put more simply, I sound like Tommy Lee Jones and she sounded like Scarlett O'Hara. I nodded.

"Come in, please. Jay is waiting for you," she pulled open the door with her right hand and beckoned me in with her left. There was a small gold filigreed band on the third finger of her left hand. I stepped inside, and onto a thick Oriental carpet. We stood in a long hallway with doors off to each side and a sweeping staircase to my right. She closed the door behind me, and I felt a gun barrel press into my back. "I'm so sorry, but would you mind raising your hands? Are you carrying a gun, Mr. Keirnan?"

I raised my hands and shook my head as she expertly and thoroughly patted me down. "What are these?" she asked, feeling my knee braces.

"Knee braces. I had a bicycling accident many years ago," I answered.

"You can put your hands down," she said sweetly. "Thank you for not making a fuss. Some people really get huffy, but Jay gets death threats daily, and we have to take them seriously."

"What happens when people get huffy?" I said as I turned. She slipped the gun into the drawer of a small wooden table and pushed it shut. There was a bouquet of carnations in a vase on the table, the blooms doubled in the mirror behind it. I watched her pale blue eyes in the reflection.

"It's usually just the guys. Having a girl search them offends their pride. Then I have to insist," she answered, smiling with her perfectly lipsticked mouth. "My name is Caron, C-A-R-O-N." She pronounced it like "Karen," with a hard C and soft second syllable.

"You drive the Jag," I guessed.

She looked at me appraisingly. "All those muscles, and a brain, too. I'll have to keep an eye on you Mr. Keirnan."

"Top," I answered.

"Top," she answered. "Jay will see you now, Top. Please follow me." She opened a set of French cut-glass doors to our left.

# CHAPTER 2

*W*e crossed *through a smallish parlor with a* fireplace and deep red walls filled with framed scenes depicting Southern life before the War, and into what was once probably the dining room. It appeared to now be Caron's office, and was dominated by a large modern-looking desk holding an HP computer. The desk sat in a sideways U in front of a huge floor-to-ceiling window. Her desktop held no pictures or personal items at all.

Facing the desk across the room was a wall of shelves filled with books. I could see the books were shelved two deep, English style. Against the far wall, beside a painted door, sat a row of black metal Steelcase filing cabinets, the shallow kind where the files run perpendicular to the wall. On them were neat stacks of papers. From a quick glance, they appeared to be academic submissions in various stages of preparation and editing.

She caught my look. "Jay still edits a journal on Southern history. They haven't taken that away yet," she said tightly. Walking briskly past me to the door, she tapped lightly and without waiting for a reply, opened the door. She stepped through and stood to the side, announcing me, "Professor Pope-Scott, Top Keirnan."

"One moment, Caron, Mr. Keirnan," said the man sitting at the desk with his back to us, tapping on a keyboard on the credenza. While we waited for him to finish pecking in his message, I looked around curiously. The corner room we stood in was blindingly bright, partly because of the yellow paint and white trim, but also because of the huge windows that filled the two outside walls. The wall behind me held four framed certificates, diplomas from Emory and Harvard, a 1991 Pulitzer Prize, and an appointment to the Latham Chair. The last certificate was hung upside down. Every frame was perfectly aligned.

Against the inside wall to my right stood a row of flags on poles. In the midst of the flags, about halfway down, squatted a horizontal, glass-topped display case about four feet square. There was also the walnut desk and matching credenza, several tables filled with neat stacks of books, magazines, and papers, and two high-backed upholstered chairs.

Several minutes later Pope-Scott finished his e-mail, sighed and stood. He turned, and I saw a handsome fortyish man, perhaps six three or four, with rounded shoulders and a thick shapeless waist. His hair was thick and wavy, brown streaked with gray, and he wore it long and combed back. He dressed in a dark, woody sport coat, cream-colored button-down shirt, and crisply creased brown slacks. Instead of a tie, he wore a brown and red paisley cravat. In the pocket of his sport coat was a neatly folded solid red silk kerchief. The clothes looked fashionable and new, but the overall effect was that of a Victorian fop.

The professor stepped out from behind the desk and sailed across the room toward me, head back, back stiff, smile beaming, and right hand outstretched. On his other hand were a large pinky ring with the Harvard crest, and a small filigreed wedding band, just like the one Caron wore. The hand I shook was soft and dry.

"Mr. Keirnan, delighted to make your acquaintance," he said. "Positively delighted."

"Bullet-proof glass, Professor?" I asked, nodding to the windows, although I knew the answer from the thickness and slightly bluish cast of the glass. The question was just theater, intended to reinforce the mercenary stereotype.

"Why, yes, sir. How did you ever know? And call me Jay, Mr. Keirnan, please. I insist," he said. Listening to his exaggerated Southern phrasing and syrupy accent, I realized I might not be the only one playing to type. "Do you do a lot of this?"

"How can I help you, Professor?" I answered. I didn't want to explain that I *had* done a lot of this, before my ex-employer Shaw's Mercantile Marine had fired me. Somehow I didn't think telling Pope-Scott that I now earned my living as a librarian would build client confidence. Behind me I heard the click of Caron's heels on the small stretch of hardwood floor between the thick carpet in this room and the one in her office. She didn't close the door.

Pope-Scott looked a bit lost at my question. He gave a quick sideways glance toward the open door that led to Caron, looked back at me and pursed his lips. After a moment he answered, "Well, how refreshingly direct. I fear I am not that used to directness, being an academic and a historian at that. Indeed, I myself have not had great success with directness." He laughed at his own joke. His laugh was a horsey thing that bared his top teeth and threw his head back.

"Please, sir, sit. Can I offer you coffee?" I nodded and he called in a slightly raised voice, "Caron, would you mind? And if we have any pastries or something, that would be absolutely delightful, my dear." He led me to the two chairs in front of the desk and turned them so they faced each other. He placed me in the one with its back to the window, facing the row of flags and the glass-topped case. "How's this?"

"Fine, thank you," I said.

He sat, crossed his legs at the knee and eyed me carefully. "Are you comfortable, Mr. Keirnan? Pardon me, but you seem to be fidgeting a bit there. Is it the chair? Perhaps that sun on your back is too warm?"

"I'm fine," I said.

"Are you sure? Perhaps you'd rather have herbal tea, something without caffeine?" He raised his hand to signal Caron.

"I'm fine, really," I said. I didn't explain that with the adrenaline rushing through my blood vessels like a subway train through a dark tunnel, it was almost impossible for me to sit still. I willed my legs to stop bouncing, and laced my fingers tightly in my lap. There was nothing I could do about the tic under my left eye.

He didn't appear completely convinced, but decided to drop it, and instead said, "Well, let us be direct. Mr. Keirnan, I need you to recover the flag stolen from that case, stolen by my cousin, Styrell Wooten."

"Why did he steal it?" I asked, leaving aside for a moment the question of how anyone managed to steal something from a building with deadbolted steel doors, inch-thick glass, and an expensive camera system.

"Why to sell it, of course, sir. Its value is incalculable. Any number of collectors would pay millions for it. Millions," he said with emphasis.

He paused and then melodramatically touched a finger to his lips and rolled his eyes skyward, before extending his hands, palms outward toward me. "Wait, let me take a step back."

He dropped his hands to his knee and leaned forward. "What do you know about the Confederacy, Mr. Keirnan?" I hesitated, debating whether or not to admit that my family had been in the South for two hundred years and two of my great, great, great-grandfathers had fought for the 25th Georgia under Johnston. Before I decided, his hands flew up, he uncrossed his legs and bounced to his feet, "Perhaps a quick history lesson would help."

He eagerly strode to the row of flags and straightened. Caron brought in the coffee, a bamboo tray holding a frail china pot and two matching cups and saucers, a tiny pitcher of milk, a small bowl of Equal artificial sweetener packets and two spoons. On the side of each saucer next to the cups were two Fig Newton cookies. Pope-Scott stood waiting impatiently, coffee forgotten. As Caron stood, she turned quickly away and I thought I saw a tear leak down one cheek.

"Mr. Keirnan, let me tell you about the Bloody Red Rag, the battle flag used to staunch the blood from General Stonewall Jackson's mortal wounds, arguably *the* most important artifact remaining from the War Between the States."

I pointed at the squat case and raised my eyebrows. He nodded, and held up a finger to keep me from interrupting his flow, "Let us start our discussion on that fateful day in May of 1863."

When the university had appointed him to the chair eleven years ago, the wunderkind Pope-Scott had just won a wheelbarrow full of prizes, including a Pulitzer for his first book, *Johnnycake: The Scotch-Irish in America*. His appointment by the university made him the youngest chaired professor at the University of Georgia since World War I and one of the most popular—his lectures were standing-room only.

But then he'd written *Dixiecaust*, which critics called "a rancid mix of half-lies and pseudohistory" and my personal favorite, "the Mein Kampf of the trailer park set." Supposedly, the university lost one hundred million dollars in alumni and corporate donations the first year after *Dixiecaust* was published. And because Pope-Scott had tenure, there was not one darn thing they could do about it. Except try to pretend he didn't exist. So Pope-Scott now gave lectures in his office to audiences of one while his wife cried in the office next door.

# CHAPTER 3

*M*y mini-course on *Civil War history took* two hours. He was a pretty good speaker, and if he was rusty now, he must have been something when he was in lecturing shape. I learned a great deal about the strange and brilliant General Thomas J. "Stonewall" Jackson but very little that might help get the flag back.

At the end of the lecture, we left it that I would confer with my partner and get back on whether we thought we could help them. I promised to drop by the next day at the same time with a decision, and if the decision was "Yes," spend some time getting started. As Caron closed the big door, it was clear from the look in her eyes that she never expected to see me again.

I eased up the driveway with both windows rolled down, and a hot humorless breeze cut through the cab. I didn't bother to turn on the air conditioner because I was only going to the bank, a few blocks away. Suddenly a horn blared, tires squealed, and I saw a red BMW whip across the near lane of traffic and into the driveway, spraying a hatful of the white marble pebbles across the immaculate lawn. I stood on my brakes and slid an inch or two on the loose surface as the BMW skidded to a stop a foot or so from the front bumper of my pickup.

The woman driving threw a fist with one finger extended skyward at whoever had blown the horn. She climbed out of the con-
vertible, slammed the door emphatically, stood and raked her thick
curly hair back over her head. Walking around to the driver's side of
the pickup, she dropped her large, round sunglasses down her beautiful nose. Gillie Marcianello Lynfield stands five ten in stocking feet,
and her eyes were level with mine. She leaned on the door, bringing
her face a quarter inch too close for comfort. She knew it.

"Hi, Top. I thought it was you," she said. "Long time no see."

"How do you walk in gravel with three-inch spike heels?"

"We've had this discussion before," she said.

"I don't remember the answer, if I got one," I said.

"So how are you? How's Benny? Maggie?"

"Fine, Gillie. How are George and the kids?"

"They're good, real good," she drawled. "Robbie's enrolled in the
Christian Academy out on 441 now. He likes it real well. He's got a
teacher that seems to be taking some interest in him. Finally. And he
gets along with all the kids in his class. The baby's started doing that
thing they do before they crawl, you know, where they scoot around
on their butt. So she'll be hell on wheels here before long. And
George is George." Her broad smile cut big dimples into her cheeks.
Gillie had been the second person I'd hired when I'd started Polymath. For five years we'd been partners in building up the business.

I started the company as a front, a way to get a W-2 for the IRS,
but it's become a real business with a building full of computers and
real employees paying real taxes. Gillie helped me build up Polymath,
and now her new company, AWS Research, is our largest competitor.
AWS, like Polymath, is in the business of fact-checking manuscripts,
speeches, and the like. Most of the revenue comes from correctly
rewording and attributing quotes.

Take "In the land of the blind, the one-eyed man is king." Last
year a national newspaper ran a story attributing it to Lincoln. People
usually think that quote comes from the Bible because it's got that
Old Testament plague-pestilence-and-mutilation ring to it. Which

isn't that far off. It was actually said in 1523 by Erasmus, the Dutch religious philosopher. Had the paper called Polymath, we would have told them that and sent them a bill for a hundred dollars. The newspaper fact checker had probably gotten lazy and searched the quote on the Internet, the world's largest source of IRIT, information that really isn't true.

Most of our researchers work in the big libraries at the University of Georgia as their primary job and for me on the side. What we do ranges from checking a single quote for a speechwriter to completely fact-checking manuscripts. We have over a hundred semiregular clients, and have annual contracts with a dozen or so Fortune 500 companies, publishers, management consultancies, and law firms. At least we had annual contracts with a dozen or so large companies; now we have half that.

"How's business?" she said on cue. She bit her lower lip and smiled and leaned an inch closer. I tried not to look down her scoop-necked blouse at the swell of her breasts. I felt a disloyal stirring in my jeans.

"Not too good," I admitted.

"You shouldn't have fired me. I wouldn't have founded AWS and taken all your clients."

"You shouldn't have tried to steal money that I was getting paid to deliver to an insane drug boss and I wouldn't have had to fire you," I said.

"You should have let us make some real money at Polymath and I wouldn't have had to steal," she said.

I shook my head, tired of the exchange. "Speaking of money, I'm going over to the bank. There's some problem with the account. You wouldn't know anything about that would you?"

She smiled and shrugged philosophically. I saw a bead of sweat start on the corner of her hairline and leak down. "Aren't you hot standing out in the sun like that?" I asked.

Her eyes flashed. "Don't worry about me. Marcianellos are genetically designed for the hot weather. Good Neapolitan olive skin."

I looked in the mirror and saw Caron standing at the window, staring out at us. "I need to get going, Gillie. Glad to hear your family is doing well."

"Fuck you, Top," she said sweetly. She spun around and marched back to her car, climbing in and quickly backing out onto Lumpkin without looking. A tan truck with a landscaping logo on the side slammed on its brakes. The trailer it towed jackknifed and slid sideways four feet. Behind it a young woman in a Hyundai compact screeched to a halt, missing the trailer by a millimeter. She sat, her mouth opening and closing like a guppy, her hands in a death grip on the wheel. Gillie peeled out without looking back.

# CHAPTER 4

*J*eff *Nelson was a large, heavy-set man, a few years younger* than my early thirties. He wore a short-sleeved yellow shirt that struggled to stay tucked into his khaki pants, a brown patterned tie, brown loafers, and horn-rimmed glasses. His hair was blond and thinning and fell unbankerlike over his forehead. His round, smooth face bore a strong resemblance to the Gerber Baby.

I'd been sitting a few minutes when he came and fetched me from the small waiting area. "Welcome to Fourth Federal, Mr. Keirnan. Great to finally meet you. I'm Jeff," he said. I shook his hand.

"Call me Top, Jeff, everyone does. Give me one minute, there's a quote I want to write down," I held the *People* magazine open with one hand and with the other scribbled a few words on the outside of the ochre folder that contained Polymath's latest bank statements. We keep our own proprietary database of quotes in addition to dozens of books and databases. While I wrote, Jeff shifted from foot to foot uncomfortably.

"Mr. Greenfell is waiting for us," he said. "Let's go this way, please." We weaved our way back through a maze of small cubicles demarcated by chest-high dividers. From the ceiling of the big room hung a dozen or so small white signs, with titles like "Corporate," "Small Business," and "Trade/Forex."

Each cubicle we passed had a small nameplate, including one that read, "J. Nelson, Relationship Banker." I glanced inside and saw a neat desk and a small sideboard with a computer. The screen displayed a news page with a picture of a man covered in blood standing in front of smoking rubble. I'd seen the picture a dozen times. The man in the picture was a doctor at an abortion clinic, and the latest victim of the serial bomber who called himself the Sword of Michael. On the desk sat a gold-framed family portrait. At a quick glance, the Nelsons had an infant and a toddler, and she and the kids were also blond. The only other personal touch I could see was a blue back-support resting on the dark gray chair.

We worked our way over to a small glassed-in office in the corner. Inside sat a thin man wearing a stiff blue pin-striped suit, a blue and red regimental tie, and a white cotton button-down shirt that was carefully pressed, but unstarched, meaning Mr. Greenfell still ironed his own shirts. Probably one promotion away from sending them out, two away from once a week dropping off a bag of shoes off to be shined. We gazed at the top of his head as he used a yellow marker to carefully highlight sentences in a densely worded contract. Jeff tapped on the metal door frame with his knuckles, "Mr. Greenfell?"

The man looked up. His face was thin and he wore a very serious expression, possibly to disguise that he was no older than Nelson. "Please, come in. Sit down," he said, motioning to two chairs in the small space in front of his desk. Jeff bumped his way into the chair closest to the wall. When we'd set up the account five years ago, there had been a different person in this office, and instead of Jeff, we'd been assigned to a woman named Naomi, and everyone had been smiling and we'd been offered iced tea. Today, even Jeff tried to look somber.

"Thank you for coming in, Mr. Keirnan. Is Gillie, er, Mrs. Lynfield, joining us?" Greenfell asked.

"Ms. Lynfield has left Polymath and gone into business for herself," I said.

"In competition?" Greenfell asked.

I nodded, not wanting to go into it. "She left around the first of March. I got this letter a few weeks later," I said.

"Why didn't you come in then, Mr. Keirnan?" Greenfell asked.

"I thought there must be some mistake. I called Jeff and asked him to check up on it and he called me back yesterday," I said. Greenfell swiveled his head ten degrees and gave Jeff a flat stare, and I felt my chair shift as the big man beside me squirmed.

"We had to pull the transaction files, Mr. Greenfell," Jeff said.

"And are our records correct?" Greenfell asked.

"Yes, sir," he answered, and laid a thick manilla folder on the edge of Mr. Greenfell's desk. Opening it, he began to read, "Eleven-acre property in Winterville, four buildings, total appraised value $1.2 million dollars, monthly mortgage payment on the property is nine thousand, eight hundred and forty-six dollars. No payments made since October of last year, so to bring the account current would require a payment of fifty-nine thousand and seventy-six dollars. To prevent foreclosure, we need to receive at least half that amount within thirty days and the remainder within the next thirty." He pulled a small flat calculator out of his shirt pocket and placed it on top of the file and began tapping.

"Twenty-nine thousand, five hundred and thirty-eight dollars," Greenfell and I said simultaneously. Jeff looked up and swung his baby face between us, then held the small calculator up close to his thick glasses.

"Twenty-nine thousand, five hundred and thirty-eight dollars," he agreed, and slipped the calculator back in his pocket.

"We keep a balance of two-hundred thousand in our checking account. Aren't the mortgage payments automatically deducted from that?" I asked.

Greenfell looked at Jeff. "Normally, yes, Mr. Keirnan, but you haven't had two-hundred thousand in your account since early last year." He nodded to Jeff, who pulled a stapled computer printout from the file and placed it in front of me. I flipped the pages and saw the monthly balance falling to almost zero in December, then to a negative number in January and February. I had looked at the same ledger two weeks ago, but tried to look as if it were new to me.

"Covered by the equity line you took out in November," he said. I nodded, no idea what equity line he was talking about, my throat too tight to speak, and felt the anger bubbling below the surface.

"For most of the time we've been your bankers, you've kept up pretty well. Steady growth, sensible expenditures. But last year your revenues jumped by about ten thousand a month, but your expenses went up by more than twenty. It looks like you expanded Mr. Keirnan, and didn't have the cash flow to support the investment," Jeff said, earnestly. Greenfell stared across the desk unblinking. Good cop, bad cop. "This year revenues have fallen to around fifty thousand dollars per month, and expenses have dropped as well. So you're keeping up, but you're just not generating enough cash to make up any ground on your loans."

I looked back and forth at Greenfell and Jeff, blood pounding in my ears, trying not to show my surprise. The only possible conclusion was that my ex-office manager Gillie had embezzled somewhere around a quarter of a million dollars from me. I thought about our chance meeting a few minutes ago and wondered.

Attempting a calm smile, I mentally channeled all that violent, adrenaline energy into my right hand, the one they couldn't see, the one squeezing as hard as it could on the square metal frame of the chair. There was a small pop as the metal weld broke loose. Greenfell started at the sound, and his stern expression fell away, to be replaced by one of nervousness.

# CHAPTER 5

*O*utside the day was getting warm. The Bradford pears had all bloomed late this year, and the trees lining the street were masses of white blossoms. A soft breeze stirred the branches, and a storm of white petals snowed down onto the sidewalk, adding to the carpet that was already there. I turned into the bank parking lot, and paused.

Leaning up against the driver's side of my truck was a thin, blond man wearing Ray-Ban sunglasses, black pants, and a dark blue long-sleeved shirt. He was talking to a beefier man wearing blue jeans and black T-shirt with a NASCAR design on it. The second man had longish red hair and several days of stubble. A "Cocks" cap from the University of South Carolina rested on the back of his head. He leaned up against a battered gold Volvo with South Carolina plates. Neither saw me at first.

Then the South Carolina man turned his head and spat a long brown stream of tobacco juice toward the mulched flower bed that bordered the lot. Swinging his head back, he saw me out of the corner of his eye, and said something. Both he and the thin man came off the vehicles and turned to face me. The man with the blue jeans slipped one hand behind his back. He gave a quick glance around to see if anyone was looking, and pulled something from his waistband. He held his hand hidden behind his leg.

I stopped where I was, about fifteen feet from the back of the truck. There was one other vehicle in the lot, a delivery van just to the right of the pickup. I dispensed with pretense, "You waiting on me?"

"Are you Top Keirnan?" said the thin man. He spoke softly, with a smooth script Midwestern accent.

"No," I said.

The man laughed. "You're right. That was a stupid question. Five ten or so, receding brown hair, gray eyes, bodybuilder upper torso, dressed in all-black, walks with a limp, nervous and twitchy, loud voice. How many of those are we going to find in a parking lot with your truck in it?"

"Six feet and what do you want?" I looked around to see if anyone was coming. In the distance I could see a line of students crossing Broad Street, and cars driving by. No one appeared interested in us and this small lot hidden behind chin-high hedges.

"To talk," the thin man said.

"Then why is Gomer Pyle packing?" I asked.

"Because you look like you might be the kind who likes to get it on, and we don't want that. Billy is fast and accurate, and we feel more comfortable with some protection. We just want to talk," he said.

"OK, talk," I said, sliding one foot backward.

"Why don't we take a ride to somewhere private?" he said. The redheaded man grinned, and spat another stream from between dirty brown teeth. It splattered on the black tarmac between us. He swung his arm around from behind his back and put both hands on the long-barreled revolver, shifting his left foot open into a shooter's stance. There was a three-inch metal tube screwed on the end of the barrel. The silencer would reduce the accuracy of the long barrel, but it would also reduce any reluctance he felt about blasting away in a bank parking lot in broad daylight. I felt an itch in the center of my back.

"Not a chance in hell," I said.

"Then come on over here, where we can have a conversation quietly," he said.

"If you want to talk, come on over here," I said. "Last offer, and then I walk away."

I felt the sudden point of a knife in my back, right where the itch had been, and behind me another Midwestern voice said, "Walk." I felt disgusted with myself—I know to pay attention to itches. When adrenaline is lighting up every nerve ending, those nerves pick up signals too subtle to be decoded by our modern, civilized brain, and they float up into our consciousness as hunches. Ignoring hunches gets soldiers and policemen killed.

The redheaded man laughed and took one hand off the gun, letting it swing down beside him. I turned my head and in the reflection from the window of the van saw another thin man in sunglasses, black pants, and blue shirt, identical to the one in front of me. He waited for me to take a step and then followed, the knife held low and angled almost at his side.

It was textbook, except for letting the knife drop out of position. That was the carelessness of someone used to pushing around those who won't fight back. But I'm no civilian. I don't mind violence. In fact, at times like now, when I'm buzzing and tight and full of anger at being betrayed by a friend, I need violence. Let the healing waters of adrenaline quench my raging fires. Can I get an amen? "Amen, brother, amen," I heard and realized I must have said it out loud. I could feel myself grinning, elated to have them make the violence decision for me, and saw the thin man in front eye me nervously.

Instead of stepping forward, I sidestepped quickly behind the van, blocking the field of fire of the man with the gun, and swiveled. The man with the knife slashed at me backhanded and traced a small shallow line across the front of my left arm. I grabbed his wrist as it flew by and jerked it, reached for the back of his neck, and when I grasped it, shoved his head as hard as I could into the side of the van.

There was a loud thump and a dimple appeared in the metal. He sagged, semiconscious, into my arms and the Ray-Ban sunglasses and knife clattered to the ground.

The redhaired man ran out and away from the van in an arc, trying to get a clear shot at me, but I swung the sagging body of the thin man toward him, lifted and pushed. The body took one or two stiff legged steps and fell facedown between us. Billy hesitated, automatically half-stepping to catch the unconscious man, and I used his indecision to scramble around to the front of the van, where I dropped to my knees. I heard the thin man to my right, still behind the pickup, say, "Vance?"

I reached my arm up over the hood and snapped off the antenna. There was a puffing sound, and I heard something thump into a branch in the hedge behind me. I dropped flat. A pair of blue-jeaned legs took two steps left. I scooted back a half step, so I could keep the van between us.

Billy shifted from foot to foot, trying to decide whether to flank me and risk another long shot, or to close. After a moment of indecision, he crept closer, moving right up to the van, turning to press his back against the side, and sliding his feet along, edging closer to the front where I hid. Working myself to my knees, I counted to five and stood, whipping the antenna as hard as I could. The antenna shuddered to a quick stop, there was a scream, and the pistol flew into the flower bed. The redheaded man stumbled backward, both hands pressed against his eyes, blood oozing from between his fingers. He lurched in a circle, screaming.

The other thin man raced around the end of the van. His hands were empty. I tossed the antenna to the side and picked up the pistol by the end of the silencer. "You better shut him up, or we're all going to end up in jail," I said. He looked at me in confusion, then ran over to the redheaded man, who was now on his knees, sobbing.

"He's blinded me, Lance, I'm blind. The reverend . . ." he whimpered.

"You'll be OK, Billy. We'll get you to a doctor. Hush," the thin man said. As he held his shoulders, a woman came around the corner from the bank. She took a long look, then turned and walked quickly away. Vance, the twin I'd rammed into the truck, rolled over onto his back, and shook his head groggily.

The thin man pried Billy's fingers away and peered through the mask of blood at the wound from the antenna. "He didn't get your eyeball, just a lid and the skin under the other one. You're going to be fine, Billy."

"You've got two minutes, max, to get those two in the car and get out of here, and to do all the talking you want to do," I said.

The thin man pulled Billy to his feet and led him away. I heard a door slam.

"Better come back empty-handed," I said, "or your brother's going to have more than a concussion and a sprained neck." I stepped behind the front of the van, waiting. Lance came back around the other end and helped his identical twin up. He stood with his brother's arm draped over his neck, using one hand to keep him balanced and cinching the other arm around his waist.

"This was unnecessary, asshole," he said.

"What do you want?" I asked.

"Leave the flag alone. It's none of your business," he hissed.

"Says who?" I asked.

He shook his head, and dragged his brother away. They bumbled drunkenly toward the Volvo. I edged around the front of my truck just in time to see Lance dump his brother in the front seat, scramble around to the driver's seat, and start the engine. He backed up, stopped too quickly, and drove away, tires squealing.

Extreme violence always has an effect, even on professionals. Just as I was climbing into the truck, the nausea hit me, and I threw up onto the flat pavement of the lot. I wiped my mouth and spat, then using the tail of my shirt to hold the pistol, I unscrewed the still warm silencer from the pistol. I walked over to the mailbox on the corner, opened the lid with the knuckles of my left hand, stood on tiptoe and dropped the pistol into the box, still holding it in my T-shirt. The silencer I tossed in the back of the truck with the trash.

As I drove slowly up Broad St., three cruisers raced by me, going toward the bank, no sirens, but lights flashing. I punched up a Mozart piece and whistled along softly.

# CHAPTER 6

*I fired Gillie for stealing. Shaw's fired me for letting* situations get completely out of control. Soames, the ex-SAS who runs the place, would have said that the situation back in the bank parking lot was a perfect example of that.

He would have argued I should have turned around and walked out of that lot the second I saw them leaning against my pickup. He would have said that going up against three men, one with a silenced pistol, with no weapon of my own, was simply foolish and guaranteed to produce either suicide or mayhem. And in his view, I semideliberately create these situations because of my addiction to adrenaline rushes, by my being what they call a "buzz junkie."

Shaw's used to be my other job, besides Polymath. Their specialty (or speciality as South African-born Soames would pronounce it) is booking mercenaries. Although I've never actually met a mercenary who uses the word "mercenary." It sounds so melodramatic and sixtyish, like "swinging" or "cat." Instead, we in the business tend to call ourselves by our specialties "co and pro," short for collection and protection, courier, electronics, cleanup, or in my case, operative.

The operative business exists because the police are really lousy at recovering lost things. Seven of ten robberies in the U.S. are never solved. The statistics are even worse when the people doing the taking are professionals, and worse yet when the crime is outside the U.S. Even when thefts are solved, the property seldom ends up back with whoever lost it. So people who lose very valuable stuff, say yachts, jewels, paintings, computer chips, or loved ones, tend to call Shaw's in London. They then send an operative to steal stuff back for the people who lost it. You'll notice I didn't say for the people who *own* it. That I'm less sure about.

Last February Shaw's fired me for burnout. They said I'd gotten to the point where I was taking too many risks, going too far out there to get the adrenaline rush, turning simple retrievals into gunfights at the OK Corral. They said I might not even know I was doing it, but they'd detected the pattern, and it was one they recognized. I don't know if they're right or not. It seems to me I never initiate the violence. But then again, if I was doing it subconsciously, I wouldn't know, would I? Catch-22.

The last job I did for them was a kidnap recovery, a rich Peruvian businessman's wife and daughter. The mother died in my arms as we ran across a cobblestone killing zone to the police barricade. A picture of her corpse ended up on the front page of the *International Herald Tribune,* my shoulder just barely in the frame. A few months after that, Soames called me to Atlanta and fired me.

I tried to talk them out of it. I could have gotten her out in one piece if her dickhead rich-guy-take-charge husband had just given me the time window he promised, instead of panicking and calling the police. My only mistake was carrying the cell phone he gave me. That allowed them to track me and follow me in. I believe it, too. Soames just chain-smoked and nodded, watched me with those pale blue watery eyes of his, and after he heard my explanation, told me again in the same flat voice that I was fired. I told him he was full of shit. But I didn't tell him that I still dream about Peru at least once a week, waking up in a puddle of sweat with the bed-sheets twisted into wet ropes. Maybe he knows; maybe it's part of the pattern.

I should have known that the Shaw's gig had to end sometime and planned for it. But I'm just not a planner. That's one thing about me that drove Gillie crazy. I just fall into things and I fall out. In high school, I fell into weight lifting because I slid down in a bicycle race and a motorcycle rolled over my knees, putting me in bed for a year. My dad put a weight bench in my room to keep me from going nuts.

I fell into being an operative the same way. I began helping my buddy Dee Lane run marijuana up from Jacksonville, which turned into smuggling bales of pot from Mexico, which turned into working part-time for a guy Dee Lane introduced me to in a bar in Belize City. His name was Edgar Haggenfuss, but everyone called him Foosball. Foosball died when he hit his head while pushing his pon-toon boat away from a dock at Lake Conroe, Texas. A month later his employer, Shaw's Mercantile Marine, called with an assignment. I even fell into Polymath because I needed to show an income to the IRS, and Polymath was a logical extension of my part-time college job of footnoting papers for other students for five bucks a shot. And I'd fallen into my affair with Gillie, or to be more precise, she fell onto me one morning when one of her heels snapped.

I put on my turn signal to turn right on to Barnett Shoals Road to go to the liquor store, but then before I turned, I realized that I had two dollars in my pocket, and couldn't afford a six-pack. I turned the signal off, and drove on to Winterville.

# CHAPTER 7

*I* *bumped the pickup across the railroad tracks in* Winterville, and edged over the washout from the highway and onto the lane that led to the school. Paving this long driveway had been the next project, and then the money had run out.

The parking lot was empty except for a tan Toyota minivan. Benny sat on the top step, his feet on the second. An old maroon blanket was spread on the concrete beside him, and on it were a tuba, a trombone, a trumpet, a cornet, and a euphonium, or what I think is a euphonium. In his hand he cradled a small square gray Sony cassette player.

Benny Culpepper is tiny and blue-black, midthirties, and the word that comes to mind when you describe him to anyone is "stillness." If asked, I would have automatically called Dee Lane my best friend. We grew up together in Arlene, came to the university together, and smuggled bales of pot together. Benny comes from the streets of Atlanta. His nickname is The Blade, and many claim he has the fastest hands on the East Coast. He has retired from a life of extreme violence to work with me at Polymath, where he lives in the old band wing with his tuba. He and I don't go back like me and

Dee Lane, but if Benny isn't also my best friend, I have no idea what to call him. I parked the truck in the circle and walked up.

"Where is everybody?" I asked.

"Everyone's gone home. We ran out of work," he said. Six months ago we'd had as many as thirty researchers working two and three shifts. Now we were down to a handful, the result of the recession and business lost to our new competitor, ASW Research. "Maggie's finishing up."

"You practicing?" I asked.

"Playing around," he answered. "What happened to your arm?"

"Tell you when I get back. I'm going to grab a beer," I said. "You want anything?"

"No, thank you," he laid the cassette player on the corner of the blanket and picked up the cornet, and began keying it idly. I returned a few minutes later with a first aid kit and cans of Budweiser beer hanging from the plastic rings that had held the six-pack. I sat down on the steps beside him. Opening one of the beers, I told him about Caron and Pope-Scott, the bank, and the three who'd jumped me in the parking lot. As I talked, he listened politely, and continued to key the instrument as if playing a piece. When he did that, it usually meant he had something to say, but didn't want to say it.

"You had a busy day," he said.

"What do you think?" I asked.

"About what?" he answered.

"Any of it," I replied.

He stretched out his leg and dug in his right pocket. I could see the outline of his prized straight razor through the cloth and saw his fingers push it aside as he dug. When the hand finally came out, he peered at the five-dollar bill between his two fingers for a second, and dropped the money on the step. "Challenge."

"You used to bet twenties," I said.

"That was when you could pay me twenty," he said. "Do you have five?"

"No, but I won't need it."

"Ready?" he asked. I nodded and he continued, "Maggie sold this one today to the governor's staff for a commencement speech. It goes 'All you need in this life is ignorance and confidence; then success is sure.'"

"Mark Twain, *Mysterious Stranger*. Too easy. Are you trying to change the subject?" I picked up the five and put it into the pocket of my T-shirt.

He turned the cornet around in his hand and peered into its silver bell. "I suspected Gillie was up to something."

I looked at him and raised my eyebrows. "Why?"

"You know. The new clothes, the car," he said.

"I never noticed the clothes and the car," I said truthfully.

"You wouldn't," he said. "You don't care about things like that. All you wear are jeans and T-shirts, and all your money goes into fixing up the school. And into your glass."

"I'll be glad when I can get back to Macallan," I waved the Budweiser can in the air, "Drinking this stuff is killing me."

He looked at the can a moment, and tilted his head a fraction. "Gillie loves money. And toward the end there, she was really throwing it around. She was acting funny, too. But you didn't notice." I finished the beer while I digested his message.

"Why didn't you tell me?"

"What good would that have done? You're loyal as a dog, Top, and think everybody else is too. You wouldn't have believed me."

"Do you think she tried to steal Dee Lane's money to repay what she'd borrowed from the till? Or do you think she was going to keep all of it?" I asked. That's why I'd fired her, because she'd stolen a million and a half dollars of our friend's money. Harlan Q. Winslow, an annoying academic who worked for us part-time, had been killed because someone thought he might know where that money was.

"Maybe," he answered.

"Gee, that helps," I said.

He smiled a small, quiet smile, and turned serious again, "What about this thing with Morton?"

"Morton says he wants me to do some work for him, but he's CIA, and supposedly all his budgets and stuff have been diverted to the War on Terror. I get the feeling he'll do what he can to help out because he wants me as an operative, but I'm not sure what he can do. Maybe not much," I said.

"Do you want me to call Elbert Day and see if he'll loan us some to tide us over?"

"If we take money from Elbert, we may never get caught up again," I said.

"What choice do we have?" Benny said.

"This job, the flag thing, that could help," I said. Benny looked down at the cornet. It was silver, with faint curlicued engraving that wound around the bell of the horn and worked its way down toward the mouthpiece. He ran his fingers down the mouth tube and along the slide ring.

"What? You have a problem with it?" I asked.

"Isn't Pope-Scott the guy that wrote that book that said Sherman's march was equivalent to the Holocaust and that white men raping slaves was a good thing because it improved the intelligence of my race?" Benny said.

"Something like that," I answered.

"That's a pretty hard line."

I thought about it a moment while I finished the last beer. "I'll call him tomorrow and turn it down," I said.

"Because I have a problem with it?"

"Yes, and because I have a problem with it, too."

Benny picked up the tuba and the cornet and stood. "Just like that?"

"Yep," I said.

"And if we lose the school? After five years of tuckpointing, rewiring, tearing out walls, reroofing, painting, and plastering? You'd risk all our hard work?" he asked.

I shrugged, and felt myself turning red. "Got to be a hundred old schools in Georgia. We'll just find another one. Start over." I looked straight ahead, too embarrassed to look back at the school I'd just betrayed. Sorry, old girl, I thought silently, and hoped she could hear me and would understand.

Benny looked at me and nodded, "So what did you tell him?"

"I told him I'd call him tomorrow after I conferred with my partner," I said.

"I thought I was an employee," he said, too casually, once again examining the etching on his horn.

"Nah. Now that Polymath is worth nothing, you might as well own some of it," I said.

"How much?" he asked.

"Ten percent? A hundred percent if we lose everything," I laughed tightly.

"Do you see what I mean? Loyal as a dog. You'll walk away from five years of work just because you don't want to hurt my feelings. You never would have believed me about Gillie," he said.

"I'm OK walking away from this one. Really."

"You're a trip, Top, a real trip. Let me think about it," he answered.

"Want some help with those horns?" I asked.

"No, you need to pay attention to that cut," he nodded to the unopened first aid kit, as he stood, picked up a horn in each hand, and tucked the maybe euphonium under one arm.

# CHAPTER 8

*I* *cleaned the cut, and said good-bye to Maggie as she* stepped around me and skipped down the steps to head home. When I'd finished dressing the wound, I went back for more beer. When the buzz starts, the alcohol just flames right off, and I don't know why I don't just drink water and save the eight dollars. But I don't, I drink more of the stuff than usual, and I probably drink too much anyway. At some point, I lay down on the warm concrete and took a quick nap, letting the sun heat up the dark shirt and keep me comfortable even as the sun dropped near the tops of the pine trees and a chill crept across the fields.

The cool air woke me around four. I woke clearheaded—the intense adrenaline-fueled dreams hadn't started yet—creaked to my feet, and went inside. Polymath is based in what used to be Winterville Elementary, an old brick school built in the thirties. It sits high on a small rise, a tall red building a story and a half high, still as imposing as it must have been to those two hundred nervous eleven-year-olds on their first day of "big" school seventy years ago. For many this would have been their last year of formal education. At twelve, they'd have joined their families in the fields full-time.

Just inside the front doorway hangs an aerial photograph of the school, and it shows a building roughly shaped like a short, fat butterfly. The concrete porch I'd napped on serves as the head and the driveway as the antennae. From the butterfly's head, double doors open into a long hall, which cuts the building in half. Just inside the doors to the left is my office, in what used to be the principal's and school nurse's offices. Across the hall is an old room that used to be a teachers' lounge, and now houses our tape backups for the computers.

Seventeen classrooms and a library are spread along the main hall and the two that cross it. Some of the classrooms now house researcher stations and a half dozen more are refurbished exactly as they were when the school was finally closed in the seventies, with long green chalkboards, high windows, lights hanging on long wires from high ceilings, and rows of one-piece metal and wood desks, each with a metal cubbyhole for books under the seat.

In one far corner of the building is the old lunchroom, nothing now except a dusty room stacked with still-graffitied tables and desks, a couple of saw horses and a table saw. Across the way, in the bottom left of the butterfly, is a suite of band rooms, where Benny and his instruments live. The other two corners of the building hold the gym and the auditorium. The gym now houses a Nautilus machine, and in the middle of the tip-off circle, my bed, along with an alarm clock and a phone. It is my second favorite room in the entire world.

My favorite is the auditorium, which sits in the other corner and is the most beautiful space I have ever been in, and I have seen the cathedrals in Milan and Paris. The heart and soul of the old school is the huge fresco mural that covers one wall of the auditorium, done by a local band of artists back in the thirties, funded by the WPA. We'd found it under a coat of whitewash, and had a local artist named Libby remove the wash and repair the cracks, and now that the tin ceiling was renovated, the pews refinished, and the heavy velvet curtains replaced, the room is simply spectacular. The idea that we might lose the school creates an icy knot in my chest. There aren't hundreds of old schools like this one in Georgia, and Benny and I know it.

I stopped in my office to check messages, noted the trickle of inquiries coming in for tomorrow, and saw a message to call Amanda. Dropping my jeans, I unbuckled the bulky knee braces and tossed them onto a chair. I tugged my pants back up. Pulling open the bottom drawer of the credenza, I removed a bottle of Jamison's, unopened, the last of the good whiskey. Tucking a small cell phone in my back pocket, I limped, whiskey in one hand and cane in the other, down linoleum halls silver shiny with the late day sun toward the auditorium, where I intended to park myself on the front steps that led up to the stage, drink the whiskey and call my *girlfriend*.

# CHAPTER 9

*T*he phone on the small table beside my bed rang at 2 A.M., and I knew it was her before I picked up the handset. I could picture her, sitting in George's old house robe, perched on the sofa in the den of her smallish brick house, cup of coffee on the table in front of her, folding clothes. Gillie worked late and rose early, and sometimes just skipped sleep altogether. I never did, and she'd never called me on the landline in the middle of the night before. The caller ID said it was a 215 area code. Philadelphia.

"I don't recognize the number," I answered.

"You taught me about prepaid cell phones," she said.

"That's for when you don't want to leave a record of the call," I said. "I'm not sure how that applies here."

"Hmmmph," she answered, noncommittally.

"Well, you called," I said, after a few long seconds of silence.

"You figure it out yet?" she asked. Her voice was low and husky, and fitted her olive skin and dark good looks. I realized how much I'd missed hearing it over the last two months.

"What? The bank?" I said.

"No, the name of my company, AWS Research. You figure it out yet?"

"I haven't tried, Gillie. I've been too busy trying to pay my bills and keep my people working," I answered.

"You will. You're the genius. I'll give you a clue: Shakespeare misattribution," she said. And suddenly I knew. AWS stood for "a woman scorned," as in "hell hath no fury like," the popular rephrasing of a line from a 1697 William Congreve play. The original was more powerful than the watered-down version: "Heaven has no rage, with love to hatred turned, nor hell a fury, like a woman scorned."

"I'll work on it," I answered, deciding discretion was the better part of valor in this case. "Any chance we can get together and talk about this?"

"Nope, you had your chance to talk to me," she said.

"Gillie, last time you were here, you were trying to convince your husband that he should shoot me. Is that the chance you were talking about?"

"Before then," she said, "and you know it. We could have talked all those times after you'd just screwed me. When we lay in bed together, we could have talked then."

"Can we talk now?" I asked.

"Maybe," she said, "I'll think about it. Let you know. Isn't there anything else you want to ask me?"

"Like what?" I said.

"Like 'what's next?'"

"What's next?" I answered.

"It's going to hurt, Top. Bad. Badly? No, bad is right. It's going to hurt bad," she laughed.

"Gillie, is this just about the money? Are you going to tell me why?"

"No," she answered, and turned quiet, saying nothing. I hung on the line for a while, no sounds but the scrape of breathing into the phone, like I had with my first girlfriend back in the ninth grade.

"Good night, Gillie," I hung up the phone softly. It rang again, and I answered.

"Did you just hang up on me?" she asked, her voice a mix of incredulity and indignation.

"Gillie, I've got an early morning meeting, good night," I said.

"I don't give a good goddam. . . ." Her voice rose.

I hung up again, and reached around behind the phone and unclipped the line, certain the next morning I'd find a dozen or so retries on the phone log. It took me a while to go back to sleep. I lay pondering Congreve, and wondering how love to hatred turned.

Gillie's theft had set off a chain of dominoes. By the time they had all fallen, one of my employees was dead and a friend, Leonard "Vinyl Man" Marks, had been kidnapped. Then when I'd taken the money back, she'd tried to get her husband to kill me. And now she was destroying the one thing I really loved, using money she'd embezzled from me to get started. Love to hatred turned. So quickly. And for the life of me, I couldn't figure out why.

# CHAPTER 10

*A*manda and I met for breakfast in the Busy Bee, on the corner of Broad and Wall. We tucked ourselves into a small booth looking out onto the side street. Mina slopped two cups of coffee and two waters down in front of us, and tossed two menus onto the tabletop, then left without saying anything. The menus were a mere formality, since the aged Mina scrambled the orders so badly that what you got bore no relation at all to what you ordered. But Veronica, Mina's sister, was an excellent cook, and usually whatever came back was pretty edible.

"Well, what about Jay? You told him you'll do it?" Amanda asked, her huge green eyes looking at me over her coffee. Her chin-length caramel-colored hair flirted with the surface of the black liquid, and the steam framed her pretty, thin face. It was early, a little after seven, because Amanda's job in the law library required her to be there at eight. That's only a five-minute walk away, across Broad and along a diagonal that crosses the huge quadrangle.

"Not yet. I had to talk to Benny," I said.

"And?" she asked.

I pulled a yellow Post-it self-stick note from my shirt pocket and handed it across. "This was on the bathroom mirror this morning."

"What does it say? I can't read it," Amanda asked, unfolding it and peering at it closely.

Benny had little formal education, but since coming to us had assiduously worked his way through our rather large library, gotten his high school equivalency diploma, and was planning on starting at the university in the fall. Still, his handwriting was a childish scrawl, painful and spidery, with poor spelling and random punctuation. "It says he's cool with me doing the assignment, but we have to talk."

"What does he want to talk about?" she said. I shrugged.

"So you are going to do it?" She dug into her purse and pulled out two small tortoise-shell barrettes, one of which she stuck in her mouth as she put the other in her hair.

"Yes," I answered. "Thanks."

"It's nothing," she answered around the hair clip. While she fussed with her hair, I sat and waited, mostly watching her. But when the adrenaline begins to build, you watch everything, hear everything, smell everything.

Any given morning sitting in the Busy Bee was enough to cause sensory overload. Today, tables were full of frat boys having loud conversations. There was the whoosh and thud of the front door opening and closing, and sizzling and dish-clanking sounds came from the kitchen. The sound on the TV was turned down, but two tables away from us an old man with white stubble and thick, smeared glasses read out loud the scrolling bar that ran across the bottom of the CNN screen. I heard something about Walter Caldwell, better known as the Sword of Michael, had escaped the dragnet and was believed to be hiding with sympathizers in the North Carolina woods. The Department of Homeland Security was considering labeling him a domestic terrorist. I tried to ignore the diversions and focus on my internal debate—whether I should ask the next question, knowing I probably would.

"Can I ask how you know Pope-Scott?" I asked.

Taking the barrette from her mouth, she smiled at me flirtatiously and worked her lower jaw, the way women do when they're deciding how much to say about something.

"We used to date, before you, before Dee Lane, even before Chip." Chip was her ex-husband. "I met him when I first came to the university. I'd read *Johnnycake,* and thought it was brilliant, and someone pointed him out in the library. I walked over to say 'hello,' and we started dating. It lasted for a couple of years, until Caron."

"Have you read *Dixiecaust?*" A note of unreasonable jealousy sang through me.

"Yes."

"And what did you think?"

"Read it yourself, and then we'll talk," she answered. "I don't want to bias you."

"I've ordered it off the Web site," I said. "You can't find it in the bookstores or even at Amazon."

Mina dropped two plates in front of us, even though we hadn't ordered yet. Digging in the front pocket of her apron, she tossed two sets of forks and spoons wrapped tightly in napkins down beside them. "Back with more coffee soon? Do you want OJ?" And moved off without waiting for an answer.

One dish was an omelet, the thin kind, with what looked like bell peppers and a white cheese leaking out of one corner. Four triangles of wheat toast sat on the side of the plate. The other was a bowl of steaming oatmeal, the top buried under an avalanche of early season South Florida blueberries. We negotiated for a moment, and finally Amanda took the omelet and a dozen or so of the berries. I scraped the berries to the side, used my spoon to create a small crater in the center, and dropped in a spoonful of brown sugar and a pat of butter. I waited until it melted, then spread it back across the top of the cereal and redistributed the blueberries. Now the buzz was beginning to build, and soon it would be hard to keep anything down. Better to fuel up now, before the throat got tight and the stomach shrank to the size of a peach.

While I did that, Amanda salted and peppered her omelet, and spread strawberry jam and butter on her toast. "How do you eat like that and stay so thin?" I asked.

"Good genes and bad habits," she answered, with a smile and a wink.

Her smoking and my drinking were ongoing friction points between us. "I thought nicotine was an appetite suppressant," I said, in what I hoped was a conversational, nonconfrontational tone.

"Not with me. With me it burns calories," she said. There was a subtle defiance in the answer. I smiled back, and spooned a glob of oatmeal. After a few seconds, her smile faded, "Top. I've got about two thousand dollars in an IRA, if you need it for the bank."

I shook my head. "I can't let you do that."

"Then what are you going to do?" she asked. She lifted her cup to take a sip.

"Pope-Scott should help. I've also got some messages out to a guy who's said he wants me to do some work. I'll ask him if I can get an advance." That would be Gerald Morton of the CIA. "I've even thought of pressuring Gillie to return part of what she stole."

Amanda broke out in a sudden laugh that caused a small geyser of coffee to spray out onto the table. She waved an apology and dabbed her mouth, then the table, with the paper napkin. "You what?"

"I think I might try to get our money back. Maggie says Gillie is getting some loan from the Small Business Administration. If we had half the money she embezzled, we'd be in pretty good shape."

Amanda looked at me incredulously. "I'd pay money to watch this one."

"You don't think so?" I asked.

"What sort of pressure? Her conscience? Let's go over this once again," she held up her fist, palm inward, and began ticking up fingers as she spoke. "You fired her, and you dumped her, and you told her husband she was cheating. Since then she's taken half your clients and two thirds of your staff, and you're now being audited by the IRS because of an anonymous tip that she probably called in. And you think she's going to help you get back on your feet?"

"I didn't dump her," I said, remembering the conversation of the night before.

"Top, it doesn't matter. The first thing you learn in law school is what happened and what the two sides think happened is never the same thing. She thinks she's the wronged party here," Amanda said patiently.

I said stubbornly, "There are other sorts of pressure."

"Such as? You won't go to court because you don't want the public attention. You won't use force against her or her family because she used to be a friend, and you won't be able to put that aside. And you can bet she's already figured that out. So, I don't think you have any pressure to bring."

"Anything else?" I asked, knowing that my arguments made no sense at all, and that Amanda was certainly right.

"Nope," she smiled.

"That's what I get for hanging out with a lawyer," I grumbled.

She stood up and tossed a five-dollar bill on the table. "Ex-lawyer. Now I'm a librarian, just like you, only in the public sector. Gotta go. Let me know how you come out with Jay and Caron." Was it my imagination or was there the slightest emphasis on the word "Caron"?

I nodded, mouth full of oatmeal.

She hooked the strap of her purse over her shoulder and paused, looking down at me. "You know why I hooked you up with Jay, Top?"

"Because I need the money?"

"That. And because I thought you two might click."

I was mildly offended. Why would I click with a pretentious racist? I asked, "Why's that?"

"You two have certain similarities."

I thought of his cravat and looked down at my T-shirt. "Such as?"

"Oh, I don't know, when he broke up with me, he did it in a very Top-like way," she smiled sadly.

"Are we breaking up?" I asked, surprised.

"No, silly, when Jay broke up with me, he used a quote to do it. He took me out for coffee, looked across the table and said, 'Non amo te, Sabidi, nec possum dicere quare: Hoc tantum possum dicere, non amo te.' Do you know it?"

"No," I lied. She bent over and held my face in her hands, and pecked me lightly on the mouth.

"That's why I like you so much, Top. All a woman wants in a man is a nice guy or a terrible liar, and with you I've got both."

"I'm a great liar," I protested, my face still cradled in her hands. She kissed me again, more sincerely, and from the corner of my eye I could see Mina glaring at us. Amanda released my face and turned and walked out.

"See you," she called over her shoulder.

The quote was Martial, the Spanish writer, and the language Latin. It translated roughly as "I don't love you, Sabidius, and I can't tell you why; all I can tell you is this, that I don't love you." Turned halfway in the booth, I watched Amanda light a cigarette, blow a long plume into the air, then dart through a gap in the traffic and through the wrought-iron fence and into the quiet green peace of the university. Maybe the jealousy wasn't so misplaced after all.

# CHAPTER 11

*T*he truck was parked in front of the Bee, and before I climbed in, I fished around in the garbage in the back and came up with the black silencer I'd tossed there the day before. I tucked it into a pocket of my jeans, hoisted myself up into the cab, and drove over to Pope-Scott's office. Only one parking space was occupied this morning, and that with Caron's Jag. The other spot, where Pope-Scott's Mini had been the day before, was empty.

Something felt wrong. Maybe it was the missing Mini Cooper. But the decision by a married couple who work together to take one car instead of two isn't that big a deal, I told myself. Suddenly on edge, I sat quietly, letting my heightened senses work, taking it all in: the newly green trees swaying slightly in the morning breeze, the perfect manicure of the small patch of lawn beside the lot, the elegant precision of the edging between the grass and the pine straw-covered bed, the tiny, neatly painted garden shed tucked into the back corner of the lot. In the bed across the blanket of lawn, daffodils were already beginning to wither and behind them something I didn't recognize was poised to bloom. And I could spot nothing out of place. Still.

The hair on my neck stood erect. I rolled down the window and listened intensely. I could hear the traffic building on Lumpkin and somewhere a church bell chimed eight o'clock, but I heard nothing that explained my sudden case of the heebie jeebies. Once more I checked my mirrors and scanned the small lawn and the black iron fence beyond. Pulling the small LG cell phone from my pocket, I checked for messages. And found none. It still felt wrong.

There was a sensation that something lurked just beyond my peripheral vision, and I swiveled compulsively. Finally, I decided it was just nerves. I shook it off, climbed down from the truck and tentatively made my way along the driveway toward the front.

I'd gone maybe eight paces when I heard the steps behind me, heavy, and coming fast. Automatically, I stepped left, turned and crouched. I saw the black muzzle of a pistol in a two-handed grip swing upward. Without thinking, I stepped into the attacker, swung my left arm up and over his arms and back around underneath. At the same time I extended my right arm to the man's throat, locked my left hand on my right elbow, lifted and dropped my left knee, causing my body to spin like a discus thrower's and tossing the man up into the air. He landed on his back on the marble shards with a loud whump. His pistol flew a few feet from his right hand, and skittered another few inches across the driveway. There was an audible whoosh as the air left his lungs.

I stared down, dumbfounded, at the prone body of a young deputy sheriff. He wore a stunned look on his face. His baseball-style cap lay at my feet. I picked it up and dusted it off. My right knee throbbed.

"Are you all right?" I said. He wore a blond crew cut, and his scalp glowed a bright red. As I watched, he struggled to one knee, holding himself up with an elbow, and fought to regain his breath. He looked around anxiously for his pistol. Without being told, I placed the hat carefully on the driveway, dropped to my knees, and laced my fingers behind my head. The deputy scrambled over to the gun and lifted it toward me. His nostrils flared as he fought to pull air into his emptied lungs.

I wondered if he would shoot. Like a strange statue, I knelt on the sharp marble pieces, staring straight ahead and down, submissive, and waited for him to decide. He held the gun out sideways and jerked it downward, motioning me to the ground. I raised my arms very, very slowly and brought them over in front of me. Slowly, I levered myself down, and lifted my hands back behind my head.

I heard the deputy climb to his feet, and walk toward me. "Put your hands, hunhh, hunhhh, behind your, hunhhh, back," he wheezed. I did so, and felt the cold steel as he handcuffed me.

"What were you doing running up behind me?" I asked. "Couldn't you have identified yourself?"

"Shut up," he panted. Grabbing my shoulder, he rolled me over and began patting me down. He found the black silencer and wrestled it out of my jeans pocket. "What's this?" finally sounding normal, but his face was still flushed, and he moved stiffly, as if he'd sprained something.

"A foot peg for a mountain bike," I said. "I'm taking it in to have a duplicate made for the other side. The other one broke."

"I think we'll take it in for evidence," he said. "Looks like a weapon to me."

"Suit yourself. Those two bales of hay looked like pot to those rookie cops in Illinois and they're still getting crap about it. You might as well have your five seconds on the six o'clock news." I fidgeted to get more comfortable. "What's this about?"

The deputy looked at the silencer for another minute, then turned and threw it fifteen or so feet into the back of the pickup. It clanged against the metal toolbox. He turned back to me, then looked up. I moved my head to see a pair of woman's feet in small strapless black high heels walking briskly toward me. This morning Caron wore an electric blue sheath, of a similar cut to the red one the day before. There was a strand of pearls around her neck, but she wore no makeup and her face looked blotchy and washed out.

"This is Mr. Keirnan," Caron said. "He works for me. Can you release him please?"

"What's all this about?" I asked again. They both ignored me.

"No, ma'am, I have to take him in for assaulting a police officer," the deputy said. He looked to be in his midtwenties, maybe two hundred and thirty pounds. No wonder my right knee felt like it was packed with ground glass. I could feel it swelling inside my jeans.

"Bad idea," I said to the young cop. "You're going to be the laughingstock of the locker room. Better off just forgetting all this happened." I watched his face to see if I'd gone too far, and saw his eyes flicker back toward the truck and the illegal silencer.

"Last night Jay went out to walk our Corgi and someone shot him. He's in Athens General. We've hired the deputy to keep an eye on the place until we know more about what happened," Caron said.

"I'm taking you in," the young policeman said stubbornly.

"Is he OK?" I asked.

"Yeah, I'm OK, just knocked the breath out of me," said the cop, gratefully.

"Not you, my client," I said.

Caron looked at the policeman, then back down at me. She stepped closer and I could see where her hose changed color up under her blue skirt. I tried not to think about garter belts. "He was shot in the right lung. It didn't hit anything vital, but the lung collapsed and they had to operate to get the bullet out. So, no, he's not OK. He's awake though, and he wants to talk to you." She stepped closer, and kneeled to brush a few bits of marble off my face.

The policeman reached for the radio mike attached to his vest and turning away, said something into it. I lay down and closed my eyes to keep from staring at Caron Pope-Scott's pale blue underwear.

# CHAPTER 12

*I*n the end, it was Caron who cajoled the young trooper into letting me go, although I think the mental image of him explaining to his fellow deputies how he lost his gun to an unarmed man might have played a role in his decision. A muscle in my shoulder hurt where he'd accidentally-on-purpose yanked my hands up between my shoulder blades when releasing the cuffs. As a peace offering, Caron had taken a fresh pot of coffee and a plate of Fig Newton cookies back to the shed where he was posted, and while she and he fiddled with his thermos, I'd surreptitiously retrieved the silencer from the bed of my pickup. There was a three-inch scratch on the metal toolbox.

Now, Caron and I sat facing each other in the two wing chairs in front of Pope-Scott's desk, the silencer balanced at attention on the edge of the desk. "Is that what it looks like?" she asked.

"Depends on what it looks like. I convinced the deputy that it was a foot peg for a mountain bike, but it's not. It really is what the professionals call a sound suppressor, a silencer in layman's terms. How well it works in silencing depends on the type of weapon and the velocity of the bullet. This one is homemade, although whoever made it has access to a pretty decent machine shop. It belonged to some guys I met yesterday," I said.

"How'd you get it?" she asked.

"I took it away from them," I replied, "along with the gun it was attached to."

"Why are you showing it to me?" she asked. She tried to hold my eyes.

"I thought you could tell me," I said.

"I don't know what you mean," she said. Her blue eyes flickered toward the ceiling. Not enough practice lying or she'd know never to look upward. Blinking once is better.

"These guys didn't know me, but they knew what I'd been asked to do. And they knew in time to drive here from South Carolina, which probably means they knew something as soon as I'd made the appointment. Then someone called them with a plate and a description when I left here. There are two people who could have told them all that, and one of them is in the hospital. So that leaves you," I said.

"I don't know what you mean," she insisted stubbornly.

I shook my head. The muscle in my shoulder throbbed and I could feel my knees swelling. "Do you have any painkillers?" I asked.

"Sure," she said, stood and walked into her office. "How many?" she called.

"Six, maybe eight, depending on what you've got," I answered. She brought back a small unopened bottle of Evian and an almost full bottle of Advil. I ate a small handful and drained the water.

"Is that healthy?" she asked.

"Great for the inflammation and the pain, not so good for the stomach lining," I answered. We sat quietly for a moment. Finally, I spoke, "All right, let's skip some of the thrust and parry and get on with it. Here's what happened: you stole the flag and sold it. Day before yesterday you called whoever you sold it to and that's who was waiting for me in the bank parking lot, and maybe who tried to kill Jay last night."

The blood drained from her face and her jaw dropped open. "Why do you think I was the one who stole the flag?"

"Because with this security system the theft had to be an inside job," I said.

"We have a maid that comes every morning," Caron said.

I looked at her. "What's the maid's name?"

"Viola. She's a Polish émigré, doesn't even speak much English," she answered.

"I can find a translator. Should I go interrogate her about the flag?" I asked. "Is that what you want?"

"No," Caron looked down. "She had nothing to do with it."

"Then it was you or Jay. You tell me it wasn't you and I'll go ask him next," I said.

"He's expecting you, but the doctors said no visitors until one o'clock or so," she said.

"So do you want me to ask him?" I asked. Persistence is the key to interrogation, not cleverness. Just keep chipping away at their story until all that's left is the truth. "Caron?"

"No."

"OK then, tell me about it," I said. She sat, head bowed, hands folded in her laps, eyes focused on the middle distance. Her chin trembled slightly. Finally, she swung to face me, and stared defiantly, without blinking.

"I did it. I gave it to Styrell and he sold it for me. I don't know the men who attacked you. I called Styrell yesterday after you left. I didn't know he was going to have anyone come after you," she looked up. "I'm sorry to put you in this situation, but I'm not sorry I did it."

"Do you want to tell me why?" I asked.

"Why bother? Your job is to get things back, right?" she asked.

"Humor me," I replied.

She paused, picked up the silencer, and turned it in her hands. Replacing it on the desk, she felt a bit of oil residue on her fingertips, and reached for a Kleenex facial tissue. I waited while she dry-scrubbed her hands. "You have no idea what it is like to be married to Jay Pope-Scott. We have no life. We come to work, we go home. In church, we sit in our own pew. We never get an invitation to a faculty dinner. We've stopped going out to eat because as soon as the staff recognizes him, there's all this whispering, and we stopped getting served. We once sat for four hours waiting for menus, Jay too stub born to leave. Four goddamed embarrassing hours. We can't even think about having children because he gets at least one death threat every single day."

"How much of this is of his own making?"

"How much is his fault? All of it is his fault. He wrote that stupid book. Then he went and found that stupid flag in a flea market in Virginia. And instead of putting it in a museum, he turned this stupid office into a shrine to the Confederacy. Every time they need someone to go on TV and defend the stars and bars on a state flag, they send a limo from Atlanta, put him on CNN and try to make him look like a buffoon. He's become the official protector of the memory of the great lost Southern empire. It's totally his fault." The phrase about the lost empire dripped with sarcasm.

"He's a hero to some," I said.

"A hero," she snorted. "You're right, he is a hero to some. To the white supremacists and the right-wing survivalists who live in compounds in Idaho. Do you know that crazy bomber Sword of Michael sends him a note every time he blows up an abortion clinic? My husband is the kindest, smartest, most decent man I've ever met, and what that flag represents is destroying him. Us." She sat quietly for a moment, looking out the window. I expected her to cry, but her eyes stayed dry. Caron looked up, over my head and out the window, and gave her head a little shake. "Save your Dixie cups, boys, the South will rise again. These nuts should drive down the Atlanta highway, the South has already risen again." She turned back to me. "They need to move on and we need to move on, too."

"And getting rid of the flag is going to accomplish all that?"

"I think it's a start. Sometimes you just need to break the cycle," she said.

"What cycle?"

"This cycle. Any cycle. Jay told you a story, let me tell you one. When I was in college, Mr. Keirnan, I hated my life. I hated my sorority sisters, I hated my classes, I hated the dim-witted jocks I dated, I hated everything. Finally, one day I decided to start committing random acts to break the cycle. That way, I thought, I'd get to breakfast five minutes late, and maybe I'd meet new people. Or I'd miss a light and cross the street a block early or something." She smiled wanly. "I know, teenage pretentiousness."

"I think it makes sense. What did you do?"

"I started picking up rubber bands. I have to say, you wouldn't believe how many rubber bands there are until you start picking them up." She looked down at her hands. "And three weeks later I bent over to pick up a little red one like they use on newspapers and there was a page on the ground from some girls looking for a new roommate. I called, moved out of the sorority house, and changed my major from art to history. So maybe it worked."

"And if you and the professor could break this cycle, what would you do?"

"I don't know. Move to California or Colorado. Jay could go back to writing brilliant history books that everyone would read, and I could stay home and have babies and change diapers." She paused and took a sip of coffee from a china cup. "Styrell was just helping me. He's a worn-out old hippie. Please don't hurt him when you go after the flag. I should have burned it, then you couldn't bring it back," she said.

"Why do you think I'll still go after the flag?" I asked.

She looked at me squarely. "Oh, please."

# CHAPTER 13

*I* *finished up at Pope-Scott's a little before nine.* With four hours to kill before I could get in to talk to my client, I decided to find out a bit more about the Bloody Red Rag and who might want it. I left my truck in the lot and walked over to the Law Library, where I had Amanda run a search for me. The search turned up Grant-Freeholder, an antique dealer based in Marietta, or May-retta as it is called by those like myself who are born and bred in north Georgia. I debated calling the dealer on the phone, then decided I might do better in person.

Despite the size of the city, Marietta is still more or less the classic old-style southern town it was before the spillover from Atlanta's growth made it into a city in its own right. Downtown is nothing much, just a bunch of stores around a square, except for a large government building on one side of the square, and a venerable bank on the other. Grant-Freeholder occupied a corner of the bank building, next to a large new Starbucks café.

The façade of the building was polished north Georgia gray granite, with fine silver flecks instead of broad black veins. Grant-Freeholder's corner was ringed with windows that ran from waist high to around seven feet above the sidewalk. Each was painted black, except for a small square area in the center that revealed a display area of cream-colored silk. There were probably a dozen displays in all. Some held coins, two held pistols, and one a dusty-looking gray glove with a little handwritten card that said it was worn by Vivian Leigh in an outtake of *Gone With the Wind*. The windows were lined with double silver bands of security tape.

The gold paint on the door discretely informed me that hours were eleven to four, or by appointment. It was just nine forty-five, but through the glass I could see a small gray-headed man wearing an open-necked white shirt, black pants, and an elaborately brocaded silk vest. His sleeves were rolled up and he wore surgical gloves. In the center of the room was a glass table, lit from beneath and above. On it was a gray infantry cap perched on an oval wooden hat stand. The small man wore a jeweler's loupe, and held a large magnifying glass in one hand and a pair of tweezers in the other. He did not look up at me. I pushed the buzzer at the door and stood back.

He looked up, smiled, put down his equipment and walked to the door. I tried not to stare at his comb-over. Each hair originated some-where over the horizon of his scalp and came straight forward, ending in short bangs that flipped up at the end. The hair was cemented into place by some sort of spray or gel that gave it an artificial sheen, like a plastic cap. One row of the hair had parted, and through the gap I could see a patch of shiny pink skin. His face was as wrinkled as a Shar Pei and his eyebrows were huge white things with long hairs that stretched up toward the bangs. He reached the door and flipped a switch beside it.

"Yes?" he said kindly. The voice came out of a speaker next to my ear.

I pulled out a Polymath business card and held it up to the glass. "My name is Top Keirnan and I run a small research business in Athens. A client has paid us to prepare a white paper on Civil War memorabilia, and I was told someone here could help me. Of course we will give you full credit in our report." Behind me was the constant hum of traffic. A warm breeze pushed down the street.

"I am delighted to help you, Mr. Keirnan. My name is Sam Free-holder, and my nephew and I own this shop." His voice was scratchy through the intercom.

"May I come in?" I asked.

"Only if you come back at eleven. Insurance, you understand. We can't let people in until we have a full complement of staff on hand. There have been so many robberies these last few years. We have to be careful." I admired his tact. If I was a seventy-year-old man working alone in a store full of rare coins and the like, I certainly would not have let in a muscular thirty-something man wearing a black T-shirt, blue jeans, Giro cycling shades, and Chuck Taylor basketball shoes. But it was polite of him not to put it that way.

"Maybe we can talk here, then?" I asked.

"Sure," he reached to one side and pulled over a high chair made of black wire and plastic. He seated himself. "What would you like to know?"

"Civil War flags," I said.

"My word, it must be true," he gasped.

"What must be true?" I said.

"The Bloody Red Rag is on the market. All the chat rooms are buzzing with it. And here you are, from Athens, asking about Civil War flags. It must be true," he said. He clapped his hands in glee, and held them there.

"What's the Bloody Red Rag?" I asked.

He grinned and gave me a broad wink, "OK Mr. Whatever-your-name-really-is, we'll play it that way." I smiled back. He continued.

"As you must know, Civil War collectibles are huge right now, huge, and flags are amongst the most desired items. The Bloody Red Rag might be the most valuable of them all, potentially worth half a million dollars at auction. Maybe more."

"Why potentially?" I asked.

"Well," he gestured extravagantly, "what drives value in this market is celebrity, rarity, condition, and provenance. The Rag certainly has celebrity and since it is one of a kind, it has rarity, and I have heard it is in excellent condition."

"So provenance is the issue?"

"Absolutely," he nodded and grimaced. "See, the Stars and Bars we know today was never the official flag of the Confederacy. It was a battle flag, popular, but not widely adopted. Each unit had its own banner with its own design. Some were white. Others were light blue or gray. Some used the stars and bars motif, others had single stars or snakes or cannons. One had a cotton bollworm. There probably are a dozen or so basic designs and maybe a hundred variations. The flag we know today as the Confederate flag was actually created and pushed by General P. G. T. Beauregard. The story goes that he sent a flag to General Jackson as a gift, hoping the famous general would take a fancy to it. Jackson stuffed it into his saddlebags unopened. That's why it was on hand when he was shot. It was used as a compress because it was clean, or so the story goes."

"But you don't believe that?" I asked.

He looked back at me in horror. "Oh no, I neither believe nor disbelieve. But I would like to see it tested to make sure it is from the right period, that the brown stain really is blood, perhaps even some sort of DNA match to Jackson's relatives, if that sort of thing is possible."

"It's never been tested?" I said.

He shook his head adamantly. "No. The skeptics say Pope-Scott is afraid it will end up discredited, like the Shroud of Turin or the Smith letters."

"What if it's not authentic? What's it worth then?" I asked.

He shrugged and made a face. "It depends. If it's a real Stars and Bars, maybe a hundred thousand. If it flew at a big battle like Anteitam or Atlanta, add another hundred. If it can be shown to be handled by Lee or Jackson, add another. Collectors are fanatical about this type of item. Sky's the limit. I just sold a drum carried at Manassas for fourteen thousand dollars."

"Who would those collectors be?" I asked.

"Goodness, Mr. Keirnan. It could be anyone. One of the biggest Civil War collectors is a Brazilian industrialist who claims descent from one of the officers who fled there after the war rather than surrender. Maybe you've seen the pictures in *National Geographic*? They still have cotillions and that sort of thing every year?"

I shook my head, "Sorry."

"Well, anyway. It could be him. It could be someone like Mike Parsons, the fellow who founded Chickeninny. He's probably got the best collection of flags in private hands right now. It could be anyone. Any number of museums would be in the bidding," he said.

"What if it was stolen?" I asked. My knees both ached and I shifted from foot to foot seeking relief, but found none.

"Stolen?" he mouthed silently. Then, "I know Jay never insured it because he refused to allow it to be tested. If it's been stolen, he must be sick about it."

"I didn't say it had been stolen," I said.

"Right," he said, drawing out the word, and winked again. "Wait here." I saw him move to a desk in the back and sit down at a computer. A few moments later he pulled a page off the printer and brought it back to me. "Here." He folded the paper twice and tucked a corner under the edge of the door. I pulled it an inch or so, but he didn't let go. "Here are the places I would go if I had the Bloody Red Rag and I didn't want to be too public about the sale. But you didn't get it from me."

"Would any of these guys resort to violence?" I asked.

The small man gave a short, nasty laugh, sending a crackling static over the intercom. "Violence? We're collectors. I would shoot you right now with one of those antique pistols if I thought it would get me the Bloody Red Rag. Assuming of course it's really Stonewall's blood covering the thing. Don't be deceived by the grandfatherly look, Mr. Keirnan. We collectors are absolute fanatics."

"What do I owe you for this?" I asked.

"Are you going to get this flag, Mr. Keirnan?" he asked.

"Yes, I am," I answered truthfully.

"You will have it physically in your possession at some point?"

"Yes," I repeated.

"In exchange for this list, then, I want five minutes. Raise your hand and swear that you'll let me have five minutes with it. This is letterhead paper. It's got my private number. Day or night. Anywhere. I have access to a private jet through one of my clients. I just want five minutes, Mr. Keirnan. Swear to me!" He stared at me through the glass, hard-eyed and unblinking.

I let go of the paper, raised my right hand and swore. Sam Freeholder shoved the paper underneath the door and I put my foot on it before it could blow away.

# CHAPTER 14

*T*he ICU at Athens General is a giant circular room, with a central control area in a glassed-in sunken pit. There a young resident sits scanning banks of screens. Surrounding the control room is a large desk where the nurses march back and forth like sentries along the Western Front. The beds stick spokelike from the round center, separated from each other by curtains hanging from metal rods connected to the walls. The room lights are muted, and each bed is a glowing island of white sheets illuminated by a single overhead spot and the red, orange, and green glow of the CRT screens that monitor every single body function, and adjust the complex system of valves, pumps, and bellows accordingly. There are no chairs to encourage visitors to linger. I was told I had ten minutes.

Pope-Scott's bed was inclined almost to a sitting position, but his eyes were closed. His wavy brown hair was dank and matted, and fell limply over his forehead. His skin was pale and paperish, and under each eye the skin was a dark brown smear. He breathed shallowly through his mouth, which was caked with dried spittle. After a moment, his eyes fluttered open, and he licked his dry lips.

"Hi," he said weakly. "Could I get you to hand me that water?"

"Do you want me to call a nurse to clean you up?" I asked. I handed him a disposable foam cup full of ice and water, and guided his hand to the straw.

He smiled weakly. "No, they don't like taking care of me. Unless one of these monitors starts beeping, I don't get much attention."

I looked around, saw a clean, dry washcloth. I ran the water luke-warm and wet the cloth in the sink. "Hold still," I said, and wiped off his lips and eyes, used the cloth to brush his hair back, then turned back to the sink where I rinsed the cloth and hung it over the side of the small sink to dry. "Don't tell anyone I did that."

"I promise," he said. He smiled weakly. "Tolerate no uncleanliness in body, clothes, or habitation. General Thomas J. 'Stonewall' Jackson."

"Not really. Ben Franklin said it first. Jackson borrowed almost everything attributed to him from Franklin or from Lord Chester-field," I answered.

"You sound certain," he said, surprised.

"I am. Want to tell me what happened?" I asked.

"Not much to tell. I was walking our Corgi, Sumter, when ahead of me a tan Volvo pulled over and two men got out. The one on the passenger side raised his hand and I saw a gun. Before I could do any-thing he fired and I felt like I'd been kicked by a mule."

"Was he trying to kill you?"

"I'm not sure," he said. "My impression is yes, and maybe they were startled by the noise the gun made and ran away. It was very loud. My neighbors called an ambulance right away. But I don't really remember. It's just a feeling."

"I ran into those same guys yesterday. This is all about the flag," I said.

He sighed and shook his head weakly. "Poor Caron, I know she never intended all this to happen."

It was my turn to be surprised, "You knew it was Caron?"

"Of course. Who else? Her and that fruitcake Styrell." A nurse came by and looked at her watch, and then at me. She held up five fingers and moved on.

"She thinks she's doing the right thing, trying to make it so you two can have a normal life," I said.

Pope-Scott lifted his head from the pillow and leaned it toward me. His eyes locked on mine. "Have you read my book, Mr. Keirnan?" he asked.

"Not yet," I said.

"Most people haven't. They just know what they've heard, but they haven't actually read it. If they did, they would know I have nothing to apologize for," he said.

"The part about miscegenation improving the 'Negro' race?" I asked.

"At the time, there was a study out that suggested the average IQ of the Caucasian race was 101.38, and the average IQ of blacks 99.43. That is a huge difference. I cited it, and noted that it was common for racial improvements to come via unpleasant social mechanisms. The example I used was the height gain achieved by the English at the end of the first millenium. That occurred as a result of Viking raids . . ." he began coughing. I stepped closer, but he raised a hand slightly and motioned me back. "I never said I approved of rape."

"Still," I said.

"No 'still.' I will not apologize for a legitimate academic work."

"So you were politically incorrect, but right?"

"No, Mr. Keirnan. Subsequent studies have shown that the tests used in that study were biased. When the bias is removed, the IQ difference is statistically insignificant. I wrote a letter to the *New York Times* as soon as I learned of it, retracting the point. No one read my letter either. I was wrong, but I am not a racist," he said adamantly. I didn't believe him. I suspect we're all racists, it's just a matter of degree. That degree and a willingness to face up to it are the only things that separate us. But I didn't argue.

"Nine hundred and seventy-three pages, and that's all people remember," he complained. "I wish they would just read the book."

"I'll read it," I said. "I've ordered it."

"Caron could have given you one," he said. The nurse passed by and raised one finger. She looked at me over her half glasses and raised one eyebrow.

"I'm getting rousted," I said. "I need to know who you think might have the flag."

"As I told you, it's very desirable. Every museum in the world wants it. Private collectors . . ." he trailed off.

"But museums no longer shoot people to build their collections. We need the names of people who might want it and could hire men like the ones who tried to kill you," I said. "My research so far has turned up three names: Mike Parsons, Herbert Willingham, and Jo Ann Wilde."

He turned and looked at me. "My goodness. How did you find that out so quickly? Mike is very, very low key. Not many people even know he's a collector. Did Caron show you the letters?"

"No," I kicked myself mentally for not asking her if there was a file.

"Then add one name to the list, Marcus Alstott," he said.

"Is he a collector, too?" I asked. The name sounded familiar but I couldn't place it.

"Goodness no, Mr. Keirnan, he's the head of the Knights of the South, formerly known as the United Konvocation of Ku Klux Klans. He wants it . . ." Pope-Scott said. Before he could finish, the nurse stepped into the pool of light and jerked her thumb over her shoulder, sending me out. Behind her stood the young resident. He held a long light brown tube. It was hard not to notice that both were African-American.

# CHAPTER 15

*I* *turned my cell phone on when I left the ICU, and* saw from the display I'd missed a call. I didn't recognize the number, but when I called back, the phone was answered immediately by Bob John Wynn, another childhood friend, and now head of the local DEA outpost. He tersely suggested we meet at the old railroad station in fifteen minutes.

The old station was long gone, as was the popular bar that had taken over the building in the seventies. Now it was just a large circular brick drive ending in an empty lot. In the center of the lot, there was a gaping hole through which you could barely make out the huge timbers of some forgotten underground structure. Orange plastic netting cordoned it off. In a better neighborhood, the hazard would have rated more than a few yards of plastic and a few fence poles.

He arrived before me and I found him leaning up against the hood of a dirty brown Dodge. Bob John looked the same way he'd always looked, thin and intense, and dressed the way he always dressed, in nondescript Dockers pants, a short-sleeved white shirt, and a brownish tie. He shoved himself off the car spryly, showing no signs of the severe bullet wounds he'd sustained two months ago.

I parked, and he jerked his head away from the vehicles. "Let's walk, Top," he said. I reached into the back of the cab and pulled out my two canes, and limped beside him to the far end of the lot, to where the concrete ended. I didn't need the two canes, yet, but if I babied the knee with the canes and the braces for a week, I knew from experience I could avoid a month of creeping around like a hundred-year-old man. An ounce of prevention.

We walked ten or so feet into the knee-high weeds and stood in an empty depression, surrounded on every side by a hundred feet of empty lot, and overlooked only by two small buildings housing a senior citizens activity center and a row of pine trees overgrown with kudzu. Bob John looked nervous and uncertain.

"What's up, Bob John?" I asked.

"You're using your canes," he said.

"My knees felt good when I woke up, so I left off the braces and sure enough twisted one this morning. It's not bad. A little time off my feet and it will be OK," I said.

He nodded nervously, and peered over my shoulder. "Bob John, we're standing out here in the middle of a vacant lot. Is there something you want to tell me? Is it about Dee Lane?"

He looked at me in surprise. "No, though you probably heard. Word on the street is that he may be back soon."

"Good, but that's not it. Is it?" I said.

"I don't know if I should be telling you this," he whispered.

"Then don't," I said.

"What?" he asked.

"I said 'don't.' You're a straight guy, Bob John, if you tell me something you're not supposed to, it will drive you crazy. That's the way you are. That's why we never tell you anything. You're not cut out for the tricky stuff."

He looked insulted, and casually fingered the silver badge that hung on a chain around his neck. "There's a lot about me you don't know, Top."

"I doubt it," I said, "but what I said stands. If you shouldn't be telling me, don't tell me."

"I don't know. You need to know this," he mumbled, looking not at me, but down. He wore thick black brogans, and one nervous foot worked a trench across a small scrape of bare clay.

"You're going to tell me that Gillie is talking me down all over town. I know. Forget it. It'll pass," I said. I half-turned.

"It's not that," he mumbled. I turned back. His eyes held a mix of pity and confusion.

"Bob John, I'm leaving. I'm not going to let you put yourself in a place you don't want to be," I said and began walking away.

"Top, wait," his voice rising. "The ATF and Clarke County went to a judge this afternoon and got a search warrant. They've received what they feel is a credible tip that you've sitting on top of an arms stash. You're going to get raided."

I sped up, swinging the canes as quickly as I could, and called over my shoulder, "Can't hear you. I'll catch you later." As I climbed in the truck, I heard him yell, "Soon." I put the truck into gear and peeled off.

# CHAPTER 16

*I* *drove straight back to the school. The truth was we*
did have an arms stash, with a fair number of illegal weapons,
including several fully automatic machine guns, and a dozen
hand grenades. Most of them I'd inherited when my mentor Edgar
Haggenfuss had died and his wife Laurie had asked me to clean out
his gun safe. The weaponry now lived in a very well-hidden secret
locker behind a false wall underneath the hidden trapdoor in the
stage of the auditorium. The only two people who knew about the
secret compartment were the two people who'd built it, me and
Benny. We were pretty confident it could survive a very thorough
search. Still, I wanted to talk it over with Benny and see if he thought
we should clean it out.

When I reached the school, the parking lot was what now passed
for full, a half-dozen vehicles. There was a note on the door asking
me to come down to the auditorium when I got back. Benny and his
two maintenance workers, E. J. and Dice, and Maggie and her five
part-timers, all of whom, like her, also worked full-time in the large
research libraries at the university. Maggie sat on the steps that led up
to the stage. Everyone else sat on the pews facing her.

"Here he is," she called cheerfully as I entered. Benny stood and turned. He gave a small, almost imperceptible, what-could-I-do sort of shrug. Everyone half turned in their seats and clapped briskly. Maggie beamed. E. J. tucked two fingers into his mouth and gave a piercing whistle.

"What are we celebrating?" I asked, working my way down the center aisle.

"We hope we're celebrating something really exciting. But that depends on you. We have a business proposition for you. An offer," Maggie said.

"What sort of offer?" I wobbled to the second pew from the front, and one of the researchers, a shy, heavy-set woman named Linda slid over to make room. I shifted one cane to the hand that held the other, and used the back of the next pew to help lower myself into the vacated space. I dropped the last six or so inches, and grimaced as one knee rapped the edge of the armrest.

"Well, two offers, actually," Maggie said. Maggie is a shaggy-haired pixie, if pixies can be forty-something and wear horn-rimmed reading glasses that hang around their neck on a black string.

"OK, let's hear it," I said. The midafternoon sun poured in the high windows above the mural, throwing it into a graceful shadow. Behind Maggie, one beam cut a sharp diagonal across the stage, and dust motes swirled in the light.

"OK, OK," she said nervously. She looked around for support. E. J. gave her a thumbs-up. She continued, "Well, here it is. We'd like to buy into Polymath."

I started to speak, and she held up a hand to stop me. "Here's what we thought. Gillie's been telling everyone in town that unless you come up with thirty thousand dollars in two weeks, you're going to lose the school. We've gotten together and scraped up about thirteen thousand dollars. That should help you meet the bank payment. We thought that we can forego our salaries for a while, too, and you can tell us how much of the business we can buy. We'll be your partners."

"Maggie, I can't," I said.

"You mean you won't. You think we're just librarians," she said, her disappointment palpable.

"It's not that at all," I said. "But all of you have families and bills to pay. I can't let you risk your money, especially when things don't look too good right now."

The woman beside me spoke, "We're grown-ups, Top. We can make our own decisions. You don't have to worry about us."

"Alright, Linda! You tell him. He ain't nobody's daddy," crowed E. J., and slapped palms with Dice.

"Guys, it's too risky. I don't know if we're going to make it," I said.

"We'll make it, Top," said a square-faced man named Dave. "Have some faith in your new partners." Everyone laughed.

I sat speechless and looked from one face to another. Benny almost smiled. Maggie sat expectantly, nervously working a nail. E. J. tried to look cool, but eyed me carefully. I looked straight up at the tin ceiling we'd replaced small panel by small panel, then down at the refinished pews, and finally at the mural. The strong young workers in the picture picked cotton, cut pulpwood, and hunted deer. The white hunter laughed and threw his arms over the shoulders of his black and red companions, whose arms were laden with game. My throat was tight, and I did not trust myself to speak. Finally, I simply nodded.

Maggie clapped her hands and danced a small circular jig. Everyone else stood up and began hugging each other and shaking hands with me. I sat, confused, and listened to my new partners talk about their plans for the business. Benny caught my eye, and attempted a smile. E. J. produced a half-gallon bottle of Diet 7UP soda and a stack of small paper cups. He poured each one half full, passed them around and we solemnly toasted the new Polymath.

# CHAPTER 17

*A*fter the meeting, I returned to my office. Idly, I picked up one of the dozens of tops that covered the shelves and windowsills of the office. Before Gillie left, the windowsills had been covered with plants. Now a single lonely orchid sat in the center of a middle sill. I threw the red Whammo top across the room, aiming at a single board in the worn flooring. The point landed precisely in the center of the board, and the top spun straight up without a trace of wobble. A few minutes later, as expected, Benny knocked softly, then entered.

We sat at the round table in what used to be the nurse's station, and I wrote down what Bob John had told me on a yellow lined pad. Writing, not speaking just in case we were bugged, and just calling Bob John "a friend in the sheriff's department." Benny nodded solemnly, then shrugged. "I think we're OK," he said. "I'll go make sure. Did you check the safe?" He nodded toward the large safe up against the far wall, where we kept our legal weaponry, my SIG, a twenty-two target pistol, and a double barreled 4-10 shotgun, what locals called a varmint gun.

"Yes," I said.

"Any idea on timing?" he asked.

"You know what I know," I answered.

"OK, then, I'm going to get back to work. A squirrel has built a nest under the eaves on the back wall of the lunchroom, and it's blocked a gutter. We're starting to have water back up into the ceiling. I want to take care of it before we have any more rain. I may have E. J. and Dice do a little dusting and polishing. What are you up to?"

"Nothing," I said. "I may go lift for a while."

Benny stood, tore off the sheet I'd written on and the ten below it and walked over to the shredder. He ran all of the sheets through, then reached down and pulled the confetti into even smaller pieces. I watched him for a moment. "Hey, Benny. You said you wanted to talk about something. Is now good?"

He shook his head. "Not now. Later. We've both got work to do now." He reached for his Nextel to call E. J. and Dice. In the end I blew off lifting, and instead I sat there most of the rest of the afternoon, spinning tops and drinking a cheap bottle of licorice liqueur someone had left behind from a Christmas party or two ago. It was one of those things people get as gifts and bring to parties to ditch, and I felt like I was drinking cough syrup.

A few hours later, my legs were stiff from sitting at the desk and I needed to go to the bathroom. As I stood, a ringing sound came from the safe, and I retrieved a large, clunky Iridium phone, given to me by my new friends at the CIA, to replace the last one they'd assigned me. The first one hadn't survived the impact of hitting a highway surface at fifty miles an hour. I wondered if that long-promised job was coming through, and if I could stall a day or two to wrap up this flag thing before I headed to Chile.

"Top," I said.

There was a pause before he answered and I knew there would be a click at the end of every sentence. "Don't say my name or anything else. Just listen," said the voice on the other end, Gerald Morton. He sounded stressed. Granted, I only had seen Morton a few times, and talked to him a few more, but every time I had seen him he'd been impeccably dressed, sardonically cool, and in control. Maybe it was the way I had the phone wedged between my head and shoulder that made his voice sound so strained.

I stopped, turned, and leaned back against the wall. Shifting both canes to one hand, I used the free hand to take the phone. "Say OK," said the voice on the phone. It still sounded stressed.

"OK," I said. My bladder suggested I put the phone back on my shoulder and continue my journey. I ignored it, and listened.

Pause. "I assume my friend got you my message. Say yes or no." Click.

"Which friend?" I asked.

"Top, I asked you not to say anything," Morton snapped. "Our friend from the Waltons." I got it. John Boy, Bob John.

"OK," I said.

Pause. "Better," he said. "It's going down tonight." Click.

"What?"

"Tonight, you're getting raided tonight. Listen to me, Top. They've set up an arterial cordon. Don't try to remove anything. If you leave, they're going to pull you and search the vehicle. If you've got any pot or anything, I'd flush it," he said.

"OK," I answered, wondering what arterial cordon meant, and concluding it must mean roadblocks.

"Top, they're coming in hard. Will there be anybody there besides you and Benny?"

"No," I answered, making a mental note to call Amanda and tell her to keep her distance.

"When they come, don't resist. Tell Benny to put anything that might look like a weapon as far away as he can. You do it, too. I'd stash this phone somewhere. This raid is being led by the ATF. They can get out of control," he said.

"OK," I answered.

"Waco. Remember Waco," he continued.

"What?" I said, incredulous.

"The ATF. Waco," he answered, distracted. Traffic sounds were in the background. "Top, I'm on my way. As an interdepartmental courtesy, I'm going to be allowed in as an observer. I'll try to make sure it goes as easy as it can," he said. I heard a loud Germanic beep in the background.

"OK," I said.

"OK," he said.

"Anything else?" I asked..

He answered, "No. As I said, clean out any illegal drugs. If you have to stash anything, get it away from the auditorium. The warrant is very specific. They're looking for an arms locker in the auditorium. Everything else is just plain sight. See you about midnight."

I stared at the phone in shock. I had assumed Gillie was behind the warrant. But she'd never seen the gun locker. I wracked my brain, but gave up when my bladder reminded me again of the purpose of this trip. Leaving the phone in the hall where I could pick it up on my way back, I made my way to the bathroom. As I walked, I tried to remember what Gillie knew and didn't know. I stared at the green tile over the low urinal. As I finished, Benny entered the old locker room, and putting his finger over his lips, motioned me to the showers.

He turned on each of the eight showerheads, standing to one side and moving nimbly out of the way to avoid getting splashed. We met in the center of the long shower room, up on the raised walk, just out of the splatter from the nozzles, knowing the hissing water would make auditory surveillance all but impossible. He stood close to me and lifted his head toward my ear.

"Linda's brother is a deputy. He just called her and told her to tell everybody she was sick and to head on home. He told her not to ask him any questions or say anything to anybody, just to get out of here. I sent everyone home," he said. "But it must be happening tonight." I nodded and told him about Morton's call. He looked back at me, as stunned as I had been. "The auditorium?" I nodded.

"Did you ever tell her anything?" he asked.

"Nope. You?" I answered.

"No. And she was never in there?" he said.

"No," I answered.

"Then it's an informed hypothesis on her part. Gillie's pretty smart, she might have seen an assault rifle and put two and two together," he said.

"Assuming it's Gillie," I said, thinking about his use of the term "informed hypothesis."

"Who else?" he answered, and I shook my head, unable to think of any other possibilities. "Do you talk in your sleep? That could make it Amanda," he continued. "Or about a dozen more women, come to think of it. We built that thing a couple of years ago."

I shook my head "no."

"OK, then. It's a guess."

"I think so," I answered.

"But this is getting pretty close to home. You still want to sit tight with the locker?" he asked.

I didn't answer for a moment while I thought. Then finally, I answered, "Benny, it's hidden pretty well. We could move the stuff into the attic or drop it in the old grease pit in the lunchroom, but the gun room was built to withstand just this type of raid. I think we should trust it. What do you think?" Clouds of steam billowed up around us.

He pursed his lips thoughtfully, tilted his head and nodded. "Might as well. But, I think I'll turn on all the lights, so they don't get confused in the dark and shoot someone."

"Good idea," I agreed. "Also better make sure E. J. and Dice aren't planning to hang around tonight. They should get out of here before the trouble starts."

\*     \*     \*

Back in the office, the phone rang. It was Mr. Driggers, the elderly farmer and neighborhood watch captain who lived a quarter mile down the road, beside the creek at the base of the ridge. There was a hollow hiss on the line, and I pictured the plump, red-faced Mr. Driggers in his overalls, plaid cotton shirt, and John Deere cap, rocking on his son Russell's front porch, cordless phone, binoculars, and notepad on one side, and glass of iced tea on the other.

"Top?" he shouted.

"Yes, sir," I shouted back.

"You and Benny been up to something you shouldn't have, young man?" he yelled.

"No, sir, absolutely not," I called back. "Why do you ask, Mr. Driggers?"

"Because they's all sorts of soldiers and policemen setting up on top of the hill, just out of sight from your place. Using that idle field next to the Ganas's to set up. Russell says they're wearing these dark blue uniforms with helmets and visors and big yellow letters on the back that say ATF. They've even got some sort of armored thing with a machine gun on it. You know anything about that?"

"Not a thing," I fibbed. "Maybe I should call the sheriff."

"I already called the sheriff and asked them what was going on. They told me not to worry about anything, that it was just a drill, but I think that's a load of horse patootie. Looks like a 'shine raid to me," he said loudly. "That's what it looks like. If you're growing pot up there in that old school or something like that, young man, I think you better clean up your act PDQ, if you know what I mean."

"I'm not, but thank you, Mr. Driggers, for letting me know," my voice slightly hoarse from shouting.

"OK, son, good luck to you and Benny," he said.

"Thank you, sir, good night," I answered, and started to hang up, but heard him call my name in his old man's croak. I put the phone back to my ear.

"Top, these ATF fellows are the ones that are always burning places down and shooting the wrong people and crazy stuff like that. Benny, him being colored and all, you know," he hemmed and hawed, "Well, you know how things can happen. You tell him not to give these fellows no trouble tonight, all right? I'd hate to see him get hurt. All right? Good night, Top." His voice trailed off as he moved the phone away from his mouth before he finished his sentence. I smiled at the phone, thinking of Caron's comment about the South moving on and proud of my neighbors, then sat down behind my desk to wait for the Bureau of Alcohol, Tobacco, Firearms and Explosives. Remember Waco, the man had said. Well that made for some cheery thoughts.

I held my bottle of Ouzo up to the light and saw I had five inches left. Good, it was going to be a long night.

# CHAPTER 18

*A*round midnight the telephone rang. Benny and I were sitting in my office, watching a rerun of the 1994 World's Strongest Man competition. At least that's what I was watching and that's the TV that had the volume turned up to an audible level. The other three in the wall were turned to Samurai Jack on the Cartoon Network, CNN, and an old black-and-white gangster movie with a very young and handsome Jimmy Cagney. Puffs of smoke and flashes of fire poured from the barrel of his tommy gun as cars of gangsters chased each around dark city corners. Take that. I muted the TV and hit the speaker button.

On the phone was Gerald Morton. "Top Keirnan?" his voice was calm, its normal mellifluous controlled self.

"Yes, this is Top Keirnan," I answered, very formally.

"This is the Bureau of Alcohol, Tobacco, Firearms and Explosives, in conjunction with the Athens-Clarke County Police and various other involved agencies, as authorized under the President's Special Directive on Homeland Security," he said. I supposed that was meant to explain why the CIA was working on U.S. soil. "We have a warrant to search the premises for illegal arms. Is Mr. Benjamin Culpepper with you?"

"I'm here," said Benny.

"Is there anyone else in the school building? Please answer carefully Mr. Keirnan, I'd hate for the ATF team to be surprised during their search," Morton continued. There was a low murmur behind him. "Sorry, the ATF and Clarke County combined task force to be surprised."

"No, we're it," I said.

"Then please step out onto the front porch, hands over your head," he said. "Immediately, if you could."

Benny and I stood up. He picked up my canes and offered them and I waved him off, preferring to walk outside empty-handed. I steadied myself on the corner of the desk with one hand, then creaked around it and alongside Benny out into the hall and toward the door. We stepped outside into the quiet spring night. Too quiet, in fact, no cicadas, owls, or any of the normal sounds that surround the school on a night like this. For a moment, we stood and sipped the cool night air and watched the lights from the Driggers' farm twinkle in the distance. Over the ridge, we could see the faint glow of Athens.

Suddenly two cars slewed around the corner and raced up the driveway, light bars on the roofs flashing. From beside us, someone shouted "Down, down, down. To your knees." As we dropped, black-clad ATF ninjas split off from the shadows below us on either side of the small concrete porch and vaulted over the railings. They motioned us down with the barrels of a scoped black M-16. "Down, down, down," one shouted, although we were already on our stomachs. We laced our hands behind our heads.

My head hung over the rampart of the first step. Reflecting on the concrete steps below me I could see bright white light, along with red, blue, and yellow flashes. We heard the powerful roar of vehicle after vehicle as each skidded into the turning circle. At one point, there was a roar and skid followed by a small crunch and tinkling sound, and I heard someone swear.

Then came a deeper, more powerful roar, and I swiveled my head to see a matte black Hummer vehicle maneuver around the traffic jam and stop ten feet from the corner of the porch. A hatch in the top flipped up, a helmeted head popped from the opening. The officer smoothly dropped a machine gun onto a small mount bolted to the roof. Someone in the Hummer flipped a switch and across the broad roof, a row of lights turned the vehicle into a single blinding blur. I squeezed my eyes shut, and focused on the large green sunspot of retina burn that floated across the inside of my lids.

I felt someone behind me pull my hands back and tug on plastic cuffs. They cinched them tight. Then someone said "One, Two, Three." I heard a scuffling sound. A moment later, hands grasped me under each arm, and the same voice repeated "One, Two, Three" and I was lifted smoothly to my feet. Opening my eyes, I saw four helmeted, black-visored men standing in front of the green floating spot. The spot now had an orange center. In my peripheral vision, I saw Benny squinting and blinking, and wondered if the trick with the Hummer lights was deliberate, to disorient and incapacitate suspects.

One of the figures lifted his dark visor. It was a smiling man of Asian descent, midthirties, with a two-day beard and walnut-like muscles in each jaw. He held up a white piece of paper about an inch too close to my face for me to read it. "We have a warrant to search this school for illegal firearms. Under the Homeland Security directive, we have a right to use necessary force, meaning we are allowed to place you in restraints without cause. Is there anyone else in the building, sir, and I urge you to be forthright in your answer."

"There is no one else in the building. No doors are locked, you don't need to break anything. If you're looking for firearms, every weapon we have is in a large safe in the office. The safe is locked, but the combination is taped to the outside," I said.

He appeared not to hear me, but politely shifted me and Benny to one side. He then keyed a mike fastened with Velcro to one shoulder of his Kevlar vest. "Go, go, go," he barked. With one hand, he pulled open the door of the school and with the other he directed in a dozen or so agents with huge, sweeping gestures, like a third-base coach motioning a runner home. I noticed some of the figures wore slightly different gear and instead of bright orange ATF letters on their back, showed CC. He turned back to us.

"Who tipped you?" he said.

"My neighbor down the road," I said. "Check the phone records."

"We will," he said, then turned and walked back into the school.

We stood there, leaning against the railing, our hands in plastic tic strings, and watched Morton climb out of a Mercedes sedan and saunter up the steps. "Good evening, Mr. Keirnan, Mr. Culpepper; I'm Gerald Morton." This night, he wore a light sport coat patterned in a tight green and brown plaid. He turned slightly, and I saw it was tailored European style, with no vent in the back. Underneath he wore a light colored open-necked knit shirt that looked like it was made of some very fine wool. His brown slacks were creased to a knife edge, and his tasseled loafers were cut very low, showing lots of sock. As always, his gray-streaked hair was neatly parted and combed up off his forehead. The urbane Morton looked completely relaxed. He turned and surveyed the scene, holding up one hand to shield his eyes from the vehicle's spotlights.

Morton smiled. "You were tipped, Mr. Keirnan. What happened?"

I decided not to mention that he'd himself called me earlier that evening. "My neighbor saw you guys setting up. Called me to ask if I knew what was going on. There's not much around out here, so I put two and two together," I tried to shrug.

He made a face. "Let's go to the auditorium. Officer, can you open the door for us."

# CHAPTER 19

*W*e paraded to the auditorium, the black-clad trooper with the M-16, Benny, me, Morton, and behind ten or so police technicians, dressed in coveralls instead of full SWAT gear. Eight of the technicians carried four large zippered cloth bags. The other two carried a telescoping aluminum ladder. As we passed my office I saw the door of the safe standing open, the guns neatly laid out on the floor, and an agent, visor now up, carefully entering the serial numbers from the guns into a tablet PC. There was a small wireless pod on the top of the device.

Morton saw me looking at the device and said, "You wouldn't believe the stuff they have now." He looked down the hall appreciatively. "You guys have done a nice job with this place. Wasn't it pretty much a wreck when you moved in?"

"Yes, it had been empty for a few years," I replied.

"Well, it's very nice now," Morton complimented.

"So sweet of you fellows to drop in," I said. "Is that wine for us? Oh, a darling chardonnay. I just love California chardonnays, don't you Benny?"

Morton looked back at me and lifted an eyebrow. "OK, I was just trying to be pleasant. But I get your point. Let's get to business."

Inside the auditorium four of the ninjas were waiting on us. Three helmets were lined up neatly on the edge of the stage, facing out into the audience. Their owners wore thin black nylon caps. In the center aisle, the ones in coveralls dropped the four bags. There was the sound of zippers, and they began unloading plastic cases onto empty pews. I watched curiously as they carefully laid out two devices that looked like nightscopes, two more that looked like titanium versions of old-fashioned divining rods, although these had small wires that ran to headsets, and a handful of things that looked like ski poles.

"What are those?" I asked.

"The aluminum things are ski poles, we use them for tapping the floor. Everything else is classified technology, and I can't tell you," Morton said. The Asian ATF officer walked over and stood beside us. He still wore his helmet. A couple of the technicians removed plastic knee pads from another duffel bag and pulled them on.

"Someone has wiped this entire place down with some sort of furniture oil with roughly the same composition as gun oil," called out one of the technicians from the back. "Unless, they've been fired and not cleaned, we're not going to get much from the sniffers."

"Should have told us," I said. "We would have told the cleaning lady to stay home this week." The corners of Benny's mouth softened into an almost smile. Morton smirked and the ATF agent gave me a flat, cop-look that told me I'd gone far enough. We stood and watched them for the next hour as they crawled all over the huge room on hands and knees, sniffing, scoping, and tapping. Two asked us how to get up into the ceiling, and Benny walked them across the stage and showed them the metal rung ladder set into the back wall. As they began climbing, he said, "Be careful when you get to the edge of the stage. The ceiling over the seats won't support your weight."

"Thanks," one called down. An officer escorted Benny back to join us.

For the next two hours, we watched the technicians systematically work the room. Two went over every inch of the stage with excruciating slowness. We feigned polite interest, and when they reached the portion of the stage where the trapdoor lived, both Benny and me yawned at the same time and looked away. The ATF agent caught it, and immediately ordered the two techs to search the area again. They called to someone on the floor, and he handed up one of the bags. The two on the stage tugged the bag up, pulled out four gas vapor lights on telescoping stands and spotted them right on the area where the trapdoor is. They carefully laid their sniffer to one side, and slipped their scopes down. Kneeling, they went over every inch in excruciating detail.

One of the tricks when hiding a trapdoor is not to make it square. The human eye is peculiarly skilled at picking man-made regular shapes from nature's irregular ones. So our door was a composite of all the boards that covered it, and rather than swinging up on hinges attached to the floor of the stage, it sat on a frame that popped up three or so inches when Benny or I hit a button back in the office. Once it popped up, it then pivoted back out of the way. In other words, they were looking for a square trapdoor with the edges blended in, and they didn't find it, because what they were looking for didn't exist.

Around 3 A.M., all the techs gathered in the center of the room, and conferred with the officers in a low voice. Two approached our little group. "Nothing left but the wall, sir," one said.

"What wall?" I asked, suddenly alert. Benny's pupils opened and he looked at me in alarm.

"That's where the tip said the locker is anyway, sir," the other one said.

"Careful what you say. Source protection," said the ATF leader. Morton casually stepped in front of me.

"What are you talking about when you say 'the wall'?" I asked. I inserted myself in between the technician and the agent. I saw Morton reach into his pocket, and pull out a small device like an inhaler.

"The wall," called one of the technicians to the others. The men in the center of the floor nodded, and unzipped the remaining bag. He began handing out sledgehammers.

"There's nothing behind that wall," I said. "It's only a foot deep. You have my word."

"Stop shouting, Mr. Keirnan," said the agent quietly. "I'm right here."

"Can't you X-ray it or something?" I heard Benny say, and turned to see him strain at his plastic cuffs. I put my hand together and pushed as hard as I could, using every one of my overdeveloped shoulder and back muscles. I felt the plastic give.

"Sorry," said the agent. Three of the techs now held sledgehammers and were making their way toward the fresco mural on the outside wall.

"That's a valuable piece of art," I said. "I will sue your asses off if you so much as scratch it."

"It's not listed on your insurance," the agent said. "I checked.'

I'd told Gillie to leave it off, afraid it would draw attention to it, and we'd have to give tours to garden clubs. It had given her the perfect way to get back at me. "Bad," she'd said. This qualified as bad. I pleaded, "It's seventy years old for Chrissake. Please." Morton looked sorry for me. I twisted the cuffs and felt them give.

"Stop!" Benny yelled. The techs hesitated and looked back at me and the agent beside me. "Stop! I will cut your motherfucking throats if you touch that wall. I will cut your wives' throats. Your children's throats. I will kill you and everybody you fucking know." Benny never cursed and I'd never seen him this angry. His face was a dark purple knot. "I am Benny the Blade Culpepper. Do you ignorant sisterfuckers know what that means? Somebody tell these ignorant bitches that they're about to fucking die . . ."

"Unless you want to end up in jail for a long time, you'll shut up now, Mr. Culpepper. I know you're upset, but . . ."

"I will cut your head off, too, you pumped up . . ." The ATF agent cut him off by reaching around his head and grabbing him across the mouth with his gloved hand. The technicians hesitated and watched as the agent wrestled something that looked like a large Band-Aid adhesive bandage made of duct tape from a pouch on his belt. He handed it to the head technician, who still stood beside us.

"Peel it," he said shortly. The technician pulled off the paper backing, handed it back and the agent slapped it hard across Benny's mouth. He rubbed it to seal it.

"Please. Morton, please," I said. "Don't let them do this." I turned to the agent. "Don't do this." I twisted at my cuffs and pushed my shoulders out. My muscles strained and I felt the blood working its way to my face. The agent nodded, and one of the techs lifted his hammer and swung it into the wall. There was a soft, fleshy thud as the steel dug into the soft plaster, and a football-sized hole appeared.

"No!" I screamed, and popped the plastic cuffs. I shoved the ATF agent aside and jumped toward the wall. From the corner of my eye I saw Morton avert his face and push the inhaler toward me. I saw he wore latex gloves. There was a small whoosh and I froze in position, one leg up on the end of a pew, the other locked in position, a hand outstretched to the wall, and another against the chest of the ATF agent, fingers spread. A second technician swung his hammer, and another hole appeared. I couldn't move a muscle in my body, not even an eyelid.

Whispered Morton into my ear, "I'm really, really sorry, Top. I can't tell you how sorry. It's a shame." He reached over and sprayed Benny in the face. Benny turned his head. Morton said, "Don't bother to hold your breath, Benny, it's a contact aerosol. Goes through your skin."

"What did you do to them?" said the surprised ATF agent.

"Nerve agent. Lasts about thirty minutes," said Morton.

"I've never seen anything like that. We'll have to get some of that stuff," he said admiringly.

"In about thirty years," the CIA agent answered. "Come on, Chinn, move them into a sitting position and turn them around so they don't have to watch this." So we spent the next thirty minutes facing a blank wall, frozen, listening to the soft thuds of the hammers and quiet rips of the crowbars behind us, as they tore our mural down.

# CHAPTER 20

*T*echnically speaking, we could move in a half hour. But we were jerky and uncoordinated for another hour. After they left around 5 A.M., Benny and I spent a couple of hours trying to reassemble the pieces of the mural on the floor of the stage. But it was hopeless. The fragile old fresco had crumbled into small dusty bits, and there were few pieces larger than a silver dollar.

About seven or so we gave up and sat for a while in a quiet, private wake. Sometime later, I stood and told Benny I was going for a ride, see if I couldn't work off some of the anger. He nodded, but didn't say anything. I changed into a riding jersey and pants and put on a pair of stiff-soled Sidi riding shoes that clip into my pedals. I bounced up and down, and my knees felt OK. Well, not real OK, but I could move them, so I filled two water bottles, pulled the Waterford down and rode.

Today I wanted punishment, so I rode the ravine. That is, I pedaled down past the Driggers' farm to the point where the road dove straight down toward the creek bed, then began a long steep climb a mile or so up and over the ridge. When I rode like this, I just rode back and forth in the saddle of the hills, climb and coast, climb and coast. Since the coasting intervals were brief, it was mostly climbing, hunched over, thighs burning, rapid cadence in small gears. The Ganas's dog, Rufus, an amiable cross between a St. Bernard and a boxer, ran with me for the first couple of circuits, then gave up and sat in their driveway watching me with tilted head and raised eyebrows, a puzzled dog-look on his face. I smiled at him as I puffed by.

After an hour, I began to feel my knees protesting, and a few circuits later, as I stood to power up the ridge, my left knee buckled. I caught myself and threw out my right heel to get out of the clip. For a cyclist, getting out of clips is a natural act, taking no more thought than breathing, but this time, my tired right leg wouldn't torque, and I fell over onto the grass beside the road. I just stopped dead, like that character on the tricycle in the old *Laugh In* reruns, and toppled sideways. The fall only scraped a knee and tore the palm of my right glove. I lay there panting, occasionally trying to reach down with my hand and catch my heel so I could twist out of the clip.

As I struggled, a Clarke County cruiser pulled up beside me and turned on a yellow flasher, directing the nonexistent traffic around us. The door opened and the blond crew-cut officer I'd tossed up Pope-Scott's driveway walked around the front of the car.

"Everything OK?" he asked.

"I'm sort of stuck here. Is there any chance you could grab my left heel and give it a little lift. Just pull it straight toward you about an inch. That's it," I asked. There was a click as the binding let go. Without being asked, the deputy reached through the frame and did the same with my right foot. He pulled my bike out from between my legs, and leaned it carefully against the car.

I sat up, and looked around to see if I'd dropped anything. There was nothing on the ground but an old blue rubber band. Remembering my conversation with Caron, I picked it up and stretched it around my wrist. The dry, sun-cracked rubber popped, and two pieces of the band fell into my hand. I tucked the two fragments into the bottle pocket on the back of my jersey.

The young deputy stood over me. "Can you get up? Anything broke?"

"Nothing's broken, but I could use a hand," I said. He walked around behind me and put a hand under each armpit and tugged me to my feet. I stood there, swaying back and forth, the big muscles on my thighs twitching and jumping as they struggled to hold me upright without much help from my weak knees.

"You want a ride back to your place?" he asked. "These Fords got big trunks. I can just put it in and go slow up the hill so the trunk lid doesn't mess up the frame."

"You ride?" I asked.

"Used to," he said, with a laugh. He patted his midsection. "Not much anymore. Now spend most of my time riding a lawn tractor and get my exercise chasing a two-year-old around."

We rode the half mile or so up to the school driveway. Carefully he eased over the washout, watching his mirror to make sure the trunk lid didn't bang up my frame. He parked close in front of the steps, and came around to help me from the backseat, then carefully extricated the bike and leaned it up against the wall. "Nice bike," he said. Now he leaned back against the car, taking off his cap and twirling it in his hands.

"I guess this isn't a coincidence, is it? You weren't just riding by," I said.

He blushed red up to the roots of his blond scalp. "No, sir, I guess not."

"What is it?" I asked.

"Well, sir, I have to serve this restraining order. Mrs. Gillie Lynfield says you've been making threatening calls. I've got an order preventing you or any agent on your behalf coming within a hundred yards of her, her family, or her staff, and forbidding you from calling, e-mailing, or writing her family, staff, and clients." He opened the front passenger side door, reached on to the seat and pulled out a folded document. "This is the formal order." He handed it to me. I sat with my elbows on my knees, hands playing with a water bottle. I didn't reach out to take it. He laid it carefully on the steps beside me, put his cap back on his head and walked around the car.

Looking at me over the roof, he spoke again, "You know, I asked for this one because I wanted to get back at your for that ju-jitsu stuff you pulled on me yesterday. But man, you look rough. Take it easy, OK?"

I tried a smile and waved him away. Using the railing I pulled myself up, went inside and took a long hot shower. I pulled on a pair of jeans and a flannel shirt, and made my way to the office. As I passed the hallway to the auditorium, I averted my eyes.

In the office were two messages. One from Caron, told me to stop by and pick up some files and a list of contact numbers for Styrell. The second, from Mr. Greenfell at the bank, told me they had heard about my recent problems with the law and were enforcing a clause in the contract that allowed them to call for the full amount due plus an additional ten percent of the balance of the loan. In other words, I now needed roughly a hundred and sixty thousand in ten business days, by April 18th. I thought about the fact that he knew at 9 A.M. the morning after, and guessed how he'd found out. "Good luck, buddy," I answered the recorded voice, and hit a key on my computer to erase it. I made a mental note to ask Caron how long this rubber-band stuff took to start working.

Then I levered my legs up onto the desk, leaned back in the Herman Miller chair Gillie had bought for me, and slept for an hour.

# CHAPTER 21

**B**enny woke me around ten with a terse "Hey." I rubbed my eyes and looked at him, each of us unsure what to say after last night.

"Sisterfucker?" I finally managed.

"Usually makes them think. 'Motherfucker' has sort of lost its punch because of overuse," he shrugged.

"Guys here?" I asked.

"Yes," he answered.

"And?"

"They're upset, but more about the idea of police raiding us than losing the wall. Raises the issue in their minds of 'is there something going on we don't know about?'"

"What did you tell them?"

"The truth. That it was Gillie causing trouble. And I told them that you and I both used to be involved with some bad people, and unfortunately that made her story believable to the cops."

"What did they say?"

"Not much. I think they'd guessed as much," he said.

"Any one bail out?"

He half smiled, "No. In fact, I think Maggie and maybe a few others are a little bit excited. These librarians have a dark side to them."

"Do I need to talk to them?" I asked.

"I don't think so," he said. There were large, dark circles under his eyes, but he was calm and measured. I met his gaze and realized he viewed this as a test of his new role as partner.

"Good," I said, seeing from the softening of the muscle in his jaw that I'd passed the test. "What are you going to do today?"

"Work, I guess," Benny said.

"You're not going to go kill those cops like you said you would?"

He looked at me levelly. "No." A pause, then, "Not today." No way to know if that was meant to be a joke. "What are you up to?"

"We're still going to need some money, even if we get evicted. I guess I will research the names I got from Pope-Scott. Run them through Infosys, Lexis-Nexis. Google them. See what I can turn up," I answered.

"Sounds good," he answered.

"Hey, Benny. We got a protection order from Gillie." I reached on to the desk top, picked up the tightly folded document and tossed it toward him. Before it reached him, he reached in his pocket, removed his good Huddie Ledbetter razor and there was a quick flash of steel. The two halves of the legal document fluttered to the floor. He stood, watching it fall, and worked the razor in his hands, twirling it, moving it from finger to finger in a blur, turning his hand into a pinwheel of flesh and steel.

"Want to teach me that?" I laughed.

"Sure. But you should know that I started with seven fingers on each hand and now I have five. That one's called the Kansas City Cakewalk," he said as he smoothly folded the razor and tucked it back in his pocket.

"Pretty cool," I said.

"Back in the old days, a knife would get a black man thirty days in the county jail, a pistol sixty. But you could claim a straight razor was just for personal grooming. All the serious brothers carried them. They used to have razor contests in bars and the winner took home all the cake. Just like the old competitive dances. There's the New Orleans Cakewalk, The Cairo Cakewalk. St. Louis. Every one requires something different with the razor. For the Chicago Double Trouble, you have to do both hands at the same time. That's probably the hardest one," he paused, unsure of himself.

"Amazing," I said with sincerity.

"I'll show you sometime. I'm out of practice, but I can still work the blade some. You look stiff. Want me to bring you anything?" And of course I did.

I settled down in front of the computer with my six-pack of Old Milwaukee, the sale beer of the week. At this rate, I'd be drinking moonshine next week, and Sterno by the end of the month. I lost myself in the work. With our high speed lines and powerful servers, it took no time at all to build dossiers on all four of Pope-Scott's suspects. I typed up a synthesis of what I'd found, and ended up with about two pages on each of my leads.

Mike Parsons was the easiest to find information on, partly because he was the CEO of a publicly held company, and also because he was a very big billionaire fish in a very small pond, Montgomery, Alabama, population three hundred thousand. In the pictures, he was a tall, dignified-looking man in his midfifties. I don't know if I'd expected a white colonel suit and white goatee, but Parsons was straight from central casting for CEOs, favoring solemn dark blue suits with white shirts and muted blue ties. Many of the shots were of him at various charity events: the opening of the new Montgomery Symphony Center, which he'd funded much of, or at the dedication of the Parsons Chair in Entrepreneurship at nearby Mid-Alabama State University.

In most of the photos, he wore a solemn CEO-like expression or a polite smile, but there was also a shot of him receiving an award from the United Negro College Fund to celebrate the graduation of the hundredth Chickeninny employee from college. All had attended on Parsons scholarships. In this photo, Parsons and Missy, according to the caption his wife of thirty-one years, hugged a tall, heavy young black woman wearing a cap and gown while a half dozen other people looked on. Parsons grinned from ear to ear, and I could see a glimpse of the charisma that is an essential part of the successful entrepreneur's tool kit. There was absolutely nothing in the public record about Parsons and any connection to collecting or to the Confederacy. It made me wonder what other secrets a man like Parsons might have.

I didn't need to spend nearly as much time on Herbert Willingham. Willingham had been the scion of a wealthy family from Thomasville who'd grown, cured, and auctioned tobacco. He was a legendary collector and the articles hinted, not a particularly nice man. But he'd also died yesterday morning in the hospital at Emory, cause unspecified. He'd been sixty-four years old. Willingham was survived by his father and a sister. There was no mention of the disposal of his collection, and I wondered why Freeholder or Pope-Scott hadn't known of his passing. I tried to decide if the timing of his death put him at the top of my list or the bottom, and decided to hold my decision until I found out the cause of death, just in case he too had been shot at close range with a large caliber pistol.

Jo Ann Wilde had first hit the public consciousness twenty years ago as a stripper from Louisville, Kentucky, who'd met and married Harry Wilde, owner of sixteen car dealerships spread across the Atlanta area. He'd died two years later, leaving one hundred million to his young bride. The skeptics predicted an Anna Nicole-type meltdown, but the former dancer had turned out to be an excellent businessperson, and she'd led the industry charge into auto malls, building Wilde Auto into one of the largest dealership conglomerates in the country. Like Parsons, she was now also considered to be a member of the billionaire club.

Jo Ann Wilde was well-known to anyone who lived in north Georgia, mostly from her television commercials. (They typically showed her, short dark hair, busty and long-legged, reclining on a leopard skin rug thrown across the hood of a new car. Her throaty pitch was "Come get Wilde with me, baby.") But she was also known for her very active and obnoxious ownership of a local minor league baseball team, the Stone Mountain Goats.

There were many articles about her collection of war memorabilia, which spanned the American Revolution to the Gulf War, with special emphases on the Civil War and Vietnam. The collection was housed in a large building next to her newest, largest, and flashiest mall down near Lithia Springs. It was open to the public once a week, on Sunday from one to five, and then only to those who'd recently purchased a new or used car from Wilde Auto. It had proved to be a pretty effective marketing gimmick, and the place was jammed every weekend. But beyond that, nada. Ms. Wilde's private life appeared to be pretty private.

Marcus Alstott was also a public figure. He was sixty-five years old, a tall, kindly looking bloodhound of a man. At fifty-seven he'd retired as a mail carrier and begun devoting all his time to restoring the Klan from the butt of jokes back to a position of glory and respect, or if not respect, at least intimidation. Over the last decade, he'd convinced them to replace their hoods with white satin baseball caps with a red KKK embroidered on the front. The caps had even gained a certain chic in the media and several hip hop stars had worn them in their videos. He replaced the robes with golf shirts, and instead of midnight clandestine konvocations , he'd initiated huge rallies in civic centers and even a march on Washington. His latest initiative was a neighborhood patrol program: think Guardian Angels in pickup trucks.

Marcus had changed the rallying cry of the Klan to "Heritage, not hate," and his argument was for a return to "recognized standards of decency." He'd hit a chord, even across racial and ethnic lines, and Klan membership was soaring. Alstott lived in a quiet, lower middle-class neighborhood in Lagrange, Georgia, a former mill town near the Alabama border. There was no mention of him being a collector.

And finally, that left Styrell Wooten, according to Caron and Jay, a harmless, old burned-out hippie. Except Styrell had known how to fence a very valuable stolen flag, and had almost gotten both Jay and me killed by some guys who carried a gun with a silencer. I found nothing about Styrell in the media databases, but when I did a Web search on him, I soon found he had his own Web site, www.styrelltattoo.com.

Styrell, it turned out, was a tattoo artist of some note. He was known as Styrell the Stencil, and the Web site indicated his specialty was American Indian motifs. There was a picture of a scrawny worn-out-looking man with long stringy white hair, wearing a leather vest and leather pants and standing in front of a Harley Davidson Fat Boy motorcycle. He held a cigarette in one hand and a beer in the other. This guy made Willie Nelson look like an aerobics instructor. The Web site listed a phone number and an address down in St. Illa, a small town built on the rim of the Okefenokee Swamp, right down on the border with Florida.

I called the phone number on the Web site. A recorded message told me "It is time to hit the road, brother," and referred me to a Web site called www.motorcycleevents.com, which lists dozens of biker events across the country. I deduced that Styrell worked the festival circuit. This week there was an event in Scottsdale, next week in Boston, and the following week in Canton, Texas. A few calls to event organizers suggested Styrell wasn't scheduled to be at any of them. He was due to be at the Leesburg, Florida, event at the end of the month, though. I made a note to ask Caron how to get in touch with him.

The work therapy helped. As I'd worked I'd completely put the mural out of my mind, often for seconds at a time. Next stop, my bedroom to work the weights for a while. Make that the second stop.

First I needed to go to the john to get rid of this load of cheap beer. As I stretched, the computer gave a soft ping. A polite tap followed, and Bob John and Amanda stuck their heads in.

"Knock, knock," Bob John said.

"What are you two doing here at three in the afternoon?" I answered.

"I talked to Morton and Chinn. They told me about last night. And it's Saturday, Top," Bob John said.

Amanda set a paper bag on the corner of the desk. From it, she pulled out a golden bottle of white wine and set it beside the bag, then pulled out a bottle of a single malt scotch named Laphroaig. "We're on a mission of mercy. Do you drink this?"

"You don't drink Laphroaig, you chew the peat for nourishment, but yes, I've been known to consume Laphroaig. But I thought you wanted me to go on the wagon?" I said.

"Not today," she said. "Today is a day to get cross-eyed, falling down, commode hugging, story-telling drunk."

# CHAPTER 22

*M*uch later, Bob John left, and Amanda and I found ourselves in my bed, drunk and clothesless. I lay on my back, the bed dipping and moving beneath me, staring at the satin banners hanging from the rafters above us. Amanda supported herself on one arm, a leg thrown across mine, and with her free hand, stroked my chest softly. Her hand floated down, across my stomach, and ducked underneath the sheet. She kneaded me gently.

"More mercy?" I asked.

She smiled, and kissed me passionately, pulled back, and with lips still touching mine, said, "Would that be a problem?"

"Not really," I answered.

"I know," she said, throwing the sheet back and gently climbing atop me. Closing her eyes, she bit her lower lip. Her head swayed from side to side as she rode. I kept my eyes open, locked on her face, afraid that if I closed them, I'd see the holes torn in my wall. We worked like that for several minutes, but then I swung on top and slowly, imperceptibly it became rougher, pounding, belly-slapping, yelling sex, as I tried to drive her through the bed, pounding into her like those sledgehammers had pounded into my wall.

Our increasingly urgent profanities and endearments echoed across the hollow gym, and bounced back to us remixed. Eventually, we both came to a shuddering finish at almost the same time. I collapsed over her and rolled off. She threw an arm across me, and lay her head on my chest, and I could feel her warm tears landing on my skin, cooling as they slid down my sweaty side.

\*     \*     \*

When I've been too long without any action, a black nasty buzz builds inside me, a negative nervousness where I can't sit still and snap at everyone in sight. Then when I get a job, it's pushed out by the light buzz, a fast rapid climb from the depths into the clouds, with lots of little swoops and dives when the action starts. But either way, at trough or peak, I get the dreams, sometimes dark and soul-destroying and sometimes bright, colorful, over-the-top musical extravaganzas that I wake from grinning from ear to ear.

This night the dream was about Dee Lane, my best friend, whom I'd grown up with, come to school with, who'd helped shape the life I now lead. Dee Lane is six and a half feet tall, always dresses in black, usually in leather and denim, accessorized with any one of at least a hundred pairs of sunglasses. He earns a living as one of the world's best smugglers, and he'd introduced me into the world of illegal and semilegal operative work. He left a few months ago, presumably to hide out in the Seychelles and write his great novel.

In this dream, we were in the gym at night and a faint moon shown through the high windows that top the outside wall. In the moonlight, I could make out Dee Lane's black cowboy boots with their silver tips lined up just inside the door, and the dull sheen of his leather jacket neatly folded beside it. In the dream, Dee Lane took a soft jumper. It missed and bounced up on to the foot of my bed.

Amanda sat straight upright. She wore a gray Redlands water

polo T-shirt she kept hanging in one of the lockers here. She rubbed her eyes, and her mouth dropped open. "Goddammit, Dee Lane," she yelled. She reached over me and clicked on a lamp, and I realized this was no dream. Dee Lane was back.

"Jet lag," he grinned apologetically.

*     *     *

I hit the remote control that turned on the big overhead lights and after a pause, they lit the room up to full brightness. That didn't phase Dee Lane, who was already wearing sunglasses, which as always raised the question of how he could see to shoot hoops in the moonlight wearing dark brown wraparound shades. But I held both hands over my eyes like a visor and Amanda ducked her head under the coverlet.

"Go away," she groaned, "I'm so hungover I can't move. Please. You guys get out of here. And turn off the lights."

I looked at the clock beside the bed. The red numerals showed 5:46 A.M., meaning that it would be getting light in another fifteen minutes or so. Dee Lane discreetly looked the other way while I stood and buckled my jeans. The room tilted quickly, then righted, and I considered the possibility that I was still slightly drunk. I'd consumed half of Amanda's wine and the bottle of Laphroaig pretty much single-handedly, a sufficient reason. But when the adrenaline dipped and surged like this, it was hard to gauge the effects of the liquor. If you drank it on a buzz peak, it had no effect at all, and in the trough, one drink could cause slurring and slobbering.

"Am I sober or drunk?" I asked Dee Lane.

He looked at me appraisingly. "Drunkish, I'd say, but not drunk. Nothing a pot of coffee and an ibuprofen won't fix," he decided. "Come on. You shower and I'll make the coffee. See you in the office in fifteen. Leave this poor woman alone to deal with her fate."

"Not too strong," I asked. Dee Lane used one scoop of coffee for every cup of water, turning every cup into a gritty bitter porridge.

"*Right,*" he grinned wolfishly, as he bounced around on one socked foot, wrestling a Tony Lama boot on the other.

# CHAPTER 23

*I* *made the mistake of closing my eyes in the shower,* and felt the room pivot. Quickly I opened them and twisted the faucet toward cold. Every showerhead in the room was at its original height of five and a half feet except the one I stood under. I'd had this one raised a foot, and installed a high volume head on it, with the result that a waterfall of cold water now poured over me. I grimaced, locked my arms into stiff columns at my side, and spun in the freezing torrent for a moment, before stepping back and grabbing my towel. Five minutes later, clad in tennis shoes without socks, blue jeans, an orange T-shirt, and a faded denim shirt missing one of its fake mother-of-pearl buttons, I made my way to the office.

Inside the room, I found Dee Lane sitting in my chair, feet up on the desk, with Benny across from him holding a coffee mug. Benny wore the same clothes he'd worn yesterday, and there were huge black bags under his eyes. He looked like hell. Dee Lane grinned as I entered, swung his long spiderlike legs down and reached inside his black jacket, coming out with a silver flask. He unscrewed the cap, poured a dollop into the bottom of a cup, and topped it off with black coffee from a thermos. Steam rose slowly over the cup.

"Drink up, Topster," he said cheerfully, thrusting the cup at me.

"When did you get back?" I asked. The coffee was as hot as it looked—he must have microwaved it after brewing, and he'd ignored my request to go easy with the scoop. I sipped cautiously and grimaced. Benny caught my eye and gave a small shake of his head, presumably a comment on the coffee.

"Good to see you, too," he answered. This was classic Dee Lane. He's in a line of work where it's in his best interests that no one know too much about where he is and what he's doing. But he has a theory that if you appear to be hiding something, you just make people curious. Part of his shtick is answering questions in a Zen-spacy and totally unhelpful way. For example, if I'd said, "How was the Seychelles?" he might have answered with something like "The weather in the Indian Ocean never changes," which seems like an answer until you think about it. And if I'd said "How was the Moon?" he would probably have answered "That light gravity can get to you." His objective in every communication is to add to the tangled haystack of misinformation in which he hides his real actions.

In this case, I still didn't know when he'd gotten back, but I didn't really care, and wasn't about to waste what little energy I had trying to pin him down. The best way to get information from Dee Lane is to wait him out. I took another careful taste of the scalding hot coffee. On the desk was a bottle of ibuprofen. I ate three. Benny sat in silent agreement and sipped his coffee beside me. After a minute, he stood and turned his chair to line up with mine. We sat side by side looking out of the windows at the pale gray sky. I walked over and turned out the lights, and we sat in the semidarkness while Dee Lane waited for us to ask him another question. We did not oblige, but instead quietly drank our coffee.

Dee Lane reached his long arm over to the credenza where the two computers sat, picked up one of my tops and examined it, put it down, and swung his feet back up onto the desk. After a minute, he brought them down again. He picked up the flask and tightened the cap, loosened it, started to pour himself a drink, changed his mind, and then tightened it again. For all his patience, Dee Lane can't take silence. After five minutes or so, he said, "I got a message through Shaw's that you were in a bind. Thought I'd come help out."

I wondered who'd sent the message. Bob John? Morton? Instead of answering, I simply nodded. Benny blew across the top of his cup and little brown wavelets rippled into the far rim. He carefully extended his upper lip over the surface like a horse and drew in a tiny drink, and winced as the hot liquid hit his tongue. Dee Lane looked straight up at the high ceiling, where globe lamps hung down on long brown cords. He turned back to our profiles.

"Gave up on the novel," he said, "after one chapter."

"Why's that?" I asked, with as much disinterest as I could muster. He paused.

"It sucked," he said. Benny started and pushed the coffee away so it wouldn't spill in his lap. A drop splattered on the hardwood floor beneath him. He reached down and wiped it up with his thumb.

"You gave up because the first chapter sucked? Think it would have gotten better if you'd worked at it?"

"It wasn't the *writing* that was the problem," Dee Lane said. "The *problem* was that the first draft was *really good*. They say to write what you know and I did. I put in lots of detail. Crossings. Drops. Diversions. Names. It was riveting, if I do say so myself."

I looked at him without expression. "Hey," he protested, "I've read a lot of books. I know *good* when I read it."

"So what was the problem?" I asked.

"There's such a thing as too good is what the problem is. When I read it, I realized that the day the book hit the shelves is the day *I'd* get hit. Think about my clientele. What would they say about me explaining all the tricks of the trade to Curly, Moe, and Larry?" he asked. Insider names for Customs, the DEA, and the FBI.

"So take all that stuff out," I said.

"I did," he said, shaking his big blond head. "And then it sucked."

Benny started laughing, not his normal quiet chuckle, but small whoops. He quickly moved his cup to the corner of the desk, placed it, and folded both hands into a tent covering his nose. Squinting, he laughed into it. After a moment, we both joined him. We sat there while the red sun climbed determinedly over the pine trees, throwing long shadows out across the freshly tilled soybean fields, and in between bouts of laughter drank our undrinkable coffee.

# CHAPTER 24

"*H*ow clean are we?" *Dee Lane said at some* point. I shrugged. "Bob John says 'very.' They had a phone tap on my line and laser mikes on the windows. Should be gone now." Laser mikes are easy to defeat anyway if you know they're there. A couple of cheap radios turned loudly to different stations, for example a Spanish rock station and Christian talk radio, and pointed toward the window creates a set of randomized vibrations that mask those caused by the voices in the rooms.

Dee Lane grimaced. "*Maybe,* but then again maybe they left one or two behind accidentally on purpose." There is a fine line between caution and paranoia, and Dee Lane is at least two long steps across it.

After some debate, we wheeled three chairs down the hall to the boys' locker room. We set them up just inside the shower room, out of range of the spray, and turned on every faucet. Dee Lane left, and five minutes later returned with a full thermos of coffee. He set it on the tiles between us. Raising his steamed up glasses and parking them atop his head like a hair band, he looked at us blandly. "Well, what now, *boys*? What's going on here?"

And I explained, starting at the point when he'd left town after dropping off the duffel bag of money for me to deliver, telling him how Gillie had tried to steal it, and how Raoul Menes had sent a crew of redneck meth heads to get it back. Benny chimed in at a few appropriate times, adding details and interpretation. We told him how the peckerwoods tortured and killed Harlan, and kidnapped Vinyl Man, and how we'd gotten Vinyl back, and retrieved the money and what we'd done with it. Dee Lane nodded in approval at my story. Benny nodded in approval at the parts of the story I left out. Then I told Dee Lane about Gillie's campaign to put us out of business, and the bank and the flag.

"Anything else you'd add to that, Benny?" he asked, when I'd finished.

"No, I don't think so," Benny said.

"OK, I need to think for a minute," he said, and tilted my Herman Miller chair back and closed his eyes.

I left, first to use the bathroom, then to check on Amanda. I found her in the girls' locker room, sitting on a wooden bench, arms crossed, hair falling across her face, one towel across her bare legs and another wrapped around her shoulders. She looked up as I came in, and I saw the greenish cast just underneath her jaw.

"Are you OK?" I asked.

"Unnh, unnh," she answered. "I've already thrown up twice. How do you do this? I'm going to go back to bed, hope to die before I wake." She stood and wobbled out of the room. A sour odor trailed behind her.

I walked down the hall, first to the office, then to a janitor's closet where I pulled out a small blue plastic bucket. I brought the bucket back into the gym and placed it beside the bed. Amanda was a long lump under the covers. On the small table I set a glass of water and the bottle of Advil analgesic. Before I could say anything, I heard a muffled "Thank you" from the blanket. I patted one likely hump softly, and went back to the showers. Dee Lane's eyes were open now and he was smiling. Benny was wearing a clean shirt, probably taken from one of his lockers.

"Do you have a plan?" I asked, knowing the answer from his smile. Smugglers are by their nature planners, studying tide tables and phases of the moon, and developing plans and backup plans and fall-back backup plans ad infinitum. And Dee Lane? Well Dee Lane was the most devious, complex, careful, creative, and all-round best planner I'd ever met.

"Not that hard a problem," he answered.

"OK, so tell us," I said.

He nodded his head, "*Right*. Well, it's not *that hard* a problem, as I said. Here's what we need. You, old son," he pointed to Benny, "need an airtight alibi for tomorrow night and some roofies. You probably know Hoffman–La Roche has added blue dye to the new ones to make them easier to detect, so if you can get Mexican bootleg without the color, that would be better."

"Why would I know anything about roofies?" asked Benny. Roofie is the slang term for rohypnol, made famous as the date rape drug that wipes out the memory of the assault.

"General knowledge. And you," he pointed to me, "need to agree to find that flag." He leaned back triumphantly, as if waiting for applause. Benny and I looked at each other. Benny shook his head as if trying to lose a mosquito.

"The flag?" I'd almost forgotten about Pope-Scott and the flag. "Why do I need to find the flag?"

"I didn't say you needed to *find it*," he said. "I said you needed to *agree* to find it. Specifically, you need to get them to give you a ten-thousand-dollar retainer."

I shook my head tiredly. "Dee Lane, we need a hundred and sixty thou. What good is ten going to do? Are you going to make up the difference?"

He held up one long bony finger, "That, *my brother*, probably wouldn't do any good anyway. If I've figured out Gillie's next move, she's going to make an offer for the school to the bank. I'd guess she has someone inside helping her. So you'll need to borrow a million next. I can't find you that sort of money. Well, I could, but you wouldn't like the interest rates."

I hadn't thought about someone at the bank being in bed with Gillie, literally or figuratively or both. Frowning, I wondered why I hadn't seen it. Greenfell or Nelson? "Explain it to me one more time then. The ten thousand?"

"That's the retainer. For Jimmy 'The Rattlesnake' Sweeney. Either of you guys know Rattlesnake?" he asked patiently, as if it should have been obvious.

My head hurt, although I couldn't tell if it was from the hangover or from trying to pull information from Dee Lane. Benny said, "I know him to speak to. He worked for Elbert some."

I didn't know Rattlesnake, but I knew of him. He is a lawyer from Atlanta. The TV channels love him, and why not? He is a bona fide character, short and muscular, with a square jaw and black moustache. He shaves his head twice a day and wears skin-tight beige silk shirts and similarly colored suits, so tight that he carries his Marlboro Light cigarettes and lighter in one hand and wallet in the other so as not to ruin the cut of his immaculate pants. His hand-painted pale ties are seldom visible, instead usually buried underneath a wreath of gold chains.

Rattlesnake is shrewd, ruthless, and not at all choosy. His practice serves drug lords, gangbanger hit men, and pedophiles. Rattlesnake is rumored to be willing to do anything, including threatening witnesses and jury bribing, to get his clients off. Although the police had never proved it. And they'd tried more than once.

"I have a lawyer," I said. "He said there's nothing we can do."

"I have the same lawyer you do, Mel Hirschman. I introduced you to him. But you don't need Mel. Mel's good for helping you decide between an S-Corp and a C-Corp. For this, you need Rattlesnake," Dee Lane said patiently.

"What's he going to do?" I asked.

"Rattlesnake? Who knows? That's why you pay him," Dee Lane

laughed. "My guess is he'll start by suing Gillie, the bank, the loan officers, the ATF, the DEA, Home Depot for selling them the sledgehammers, Clarke County, your HMO, the tobacco companies, the UN. Pretty much anyone he can think of."

"And?"

"We need to slow down the foreclosure process, and keep Gillie occupied. Rattler will do that."

"Why would he take a little case like this?" I asked.

"He owes me, number one," Dee Lane said confidently. He held up a finger to indicate that was as much as he would say on that topic.

"And number two?" I asked.

"He's a real misologist," Dee Lane said.

"He hates to argue?" I asked, confused.

"Do you mean misogynist?" Benny asked. He said it so casually I knew he was showing off.

"Right. He's on his eighth wife. To add insult to injury, the seventh blew up the prenup and took his antique Bentley. He's still pissed about it," he said.

"Ten grand?"

"Point of pride with this type of lawyer. They want some cash up front. The jury may have reasonable doubts about these clients, but their lawyers don't," he said, standing. He picked up the thermos and empty cups and placed them on the seat of his chair. "I'll take this stuff back to the office."

"Is this meeting over?" I asked, surprised.

"Well, you need to put on some socks and go find Caron and get your money. Have them make the check out directly to Rattlesnake if you can. And Benny and I need to talk. 'Come, Watson, come. The game is afoot,'" he said, raising an eyebrow to ask me if he'd gotten the quote right.

"Perfect. *The Adventure of the Abbey Grange*," I answered.

"Maybe I'll apply for a job," he said.

"It's a thought. Dee Lane, you're going to call a top criminal lawyer at," I looked at my watch, "seven-twenty-eight on Sunday morning?"

"Top, when do you think a lawyer like Rattlesnake gets called?"

I looked at Benny and shrugged. He shrugged back and said, "It's better than sitting here and waiting to see what crap Gillie pulls next." It is indeed, I thought.

# CHAPTER 25

**R**attlesnake lit a new cigarette off the butt of the one he was smoking. He ground out the old cigarette in a small red tin ashtray. "You know what this guy did for me?" He pointed to Dee Lane with his open hand.

"No." We sat in a Waffle House just outside of Stone Mountain. Rattlesnake wore a tuxedo. He'd ducked out of a charity event being held at the monument to come meet us.

"Third wife? Fourth wife? No, third wife. Malaysian dancer named Tam. Well her real name was some fourteen-syllable thing with about thirty A's in it. Her family nicknamed her Tam. Pronounced as a cross between a tee and a dee. Spelled with a tee. Tam and me split up and she takes my four kids to Kuala Lumpur. Not just the kid we had together, but all my kids, including three from my first marriage. Takes them to KL and says she's going to raise them Muslim. I tell my mom this and she freaks. She's calling me ten times a day, telling me what this priest says and that priest says, and she's eating tranquilizers like candy corn. So I'm trying to keep her from going off the deep end, and at the same time I'm calling Interpol, the FBI, every law enforcement agency I can think of. And I'm hiring lawyers by the platoon. Before it's done, I've got Malaysian lawyers, Singaporean lawyers, Swiss lawyers, lawyers with long beards that work exclusively in the Islamic religious courts. My lawyers have lawyers. Nobody can do shit. My ex-wife's brother-in-law is a sultan or something and he's got too much ooomph." He took a drink of his orange juice and licked his lips.

"My oldest kid, Leeza, slipped a letter to a British kid at school. This kid's parents called me and read it to me over the phone. terrible. She's twelve and they're talking about doing that operation they do on girls there and finding her a husband when she turns thirteen and crazy stuff. I can't tell if it's for real or if the whole thing is something Tam cooked up to drive me over a cliff. If that's what it was, it sure worked." Rattlesnake drained his orange juice and held up his glass. He waggled it toward the woman behind the counter. Something on the glass caught his eye and he held it up to the light.

"Must have been tough," I said, looking over at Dee Lane. He looked uncomfortable.

"You don't have any kids, right? You can't imagine. You just can't imagine."

"Probably not," I said.

"Damn straight. You can't, unless it happens to you. I can't sleep, I can't work, I can't even screw. One day I ask one of my clients what to do. And he asks me if I can get them out of the house. I say sure, Leeza can get their nanny to take them to McDonald's or something, but that doesn't help, because Tam's got their passports. He says he knows a guy that can smuggle anything. Guy's moved drugs, high tech, weapons, anything that needs to get from point A to point B, this guy can get it there."

"Dee Lane."

He nodded, "Dee Lane. So I call him and tell him about it and ask him if he'll do it. You know what he says?"

"Yes?"

"No, he says that he will go over there and ask them if they want to come home, and if they do, he'll bring them back."

"And?"

"Three of them said yes. The youngest, used to be Casey, now he's Khassim, said he didn't want to leave his mom. Fair enough. So Dee Lane doesn't bring him. Nanny came back, too."

Rattlesnake picked up the menu, gazed at the back for a second and put it down. "I feel like having a piece of pie, but I have to tell you, this lipstick mark on my orange juice glass isn't inspiring any confidence in me. Anyway that's why a big swinging dick lawyer like me is going to work for a nobody like you. See, my thing is 'my word is my bond.' If I threaten you, I want you to believe it. So I make sure I do what I say I'm going to do. When Dee Lane brought my kids back, I told him he had one phone call. One." He held up his index finger for emphasis. "That no matter what I was doing, if he ever used it, I'd come. He used his phone call for you, Kiernan. I hope to hell you appreciate that." Rattlesnake flipped open his wallet and showed me a picture of three smiling blond children and one dark complexioned one, the oldest a girl of twelve or thirteen. "Pretty kids, huh?"

I admired the picture a moment, then turned to look at my friend. He was more interested in trying to decipher the menu. The waitress set down a new glass of orange juice, sloppily poured me some fresh coffee, and pulled a rag from her pocket and wiped up where she'd spilled. After a moment, he stood, "Where's the john in this place? I've got to pee like a racehorse." With the hand that held the rag, the waitress pointed to a corner.

Rattler laughed, "He hates that shit, huh? Talking about himself. Well, to hell with him. You should know."

# CHAPTER 26

*I* *gingerly* *removed* *the* *hot* *Starbucks* *latte* *from* between my thighs and held it suspended in air, as Dee Lane carefully crept his '92 512TR Testarossa car over the wash and up onto the pavement without bottoming out. Once on the pavement, he came up to speed slowly as he steered with the hand that held the coffee and shifted with his right.

"DeWayne Lane. Seen up and dressed before noon two days in a row. Call Ripley," I said.

"Enjoy it. La Digue is a nine-hour shift. So day is night and night is day to me, and since I normally stay up all night and sleep all day, it means I'm waking up at 4 A.M. and going to bed at 9 P.M. But I don't expect it to last long," he smiled. We drove a sedate seventy miles per hour. "I'll take it easy until we finish our coffee. This European thing of no cup holders can be a pain in the ass sometimes."

"This coffee is a treat," I said, taking a sip. It was very hot, triple cupped, and tasted like it had a couple of extra shots in it, which it probably did. "I've been too broke to buy Starbucks coffee."

"I am so pleased you are pleased, sir. *Cheers*," he said sincerely, lifting his cup. "What did you think of Rattlesnake?"

"You could have told me he actually looks and sounds like a rattlesnake," I said.

"No, it's too much fun to see people meet him for the first time. They get mesmerized watching his little black eyes go back and forth and his tongue lick his lips. Did you see the waitress jump when he spoke to her in that sibilant voice of his?"

"Did you see me jump?"

"*What-e-ver*," Dee Lane pronounced in his best Valley Girl accent. He grinned from ear to ear and took a slug of his coffee.

"I thought you sold this car," I said.

"I couldn't part with it. I've already had the seat lowered and the rails extended so I could fit inside," he said.

"Nice ride," I said, half-truthfully, since I find sports cars noisy and bumpy, and hard to get my stiff legs into and out of. This was even a little more cramped than normal. Dee Lane has Schedoni luggage made to fit into the miniscule front trunk, but my small duffel was tucked into the microscopic luggage compartment behind us. I'd had to slide my seat slightly forward. "You want to tell me where we're riding to?"

"Anywhere you like, as long as it's at least a seven-hour drive away, we're seen by about a hundred witnesses and we get receipts for dinner and the motel," Dee Lane said.

"What?" I asked.

"Top, if Benny and his crew need an airtight alibi for tonight, you do, too," he said. We'd increased our speed to about eighty-five, and tore along the curvy two-lane roads.

"Want to tell me what's going on?" I asked, not really expecting an answer. In fact, I didn't expect Dee Lane to acknowledge the question. He surprised me by answering directly.

"No, I don't. Not yet," he said. I looked at his barracuda profile. He'd slightly cracked his window, a habit from the old days when he'd smoked, and the wind whipped his earlobe-length blond hair about his head. He glanced over at me, then back at the road. "Hey, you can get squeamish about stuff."

"This from a man who hates to look at a paper cut?" I said.

"Different kind of squeamish," he answered.

"So you're telling me what? You told Benny to do something you knew I wouldn't like. Probably something that could put him in jail. Is that what you're hinting at?" I felt myself getting angry.

"Come on, Topster. Benny isn't *Tonto* and my name isn't *Kemosabe*. I didn't tell him to do anything. I laid out a plan and he bought into it," he said.

"Want to tell me what it was?" I reached out with my left hand and grabbed the steering wheel. I gave it a twitch and we fishtailed across the road, tires squealing before we straightened out.

"Nope, your name isn't Kemosabe either," he said, pulling both hands off the wheel and using them to adjust his sunglasses. "Go ahead if you want to be an asshole, kill us."

He pressed on the gas pedal and we sped up. I couldn't take my eyes off the road, but from the corner of my eye I could see fence poles flying by at an alarming rate. He pressed harder and I concentrated on steering. "Tell me if you want to brake or something." I glanced down for a microsecond and saw the speedometer at one o'clock. On the Testarossa, one hundred mph is at high noon. I looked back up in time to see a yellow sign with a curve on it, and just past it, a sign that said "Speed Limit 25."

"Brake," I barked. He slowed to fifty a few feet before the entrance of the curve and accelerated us evenly through it as I managed the wheel. Even so, we could feel the back end float a bit as we hugged through the curve. Once we straightened out, I let go of the wheel.

"So where are we going?" he said, smoothly reaching out to take control.

"How about St. Illa to find Styrell Wooten?"

"So we're really going to find the flag? Hot diggity dog," he said.

"I don't know what we're doing, but St. Illa is plenty far from whatever crap you and Benny are up to," I said, still miffed at being left out of the plan.

"Nice driving back there," he said, grinning, flipping up the cover and turning on the concealed radio. "Why don't you find us something to listen to before we get out of range?"

I fiddled with the tuning button. "We're headed in the wrong direction. You can either turn around or take a right when we get to 22. We can then go down to 129 and catch I-75 down to Valdosta."

# CHAPTER 27

*S**t. Illa is tucked away at the very bottom of* Georgia near the Florida line. According to the topo map, it straddles a little suppository of dry land extending up into the backside of the massive Okefenokee Swamp.

At the turn of the last century, the Okefenokee was seven hundred square miles of shoulder-deep water, floating islands, alligators, and virgin cypress trees. In 1906, two companies began a race to harvest the timber. On the northeastern side, the Hebard Cypress Company built twenty miles of railroad running from their mill in Waycross down to Hopkins, a tiny village on the edge of the swamp, and later extended a small spur down to Billy's Island, inside the swamp itself.

On the southwestern side, Portland Timber and Pine built a camp called St. Illa. Their plan was to float the logs out using tiny tugs, 240 miles down the Suwannee River to Cedar Key on the Gulf of Mexico. It never was very successful. Cypress doesn't float well, and the Suwannee is crooked, narrow, and shallow much of its length.

Still, St. Illa found ways to get by. For a while the town was the unofficial moonshine capital of America. Turpentine is also made in a still, and the numerous turpentine stills in and around the swamp provided perfect camouflage. In those days, St. Illa was a wild and lawless place, full of gangsters from Atlanta and Cincinnati who came to pick up their loads.

But by the early thirties the cypress was gone and prohibition ended, and St. Illa shrank from thirty thousand down to its current size. Now the town grows a few peanuts and calls itself the "Backdoor to the Okefenokee, a Hunters' and Fishermen's Paradise." I recited all this to Dee Lane as we drove down I-75. He's one of the world's great listeners and appeared completely engrossed in this miniature history lesson.

"Very interesting," he said when I finished. "St. Illa. Isn't there a river with a name something like that down there?"

"Satilla. Same derivation, but it's on the other side of the swamp and flows to the Atlantic. Not even close," I said, examining the map on my lap.

"St. Illa has a rep. Lots of pot grown back in the swamp. Ragweed. Not my sort of thing, but that's what they say. Do we know exactly where to find Styrell when we get there?"

"Nope. That's what all this history I'm rattling on about is for, to disguise the fact that I spent four hours researching and learned not a darn thing we can use. His mail goes to a P.O. box, even though his phone listing says rural route four," I said.

"Well, it's very interesting, anyway," he said happily. "How are you going to find him1?"

"Two options. We can find rural route four and go ask around. Or we can work the bars," I said.

"Let's work the bars," Dee Lane said, "I'm thirsty."

"St. Illa has twelve of them," I said.

"Isn't that a lot for a town of five thousand?" Dee Lane asked.

"Seems like a lot," I agreed. "Maybe it's the 'hunters' and fishermen's paradise' thing."

"Or the fact that St. Illa is only a few miles from Florida and Georgia is dry on Sunday, and the Georgia State Patrol sets up traps just across the line," he said.

"So what you're saying is the fine citizens of St. Illa may save people the trouble of running the gauntlet and just bring it across for them," I said.

"It's an idea," Dee Lane said. "I'm just raising the possibility that St. Illa may be one of those places where things are a little loose. Little border action, pot growing, moonshine. You know, these little towns that cater to hunters and fishermen usually have some back-room poker, strippers, maybe some prostitution going on, anyway. I'm thinking, 'Styrell is a biker.' Why would a biker choose to live in the middle of a swamp if there wasn't some action around?"

"Good point," I said, folding the map up and tucking it beneath my legs on the floor. We passed a white van and I looked over to see a mom and what looked like a fifth grade girls' soccer team. Dee Lane slowed for the truck in front of us and we rode beside the van for a moment. The uniformed girls pressed against the windows, admired the car, and mouthed things like "Wow" and "I love you." We grinned back and waved. As we pulled level with the driver, the pretty young mom turned and looked down at us, smiled and mouthed, "Take me, please." And made a kiss. Dee Lane blew a kiss back. The girls collapsed into giggles, the mom laughed, the truck in front of us slid over, and we roared on by.

It took us just over five and a half hours to reach Valdosta. From there we took a state road southeast through Fargo, turned due south toward Florida, and then angled east again into the swamp. The last ten miles into St. Illa was an empty sun-bleached tarmac road that cut a straight line through cultivated timber plantations. We flew at ninety miles per hour past towering toothpick-thin pine trees in neat rows. The broad grassy ditches along the road were full of murky water, and the only sign of life was the occasional buzzard floating in the blue cloudless sky. This far south, it was ten degrees warmer than Athens, and we rode with the windows open, fast, the roar of the Testarossa's special Tubi stainless steel exhaust providing an appropriate soundtrack.

# CHAPTER 28

**D**ee Lane loves bars. Every night he parks himself at Sluts and Mullets or one of his other Athens haunts and nurses a beer until the wee hours. The local Athens alkies love him because he smiles a lot, is always willing to listen, and buys a few more than his share of rounds.

As soon as we hit the outskirts of St. Illa, he spotted a bar on our right, a small white building with a sign that said "Sally's Lounge." He took his foot off the accelerator and downshifted. His disappointment was obvious when I suggested we drive around a bit first to get a feel for the place. Dee Lane swiveled his head wistfully as we drove by. One of the four trucks in the lot had a Confederate flag in the back window, and a bumper sticker that read "Heritage, not Hate."

We rode on through a mile of brick homes set back from the highway on big lots with small ponds in the front. The houses got closer together and closer to the highway, and we passed the local Hardee's restaurant, Chevrolet dealership, and farm supply store and then we were in downtown St. Illa. Dee Lane drove slowly back and forth along empty streets through a downtown of two-storied buildings dating from the twenties.

"It's like that episode from the *Twilight Zone*. Look around, Top. It's two in the afternoon and the place looks like a ghost town," Dee Lane said.

He was right. The streets were almost empty. An old, sun-faded Greyhound bus sign hung by one rusty metal hook from a pole in front of a defunct gas station. Roughly half the buildings were boarded up. On one storefront, someone had hand-painted "St. Illa Youth Center" and the windows were decorated with painted flowers, peace signs, and oddly proportioned children of various colors holding hands. Beside it was the largest building in town, the Portland Hotel, five brick stories of empty windows pockmarked with BB holes. The hotel was abandoned, and the glass front doors hung slightly open.

Right next to downtown was a dark gray neighborhood, once white but now apparently black. Looking at the people rocking on porches, I'd guess the only whites who lived here were older people who couldn't afford to move to the newer brick houses we'd passed on the way in.

"Azalea bushes everywhere. This place was probably pretty during the spring bloom," Dee Lane said.

"Sure," I said, unconvinced.

The neighborhood was an architectural hodge-podge. Many of the homes were classic coastal hot weather houses, big, rambling wooden things with tall windows, central breezeways, and wraparound porches. Sprinkled among them were more modest structures, some of them squat rambling Florida-style cinder-block constructions with open aluminum carports and jalousie windows.

As we rode, the proportion of cinder-block and run-down homes increased and the neighborhood eventually petered out into a long ugly row of two-story brick projects. We turned around in an empty lot across the street. Hard-eyed black kids in dirty white T-shirts stopped skateboarding and watched us pass. One gave the car a thumbs-up and Dee Lane smiled and waved back.

"Why do you think people would choose to live in a little back-water like this? You think they're hiding from something?" Dee Lane asked.

"Yeah, evolution." I looked over to see if Dee Lane appreciated my razor wit. But he looked sad, weighed down by the tiredness of St. Illa.

"I haven't seen but the one bar," I said. "I wonder where they all are."

He brightened, "Well, that's one thing I can help with." Smoothly he took us back to the crossroad, pursed his lips and looked in both directions, then turned right toward the swamp and drove a half mile down. There two bars faced each other across the highway and another was set a hundred yards down. He looked at me and smiled, "Voila. Now *that* is natural-born talent, old son." He turned us into the gravel lot for The Gator Hole, the one with the most cars and trucks, and parked in an empty slot.

We climbed out and stretched. I walked stiff-legged in a big circle trying to loosen up my knees. On the gravel lay a brown rubber band which I picked up and slipped over my wrist. Taped to the inside glass of the main door was a computer-printed sign that said, "No Tan-ners." As we opened the door, a blast of refrigerated stale air redolent of beer and cigarettes slapped us in the face. Inside, a dozen or so patrons looked up as we entered. Dee Lane smiled so broadly I was afraid his chin might fall off.

We stepped up to the bar, and a tall broad-shouldered woman with curly brown hair, a small butt, and a gray cut-off T-shirt spread tight over outsized breasts wiped the space in front of us with a damp cloth.

"What can I get you, boys?" she drawled at Dee Lane. Behind her, beside the register, a long thin white cigarette burned in a glass ashtray. Alongside it sat a glass jar of neatly creased dollar bills standing on their ends.

"Two beers. Heineken," he grinned back.

She opened a case and pulled out two wet green bottles. When she turned to get the opener, I saw an elaborate tattoo stretched across her lower back, and wondered if that was Styrell's work. She dried off the bottles, tossed two coasters down on the bar, and said, "Seven dollars, please."

Dee Lane peeled off a ten and tossed it on the bar, "Keep the change." She smiled thanks, made change, and slid the three creased dollar bills into the jar. She took a puff of the cigarette, replaced it in the ashtray, exhaled toward the ceiling and checked the drinks and ashtrays of her other customers with a quick, professional eye.

"What brings you guys to St. Illa?" she said, leaning on the bar across from us.

"Fishing," I answered.

"Bullshit," she smiled.

"Bullshit?" Dee Lane replied.

"Absolutely bullshit. I spend forty-two point five hours a week standing behind this bar getting hit on by out-of-town fishermen. Fishermen have pot bellies, beards, and not one ever left a three-dollar tip in his life. I can smell a fisherman as soon as he pulls his truck into the parking lot."

"So what are we?" Dee Lane said smoothly over the mouth of his bottle. "What's your name?"

"I'm Darlinda. And you're?"

"Wayne, and this is my friend Kevin," he said.

"Let's see. What are you? Cool, friendly, laid-back, thousand-dollar leather coat, black T-shirt and pants, custom-made boots. I'd guess you're here to pick up a bale of pot." She jerked a finger at me. "But he looks like your gardener. Too many muscles, raggedy old Daffy Duck T-shirt and worn-out jeans. Intense, can't sit still. I don't know what he is."

"None of us do, Darlinda darling, none of us do," Dee Lane said with mock sadness.

# CHAPTER 29

*D*arlinda sent us to another bar, the Lemon Tree, on the same road as the Gator Hole, but further on into the swamp. Outside of town, pine trees gave way to huge patches of wetland, open fields of shallow black water interrupted by occasional islands of small cypress, scraggly water oak, and a few pine trees. After a few miles of this, a sign said "Scratch Island," and the land around us turned back into pine forest. I looked for the sign for the Boara-boara Hunting Camp, our landmark to the Lemon Tree.

Every half mile or so, a road perpendicular to ours stretched into the distance. On the corner of each was a handmade sign advertising a Baptist or Pentecostal church.

"Who do you think starts all these churches?"

"Entrepreneurs," I guessed. "It's the south Georgia equivalent of dotcoms." A few minutes later, I said, "There's the sign. Now a half mile down." Dee Lane turned smoothly and we slowly rode along a canyon of tall straight trees crowding close to the gray sand road on which we rode.

"I hope we don't meet anyone coming the other way," Dee Lane said. "This vehicle is not designed for ditches. I wish I'd given Benny the Ferrari and we'd taken the truck."

"You won't let me drive this thing to the 7-Eleven and you're going to loan it to Benny?" I asked.

"Don't sulk," Dee Lane smiled. The trees began to get thinner and the ground wetter. Ahead we could see clear space, and soon, we could also see a double-wide mobile home on the left. A portable lighted sign with an arrow pointed at the trailer and said "Lemon Tree." In front of the sign grew a tiny tree, protected by a half-buried truck tire painted white. Behind the trailer stretched what Darlinda had called prairie, a large expanse of open swamp.

Outside the bar were a half dozen pickups, most of them huge jacked-up four-wheel-drive vehicles with enormous tires, massive shocks, and long whip antennae. The sides of every truck were decorated with sprays of dried wet mud. In the back of two trucks were large metal cages. One held a large redbone hound with a scarred face. He opened an eye as we drove by, confirmed his suspicion that we weren't wild hogs, and went back to sleep.

Dee Lane parked carefully. The earth beneath us trembled as we walked across the lot and negotiated our way around the standing puddles. Things too small to see zipped across the surface of the water. Two gleaming Harleys were butt-ended against the trailer. Under each foot peg was a round circle of plywood the size of a Frisbee. A faded twenty-year-old Chevrolet hatchback sat at the rear of the lot, next to a small blue Dumpster trash container, which rested on a lattice of boards. Dee Lane looked back over his shoulder, as if unsure whether his Ferrari would sink out of sight in the soft ground.

From inside the trailer, we heard the faint sounds of Lynyrd Skynyrd. Dee Lane winked at me, and led the way up a set of simple unpainted steps made of pressure-treated lumber. Conversation stopped when we entered.

Dee Lane smiled around the room, "Howdy." Only one of the ten or so people in the room grinned back. The grinner was a young giant, taller than Dee Lane and seventy pounds heavier, most of it muscle. He wore a cotton work shirt with sleeves chopped off to reveal biceps the size of my thighs. His long brown hair flopped across his friendly face.

He said, "Howdy." And then he stepped back a pace or two to make room for us at the bar. Conversation resumed. At one of the three tables sat two middle-aged bikers wearing colors I didn't recognize, filthy jeans, and black boots, but neither looked like the picture of Styrell from his Web site. Two twenty-somethings with beards, Lite beers, and disposable foam spit cups worked a pinball machine in the corner. Ranged along the bar with us were six or so ropily muscled men, all over six feet and all of whom looked vaguely alike.

"I'm Buddy Tanner, and these here are my cousins and brothers and fuck-buddies and all that shit," he said. The men laughed. Behind the counter hung a Confederate flag, and in front of it stood a thin black girl with a short 'fro. She smiled at us nervously, and shifted from foot to foot.

"My name is Wayne and this is Kevin," Dee Lane said.

"What you doing way out here, Wayne?" Buddy said.

"Just riding," he said. "You know, seeing what there is to see."

"Funny, cause when Darlinda called, she said ya'll was looking for old Styrell," Buddy smiled sweetly. He reached over and hugged the scowling man beside him, "Ain't that what she said, Leeson?"

I saw the bartender slip to the side. She nervously fondled the phone. I said, "Where's your john?" She nodded to a door in the far wall.

"Unithexth," she lisped. When she opened her mouth, I could see a heavy gold cap on the two upper front teeth.

I left Dee Lane at the bar, walked to the bathroom and locked the door. Inside, I pulled my cell phone from my pocket and dialed 911. A woman's voice answered and before she could say anything else, I said in my thickest drawl, "My name is Leeson and I'm calling from the Lemon Tree, out on Swamp Road. There's been a murder, Buddy

Tanner's shot some old tourist from Florida, and now they're raping the old woman on the bar. It's terrible, please get somebody out here. It's terrible . . ."

I hung up just before a knock came at the door and a voice yelled, "You fall in or something?" I flushed and came out. One of the bikers stood close, and I had to turn sideways to pass between him and the jukebox. I didn't meet his eyes, but noticed he had three teardrops crudely tattooed under his right eye. That meant he'd either killed three men in prison or wanted to make people believe he had. If it was just bragging, it was a pretty dangerous conversation starter. I thought I saw the butt of a pistol beneath his vest.

Back at the bar, Dee Lane coolly sipped a Miller Genuine Draft beer. "No Heineken," he said apologetically, and pushed a Miller beer toward me. I noticed that Buddy Tanner also held a beer, but it was impossible to tell what brand because his hand obscured the entire can. He was still turned toward us, smiling. On either side of us, his crew watched Buddy and watched us.

"Mind if I get one in a bottle?" I asked. I could hear the roar of the buzz building in my ears.

"No bottleth in thith bar, mither," the girl said. Buddy smiled at me. His head touched the plastic banners hanging above the bar. He was at least two inches taller than Dee Lane. Six eight, maybe more.

"Not much to do around here out of season, Wayne, you know what I mean?" Buddy said.

"That so?" answered Dee Lane warmly.

"Yeah, sometimes I bet hunters that come through here twenty dollars I can set the jukebox on the bar. None of these guys will bet me because they seen me do it too many times," he said. I glanced down at the bar and saw deep gouges in the surface.

Dee Lane laughed, "Well, I'd sure like to see it. Maybe I'll bet you."

"Nah, I don't feel like it, today. Today I feel more like fucking or fighting. You up for either one of those, Wayne?" he looked around and his posse laughed appreciatively.

"A round for these boys. Everybody." called Dee Lane. He turned to the bikers, "What you fellows having?" He dug in his jeans and tossed a hundred-dollar bill on the bar.

"I can't bweak that," the bartender said.

"Don't worry about it," Dee Lane smiled, "I'm sure we can drink it."

"I ast you a question, Wayne," Buddy said patiently. "You want to fuck or you want to fight? Or what about your friend here with the weak bladder, Smoldering Volcano Boy?" He laughed, a huge booming sound. "Yeah, I seen that look. You didn't think dumb-ass rednecks like us would know them big words like 'smoldering,' did you? What do you want to do, Volcano Boy?"

I listened hard, hoping to hear sirens in the distance. In *Little Big Man*, Tom Berger says that any time you hear about a fight where one man beats more than three, what you have just heard is a lie. I looked over at Dee Lane. He was still smiling, hoping he could talk us out of this.

I didn't think so. It was a trap, quickly planned but lethally efficient. I'd guess most of these beers were full and these trucks had preceded us by a few minutes at most. We'd be lucky if all we got out of it was a good stomping. No sirens. All I heard was the mutter of voices, the ping and clang of the pinball machine, and Grand Funk Railroad promising to come to my town and party down. I felt the adrenaline rushing to battle stations, honing my senses and tightening my muscles.

I picked up my beer and took a long sip. I couldn't really taste it, but the cool liquid felt good going down. "Oh, I'm partial to fucking, Buddy. And I'm going to start with you, you little tease," I said, smiling.

# CHAPTER 30

**D**ee Lane spit a line of beer across the bar, and coughed furiously. The bartender scooted to the far end of the bar and reached beneath it, coming out with the lower half of a pool cue wrapped with stained adhesive tape. She passed it nervously from hand to hand. Conversation ceased, and in the semiquiet I listened, trying to tell if that wailing was Mark Farner singing or sirens. Buddy flushed red, set his beer on the bar, and stood up to his full height. I straightened, too, which brought me eye-level with the top button on his shirt.

"You being funny, Kevin? You think that's funny?"

I slapped him as hard as I could across the face with the almost-full can of beer, felt the can crumple and the cold beer shoot up through hole and rain down on my hand and arm. Buddy shook his head as if my hit were the bite of a gnat. I head-butted him in the jaw. That made him step back against the bar.

Before I could reset, he came down on the back of my neck with both hands, knocking me to my knees. I reached out and grabbed his jeans to steady myself. He grabbed me under the arms, lifted me off my feet, and swung me. I flew across a table, bounced off the cigarette machine, crashed through the flimsy metal trailer door, landed backward on the ground, tripped, and rolled across the muddy lot.

Behind me, the bar patrons foamed out of the small door. The two bikers each held Dee Lane by an arm. The hound woke up and started barking, a series of deep bass aaarrrumphs. Last one out of the bar was Buddy, who casually stepped directly down from the porch to the ground, a two-foot drop. A trickle of blood ran down the side of his enormous head. "Kevin, you got some balls, I'll give you that. But now I am going to beat the living shit out of you, and then we're going to cut your narc asses up and drop off the pieces back in the swamp for the gators," he said. I stood up and tested my legs. They felt fine, adrenaline fine.

"What we gone do with the car, Buddy?" rasped the one called Leeson.

"My name is Top, not Kevin," I said.

"We'll decide about the car later. You fellows spread out so he can't run. I don't mind killing him, but I don't want to have to chase him all over Clinch County to do it," Buddy said.

Above the barks of the excited dog I now clearly heard the wail of sirens, and in the gap between the front of one of the trucks and the trailer, saw red and blue lights flying down the dirt road. Leeson looked back over his shoulder, and said, "Damn, Buddy, it's the police." Buddy straightened up and stared at me, then looked back at the approaching vehicles.

I smiled back, and edged over to the nearest pickup truck, one with a missing tailgate, and looked inside. It was full of trash—Miller Lite beer bottles, chicken wire, an old electric motor, and an aluminum baseball bat with a big kink in the barrel and no tape left on the handle. Two brown and tan SUVs swung into the parking lot, and four officers got out. One leveled a shotgun across the hood.

"Everybody freeze. Where are the old tourists, Buddy?" shouted one, a tall thin, man with a moustache.

"What old tourists?" Buddy replied, genuinely puzzled, eyes on the tall man. No one was paying any attention to me, so I reached in the truck and grabbed the bat, skipped two steps and took a Sammy Sosa swing at Buddy's left leg. There was a loud thud quickly followed by a scream and he crumpled to the ground. One of the officers swung his pistol around to me, but the one in charge held up his hand.

"Don't hit him, again," he said flatly, in a voice barely above a whisper.

I smiled and swung my bat into his kidneys. Buddy screamed and arched his back toward the sky. The dog stopped barking, and his hackles rose. Up on the porch, the thin black girl stifled a laugh. Leeson danced back and forth behind Buddy, looking between me and the policeman.

"I said 'Stop,'" the policeman said quietly. He kept his hand up to the officer. I walked around and booted Buddy lightly in the stomach. There wasn't much in it, and he didn't react.

"OK, that's enough. Arrest him," the policeman said in a different voice, dropping his hand.

I leaned down over Buddy and said in my best Sammy Sosa accent, "Bessboll been berry, berry good to me."

"You with him?" the policeman spoke to Dee Lane. Dee Lane nodded. "Harry, ride with this fellow in their vehicle back to jail. Search him first to make sure he's not carrying some sort of weapon. William, put Tough Guy in the back of my car." As far as nicknames go, I decided I liked Smoldering Volcano Boy better than Tough Guy.

William one-cuffed me and led me away. "Hey," the policeman called to me as we reached the vehicle, "You make the 911 call?"

"Yep," I said. I assumed the position against the SUV. The officer kicked my right leg out and patted me down, holding my jeans at the waist to keep me from turning on him. The nausea hit me, and I fought it until he stepped back, then I threw up on the wheel of the vehicle. The policeman wrinkled his nose in distaste, pulled me back, and opened the door.

"First, you make a false emergency call. Then you deface public property. I'm starting to think you have a problem with authority, son," the top cop said, trying to hold his face straight.

"Nawsuh," I said.

"We can talk about it back at the jail. Take off that muddy shirt before you get in my wagon. Hey," he motioned to the biker with the teardrop tattoos. "You come, too. Parole violation."

I climbed in and the deputy closed the door with a solid thunk. The wire separating the prisoner compartment from the front seat was made of the same material as the cages in the back of the pickup, and I thought I saw the hound dog give me a brotherly wink as we drove away.

# CHAPTER 31

*T**he police chief did not say a word to me on the** ride back or once we reached the jail. They let me bring in my new copy of Pope-Scott's book, *Dixiecaust*.* Myself, Dee Lane, and the biker were put in separate cells, bright, well-lit little cages roughly five by eight. In each cell was a stainless steel toilet with no lid, a bare metal shelf thirty inches wide for sleeping, and a small sink with a push-button cold-water faucet. Dee Lane was placed in the cell farthest from me.

At six o'clock the jailer came by and handed each of us a soft plastic cup along with two plastic-wrapped triangles of sandwich made of sliced cheese and white bread. I filled the cup from the sink and managed to chew down half of the tasteless sandwich as I read. Like all jails, this one smelled of vomit and Pine-Sol disinfectant cleaner. I went to sleep to the sound of the biker's voice, as he explained his sad life to a sympathetic Dee Lane.

The next morning I woke at seven to the low-pitched mumble of the officer named William unloading to Dee Lane about the limited job opportunities in St. Illa. He leaned up against the back wall, one foot on the wall and gesticulated with his hands. Dee

Lane held his eyes and nodded at all the right places. The biker's cell was empty.

At eight thirty, William took us to a small interview room with a metal table bolted to the floor and four flimsy metal chairs. In one chair sat the tall thin man with the moustache. In front of him were a carafe of coffee, a stack of white paper cups, and two brown folders.

"You know what I find most amazing?" he asked, pouring two cups of coffee and pushing them across the table. "That two fellows like you could have files this thick and not a single conviction. That tells me . . . heck, I don't know what that tells me." He smiled, put his elbows on the table and rested his chin in his hands. "So maybe you can help me out. Who are you?"

"Just two guys with a fast car looking for a little empty road. I run a research business and he runs a record store up in Athens," I said.

"Then why don't you tell me about the little scene out at the Lemon Tree? What was that all about?"

Dee Lane looked at me, then sipped his coffee. I spoke, "We were driving around, saw the bar and decided to have a beer. Tanner went nuts and threatened to kill us. I was afraid if you didn't get us out of there, he would."

"Why did he want to kill you?"

"Thought we were undercover police. He said he was going to chop us up and feed us to the alligators."

The cop pursed his lips, raised a single eyebrow, and tilted his head, "We think he's done that before."

"We believed him," I said.

"What if I told you he's in Valdosta Hospital with a broken leg and a badly bruised kidney?" he asked.

"I broke his leg? How bad?" I asked.

"Tut, tut, tut. Don't you think a little remorse is in order?" the policeman said.

"Oh, my. I broke his leg? That's terrible. How bad?" I said in the same voice.

The cop leaning up against the wall broke out in laughter and hid his face. The policeman sitting across from us gave a smile. "I could put you in County for this, aggravated assault." There's no answer when a policeman says that. They either will or they won't. "You have anything to say about that?" he continued.

"Preemptive self-defense," I answered.

"Good try. What about him?" he nodded to Dee Lane. "Does he talk?"

"Sure, he's just not quite awake this time of the morning. Catch him after lunch and he's a real chatterbox," I said.

"William," he spoke to the officer leaning against the wall, "bring these guys their stuff. I think I want them back up in Athens where they belong and out of my town."

A few minutes later William brought in our keys, wallets, coins, and cell phones. The SIG from my duffel bag was disassembled inside a thick plastic baggie. I turned my cell phone on and saw eight missed calls. I paged down. Four of the calls were from Gillie's number and the others from a number I didn't recognize. As I held the phone, it rang and the strange number popped up on the display. I raised my eyebrows to the police chief. He said, "Go ahead."

# CHAPTER 32

"*Top,*" *I said.*

"Mr. Kiernan, this is John Slocum, Athens-Clark County Police Department. We need to talk. I want you to come in right now."

"Sure, but I'm six hours away," I replied. "Mr. Kiernan," he'd said. That sounded serious. My first thought was that they'd searched the school again, and this time found the gun locker. Then I remembered Dee Lane's plan.

"Where are you?"

"St. Illa," I answered.

There was quiet at the other end of the phone. "When did you get down there?" he asked.

"Yesterday afternoon," I said.

"And you've been there ever since?"

"Yes," I answered.

"Anyone who can vouch for that?"

"My friend, DeWayne Lane," I said.

"Anyone else?" he asked.

"Sure," I said, and handed the telephone to the police chief. "Clarke County Police. He wants to talk to you."

They talked for a few minutes. I heard the police chief say Gillie's name and briefly explain the episode at the Lemon Tree in clipped cop language. After a few minutes, the policeman handed the telephone back to me.

"I'm back," I said.

"Thanks for your cooperation. If we need to talk to you again, we will let you know," he said.

"I've got two calls on my phone from Gillie Lynfield. Is she alright?" I asked.

There was a moment of hesitation, and then he said, "Last night someone broke into her home and tied up her and her husband. Poured red paint over her children's beds. They worked loose this morning and went hysterical, saw the red paint, and thought . . . Well, you can imagine what she thought. Insists you did it. Positive visual identification."

"Nope."

"I can see that. Maybe it was a fraternity prank or something like that."

"But she said I did it," I repeated.

"That's all I'm willing to say right now. We'll let you know if we need to talk to you again. Thanks for your help, Mr. Kiernan." He hung up.

The police chief sat across from me smiling. "Whatever you two are up to, I don't want it around here. How long are you staying?"

"I'm thinking about getting a tattoo, wanted to talk to Styrell Wooten about it," I said.

"William, draw them a map to Styrell's house. Then Top, get your tattoo and get out of my town. I'd rather not see you here again. You got me?"

"Yassuh," I said.

# CHAPTER 33

*T*hey'd put the Ferrari under a long metal sunshade inside a chain-link compound behind the jail. We sat there while Dee Lane started the car and let the engine warm up.

"Pretty intense," he said.

"Which part?"

"I was talking about the part where you went *psycho* with the bat," he replied. He checked his gauges as we spoke, not quite looking at me.

"You said we needed an airtight alibi," I answered.

"That's not what that was about," Dee Lane shook his head. "You're a man of *extremes*, my friend. And sometimes those extremes scare me."

"This from a man who hatches a plan to pour red paint over the beds of children? That was pretty intense, I think," I said.

All the blood drained from Dee Lane's face. "What did you say?"

"You heard me," I said.

"That wasn't the plan," he said, an uncharacteristic tremor in his voice. He pulled off the brown wraparound shades he was wearing and reached beneath the seat. He came out with a small chamois bag, from which he removed a pair of wire rims with rose-colored lenses.

Laying out the fresh glasses on his leg, he placed the pair he'd removed in the bag, and slipped it back under the seat. Deliberately, he removed a lens cloth from his pocket and carefully polished the glasses, not looking at me.

I looked at him, "That's what happened. Someone tied up Gillie and George and then poured paint over the kids."

"Say *what?*" His surprise was genuine.

"Dee Lane, you said it. Benny's not Tonto. He's not going to do what you *tell* him. Whatever your plan was, it changed. Don't worry about it. It could have been worse. What if Gillie had pulled out that little 32 she's got and popped off a shot? You think it would have been red paint on the walls then?"

"But Benny . . ."

"Is also a man of extremes, and his are far beyond mine. Benny is my friend, but even I don't want to wake up and find him in my bedroom."

"Top, I would *never* have suggested he touch the kids. Man, you know me better than that."

"Dee Lane, when we get back to Athens, you should get down on your hands and knees and thank whatever god you're praying to this week that all you caused was home invasion and assault. This was a very bad idea," I said.

Dee Lane turned and looked at me. He continued to rub the spotless glasses. He opened his mouth to say something, stopped and looked down at his shades.

"Write it off. You got lucky. And Gillie got real lucky," I said.

He licked his lips, and offered a tentative smile, "Reckon we can find a decent cup of coffee in this town?" He slipped on the now immaculate glasses.

"I doubt it."

"Maybe there's a Dunkin' Donuts donut shop somewhere." He checked the engine temperature, and satisfied, slipped the car into gear. William held the gate open, smiled and waved good-bye to Dee Lane as we passed.

# CHAPTER 34

**W**e followed William's map, driving back to the crossroad and heading southwest, along the only major road we'd not yet driven. To Dee Lane's delight, we soon came to a cluster of motels and chain restaurants. We stopped in a Denny's, had two huge, cheap breakfasts, and then bought two cups of Seattle's Best dark roast from the Mobil gas station next door. Thus fortified, we followed William's very precise directions: 3.2 miles, turn right on a narrow paved road signed County Road 21, follow that 1.6 miles and turn right again on a sandy dirt road with a neat, professionally painted sign that reads, "Our Redeemer's Church of the Chosen" over a red, white, and blue arrow. We turned the corner and drove by a recently plowed field. Hanging on the wire fence like laundry was a row of carcasses of big diamondback rattlers killed by giant tractors pulling disk harrows.

We drove down the dirt road carefully. On the map William had marked the church with the words "fenced compound," and before too long we saw a long double row of twelve-foot-high chain-link fence topped with razor wire, a large automatic gate, and a small sign with the church's name on it. A few hundred yards farther along, we saw a blue and white mailbox with Wooten painted in faded block letters. The post that held the box had rotted away and someone had driven several stobs around the base. They'd then wrapped wire tightly around the old post and the supports to hold it up. We turned into the narrow driveway beside the box and crept slowly up to Styrell's shack.

In the front yard, a new dark green GMC truck with dualies in the back floated in a sea of old junk. The truck gleamed in the morning sun. Attached to the fifth-wheel hitch in the center of the truck bed was a worn white goose-necked trailer. On its side was a large caricature of Wooten and the words "Styrell the Stencil, Tattoos of the American West." We parked on the grass. The front yard was muddy, and someone had laid out pieces of wood to form a semblance of a walkway. We followed that to the front door and knocked.

A skinny, breastless girl wearing a tight white T-shirt opened the door. "Hello," she said in the careful, nasal way mentally retarded people sometimes speak. One of her bare arms bore a small tattoo of a heart underlined by the words "Daddy's Girl."

Dee Lane stepped forward. He spoke in his warmest voice, "Hi there. My name is Dee Lane and this is my friend Top. What's your name?"

"Pam," she said.

"Pam. Is your mom or dad home?"

"My momma's dead," she said without inflection.

"Is your dad here?"

"Yes, sir, let me get him," she said, turning.

"Can we come in?" Dee Lane asked.

She turned back and looked at us with empty eyes, "Yes, sir." We opened the screen door and stepped into the small neat, living room. In one corner sat a television, and on top of it a bowl of plastic flowers. A reclining chair, a rocker, and a sofa surrounded a rectangular wooden coffee table with a remote control on it. On one wall hung a set of shelves, covered with small framed school pictures of the girl who'd let us in. On another was a framed poli sci degree from University of the Pacific. A clean cloth curtain strung on a tight wire separated the living room from the back of the house.

Styrell stepped into the room, a Colt forty-five pistol held loosely down at his side. "What are you doing in my house?" he rasped. Up close, Styrell looked even worse than he had on the Web site. His cheeks were sunken and his nose was a bulbous purple mass of broken veins. His arms were bony sticks covered with inked designs. He reached up with his free hand and raked his long gray hair back over his head. We could smell the vodka from across the small room. He raised the gun to his waist. "What are you sons-a-bitches doing in my house?"

"Caron sent us," I said. I could feel the reassembled SIG jammed in my waistband in the back, covered by my T-shirt. Dee Lane stepped right to give me room.

"You liar. I know who you are and Caron never sent you," he said. The gun dropped a few inches.

"The flag," I said. "I just need to know who you sold the flag to."

"Or what? You'll hurt me like you did Buddy Tanner? Word gets around."

"Styrell, I'm just a man doing a job. Give me a name," I said.

"I did a favor for Caron and now she's sicced you on me. I did what she asked me to, and that should be the end of it," he whined.

"You know it doesn't work like that, Styrell," I said.

"Well, I'm not going to give you a name and you can't make me," he said stubbornly.

"I wouldn't be sure about that, Styrell," I said. I slipped my hand behind my back.

"I spent my entire life around scary people and I'm telling you friend, these folks make you look like fucking Cher. You don't know who you're messing with, mister," he said. "You may think because you put Buddy Tanner in the hospital that you're some sort of . . ."

"Daddy," came a call from behind the curtain.

"Just a minute. She's using the stove," he said, ducking behind the curtain. Dee Lane stepped over to the shelves and examined the pictures. I slipped the SIG into my front waistband, making sure it wasn't cocked, and checked my cell phone again to see if Benny had called. We both jumped when we heard the ATV motor start.

"Oh, hell," I said and dove through the curtain. I ran through the small kitchen and burst through the back door just in time to see the taillights of an ATV vanish around a corner and into the woods. Leaning up against the rear wall stood a battered Huffy mountain bike. I pinched the tires, and satisfied, jumped on it and pedaled furiously after the ATV.

The well-worn trail wound through the flat pine woods. It was a lousy bike, too small by two sizes and without clips to hold my feet, but I was a cyclist, and I rode aggressively, cutting corners through the trees to follow the sound of the ATV engine. After maybe a half-mile, the trail came out of the forest and into a field of six-inch-high corn. A grassy strip ran along the edge of the field. Across the planted area, I saw the ATV speeding along a fence line toward a gap in the trees. I pedaled to the corner of the field, jumped off the bike, picked it up on one shoulder, and scrambled through the woods and across a small stream. The stream looped back and I splashed across it again. I heard the pitch of the ATV engine climb.

On the other side of the water, I threw the bike across a waist-high metal fence and dove over after it, climbed on, and pedaled through the underbrush to the trail on the other side. I flew out of the brush and, as expected, saw the ATV racing straight toward me. I dropped the bike, pulled the SIG and leveled it. I thumbed back the hammer. The small vehicle slid to a halt five feet away from me and the engine died.

I yelled, "Get off."

The leather-jacketed figure on the bike pulled off the full face helmet and said, "Please don't hurt me, mister. Please don't hurt me." It was Styrell's daughter.

I uncocked the pistol, slid it back into my waistband and walked toward her. "It's OK, nobody's going to hurt you. It's all right." She jumped off the ATV and threw her arms around me, burying her face in my shirt.

"Please don't hurt me. Please, mister, please," came the muffled sob. "And please don't hurt my daddy."

"I won't. I promise," regretting the oath as soon as I'd spoken it. I held her and felt the front of my T-shirt growing wet.

I rode back slowly and by the time I got there, the truck and trailer were gone, and Dee Lane knelt beside his front tire. "What happened to you?" he said.

"Nothing," I said shortly, pulling off the T-shirt, jeans, and shoes and tossing them into the space behind the seat. I dragged out the small duffel and tugged a dry shirt and jeans on. I had no extra shoes, so I stood barefoot.

"Son of a gun ice-picked my tire," Dee Lane said. "When you catch him, he owes me $381. Plus mounting and balancing."

"Only one tire?" I said.

"Yes," Dee Lane answered.

"That was nice of him," I said, and watched Dee Lane fix the flat using the can of aerosal goop Ferrari provides instead of a spare tire.

# CHAPTER 35

*D**ee Lane was preoccupied on the return trip.* We drove slowly, eighty or so, and made little conversation. He called the manager of his record store, Vinyl Man, once on his cell phone, had a brief discussion, then turned the telephone off and tossed it onto the console. Around three, we pulled into the driveway of the school.

It was a perfect spring day, warm and clear. The lot held more cars than usual. Benny sat on the front porch, this time with a slightly different assortment of horns. Dee Lane gave a brief toot at Benny and pulled away. I smelled brass polish as I walked up the steps.

"What's up with all the cars in the lot?" I said.

"It's our new partners," Benny answered. "They've got a plan to call everyone who's ever been a client trying to gin up more work. Maggie set them up with a little bell. Whenever anyone makes a sale, they're supposed to walk over and ring it."

"You heard anything, yet?" I said.

"No, but I'm impressed. There's a whole to-do list on the chalkboard in Classroom Two. Brochures, new Web site, lots of stuff."

I tossed my duffel up on the porch and turned to sit. "How'd it go?" I asked him, and he briefly described his night in Atlanta, and how he'd sneaked away at 2 A.M. to raid Gillie's house, getting back to Atlanta in time to crawl back into bed before dawn. I told him about St. Illa.

"Buzz funk," he said.

"What's that mean?"

"Usually, when you get this much action, it calms you down. You walk around smiling, friendly, like you don't have a care in the world. But this time it looks like you're still stuck in the buzz funk." He put the horn to his lips and played a riff of deep burps, and then repeated it twice, a little lower each time. It was melodic in a Miles Davis sort of way. "I'll have to remember that. The Buzz Funk."

I didn't answer. Benny put down the cornet and fished in his pocket. He pulled out a thin fold of bills. "Here, I'll cheer you up. Progressive." He tossed a dollar on the step.

"I can't match it, I'm broke," I said.

"You can owe me. This one's pretty good," he answered. I didn't respond. "The category is misquotes. You have to tell me if it's right or wrong, and if it's wrong, correct the phrasing of the quote." I nodded to show I understood. Benny pulled a wrinkled piece of paper from his pocket and unfolded it.

"Mae West," he said.

" 'Is that a pistol in your pocket or are you just glad to see me?' is the popular version, but it was really 'Is that a gun in your pocket,' " I answered. " 'Come up and see me' is also a misquote."

"You could at least wait until I read the quote," he said, tossing another dollar on the pile. " 'Play it again, Sam.' "

"*Casablanca*. Ingrid Bergman says 'Play it, Sam,' and later in the movie, Bogart says, 'If she can stand it, I can. Play it.' You got any hard ones in here, or are they all lollipops?"

"The harder ones are coming. You see I'm just betting ones right now. These are just to warm you up. We haven't played a progressive for a while," he said. "Beam me up, Scotty."

" 'Beam us up, Mr. Scott.' First used in 1966 in the *Gamesters of Triskelion*." Then repeated. "I'm waiting for the hard ones."

He smiled and threw a five on the pile, "Elementary, my dear Watson, elementary."

"Now you're getting tricky. That's not really a misquote. It's a correct quotation of a phantom quote. Sherlock never said it, but P. G. Wodehouse said Sherlock said it. Is that it?" I held my hand over the pile of bills.

"One more. 'You dirty rat,' " he said, tossing a ten on the pile.

"Tricky again. Jimmy Cagney never said that or anything like that in any movie. The best guess is that it was coined by some vaudeville impressionist." I picked up the eighteen dollars and rolled it up. Benny shook his head and clapped softly.

"I thought the red paint was too much, Benny," I said, looking him straight in the eye.

"Me, too," he said, looking back at me.

I stared back, "I don't get it."

"I didn't do the red paint. I left a bouquet of dead roses on her dresser. You know, a message, like in the *Godfather*."

I nodded. "Where'd you get dead roses, a cemetery?"

"I went to a florist and dug the oldest ones they had out of a trash can, then I microwaved them," he said.

I smiled. "They look dead?"

"They looked pretty bad."

"So how did the red paint get there?"

"I have no idea. When I left, everybody was asleep and everything was fine," he said.

"Did you dose them?" I asked.

"Of course not," he said. "That sort of stuff may work for Dee Lane, but it's too complicated for me. What was I supposed to do, wake them up and force pills down their throats?"

"Gillie lied to Slocum and said I did it. She said she saw me do it," I said.

"So she poured red paint over her own kids' beds?" Benny asked.

"Who else could it have been?"

"Her credibility must be dropping. First the raid, now this," he answered.

"I'd guess," I said, knowing that he was right and wondering if there was a way to use it.

"There's more," Benny said.

"What?"

"Jeff Nelson's home number and cell phone are in her PDA," he said.

I stood up.

"Where are you headed?" he asked.

"I'm going to call Dee Lane. He'll be relieved to know the paint thing wasn't us. I also need to tell Sweeney about Nelson. Then I'm going to lift for an hour, then I'm going to shower and go see Pope-Scott. And maybe I'll have dinner with Amanda after that," I said.

"You still chasing the flag?" he said.

" 'Anybody who has traveled this far on a fool's errand, has no choice but to uphold the honor of fools by completing the errand.' *Sirens of Titan*. Kurt Vonnegut," I said.

"If you say so." He put the horn back to his lips and played the Buzz Funk riff.

# CHAPTER 36

*A*fter spending twelve hours bumping along at hubcap level, the cab of the truck felt plush and remote. I called Caron again, and again got no answer, so I decided to try Athens General. I had just parked in the visitor's deck and climbed out of the truck when the phone rang. I answered it.

"This is Sweeney. I've already filed suits against AWS and the bank, and asked for a temporary injunction on the foreclosure, but it's all civil stuff. Nothing that's going to do much to slow her down. That it?" He sounded exasperated and irritable.

There was a giggle in the background, and I pictured Rattlesnake and wife number eight at the other end of the phone. I tried to stop my imagination there. I said, "I've got some news."

"Go." In the background I heard the click and snap of a lighter.

"I found out that Gillie's got a personal connection to the banker, Nelson."

"How'd you find out about Nelson?" he asked.

"Bar talk," I answered. "And I can't remember who, where, or when."

There was a pause while Sweeney decided whether or not to press for the truth. Or maybe the pause was for something else. I heard more giggles in the background. Perhaps it was wife nine-to-be. Finally, he said. "You do know this conversation is privileged?" I heard him exhale smoke onto the microphone.

"I know you're an officer of the court," I answered.

There was another pause, and then he said, "That it?" And I told him about Gillie trying to pin the break-in on me. I didn't tell him that she'd probably partially staged the setting, because there was no way to explain that without giving Benny up. He listened quietly.

"I'll try to get Slocum to bring Gillie in for filing a false police report. He won't, but it'll get him thinking. Let me think about what to do with the other. I may have an investigator independently surface the Nelson connection. Be a couple or three grand. That OK?"

I explained my current financial situation. He said, "I think it's worth it. Get back to me if you can scrape up the money." And he hung up.

At Athens General, there was a small crowd outside the closed door to Jay Pope-Scott's room. Caron spoke to a tall gray-haired woman in a long white lab coat. A few yards away, Bob John Wynn gave pointed instructions to a short Latina with a badge hanging around her neck. He saw me and raised a hand telling me to wait. After a minute, he finished up and walked over to me. "What are you doing here?"

"Pope-Scott's hired me to find a flag someone pinched from his office," I said. "A little errand to pay the bills. What are you doing here?"

"I've been temporarily seconded to Homeland Security. Pope-Scott got another letter from the Sword of Michael," Bob John said.

"I don't get it," I said. "Why Pope-Scott?"

"There doesn't have to be a reason. Bombers are nuts. They fixate. He could have chosen Ginger or Mary Anne. Before Pope-Scott, the Sword sent letters to a convicted bank robber named Ben McShane, an ultra-right wing preacher from downstate."

"Why'd he stop?"

"McShane was shanked in the shower at Arrendale on Christmas Day. In January, Pope-Scott began getting letters." He looked back over his shoulder at the woman agent, who spoke into a walkie-talkie. "This is going to take a while, Top. If you need to talk to Pope-Scott, you better come back later."

"Can I talk to Caron?" I said.

"Sure," he said.

I nodded, and jammed my hands in my pockets. "Dee Lane's back. You want to play ball? Maybe Thursday?"

Bob John gave a big smile. "Have to let you know." He turned and walked back toward the woman, who now was poring over something on her clipboard. When he was almost there, he stopped and turned, "Like old times, eh?" I smiled noncommittally.

Caron split off from the doctor and walked over to me. Today she wore a light green sheath with matching shoes. Her face was red and puffy, and her mascara and eye shadow had mingled with tears and run down her cheeks, creating long green and black streaks from the corners of her eyes to her chin line. Her lipstick was worn off, and her small, pale lips blended into the background of her face. She blew into a Kleenex facial tissue. "I must look awful."

I didn't say anything. She smiled and sniffed, "You're supposed to tell me I look fine."

"Sorry," I said. "Is the professor OK?"

"Yes. He's coming home tomorrow."

"I hate to ask right now, but did you work on the list?"

"I did. Let's walk down to the car. I've got a folder for you," she said.

"What's Homeland Security doing outside your husband's room?" I said.

She walked briskly and held her head high. Heads turned as we passed. "The nut who's been sending Jay a note every time he bombs a clinic, just sent him a map and a letter."

"A map of the clinics he'd bombed or is going to bomb?"

"Already bombed. There are twenty-one red dots on the map. Columbia, Greenville, Knoxville, Huntsville, Birmingham, Tallahassee, Macon, Columbus, Augusta, Atlanta. Yesterday, he did one in Albany."

"I get it," I said, "It's a cross."

She turned and smiled tightly. "That's it. He calls it a cleansing cross. He's going to rid the south of evil by branding a 'cleansing cross of righteousness' on it."

"And he says where he's going to bomb next?" I asked. We reached an elevator and she pushed the button for down. It opened immediately and we stepped inside.

"Not exactly," she said, "But it says how many. A cleansing cross has twenty-seven in it. The number of books in the New Testament."

"So he's going to bomb six more clinics?"

"They think that's best case," she said. "He's killed eighteen so far, it could mean he's going to kill nine more. Or he's killed five doctors. Maybe he will kill twenty-two more."

"It doesn't matter," I said.

She stopped, turned and looked at me, "What?"

"He's not going to stop until he's caught. He'll just find a new reason or a new place to do it," I said.

"That's what they think, too," she said. "And what really scares them is that the pace of bombings has picked up. I heard them talking. Either he's got a stockpile of devices or there's a bomb factory supplying him. They think he's got a factory."

"Why?" I asked. We walked across the lot to her Jaguar car, and she unlocked the trunk.

"Apparently bombs have what they call signature elements. Not just how they're constructed, but how the wire is cut and twisted, that sort of thing. And the last few bombs are different from those he started with."

"Athens, Lagrange, Rome, and Valdosta," I said. "Those are the last major towns in the cross untouched."

"Or maybe he'll go back to Atlanta." She reached in the truck and pulled out four files. "Here is the correspondence from Willingham, Alstott, Wilde, and Parsons. I e-mailed and called all of them and asked them to meet with you. You should have copies of the e-mails."

I flipped through the files. They were neat and well-organized. Caron smiled and pointed to the brown rubber band on my wrist. "Is it working yet?"

"Hard to say," I answered truthfully.

"OK, then, I'm going back up to be with Jay." She slammed the trunk lid.

"Aren't you going to ask me about Styrell?" I said.

"He already called me," she admitted, "After you left."

I didn't say anything. Her eyes flickered upward, then dove down, trying to hold mine and failing. "Pam is staying with her aunt. She said you're a nice man." I didn't speak or shift my gaze.

"I don't know where he is and he wouldn't tell me who he sold it to," she blurted.

"Caron?"

"Yes, Top," she said.

"Try not to get me killed over a flag, could you?" I didn't wait for an answer, but left.

On my cell phone was a message from Amanda saying she'd love to have dinner, and suggesting steak, since she was ravenous. It was her treat, to celebrate going twenty-four hours without a cigarette. Good thing, in that if I were buying it would have been steak tacos at El Neato Burrito.

# CHAPTER 37

*I* *woke sweating, knotted up in my sheets, and knew*
the dream had been bad. But all I could remember of it was
Benny conducting an orchestra playing Buzz Funk. He'd worn
a topcoat and tails, a la Cab Calloway in the Blues Brothers. I shook
the foggy memory off, had two cups of coffee, and worked out.

An hour later in the office, my sweaty forearms made little
sucking sounds as I moved them across the desk while making my
list. I say "list" because it was too simple to be called a plan. Wilde,
Alstott, and Parsons and I all live along a two-hundred-mile stretch
of I-85, the road that runs from Richmond to Mobile. Throw in the
hospital where Willingham died, Danny's Bar where Morton does
most of his business, and the Great Southland Mega-Mega Tattoo
Fest, starting Wednesday morning at eleven in the King Convention
Center near Turner Field, and that was everyone I needed to see.

I packed a clean T-shirt, toothbrush, and a sleeping bag, since
it was unlikely I would catch them all on the down stroke. It was
unlikely I would catch Styrell at all, since I'd just picked the festival from a list on a tattoo-oriented Web site, but I had to start
somewhere.

At exactly nine A.M., I turned onto I-85, driving with my left hand and punching numbers into a cell phone with my right thumb. I finally negotiated the phone maze at Emory Acute Care Hospital only to reach a polite young woman with a recently acquired drawl who told me they could tell me nothing about Willingham, not even the name of the doctors who'd treated him, and suggesting that I reach for the next of kin. No, she was not allowed to tell me who that was or how to reach them, either. She did want me to have a nice day, though, and appreciated me calling Emory ACH, where people care.

I had better luck with some of my other calls. Morton invited me to a late breakfast. Jo Ann Wilde offered me lunch, and Mike Parsons's assistant's assistant suggested I drop by the office for a drink at the end of the day. Since I had eighteen dollars in my pocket and a gas gauge hovering around "E," the meal invitations were probably a good thing, although with the adrenaline running I could actually do pretty well without food. I was looking forward to Mike Parsons's drink, though.

I met Morton at the Ritz Carlton hotel in the Buckhead neighborhood, northeast of downtown. To save five bucks on the valet parking, I left the truck across the street in the Lenox Square Mall lot and walked the hundred yards or so over. At the Ritz Carlton, the desk manager unobtrusively sized me up, costing out my Lee jeans, Russell T-shirt, and Converse sneakers (conclusion: not a guest,) scanning my face (conclusion: not a slumming rock star whose face is in the album under the desk that they study during breaks,) analyzing my walk and demeanor (conclusion: not a con man or a bum, probably) and in those few seconds it took me to walk from the door to the desk, decided to offer a smile.

"Looking for someone, sir?" he said smoothly and a few seconds later, directed me to The Café. The restaurant was almost empty, and Gerald Morton sat against the far wall looking out the window onto the patio. He wore a gray double-breasted suit, with a cuffed shirt striped in a color Amanda calls cranberry. The small maroon kerchief in the coat pocket matched the color of the jackets worn by the little jockeys on his blue tie, and the blue in his tie was the same color as his cuff links. He drank coffee from a china cup. He stood to shake my hand.

"Top."

"Morton," I said.

"Are you OK?" he asked.

"I was better before your people redecorated my home with sledgehammers," I said.

"Not my people, and you know that. I'm CIA," he said. On my left, a man in a white coat filled my glasses with water and orange juice. On the right, a similarly dressed man with a silver pot lifted an eyebrow toward my cup, and I nodded. Morton pushed the container of sugar and the small pitcher of thick white cream across to me. I ignored it, and drank half of the coffee in a single swig. By the time I'd replaced the cup to the saucer, the man with the silver pot returned to refill it.

"Distinction without a difference," I said.

"I think you know better than that," he said. I turned to find the waiter and found him already gliding toward my elbow. I asked for some dry toast and a bowl of fruit, and he moved away.

"You've moved up from Danny's," I said. Danny's is a dive on the east side of Metro Atlanta that serves as Switzerland for those who live on the wrong side of the law. That is, that's the neutral ground where they meet. I'd first seen Morton there about six months ago. At the time, I'd been getting fired by Soames and Morton was meeting with a bevy of young men in horn-rimmed glasses and blue suits who turned out to be KGB. Danny was dead now, although Benny, E. J., and I were the only people who knew, and we had no intention of reporting it. The bar was now run by Danny's daughter Moira.

"This really is the best hotel chain in the world," sighed Morton. "Not the best individual properties, perhaps, but absolutely the best chain."

"It's a dressed-up Marriott," I said. "Just another motel. Only difference is it's been decorated by a guy who owns a Ralph Lauren catalog."

"You don't really believe that. I've seen your file. You do just fine in a tuxedo when you need to," he smiled.

"I need the work we discussed," I said. "Lawyer's fees."

He laughed, "Yes, I heard. The Rattlesnake." The white napkin perfectly draped over his elegantly crossed leg.

"Well?" I asked.

"Well. Times are tough, Top. As I told you, most of the funds have been diverted to the Al Quaida effort. Latin America is very much on the back burner at the moment. We still want you to do the job, but I'm having a hard time getting it up the priority list," he said.

"Fifty thousand is chump change for you guys," I said. "You probably could fund that out of your brunch budget."

He laughed, "Yes, I could. It's not your payment that's the problem, Top. It's getting the international warrant, booking space at Guantanamo Bay to house the prisoner, and convincing the Chileans to look the other way if something goes wrong. You have no idea how pissed the Swiss and Germans are at us right now. With Iraq, we're not getting a lot of international cooperation. An operation like this is very complex."

"God, Morton. I've done a half dozen of these for Shaw's. I go get him. Period. No navy. No army. No nothing. Give me the drugs and I'll find out whatever it is you want to know."

Morton shook his head, "This is the U.S. government, Top. It doesn't work that way. Can you believe there's an official form to request an assassination? In triplicate, so help me god."

I took a sip of coffee from a cup that was magically full again. "When? Next month? The fall? What's the plan?"

"I'm hoping six weeks. This guy is old. He may not live too long, and we don't know who's next in line. We'd have to start almost from scratch."

"Two weeks is better," I said.

"Here," he pulled an envelope from his pocket and laid it on the table. "It's an advance of five thousand. That's the best I can do. If the job doesn't go, at some point I will need to get it back."

I hefted the envelope, tempted to ask if this was really an advance or just guilt money because of the damage they'd done. Then I decided it didn't matter. I needed to pay Rattlesnake's investigator. "Thanks," I said. "Do you need some sort of receipt?"

He looked surprised, and said, "No, of course not. . . ." Then he looked at my face and laughed. "Very funny. You know, that dry sarcasm of yours takes a bit of getting used to."

"That's what they say," I stood up. "Is there any chance you could do me one more favor?"

"It depends," he said warily.

"A guy named Willingham died in Emory Hospital last week. I need to know what killed him. He was pretty well-to-do but there's nothing in the news media and the hospital isn't talking."

"Want to tell me what this is about? No, of course you don't want to tell me what this is about. Let me see what I can do," he said. He removed his napkin, stood up, and brushed a nonexistent crumb off his immaculately creased pants. We shook hands and I left. In the lobby, I picked up a small red rubber band off the carpet beside the bell desk and stuck it in my pocket.

# CHAPTER 38

*T*he Wilde estate was situated a few miles from
the Ritz Carlton. It was a huge antebellum mansion, set
back from the road behind a ten-foot wrought-iron
fence. A guard in a black windbreaker hit a button and the huge gates
swung majestically open. I drove up a lengthy brick driveway, past a
sloping lawn large enough to hit a three wood on, to a small lot beside
the house. There another security guard in a windbreaker showed me
where to park, and led me down a few steps to a side door that opened
into a small office.

"I'm Susan," said the assistant, a thin, elegantly beautiful redhead.
She wore a black pants suit. A long dark cigarette burned in the ashtray on her desk. "I'll tell Ms. Wilde you're here." She left through a
glass door in the wall behind her.

A few minutes passed, Susan returned, and I was led into a larger
room that held a conference table covered with papers, a large white-
board, and a small sitting area. Jo Ann Wilde sat on the leather sofa.
She was tiny, except for her breasts, which tumbled half out of a half-
open work shirt. In front of her sat a large glass ashtray filled with the
butts of dark cigarettes just like the ones Susan smoked. She stood

and smiled, "Mr. Keirnan, please sit down." She motioned to a chair across from the sofa. Susan settled in another chair to my right, and set a black IBM laptop on the coffee table in front of her.

"So Jay is finally going to sell me that damn flag," Jo Ann Wilde smiled. Her lipstick was dark brown.

"I'm sorry?" I said.

"Jay and Caron asked me to see you concerning the Bloody Red Rag," she said. "I assume this is a discussion about price, Mr. Kiernan."

It was not easy to tell if she was genuine. "Call me Top, Ms. Wilde, and I'm here because the flag has been stolen. I've been hired to get it back."

She slapped her hands together and laughed, falling back on the sofa. "Son of a gun, the rumors are true. So you're a professional flag retrievalist, Top?" Her eyes twinkled and she played with her tongue inside her cheek. I wondered if she was flirting deliberately, or if it was automatic for her.

"I get things back for people," I said.

"Let me understand here." She sat up, shook loose a cigarette and lit it. She offered me one and I shook my head. She tossed the pack down toward Susan and slid a gold lighter behind it. "I used to have a friend named Lars who was always running off with the little bunnies he met in the hot tub. Would you be the person I would send after Lars?" From the corner of my eye, I saw Susan fidget.

"Sure," I said.

"And you'd bring him back for me?"

"That's right," I said.

"So you're a kidnapper for hire," she smiled.

"In a narrow-minded sort of legal way, I suppose," I said. It was easy to see how she'd charmed old Harry. She was even making me look good at this game.

"Not really," she said with a laugh. She folded her legs underneath her on the sofa, and held her hand so that the cigarette pointed toward the ceiling.

"No, not really," I said. "But I have been hired to find the flag and bring it back, and you're one of the people that might have it."

"You bet your pony I wish I had it, cowboy," she said. "I'd buy it in a New York minute. Here's how the Wilde world works, Top. We usually sell a thousand cars a week. Recession's got us down to eight hundred and fifty. With that damn flag, I could sell two, maybe three thousand a week."

"What if it were stolen?"

She grinned, "It would take Jay's lawyer six months to get it back. Twenty-six weeks times an extra two thousand cars a week times five hundred dollars gross margin per car is what, twenty-six million dollars? Less ten for advertising, legal fees, and so forth. Even if I'm off by fifty percent, that's still three mil. I would buy it, stolen or not stolen. And I don't even care that it's probably a fake."

"You'd buy a fake?"

"If it was the flag in question, why not? Those who believe, believe, and will no matter what the tests say. And the historians and skeptics who don't believe, will come see it anyway."

"But you don't have it?" I persisted.

She took a long draw on her cigarette and let it out. "No."

It seemed as if she wanted to say more, and I waited for her to make up her mind whether to continue. She picked at a nail while she decided. "A week or so ago a man called me, another collector like myself, and said he'd been offered the flag, but under conditions he could not accept. He asked me if I wanted it. I told him I did, but I haven't heard from him again."

"Herbert Willingham?" I said.

She looked at me in surprise. "Yes, it was Herbie."

"He died last week at Emory ACH."

"That's impossible. I would have heard," she said.

"It's being kept very quiet," I said. "What were those conditions he couldn't accept?"

"An initial down payment of a hundred thousand upon delivery. Then a million upon testing and verification. I had two weeks to do the testing. But I had to keep the purchase secret for three months, and keep the results of any testing secret for a year. He called me, I think because Herbie had finally run through the family fortune buying up old junk."

"What do you make of those conditions?" I asked.

"What do you think?" she said. "It sounds like they planned to sell me the real flag and sell a fake to someone else, and wanted to make sure they had enough time to get clear."

"Or they planned to rip you off for a hundred thousand?"

"Or that, although I assume that's why Herbie was in on the deal. He's not known for handling fakes."

"Did Willingham often do you favors?"

She hooted, "That nasty slug? Absolutely not. As payment for the introduction, he wanted a piece from my collection—a battle dispatch signed by Lee."

"And what did you tell him?"

"Deal. Only historians care about battle dispatches. Flags are sexy. Everybody likes flags. A flag would sell sedans and minivans. But I never heard back from him and now you tell me he's dead, which I'm still not sure I believe," she answered. She continued to smile, but her eyes were hard, and the little tricks with the mouth were gone now. Reaching down, she absentmindedly buttoned two buttons on her work shirt. Susan gave a small smile.

"Whoever he was representing hasn't contacted you?"

"Not yet. When I got Caron's call, I just assumed the rumors were wrong and you were some lawyer or auction type sent to peddle it. Sorry," she shrugged.

"Would you let me know if someone does get in touch?" I asked.

"Probably not," she grinned. "Will you let me know when you find it, and maybe I can rent it from you for a little while before you return it?"

"Sure," I said.

She shook her head, "I don't think so. I didn't do four years dancing around a brass pole and twenty peddling cars without learning how to read men, and I think you're as straight as an arrow, Top. Tell me I'm wrong."

"Aw, shucks," I answered.

She laughed again. "Are you still going to join me for lunch? We'll eat upstairs in the dining room." She stood and came around the table, and when I stood, linked her arm through mine. "You know, muscular, violent types like you used to be my weakness before Captain Duracell and sweeties like Susan here convinced me males were obsolete. Come on," she rested a heavy breast against my arm, "Let's go flirt some more, it drives Susie crazy." She looked up and gave me a broad wink.

# CHAPTER 39

*L*unch *was good, in a fifty-year-old-beauty-*trying-to-keep-her-figure-and-an-anorexic-model-picking-at-her-food sort of a way. In other words, it was all greens and broiled fish, no carbs at all, and they drank water, although there was an open bottle of chardonnay on the table for me. I didn't have much of an appetite after eating that piece of toast with Morton, so I concentrated on polishing off the wine. Around two, I left, assuring a skeptical Jo Ann that the alcohol just burned off, and I was fine to drive. Susan looked relieved to see me go, which I took as a compliment.

To avoid the perpetual snarl that is downtown Atlanta traffic, I went back up to I-285 and skirted the city. It took under two hours to get to Montgomery, actually to get to Parsons, a small town eight or so miles northeast of Montgomery. On the way I checked my messages. One was from Sweeney, and I called and told him I'd found the money for the investigator. He hissed agreement and hung up. The rest of the time I listened to Isaac Stern playing Otto Kreisler.

Parsons was tiny, only a dozen blocks long, and consisted mostly of a handful of T-shirt shops, restaurants, and a small theme park called Chickeninny World. Interspersed with the tourist attractions were a number of factories and office buildings housing the Chickeninny empire. The streets of Parsons were named things like Thigh Lane and Special Spices Drive, and the street signs were all in the shape of drumsticks. The main office building, a large, gray five-story Art Deco, sat on Parsons Circle, dominating downtown. But when I checked in there, I found that Mike Parsons's office was in something called the Executive Center. I'd passed the sign for it on my way in. I turned around and drove back out.

The Executive Center was a small limestone building at the end of a long driveway that wound through a half mile or so of woods. After showing my ID and signing in, I was told to make myself comfortable, that even though I was a bit early, someone would be out to escort me in a few minutes. I helped myself to a Coke from the fountain in the lobby, and settled down with a two-month-old copy of *Restaurant News*. A few minutes turned to fifteen, then to thirty. I refilled my Coke, then switched to water.

As five o'clock approached, a small stream of staff passed me, and gradually the stream thinned and stopped. Every so often, the security guard and I smiled at each other. It was almost six before a middle-aged woman came into the lobby and spoke to the guard, then turned and walked over to me. "Mr. Kiernan?" she asked.

I said I was. She said she was Carol, and worked with Mr. Parsons on his philanthropic and personal affairs. She apologized for the lateness, but the governor had called. She gave me a knowing shrug that implied we all knew what a pain the governor was. And beckoned for me to follow her.

The building was a single-story square built around a large central garden. The interior walls of the building were made of glass and faced the garden. On the other side of the hall from the glass were cubicles for assistants and behind them, offices. Parsons occupied a suite at the farthest end of the square. Carol led me through and I could see several small offices, a large boardroom, and a massive office furnished with leather chairs and dark wood furniture. The walls of the big office were densely covered with grip-and-grin photos of Parsons and various celebrities and power brokers.

Carol directed me through the office to a sliding glass door that opened onto an outside patio with a small metal table and four metal chairs. "Is this OK, Mr. Kiernan? Mr. Parsons likes to sit out here this time of day and smoke one of his stinky cigars. Can I get you a drink? He's just stepped into the little boys' room and shouldn't be a minute."

Before she could get back with the drinks, Parsons made his appearance. He looked exactly as he had in the pictures, tall, thin, patrician. His skin had a slightly yellow cast to it, and after shaking my hand, he pulled out a leather cigar case. "Do you mind?" I said I didn't and declined his offer of one for myself. A minute later, Carol came back carrying a tray with an unlabelled bottle, two cut-crystal glasses, and a small carafe of water. Parsons fussed with cutting and lighting his cigar.

"Scotch?" she asked.

"I expected bourbon," I said. Parsons squinted at me around the flame and billowing clouds of smoke.

He smiled. "Carol, could you get some bourbon for Mr. Kiernan?"

I took a sip. "No, Carol, twenty-five-year-old single-cask Highland scotch is just fine for me." She hesitated, glanced discreetly at Parsons, then at some unseen signal, smiled and left. She pulled the glass door shut behind her.

Parsons leaned back and looked at me evenly, "You assumed I would be a bourbon drinker, Mr. Kiernan. Just like everyone assumes I am a Republican, and a Baptist, and they figure I send my smart children to Harvard and the dumb ones to Yale. But I drink scotch, I'm a Catholic, and all four of my children went to the University of Alabama. Now I look at you and I see someone who looks and dresses like he works on one of my slaughter lines, but who can tell Highland and taste the difference between single malt and single cask. So I reckon I need to be just as careful making assumptions about you."

"My given name is Honus, but everyone calls me Top."

"Call me Mike. Now let's get to it, shall we? I don't have the flag, Top, but if I get the chance to buy it, I will," he said.

"Even if it's stolen," I said.

"In the world of collecting, it's finders keepers," he answered.

"I can't accept that," I said.

"Why not, Top?"

"To be honest, because I need the money I'll get from bringing it back," I said.

"What if it gets rough? Will it be worth it?"

"It's already gotten pretty rough, Mike. Pope-Scott's got a bullet hole in him."

He nodded, poured himself another three fingers of whiskey and held the bottle over my glass. "You got anywhere you have to be tonight, Top? Because if I pour this, it's going to turn into a coon hunt." A coon hunt is an all-night affair, where the men sit around the fire drinking whiskey and telling stories, and listening to the dogs barking and yelping in the distance.

"Got a sleeping bag in my truck, Mike," I said, and he smiled and filled my glass.

# CHAPTER 40

"**O**nce you've been drunk with a man, you're stuck with him for life," Mike said an hour later. He'd told me about Chickeninny and Montgomery. I'd told him a bit about Polymath and he'd listened well, asking questions at the right points.

"John O'Hara," I answered, and sipped my drink.

"Whoa," he said. "How'd you know that?"

"I told you, Mike, quotes are my day job." I said. Parsons nodded, his head moving a little too far up and down.

Carol appeared, "I'm leaving now, Mr. Parsons. Do you need anything else?"

"Another bottle, Carol, in case this one runs out," Mike slurred. "And would you tell Jeff to go get some dinner and come back? It's going to be a while before we finish up here. Neither me nor Mr. Kiernan is going to be up to driving by the time we're done." When she left, Mike turned back to me and worked to focus his eyes.

I said, "Tell me, Mike. What do you collectors do with all the stuff you buy? Keep it in a room and play with it from time to time?"

"Nossir, nothing like that," he said, a hint of a slur in his voice. He looked at me appraisingly, "If I tell you, you'll think I'm a nut."

"I already think you're a nut. You pour great whiskey for somebody you just met," I said.

"Fair enough," he nodded, then looked into my eyes with drunken solemnity. "I'm going to trust you, Top, and not just because of all this fine alcohol sloshing around in my brain. I size men up and I either trust them or I don't. I trust you and I'm going to tell you what I haven't told anybody except Missy." He wagged a drunken finger at me. "Here's what I do with the stuff I buy. I put it in a sealed glass box with all the oxygen removed and place it in an underground vault. Now I don't trust you enough to tell you where the vault is, I can't say I trust you that much. But I will tell you that when I die, they're going to lock that vault for five hundred years."

"Why is that? Some collector thing?" I asked.

"Oh, no. No, no," he narrowed one eye, and worked to light another cigar. "It's a civic duty."

"I don't get it," I said.

"Where are you from, Top?"

"Arlene. Born and bred. Ten generations."

"Family own slaves?"

"I don't know, why?"

"Do you know what the South before the war was really like, Top?"

"Gone with the wind?"

"That's what most people think. They have this sort of misty idea of beautiful women in frilly dresses and handsome men on quarter horses and happy slaves playing banjos and it's all a load of crap, Top. Ninety-five percent of the land was owned by a handful of imbeciles whose great-grandfathers had bribed bureaucrats for land grants. Slaves lived in filthy barracks with no sanitation, ate corn meal and water, and were subject to daily rapes and beatings. When the crops didn't come in, they ate clay to fill their bellies and keep them from hurting. They ate dirt." He filled my glass and his own, rattling the neck of the bottle on the rims of our glasses, carefully replaced the bottle on the small table, and tried once more to get the cigar going.

"And most white people were like my ancestors, what they called white niggers, English and Irish farmers brought over as sharecroppers after the slave trade stopped in 1808. They worked the most marginal land and lived their lives in debt to the plantation store. A few whites were shopkeepers or doctors, but not many."

"Hummph," I grunted, and drank half my glass.

"We can't imagine. Even the rich didn't have it that good. Half their children died before age twelve. Malaria. Typhoid. Cholera. The main topic of conversation at most dinner parties was the possibility of a slave revolt. It was a hot, humid, dangerous hell hole. The truth is the Yankees did us a favor by kicking our stupid asses out of the stone age."

He leaned toward me and opened both his hands, trying to make me understand. The lean made him almost topple over into my lap. He caught himself on the table with the hand that held the burnt-out second cigar. I carefully guided the glass of scotch to my mouth and sipped, then said. "What in the hell are you going on about, Mike?"

"Don't you see? This thing," he waved a hand, "this myth, is holding us back."

"You should talk to Caron," I said.

"Beg your pardon?" he asked, looking at me with glassy eyes.

"I said it sounds like we need to be educated," I said.

"I do that, too, sir," he squinted at me and held up a finger. "One hundred kids graduated from school this year on Parsons scholarships."

"That's very cool," I said.

"Thank you," he gave a modest nod, except his head went sideways as much as it went down. "But I think, Top, that the best thing I can do for the South is to erase this silly memory of a golden era where white men got respect and life was easy. So I try to buy every important piece of antebellum memorabilia I can find, and I lock it in a vault, because I figure that in about five hundred years we'll be ready for it."

I didn't know what to say to that, so I said nothing. Instead, I let my head sag and eyes close, then jerked them open again, pretending to be drunker than I was. Parsons appraised me.

"Top, I want you to think about that. When—you notice I said when, not if—you find that flag, I want you to consider selling it to me. I'll settle up with Jay and Caron and you'll do all right in the deal, too," he said carefully. I noticed that he wasn't slurring now. He lifted the bottle over my glass and I nodded. "I'd like you to think about that, friend."

It was a crazy story, but they don't call rich people crazy, just eccentric. He poured more whiskey, we drank and pretended to be drunker than we were, and spent the next hour agreeing that it was a travesty that Auburn, not Georgia or Alabama, was being picked by the experts to win the SEC in the fall.

# CHAPTER 41

*I* *woke under a fluffy white coverlet in a large bed in* a room the walls of which were painted a robin's egg blue. Sun poured in through open windows flanked by gauze curtains. After a few attempts, I successfully focused on my watch dial and saw it was almost eight A.M. At some point the night before, I remembered Mike saying it was two, but I recalled little after that. I looked around the unfamiliar room. My clothes were neatly folded on the foot of the bed. The jeans had a crease in them, as if they'd been ironed. My small duffel bag from the truck sat on a luggage seat against the wall.

After a shower, I dressed, packed, and made my way down a sweeping staircase to the first floor. I stood for a moment, listening, but heard no sound but the ticking of the grandfather clock in the hallway with me. "Hello?" I said.

"Oh, goodness," I heard someone say, then the rattle of silverware, and a moment later a pretty woman with blond-white hair pulled back into a tight ponytail joined me in the hall. She wore a simple white cotton top and black pants of the type that end somewhere between the knee and the ankle. Although she must be in her late fifties, she moved like a much younger woman. Fashionable heavy-framed reading glasses rode her straight nose.

"Top," she drawled, "I'm Missy Parsons, Mike's wife. He's already gone to work and asked me to make sure you were taken care of." She gave me a warm smile and a firm handshake. "Come on, we'll get you some coffee. You do drink coffee?" I nodded.

She led me through a huge, formal living room and several smaller ones to an attached breakfast room. Just inside the door sat a table with a white tablecloth and two settings. She motioned me to one. "We have breakfast here. It's still cool enough this time of day, but it's east facing, so in an hour or so, it'll get stinking hot." I sat down and tossed the small duffel against the stone casement behind my chair. On the table sat a huge pitcher of water. I filled my glass, drained it, and repeated the process twice more. Then I poured a cup of coffee and drank that.

"Good morning," I said.

"Good morning," she laughed. You read about silvery laughs. Hers was the first one I'd ever actually heard. She looked at me with a mischievous smile. "You boys had yourselves a night, I take it?"

"The part of it I remember, yes," I answered, and drank another glass of water.

"I hope you don't mind that we did your laundry, but you must have gotten downwind of Mike's cigars, because your clothes reeked. So we collected them from the floor and ran them through the washer."

"We?"

"Me. It's a habit. When the kids were young and we traveled a lot, we had permanent live-in help, and it really was a 'we.' But she retired, and now I just do most of the housework myself," she said. I looked at the three-carat diamond on her finger and the Piaget watch on her arm and said nothing. She saw my glance, "Oh, we still have people come in to help, just not full-time."

"Thank you for doing my laundry," I answered.

"The smell is terrible, isn't it? Although I'm not really one to talk. Do you mind if I smoke? It's my one of the day and I can wait if you wish, but I usually have it with my morning coffee," she said. And then, "Mike said he told you about his idea to buy up all the Confederate artifacts. You should be honored. He doesn't tell many people about that." She held the cigarette, waiting for my answer.

"Go ahead," I said.

She lit her cigarette and washed the smoke down with coffee. "Thank you. What do you think of his plan?"

"Not much," I said.

"Why not?"

"Leaving aside the practicality of how a vault stays sealed for five hundred years, I think even if he bought every old uniform, rifle, and whatever else is out there, some enterprising soul in Taiwan would start making fake minié balls and slouch caps the next day. The problem is demand, not supply," I said.

She sighed and waved away her cigarette smoke. "That's what I think."

"Have you told him?"

"Of course not."

"Why not?"

She looked at me with a wry grin. "You must not be married, Mr. Kiernan. You don't stay married as long as we have by poking holes in your partner's dreams. Mike's worked hard all his life. He's been a great husband and father. He's never gotten a case of the testosterone poisoning and bought a fast red car or run off with his secretary or injected botox or anything like that. He's just worked hard and tried to help people. Along the way, he's made more money than God. Now we've got more in the bank than we can spend or our grandchildren can spend or their grandchildren can spend. So I figure, if he wants to piss some away on old Confederate junk, who cares? Not me."

I nodded and drank more coffee.

"Mike likes you," she said.

"I like him," I answered. "And you, too."

"I know. All the boys like me. Always have," she answered. "It's the blond hair and the figure." She gave me a wink, but this time I knew it was just habit, and there was nothing in it.

"Any chance you could give me a ride from wherever I am back to my truck?"

"Your truck's here," she said. "And Mike had Jeff put a case of that whiskey you were drinking in the front seat. Do try not to get stopped. The bottles aren't sealed because we fill them from a big cask in the cellar. That makes each one an open container under Alabama law. Twelve traffic tickets. If you do get pulled over, there's a little piece of paper in the bottom of the box with a note explaining why there's no tax stamp on the bottle."

"Thank you very much," I said.

She waved a hand, "It's nothing. There's half a dozen casks down there. Enough whiskey to fill a swimming pool."

"Still, thank you," I said. I drank some more of my coffee. "I need to get going. I've got to see a man about a tattoo."

"Are you sure I can't make you breakfast? At least, let me get you a bottle of water to take with you." She skipped away, and a few minutes later returned with a large bottle of Evian water. We walked outside. On the step, she bent smoothly and picked up a tightly rolled-up newspaper. "Our weekly *Parsons Gazette*. Say, I couldn't help noticing when I did your jeans that one of your pockets was full of old rubber bands. Are you collecting them for something? Do you want this one?" She stripped the small red band off the paper and held it out in her open palm.

I stopped and thought, then said, "No, thanks. An acquaintance suggested I pick up rubber bands to change a run of luck I'd been having. I think it's starting to work, so I better stop now. If I keep going, I might go full circle back to bad again."

She nodded, "Of course." I knew she'd just decided I was as goofy as her husband.

# CHAPTER 42

*I* *reached Lagrange by eleven. Lagrange grew to*
prominence as a textile town, one of many such communities
located on rivers and streams of the Fall Line, the long
narrow geological belt where the Appalachian mountains abruptly
drop to the Southern coastal plain. It's a quiet, pretty place, full of
red brick houses perched on little pine-covered hills. But just like
those quaint little places, there's a feeling that its best days have
come and gone, and no matter how many tax breaks the local government offers to Japanese auto plants, those days are never coming
back again.

Alstott lived in a subdivision that appeared to have been built in
the sixties. 714 Homeridge was an immaculate ranch, with an open
carport and a large backyard visible through a chain-link fence. When
the house was built, it was probably a cookie-cutter copy of its neighbors—fifteen hundred square feet with three bedrooms, a bath and a
half, and built-in Kenmore appliances. Now people like bigger
homes, and the houses on either side had vinyl-clad second stories
added on. In a few backyards, the tops of pool slides and trampoline
cages peeked over palisade fences.

There were two cars in the driveway. Under the carport was a dark blue Buick Regal. And sitting on the concrete pad, parked facing the street, was a large black Ford Navigator with a tinted windshield. The windows were rolled down, and smoke curled out of both windows. Inside I could see two young men. Each wore a white satin baseball cap with a red KKK embroidered on the front and a pair of white rimmed Oakleys with orange lenses. Their identical T-shirts read "Heritage, not Hate." As I parked, they got out of the truck. The passenger, a thin man with wispy goatee and a mullet haircut, stood behind the passenger-side truck door, his hands together below the window line. The heavy-set driver came over to me.

"Can I help you, sir?" he said. He was a redhead, and the color of the hairs on his arm matched the lenses of his glasses. There was a badge clipped to his belt, right next to the holstered pistol. I explained the purpose of my visit and said I was expected. He asked for identification and when I provided it, studied my driver's license without emotion. "Just one minute, sir."

I waited at the curb while he walked up to the door, knocked, and spoke into the screen. After a moment, he turned and motioned to me. I walked carefully up the driveway, ignoring the man behind the truck door, and continued on the neat stone walkway. Waiting at the door was a pleasant-looking woman around sixty with short hennaed hair and immaculate makeup. She wore a sleeveless pink top, jeans, and white Keds sneakers. "Hi," she smiled, holding the screen door open for me. "Please come in."

In the small living room were several chairs, a sofa, a bookshelf, and a 27" television. On top of the television sat an arrangement of silk flowers, a *TV Guide* with a white mailing label and, peeking out from underneath, a thick stack of religious pamphlets. The walls were covered with framed photos, several of them Olan Mills portraits of the woman who'd let me in sitting beside a kindly looking man with drooping, bloodhound features. On a far wall, next to a plaque from

Mary Kay, I saw a posed school photo of two blond teenagers sitting together. "Can I get you anything?" she asked, "I just made a pitcher of iced tea."

"A bathroom would be nice," I said. I returned a few minutes later to find a glass of iced tea sitting on a coaster on a coffee table, the tall, droopy-faced man from the pictures standing in the center of the room, and an empty spot on the wall where the picture of the twins had been. The man extended his hand and spoke, "Mr. Kiernan, I am Marcus Alstott. Welcome to our home."

We sat down on the plastic covered sofa. "How can I help you, sir?" he asked. I briefly explained my mission. The plastic made crinkling sounds under me as I reached forward for my tea. He shook his head, "Sorry, friend, I can't help you. I don't have the flag. I'd love to have it, but I don't. And I could never afford it. As you can see, sir, we live a pretty simple life."

"I was told you are a collector," I said. The iced tea was instant, and had a hard edge to it like it had been sitting too long in the refrigerator. But at least it had been sweetened properly, that is, Southern-style, before the ice was added. I drank most of the glass.

"Not exactly," he laughed. "The UKS has a collection and I choose the pieces for it. It's housed in the basement of a church up in Carrollton. But we could never afford anything like the Bloody Red Rag." His eyes were kind and his voice was a deep rumble. I nodded to show I understood. "Can I ask why you are looking for it?" he asked.

"It's been stolen," I said.

"I meant, 'why you?' "

"I'm being paid," I said.

"And what will you do with it if you find it?"

"Give it back," I said.

"And what will they do with it?"

"I don't care," I answered truthfully.

"But you're a Southerner," he said.

"I still don't care," I said.

"Many would think you should show a little more reverence for an important symbol like the Bloody Red Rag." His bloodhound eyes stayed fixed on mine.

"I'm not the sentimental sort, Mr. Alstott," I said. He smiled and put one hand on my shoulder.

"All Southerners are sentimental, Mr. Kiernan. It's part of our national character."

"We lost, Mr. Alstott. We don't get a national character. We get a regional character."

He laughed, and used the hand from my shoulder to slap his knee. "Oh, but it was pretty darn close, Mr. Kiernan. Did you know that the week before Stonewall died, over a million dollars in gold, one-hundred million in today's currency, was withdrawn each day, each day I said, from the Triangle Bank of New York by its wealthiest citizens and packed in steel-banded cases to be shipped to the Continent? They thought that General Thomas J. Jackson was about to march his army into New York, and win the war for the Confederacy. That's how close it was." There was a pregnant air in the room, like the feeling in my office every October when Benny's aunt Marilyn, a devout Jehovah's Witness, drops by and sits talking about the weather. I could feel the recruiting pitch coming.

"Thank you for your time, Mr. Alstott," I said, standing. "If you find out anything about the flag, could you give me a call?" I placed a business card on the table.

"Are you a South hater, Mr. Kiernan? Many of your generation are. The educational system has created this false idea that the war was about slavery and that those of us who love our heritage are just a bunch of ignorant racists."

I stopped. "I love the South, too, Mr. Alstott. But I don't spend any time wishing for a South that disappeared over a hundred years before I was born."

"So you're happy with the South we have today, Mr. Kiernan, with crack cocaine in our high schools and children being murdered in drive-by shootings? You don't have a problem with turning on the television and watching those shows where every other sound out of some teenage girl's mouth is eff this and eff that? You don't think about the tens of thousands of babies that get flushed down the toilets of abortion clinics every year? And it doesn't bother you that decent men can't earn a living wage because all the jobs have been shipped overseas? You're happy with that?"

"Thank you for the time, Mr. Alstott, and thank you for the iced tea," I said, standing.

"We're having a convocation on Monday night in Atlanta. It will be at the Convention Center, fifty thousand of us. You should think about coming. See what we're all about," he said.

"Thanks again," I said, and let myself out. Alstott followed me to the door and stood behind the screen, watching me walk back to the truck. The two guards got out of the truck again and looked back and forth between me and Alstott. I climbed up in the cab, turned the truck around and drove off. I put up my middle finger to the bodyguards as I passed. They stared at me impassively.

When I hit the interstate, I rolled the windows down, turned the radio to an oldies station and sang loudly as I drove. I wondered if those blond twins in the school photo were the same ones who'd tried to knife me in the bank parking lot. And I found it curious that Alstott was the only one so far who hadn't tried to buy the flag from me. That could be because he was a fine, honest, upstanding man. But it could also be because he already had it, or at least knew where it was. Styrell to Herbie to Jo Ann? Maybe, and maybe the man I'd just met might be somewhere in the mix. It was progress.

I checked my mirrors for the black Navigator or a gold Volvo, but saw neither as I drove back to Atlanta. I drove well within the speed limit, very aware of the case of fine whiskey on the seat beside me.

# CHAPTER 43

*I*-75 south was a slow crawl. The cause was a gaper's block just past the Fulton Street exit. Up on a hill above the highway sat dozens of emergency vehicles. Clouds of steam and smoke billowed up through arches of water made by the water cannons mounted on fire trucks. The red, blue, and yellow flashing lights reflected off the mist from the jets. Two firemen in black coats with yellow reflective stripes and no helmets walked back and forth along the fence line gesturing and talking.

A dozen uniformed policemen paced a grid up across the hillside above the interstate. They stuck tiny red flags on thin wires into the ground to indicate potential forensic evidence. There was already a forest of little flags on the hillside above them.

Through the smoke, I could see a scorched billboard that read "Unwanted pregnancy? We can help." I tuned the radio to a news station, and learned that the Sword of Michael had claimed responsibility for another clinic bombing. I didn't want to think about what might be next to those little red flags stuck into the grassy hillside. The wind caught spray from the water cannons and sprinkled the windows of the cars on the interstate.

Two exits later, I left the highway and wove my way east toward the convention center. Even though I kept an eye out, I didn't see Styrell's truck and trailer. There was no reason to expect to find it in the outside lots. His rig could just as easily be back at his motel or inside the center. Eventually I found an empty space, parked, and followed the signs inside to a long line of registration booths. In one sat a grandmotherly looking woman with no obvious body art. I gave her my best smile, "This is my first convention and I'd hoped to see an artist named Styrell Wooten. Can you tell me if he's here?"

She looked down at her sheet. "Last-minute entry. Way in the back. Aisle VV, booth 38. One day registration is twenty dollars, and that doesn't include any tattoos or other purchases." I paid and was given a bar-coded badge, a plastic holder on a neck cord, and a little plastic orange band that snapped on my wrist. A young woman in an oversized maroon windbreaker flashed my badge with a laser bar code scanner, and waved me through the turnstile.

I felt underdressed, even though I had on more clothes than most of the others in the place. Most of the women wore thongs and halter tops, although one was dressed in just pasties, a black bikini bottom, and leather chaps. The men tended toward shorts and leather vests. Everyone except me was covered in tattoos of every conceivable style and hue. That wasn't true actually—there were a few clumps of nervous-looking people of both sexes wandering from booth to booth, trying to decide whether to go through with it.

Some of the tattooes were old and faded to a blurry, monochromatic blue, like those on an ancient sailor with a white ponytail and Elvis sideburns. He waddled along in front of me, his purple Speedo swim trunks almost hidden under rolls of overhanging fat. Other tattooes were bright and fresh, like the brilliant red, yellow, and green parrot that started just below the shoulder of a young Asian woman and covered her entire back. The bird's tail feathers ran down to her ankle.

I oriented myself using the signs hung from the rafters. At VV 36, I slowed, and ducked into a small booth. A pretty, bored woman sat in a folding chair. She was about thirty, with bright, unnaturally red hair. Tattoos covered her arms and legs. On the walls of the booth were dozens of designs. Most involved large tropical flowers, hearts, angels, and cutesy animals. A row of blue and red prize ribbons were taped to the aluminum divider pole. She looked up as I stepped inside.

"Looking for a tattoo?" she said. Smoke leaked out of one nostril, and behind the wooden box that held her gear I could see a faint gray ribbon winding upward. She saw me looking and said, "It's stupid. Every artist smokes. Every customer smokes. So we have a tattoo convention in a nonsmoking building. How stupid is that?"

"Pretty stupid," I agreed.

"You want to sit down?" she asked.

"I'm not really a customer," I said.

"I know," she answered. "My stuff is for college girls and house-wives, and that crowd doesn't come in until after the first round of drinks anyway. So I'm just killing time." She blew smoke straight down in a long jet.

"I better get going," I said.

"You'd be a lousy canvas, anyway. I can see all those scars through the T-shirt," she said.

"You can see scars through a T-shirt?" I asked.

"Give me a break, dude. That's my job," she said. I nodded and left. I wandered toward Styrell's booth. When I got close I could hear the buzzing sound of the needle and see a crowd around the booth. I found an opening and stepped close. Styrell stood in a pool of bright light, bent over a folding table. In one latex-gloved hand was a tattoo machine and in the other a bloody white wipe. I angled for a better view. It appeared he was tattooing an Indian on a horse onto a girl's behind. The girl was pale and there was a tight grimace on her face. The crowd, mostly men, looked on in rapt interest.

"Easy, easy. The endorphins will kick in any minute now, and it'll just be a little push. You won't even feel it," rasped Styrell.

The girl winced, "That's what you said fifteen minutes ago, you lying fuck. Don't worry about me, I'm OK."

"You're tightening your ass muscle, baby, that messes up my lines. You need a break?"

The girl didn't answer. She squinted and I saw tears in the corner of her eyes. Styrell didn't look up. As I stood watching, engrossed like all the other voyeurs around me, four hands grabbed my arms. Before I could react, someone jammed something hard and cold into the center of my back. On either side of me stood a massive biker wearing dirty jeans, a leather vest, and a tight silk bandanna. One sported a short goatee and the other an enormous, waxed handlebar moustache. "Come with us, fella. Styrell wants to talk to you," said handlebar.

I started to say something, then thought about the fact that I wanted to talk to Styrell, too. I closed my mouth. They spun me around and frog-marched me toward a huge white cloth partition that divided off this part of the center from the rest. We ducked through a cut in the canvas.

The gun in my back went away, and a huge arm moved around my neck. I kicked as hard as I could behind me, and hit nothing but air. I twisted my arms and felt the grip of the goateed biker loosen for a fraction of a second, then tighten. A beard tickled the back of my neck and a voice whispered in my ear, "I'm going to put pressure on your carotid artery. It will knock you out, but it won't hurt you, unless you fight. Do that, and you can end up in some home drooling on a bib for the rest of your life. I used to be a pro wrestler. I know what I'm doing. Hold still." The hands on my arms dug in and the arm around my neck tightened. "Nighty night," came the whisper.

The cell phone woke me. From the look of the sky I guessed it was about four P.M., two hours or so after I'd gone into the convention center. I lay in the back of my pickup truck. My forehead burned as if I was sunburned. A cautious fingertip said it was puffy and swollen. My first thought was for the truck keys and the three hundred dollars I'd had in my pocket. I found the money gone, but the keys remained. I could feel my wallet in my back pocket. The phone stopped ringing, probably flipped over to voice mail. I rolled over and rose to my hands and knees. The phone started ringing again and I answered it.

"I told you to leave me alone. I would have had them boys kill you if Pammie hadn't made me promise," Styrell said.

"Don't knock it. My promise to her is the only thing keeping you alive right now, too, dickhead," I croaked. I crawled over the wall of the truck and dropped to the ground. My left leg buckled and I dropped to my butt. The phone skittered across the pavement. Using the edge of the wheel well, I pulled myself up to standing. I retrieved the phone, unlocked the truck door and opened it.

"You can tell I'm scared," he said. I reached under the seat and felt the roll of bills I'd stuffed inside the springs. I sighed in relief. "You looked in a mirror yet?" he said. I closed the door and looked in the truck mirror. Across my forehead was "Leave Me Alone" in dark brown-red ink.

"I'm going to kill you anyway. Never mind what I promised Pam." I said.

Styrell laughed, "Probably I shouldda done it in bright colors, so people would notice it."

I looked at the tattoo again, this time more carefully, and could see it was slightly smeared where I'd touched it earlier. I licked my finger and reached up and rubbed. A spot of clean skin appeared. Styrell laughed in the phone.

"It's just temporary, the stuff we use on kids at county fairs," he said.

"What's with my forehead?"

"I used the lamp to give you a little burn, make it feel like you really had been tatted."

I walked around to the other side of the truck and opened the door. Inside the glove box, I found a Starbucks napkin. "Reverse lettering.

Now that was cute," I said. I laid the phone on the hood and used the last of Missy's Evian to wet the napkin. Picking the phone back up with my left hand, I used my right to scrub my forehead. It felt like I was scraping off my skin, but when I looked at the napkin I saw nothing but brown-red ink. I drank the last little bit of water.

"I'm serious, here, Kiernan. I'm not going to shit on my own doorstep, 'specially not with a kid like Pammie. I'm not going to tell you nothing and you're wasting your time chasing me."

"When I catch you, you scrawny old bird, we'll see what you tell me." The ink was mostly off, but there was still a faint shadow of the letters left behind on my forehead.

"I told you, Pammie or no Pammie, next time I'll have them kill you."

"Styrell, tell me who's got the flag," I said.

"You want a flag? Is that it? Well, dog, check out your arm. Don't go spitting and rubbing on that one or you'll get it infected," he laughed. I looked around. He must be sitting somewhere with binoculars. There were hundreds of cars in the huge lot. He could be anywhere.

"What?" I said. I looked down at my right arm. A little rectangle of white gauze and tape peeked out from under the sleeve. Carefully, I peeled the gauze away.

"That's what the two hundred and eighty dollars was for, Kiernan, for your tattoo," Styrell answered. "Now leave me the hell alone."

"Styrell . . ."

"And be careful driving. We gave you a little injection to knock you out while I worked. It's the same stuff doctors use for outpatient surgery. No big deal, but you might be a little woozy for a while. You take a drink of that whiskey before it wears off and you're going to be on your ass. " The line went dead.

Under the gauze was a small, perfect tattoo, the size of a postage stamp, of the Confederate flag. Over the top, he'd tattooed "The

Republic of Dixie," and beneath it, in small red italics, "Heritage, not Hate." I leaned against the truck and laughed. One thing about Styrell. He had one hell of a sense of humor.

# CHAPTER 44

*I* *didn't get back until six-thirty, and Bob John, Dee* Lane, E. J., Dice, Benny, Amanda, and Russell and his wife were already there. They'd moved my bed back to the corner with the Nautilus machine, pulled out one section of the bleachers and laid out five pizzas and a big Igloo cooler with pop and beer. Russell's two-year-old daughter, Rachel, ran back and forth down the court trying and failing to pick up a basketball. Every time she grabbed it, she'd get it about an inch off the floor and it would squirt out of her hands, and she'd chase along behind it, laughing uproariously. A boom box was tuned to a radio station playing Sheryl Crow.

"You guys eat pizza before you exercise?" I asked. Amanda jumped up, smiled and threw her arms around me. She gave me a loud unromantic kiss. E. J. made a dismissive gesture and I shot him a warning frown. Uncowed, he grinned back at me. The phone rang, and Benny went down to the end of the room to pick it up. He gave E. J. a little slap on the back of his head as he passed.

"We started playing an hour and a half ago. We got hungry and ordered from Domino's Pizza," Dee Lane said. "You eaten? There's plenty left."

"Been two months since we had a good game. We got started without you," said Russell. He, Rachel, his wife, and his elderly father lived on the family farm just down the road from the school. "What's in the cardboard box?"

Benny held his hand over the receiver, and I saw his lips move, but couldn't hear what he said.

"Provisions. For me. Turn that down, could you?" I said, placing the box of whiskey up against the wall. Dee Lane reached a long arm over and turned the radio off.

"Susan English," Benny said.

"Yeah, I'll take it," I said. Amanda arched an eyebrow. Benny walked toward me with the cordless phone and I met him in the tip-off circle. "Top," I said into the receiver.

"This is Susan English. Do you remember me?" I pictured the tall redhead from Jo Ann Wilde's office.

"Sure," I said.

"There's something I thought you should know," she answered.

"What's that?"

"Jo Ann's supposed to get the flag next Tuesday," she said. "A man is bringing it here. I've spent all day lining up experts to inspect it when it arrives."

"Who's the man?" I said.

"A dealer she does business with. I don't know which one. She took the call on her *private* private line," she said.

"Am I invited to the party as well?" I said.

"Why would you think that?" she answered.

I thought for a moment. "Are you making this call in an official or unofficial capacity?"

There was a harsh laugh. "Very, very unofficial."

"So I should not mention this," I said. Rachel rolled the ball over my feet, put one hand against a knee to steady herself, looked up at me and grinned. I held up a finger over my lips. She did the same and blew a wet "Shhhhhh."

"I don't care what you do," Susan said. "Forty-five minutes ago, Jo Ann told me that from now on ours is strictly an employer, employee relationship. That bitch. I didn't graduate cum laude in communications arts from Vanderbilt to be a damn secretary. Let that slut Randi answer her phone calls and print out her e-mails. Jo Ann can't even use a computer. I print them out, she handwrites the answer, and I have to type it back in. Can you believe that in this day and age?" She used the profanities awkwardly.

"What time on Tuesday, do you know?"

"Just after lunch," Susan said. "But I've also been asked to beef up security, so if you're planning on dropping by, be warned. There's going to be a lot of extra security. And not just minimum wage rent-a-cops, either." She stressed the word "lot."

Benny walked down to the free throw line and shot a few air balls. Russell wiped his mouth on the back of his hand, snagged his daughter as she ran by and handed her to his wife. He picked up the basketball and dribbled in a loose figure eight. E. J. stood up, wiped his hands on his shorts and walked over to join him. The squirming child arched her back and tried to slide out of her mother's arms, and when that failed, howled in protest. I put my finger to my lips. Mary, Rachel's mom, grabbed her up and scooted toward the double door at the end of the room. Russell gave her a what-do-you-want-me-to-do shrug. Mary glared back and carried the angry toddler out. You could hear screams through the closed door.

"Are you a family man, Mr. Kiernan? Somehow that doesn't fit my image of you," she laughed.

"No, I'm not a family man. It's our weekly basketball game and one of the guys brought his daughter," I said.

"How sweet. Good luck, Mr. Kiernan. You look like the sort who could cause all manner of hell without even meaning to, and I hope you do." There was a click, and she hung up. I stuck the receiver in my pocket, walked over and sat on a bleacher seat beside Amanda.

She handed me a slice of pizza piled high with everything on it and an open Budweiser beer.

"What happened to your forehead? It looks like you got in a fight with sandpaper. Wait, is something written on your skin?"

"I'll explain later. You already eaten?" I said.

She nodded her head. "One slice and that's it. Since I quit smoking, seventy-three hours and twenty-two minutes ago, I've already gained two pounds. Can't you see it?" Her face definitely had a little more round to it.

"No," I said. "You look the same to me. I think it's all in your head." Dee Lane, Bob John, and Dice milled around on the court.

"You are such a bad liar. I think you were lying about the family thing, too. You'd make a great dad," she smiled. "Rachel adores you, and kids can tell."

"Let's play horse for a while," Dee Lane said. "I don't want to run around like crazy and then throw up all this cheap mozzarella."

"You playing, Top?" asked Benny. Before I could answer, the phone rang. "He's not playing," he said and told the group, "Left baseline, left-handed, swish."

"No way," said Bob John.

# CHAPTER 45

*I* *punched line one on the phone, and said, "Polymath."*
"Top? It's Gerald Morton," a voice said. Benny shot from the corner and the ball dropped through the net without touching the rim. Bob John made a face and E. J. pinched his nose and waved his hand as if shooing away a bad odor.

"Hello, Morton," I answered. Amanda stood and walked around me to get to the cooler. She saw my right arm and did a double take. Gently she peeled up my T-shirt sleeve. She waved the others over.

E. J.'s eyes opened wide when he saw the tattoo and I heard him stage whisper to Benny, "See, I told you he was a cracker on the inside. It's busting right out of him." Benny put up a hand to quiet him.

"Herbert Willingham died of twelve stab wounds to the abdomen," Morton said.

"Who did it? Do they know?" I asked. I rolled my sleeve down and shooed them away.

"That's why it's being kept so quiet. An eleven-year-old hustler named Vicki. Not too smart, goes to a special school, runs away from time to time and goes back to working the streets. Apparently Herbert Willingham was a bunnyman, never caught, but known to the Atlanta PD."

"Bunnyman?" I asked.

"Prison slang for pedophile," Morton replied.

"I thought that was short eyes?"

"Short eyes is the generic term. Chicken hawk is for perves who like young boys. Bunnyman for those who prefer girls. Dippold-dick for those who like to inflict pain."

"From dippoldism, the psychiatric term for teachers who become sexually aroused while disciplining children."

I heard Morton chuckle. "How in the devil did you know that?"

Rather than answer, I asked, "You were saying?"

"Willingham kept an apartment up here. Vicki was a favorite. This time, Willingham finished, nodded off, Vicki went to the kitchen, came back with a butcher knife and stabbed him repeatedly. Stole what she could carry, ran out the door covered with blood, and got picked up a block away by a squad car. Tough old bird didn't die right away. But Vicki's attack perforated the colon and that caused peritonitis. The kid's in juvie hall now. Cops would love to call it self-defense, but they don't want to let a retarded kid with lots of rage and a history of extreme violence back onto the streets. One of those sad cases."

"Too much information," I said.

"Let me save you the trouble of asking the obvious. As far as the cops can make out, no one put Vicki up to it. She just snapped," Morton said.

"Do you have an address on his apartment?" I asked. Morton read out an address in Marietta.

"Thanks, I owe you one," I said.

"You owe me five-thousand-and-one, soon to be fifty-thousand-and-one," he answered. "And the good news is I'm going to give you a chance to repay it."

The other line rang, and the caller ID said it was Rattlesnake Sweeney. "Can you hold for just a minute, Morton? I'm sorry, but I need to take this call." I didn't wait for his answer but switched over to Rattlesnake.

"Rattler," I said.

"Don't call me Rattler. My friends call me Rattler. You can call me Rattlesnake or Jim or Jimmy or Sweeney or butt-ugly or I don't care what, just not Rattler," he said.

"My mistake," I answered.

"No problem, just getting clear. Now, to business. Bingo on the Nelson connection," Sweeney said. "My man rode over to Athens. Got there at 11:30, followed her to a motel at 12:30, snapped pictures of them through a crack in the curtain at 12:42 and was back here getting them developed by 3:00."

"Do I get a break on my three grand?"

"No way. You got your money's worth," he hissed. "I need you here tomorrow to run through things. We need to talk about how to use these pics. And, we have an injunction hearing at eleven on Monday. If we can't get a stay, foreclosure proceedings will start next Friday." We set a time for the next afternoon in a bar near his office.

"Sorry," I said, punching the line that had Morton on it.

"A week from this Sunday, I need you to catch the first flight to Miami for a connection to Montevideo."

"I thought you said Santiago," I said.

"Different assignment," he said. "Can we do a briefing next Wednesday? I'll get a room in that hotel we met at."

"OK." My heart raced in excitement. I hung up the phone. I could feel my mouth getting dry, and fought the grin. I took a tiny bite of the pizza and chewed determinedly. Amanda looked at me expectantly. "What?" I said. "What?"

# CHAPTER 46

*A round ten or so, we gave up the game. Russell* picked up a sleeping Rachel from a blanket on the floor. She balled up her fists and burrowed into his chest without waking. Mary scooped up toys and blanket and smiled good-bye. The door clanged behind them. The rest of us lifted the bed and nightstand and replaced them in their proper place, in the center of the tip-off circle. Dee Lane and E. J. left for the trash cans with their arms full of pizza boxes, and Benny trailed behind with a plastic bag of aluminum cans.

Bob John was the last one out. He paused while he strapped a shoulder holster on over his sweaty T-shirt. "Gosh, I'd forgotten how much fun this is. It's good to have him back, isn't it?"

"Yeah. It's good to have you all back. You looked pretty good out there. Considering."

"No wind, yet, but that'll come."

"No doubt," I answered.

"Good night," he said. Amanda smiled and fluttered her fingers.

We shucked off our clothes and crawled under the covers. Amanda gave me an encouraging kiss, but when I tried to prolong it, pulled away, saying, "Unnhh, Unnh. Not tonight. I need some time to get used to sleeping with that tattoo." I spooned against her back, hoping she might change her mind, but drifted off, then slept like a log until the ringing woke me. Or rather, until the ringing woke Amanda and she threw an elbow into my ribs. I was stuck in some deep dream, and it took me a moment to swim to the surface. Blearily I looked at the red numbers on the clock dial. They said 4:29. Amanda opened one eye and looked at me, made a face, then pulled a pillow over her head.

"Hello," I croaked into the receiver.

"Dead roses? You're getting a little melodramatic in your old age," Gillie said.

"I have no idea what you're talking about," I said. With my free hand I scrubbed my face to wake up and sat upright in bed.

"Of course you don't," she laughed.

"What do you want, Gillie?"

"I wanted to know if you'd figured it out. AWS?"

"I haven't really had time to think about it," I answered.

"You disappoint me, Top. I've gotten used to thinking of you as some sort of muscle-bound Einstein, smart enough to figure out anything, and now you can't figure out a simple thing like that. Tut, tut."

"Gillie, it's the middle of the night. What do you want?"

"I wanted to tell you that having your guys call my clients and solicit business is a direct violation of the restraining order."

"No, it's not," I said.

"I've got a call into Slocum," she retorted.

"Did he call you back?"

"Not yet, why?"

"Cops don't like people who make up stories to get other people in trouble."

"What does that mean?"

"Figure it out. While you're thinking about that, I'll work on AWS."

There was a pause, while she thought. When she spoke the next time her voice was thin and spiteful. "Go back to bed, Top. Lay on your back and look up at those stupid satin banners you love so much and think about the fact that they'll belong to me in exactly one week and four and a half hours."

"I wouldn't move in yet," I said. "I've still got a week." Amanda squeezed the pillow tighter to her head and flipped over.

"I'm not going to move in at all. I'm going to tear it down and build condos on the property."

"You're kidding, right?"

"Watch me . . ." Gillie said. Amanda threw the pillow on the floor, sat up, and grabbed the phone from my hand.

"Gillie, enough is enough. You've got a husband and a family and a good life. Stop acting like some crazy bitch from Jerry Springer. Listen to me. You and Top are over. Finished. Done. Get a new life, alright?" She punched the off button on the phone and tossed it onto the foot of the bed. "You big wussy. You should have done that five minutes ago." She leaned over and kissed me softly on the cheek. Turning away, she porpoised back under the covers and dropped her head heavily on to the pillow. "Whew," she stared at the ceiling. After a moment, she ran her fingers through her hair, and exhaled again.

"You OK?" I asked.

"I think I'm going to be sick," she said. "I didn't have even a sip of beer. Maybe it was the sausage pizza. You ate some. Do you feel OK?" She didn't wait for an answer, but climbed out of bed, threw the blanket over her shoulders, and raced for the bathroom.

I watched her, and thought about sudden weight gain and morning nausea, the questions about children, the abstinence from alcohol and cigarettes, and all those little red plastic flags on wires on the hillside below the abortion clinic on I-75.

# CHAPTER 47

*A*t nine, Maggie, Benny, and I met in my office to sort out the day's inquiries. There were two hundred and forty, the most we'd had since AWS began stealing our clients. A few dozen we corrected and sourced off the top of our heads—people tend to misquote the same things over and over again. Then we quickly ran down the list and assigned the rest out.

"We'll have to either work some OT or bring a few more people in," Maggie said proudly. She sipped her cup of coffee carefully and looked around again. Her skin was the same light brown shade as the coffee. This wasn't her first time in the office of course, but it was the first morning conference we'd had since Gillie left, and the first one Maggie had ever attended in her new capacity as partner. She watched as I wound up the blue spinner and lateraled it on to a bare corner of the large oak desk. It whirled there on a small worn area the size of a saucer.

"Is this jump in business the result of your marketing?"

"Probably," she said. "Have you been in Classroom 2?"

"I have. It's very impressive. I saw the storyboards for the new Web site and I like the postcards. Who's doing all the graphic design?"

"Linda, the girl who told you off," Maggie smiled impishly.

"She didn't tell me off. We were negotiating. You researchers don't understand the world of business. You make it too personal," I sighed. "Benny, what's the status of the partnership agreement?"

He sat staring out of the window. "Mel's working on it. It should be ready by the end of the month," he said.

"There's no hurry, Top," Maggie said. "We trust you."

"Yeah, well, no need to delay, either," I said. The top began wobbling, and I reached over and snatched it before it careened over the edge and onto the floor. Without looking, I wound it up again. "Maggie, I need a search done today."

"We're going to be busy," she protested

"He knows, Maggie," said Benny. Maggie looked chagrined and nodded.

I said, "It shouldn't take that long anyway. The Ku Klux Klan is having a rally Monday night in Atlanta. I need to know logistics, who's going to be there, what the theme is, all that sort of stuff. Leave me a voice mail if you could."

"Got it," she said. There was a muffled brass barrange from down the hall. Maggie jumped up and ran over to the door, threw it open and yelled, "Yee-high!" She had a big yell for a woman the size of a small nine-year-old. I heard a chorus of "Yee-high's" echo down the halls. When she turned back and saw my face, she grinned, "That's the 'Sell Like Hell Bell.' Everyone is taking a turn working the phones, calling potential clients. It's very painful work, especially for a bunch of shy librarians. Whenever one comes through, whoever got it rings the bell and we all yell 'Yee-high.' It keeps morale up. I read about it in a book."

"Sell Like Hell Rebel Yell," I said.

Benny said, "Better stick to your day job, Rapmaster Top."

I gave him what I hoped was a withering stare and turned back to Maggie, "Why is it that if I call you 'librarians' instead of 'researchers' you go for my throat, but if you say it . . ."

"You know why," she answered.

"Benny said the bell was a little silver thing," I said.

Maggie shrugged, "We scaled up. I wanted the guys at the stations to be able to hear it." She stood while she finished her coffee. "Hey, Top? Do you like this room like this?"

"Like what?"

"You know, Gillie used to have all those plants in here. Now it looks a little barren. If you don't mind, the team and I thought we might bring in a few plants from home, fill the sills back up again."

"Be my guest," I said. "Just don't rearrange the bookshelves with the tops on it."

She looked horrified, "Oh, no. We would never do that." Before I could answer, she looked down at her orange Swatch, and said, "Got to go. My turn on the phone. Bye." She scurried out.

Benny turned to me, "What do you think of all this? Too little, too late?"

I thought for a moment, "It's worth a try."

"Then as long as we're still fighting, I have a Dee Lane idea," Benny said.

"What's that?"

"Do you remember Gillie used to ride the exercise bike at lunchtime? She kept her leotards, water bottles, and all that stuff in a locker in the girls' bathroom."

"So?"

"So I checked yesterday, she never cleaned out her locker," he said.

"Double so?"

"What if someone poured red paint over her boyfriend Jeff Nelson's bed tonight, and what if when the cops came, they looked in the bushes and found a water bottle full of red paint, and Gillie's fingerprints were all over it?"

"How would they know the prints are hers?" I asked.

"Didn't she used to be a volunteer for that community emergency thing? Remember her talking about the background check and all that?" he replied.

"That is brilliant," I said. "Dee Lane has taught you well, grasshopper."

Benny gave a small smile. "Probably says you should have a good alibi for tonight, say one A.M.?"

"Airtight," I said.

"And Top?"

"Yeah?"

"I hung a canvas across the wall in the auditorium and chained the doors. Keep people out while we decide what to do with it."

"Good idea," I said. We heard the bell ring, and I yelled "Yee-high" at the top of my lungs. Benny smiled and shook his head.

# CHAPTER 48

*J*ay Pope-Scott and Caron lived in a large brick home on a corner lot near the university. In front of their house idled a car from the campus police, and in it a bored young officer read a copy of The Red and Black. He glanced up as I arrived, quickly checked my license plate against a list on a clipboard, and returned to his paper.

Caron answered the doorbell. Today she wore a color close to white from head to toe—white shift, white shoes, white enameled bracelet on her left wrist. The weeping, bedraggled woman of a couple of days ago was gone, and this morning every blond hair was in place, and her perfect makeup looked as if it had been applied with a laser. She gave me a big smile as she swung the door open, and reached up to peck me on the cheek. "Hello, Top, how are you?" She drew out the last word playfully and gave me a pat on my shoulder, thankfully not the one with the new tattoo.

"I'm fine, Caron," I pulled the SIG from my waistband and handed it to her, butt first. She took it from me, turned it to see if the safety was on, and laid it casually on the upholstered seat of one of those pieces of hall furniture that hold hats, boots, and have a mirror built into the back.

"Jay's in back," she said. "Come on." The immaculate lawn was surrounded by an eight-foot black metal fence buffered with flower beds. It looked familiar, and I realized the backyard was a very similar layout to the one at his office, only larger. On a chaise lounge in the center of the lush green carpet lay the professor, also dressed from head to toe in white, white duck pants, white cotton shirt, and a white silk ascot. A tan canvas umbrella on a wooden pole blocked the morning sun, as well as shading a small table holding two half-filled coffee cups and a canvas director's chair. On the ground beside him stood a stack of Barbara Tuchman's books. "Can I get you some coffee?" Caron bubbled. I said yes, and she bounced away. I smiled.

"Good morning, Top," said Pope-Scott, extending a languid hand. I stepped over to shake it, and then stepped back and sat down in the director's chair.

"How are you?"

The smile on Pope-Scott's face froze as he swung his feet to the ground, holding his arm tight to his side. He winced as he moved. "So-so. The doctors say I'm doing well, but I'm still very sore."

"I'm not surprised. Even when you're wearing a vest, a large caliber pistol at close range causes a bruise the size of a dinner plate that lasts a month."

"I'm not the least bit surprised that you know that," he smiled.

"I read a lot," I said with a grin.

"Speaking of reading, have you made any progress with *Dixiecaust?*" he asked. As he said it, he shifted his eyes away from mine toward a point in the middle distance.

"Almost done," I said.

"And?" He licked his lips and looked back into my face.

He was in rough shape, both physically and emotionally. I answered, "It's brilliant. Brilliant premise, brilliant research, brilliant writing."

"But did you like it?" he pushed.

"Not really," I said.

"Because?"

"Because I think it lends itself to misuse."

"That's absurd," he snorted.

" 'As long as people believe in absurdities, they will continue to commit atrocities. Voltaire,' " I said.

"Misplaced cleverness on your part. I said your point was absurd, not my work. My book was based on years of careful study and original research. Every fact was well-sourced, every argument well-supported. It is the most truthful history of The War ever written. 'Vincit omnia veritas.' That means . . ." he said.

"Truth conquers all things. Latin proverb from the first century." I said.

"Very good, Mr. Kiernan. I should not have assumed that your knowledge was confined to body building," he said. He leaned forward and smiled, still holding his elbow tight against his side. Debate was sport to him, his sport, the game in which he'd made his reputation. "And your response?"

"Exactitude is not truth. Henri Matisse."

"So what do you think is the truth about the war, Mr. Kiernan? Do you think I lied about the rapes and the massacres and the mass graves? Are you one of those who believes the news media made up the Holocaust and Cambodia and Bosnia? Do you think the moon landing was filmed in a studio in Manhattan Beach?"

"No, and I don't think you lied," I said.

"Then, Mr. Kiernan, 'don't join the book burners. Don't think you are going to conceal faults by concealing evidence.' "

"Eisenhower," I answered.

"Correct," he snapped. "Now tell me why you didn't like my book."

"I told you, because it lends itself to misuse. Assholes like Alstott can use it to make themselves respectable."

"Knowledge is neutral, Mr. Kiernan. I cannot be responsible for how people use my work," he answered.

"That's facile bullshit. I'm not talking about three academics sitting around some empty conference center in folding chairs debating what would have happened if General A. P. Hill had arrived at Antietam on time. I'm talking about dangerous characters like Alstott using your words to stir up people to bomb hospitals and drag people behind trucks," I said.

"I see," he said stiffly, wounded I suspect by the reference to the Sword of Michael. He looked down at his open hands, and turned one over and studied its back.

I let the silence grow. Finally, I spoke in what I hoped was a neutral, formal tone, "You paid me to recover a flag. Do you want to hear how that is going?"

Pope-Scott carefully lay back on the lounge. I watched as he painfully swung his feet up. The muscles around his mouth tightened and a long sigh escaped as he settled back on the chair. "More than you can guess."

"Sorry?" I asked.

"I hired you to get the Bloody Red Rag back because I intended to put it back in its case and resume life as usual. Our plans have changed. When you get the flag back, I'm going to sell it."

"That is a change," I said. Caron brought back a small tray with a coffee cup and a glass coffeepot with a plunger. She pushed the grounds to the bottom and poured me a cup of thick rich coffee. She offered a warm-up to Pope-Scott, but he declined. After a pregnant moment or two, she excused herself.

"I'm resigning the Chair at the University and putting the house on the market. We're moving to Palo Alto. In California," he said with studied nonchalance.

"Stanford?" I asked.

"No. Santa Clarita," he smiled.

"Quite a change," I said.

"Think of it in baseball terms. I'm coming off the DL and going down to the minors for rehab." He motioned to the books beside him.

"Hopefully I'll be able to latch on at Stanford or Cal Berkeley at some point. I'm planning a new book."

"Southern history?"

"Absolutely not," He nodded toward the house. "Caron is very happy about it."

"The book or the move?"

He didn't answer, but instead said, "We will need the money the flag will bring. I'm told housing prices there are outrageous."

"That's what they say," I agreed. I drank half my coffee.

"Have you found it?"

"I know where it will be, but not where it is," I said. "Marcus Alstott plans to sell it to Jo Ann Wilde next Tuesday morning. Herbert Willingham was to broker the deal, but he's dead and someone else is in the picture. My guess is that's who has the flag at the moment."

"Styrell sold it to Alstott?" Pope-Scott frowned.

"I don't know. Styrell sold it. Alstott has it, or will have it, by Tuesday. I don't know if that means he sold it to Alstott or to Willingham or to someone else. Why?"

"I don't know. I just wouldn't think he'd know Alstott," Pope-Scott shrugged.

"He's a biker, and bikers have a long-standing link to white supremacists. But I'm just guessing. I don't know all the details yet."

"How do you plan to get it back?"

"I don't know that yet. If I have the option, do you want me to take it back or buy it back?"

He pursed his lips, "I've been thinking about that. I think the only fair thing to do is to buy it back."

"That's the cleanest thing. Otherwise, it could get hung up in court for years."

"Try to buy it. Styrell told Caron he sold it for two-hundred-thousand dollars. Our two-thirds share is sitting untouched in our checking account. Do you need a blank check now?"

"No," I shook my head. "But you might want to get it available on Monday. My guess is we'll need cash, and banks drag their feet about handing out a shoebox full of hundred-dollar bills." Pope-Scott nodded. I finished my coffee and after an awkward exchange of pleasantries, left.

# CHAPTER 49

*I sipped the whiskey the bartender had poured from* the Johnnie Walker Black bottle and wondered why it tasted like the cheaper Johnnie Walker Red while I looked across the corner of the padded bar toward my lawyer. Dee Lane's drink was on the bar on my other side, waiting on him to return from the bathroom.

"So where do we stand, Rattlesnake?" I asked.

"Good news and bad news. Which one you want first?" He finished his rum and Coke and motioned for another. This guy made me look like an advertisement for moderation.

"Good news first," I said.

"I can get you two, three mil. The ATF and Clarke County were way out of line on the search. Informant with an agenda, no substantiation, excessive damage. Right now with the whole Patriot Act thing, judges will give a warrant for anything. All the cops have to do is put in words like 'explosives' or 'heavy weapons.' But sooner or later, the Court's going to notice that most of what Ashcroft has done is un-Constitutional, then that pendulum's going to slow down, and when it swings back the other way, government's going to be throwing money at guys like you to shut you up. I'd say eighteen months, two years, and you're not going to have to work again."

"Uh-oh," I said.

"Uh-oh, is right. Bad news is we have an injunction hearing on Monday morning at eleven. I think we're going to lose, give it four to one against, and they're going to formally start the foreclosure process."

"What about the embezzlement?"

He ground out his cigarette. "We can't prove she embezzled anything. And even if we could, it's not germane to the foreclosure."

"We can prove she and Nelson cooked this up between them," I said. Dee Lane came back from the bathroom and slid onto his stool.

"We can prove that she and Nelson have an inappropriate relationship and I've got a suit filed against the bank for breach of fiduciary duty. I think they'll settle, too, eventually. That'll get you another few hundred thou. But it's not going to prevent foreclosure."

"Because?"

"Because your loan contract is completely legal. It's like this: Consumers have laws to protect them, and big corporations can protect themselves, but small businesses have no clout and no protection. Local banks make all their money screwing over small businesses. And farmers."

"So I'm going to lose the school in a week?"

"Not exactly. You're facing a nonjudicial foreclosure, and next Friday is the start of that process. There will be four weeks of advertising the foreclosure in local papers, you'll get a certified letter, and then at the end of it, the property will be sold. You waived your right of redemption. Normally there would be a public auction, but your contract permits sealed private offers. That was dumb, by the way."

"So I'm going to lose the school in five weeks?"

"Unless," he said.

"Unless what?"

"Unless you can come up with a really big chunk of money."

"But you said we have no right of redemption."

"You don't, but bankers hate to have borrowers default on loans. It makes their financial results look bad. If you can find enough money, right or no right, they'll probably agree to letting you make the loan current and putting a series of future payments into an escrow account. We'll drop the lawsuit and sign a confidentiality agreement. Everybody will be happy. Probably need a quarter of a million dollars to make that work. You think you can do that?" he hissed.

"Maybe," I said. Rattlesnake and Dee Lane both looked at me in surprise. I smiled and raised my glass of raw Scotch.

# CHAPTER 50

**D**ee Lane and I left Rattlesnake in the bar, and fought rush hour traffic north to Marietta. We reached May-retta just at dusk, and joined the muddle of traffic circling the square.

"You don't really think we're going to find anything at Willingham's apartment, do you?" he asked. "You know the cops will have taken every scrap of paper and computer disk down to the lab."

"You never know," I said. "Maybe the flag is thumbtacked to the living room wall."

"Right," he answered, giving me his best grin.

"OK, then. The truth is we're killing time until the tattoo convention shuts down for the evening and we can go brace Styrell again. I'm hoping to catch him away from his gorilla entourage. So, no, I don't really expect to get much from Herbie's place." I read the Mapquest directions to Dee Lane, and he smoothly maneuvered us through the tangle of traffic.

To my mild surprise, Willingham's former apartment was not in one of the ubiquitous complexes that seem to be tucked behind every dogwood in Metro Atlanta. Instead it was a walk-up above a small pharmacy in a poorly lighted neighborhood of ambiguous prospects. We drove by, made the block, and parked in front of a travel agency a hundred yards or so up from the door. A large, elaborate display for Carnival cruises filled the front window. In it, a cutout girl wearing a bikini had toppled forward and now leaned her cardboard head against the glass. Behind her, her handsome cardboard boyfriend smilingly offered her a pink drink with an umbrella in it, apparently not noticing that she'd had plenty already.

"You see any police?" I said.

"No, but they use a lot of electronics now for this type of thing, don't they? Aim a cheap camera at the door and send it back to the station over the Internet?"

Before I could answer, the door to the stairwell opened, and a small dapper man let himself out. He wore a pink shirt, a brocaded vest, and a string tie. The dandy with the quick, snappy step was the antique dealer, Sam Freeholder. He strutted with butt tight and shoulders back to a new green Jaguar XJ sedan. As he approached the car, the trunk popped open. He raised the lid and flipped a wrapped parcel into the space.

"Slide down," I said, and we ducked as low as we could behind the dash. Sam took a slow turn, looking up and down the street. He checked his watch, and climbed into the Jag.

"Go inside the apartment or follow him?" Dee Lane asked.

"Let's see what he's up to," I said.

"Next time you want us to shadow someone, tell me and I'll leave this thing at home and rent a beige Taurus." I knew he was right. Even at night, the low slung Testarossa turned heads. Especially in a quiet neighborhood like this one.

"Let's roll the dice. Head back to downtown Marietta. Maybe he's headed back to his shop. If we don't pick him up there, we'll double back and do the apartment."

"Do you think the package is the flag?"

"The fake one maybe," I said.

"How do you know it's not the real one?" Dee Lane asked.

"I don't for sure, but I think he would treat the Bloody Red Rag with a little more respect," I said.

Dee Lane wound his way back through side streets. We saw no sign of Freeholder en route, but when we reached the square, the Jaguar was parked directly in front of the store. "Are we going in?" Dee Lane asked.

"I don't think we can," I said truthfully. "The place is sealed up like Fort Knox. Do you have a screwdriver?"

"There's a Leatherman in a case up against your seat," he answered.

I groped around for a moment, found the small leather case, and extracted the all-purpose tool. "Be right back. Give me a light beep if he comes out." Quickly I walked up the street to the Jaguar and knelt at curbside as if to tie my shoe. From the Leatherman, I unfolded a short sharp metal spike. The headlights from the few passing cars lit me up and threw dark moving shadows across the back of the car.

Taking one last glance, and seeing no one on the sidewalk in either direction, and no movement in the shop, I punched a small hole in the taillight cover, down near the bottom, where Freeholder would need to bend over to see it.

Back inside the Ferrari, I returned the Leatherman to its case and slipped it under the seat. Dee Lane said, "Why'd you do that?"

"It makes him easier to follow. The trapezoidal shape of the tail-lights aren't that distinctive. They look too much like the other cars in the Ford line, Taurus, Lincoln, Hyundai. You'll be surprised how visible this is," I said. As I spoke, Freeholder exited the shop. He turned back to the door, locked two bolts at waist level, knelt to lock another one, and set the alarm using another key inserted into a panel to the side. "Better get down." Freeholder walked around the front of the car to the driver's side door.

"Why don't we just take him now?" Dee Lane mumbled from his slumped position.

"I don't know," I answered truthfully. "Buzz hunch."

Even with the white star shining from the taillight, it was still difficult to follow Freeholder. He whipped the big Jag around the square and quickly worked his way to the North Marietta Parkway, following that to I-75. There Freeholder impatiently waited for the light to change, staging his car ahead a foot or two, jamming on the brakes, and then easing forward again. We sat four car-lengths back, behind a dark blue Saturn inside which a silhouette held a cell phone.

As the light changed, the Jaguar shot forward and dove toward the ramp. The two cars behind it accelerated. The blue Saturn in front of us didn't move. Ahead, we saw the big sedan with its distinctive taillight slice into the stream of traffic headed toward Atlanta. Dee Lane beeped his horn, the Saturn driver waved, and slowly ambled toward the ramp. Dee Lane rode a foot from the other car's bumper. The car in front of us crept along, apparently oblivious. As we approached the merge lane, we saw his brake lights come on, and the car slowed to a hesitant crawl.

"Hang on." Dee Lane whipped us onto the shoulder and blew around the nervous driver, accelerated smoothly, and slipped us into a gap between two barreling semis. He slid over into the next lane. "Do you see him?"

"No, but I think he should have twenty or so cars on us."

"All right, I'll work us forward." He slipped left and moved up five car-lengths, slid in front of a white refrigerated truck to our left, and dodged back inches in front of a gray van.

I peered through the traffic in front of us. "We're too low, I can't see anything but SUV tail pipes."

"OK, I'll move up some more." He whipped the car through traffic. Ahead of us huge green signs indicated the intersection with I-285 one mile ahead. "Stay on or take the perimeter?"

"It's a crap shoot. Let's stay on," I said. I glanced over and saw the speedometer climb past ninety. We cut through the slower traffic. Ahead, I thought I saw a white taillight two lanes to our left, I pointed it out to Dee Lane. He nodded and slipped around a big orange semi and accelerated down the right. Ahead of us, traffic from 285 poured onto I-75, and Dee Lane merged left. The white taillight moved back and forth across the lane.

"Is he drunk or crazy?" Dee Lane said, accelerating again.

"It's a motorcycle," I said. We pulled up close and saw the small white light over the license plate was bent slightly upward, creating a small white gleam under the red taillight. It was a huge Honda Goldwing, piloted by a couple wearing helmets that matched the paint job on the bike. In the glow of the overhead lights, I could see a little antenna on each helmet. We blasted by them and drove without speaking for another ten miles, my head on a swivel. Dee Lane moved ahead, sliding back and forth through the alternating gaps in the traffic flow. A new set of big green signs warned us that we'd soon be merging with I-85, meaning downtown was only a few minutes ahead. "Might as well take it easy," I said. "He's gone." We shot by the I-85 interchange.

"There!" Dee Lane pointed, and a quarter mile ahead and five lanes over I saw a green Jag with a broken taillight flashing up an exit ramp. Dee Lane cut a diagonal across the traffic. From the corner of my eye, I saw the car next to us brake hard, and the panicked face of the young driver. Her brakes squealed in protest, and behind her a semi blared its horn. I held my breath as we missed a series of cars by inches, bumped over a row of warning strips and fishtailed up the ramp. Dee Lane pumped the brakes. Behind us, I could hear a fading chorus of horns. "Piece of cake," Dee Lane grinned.

"You do that again, and I'm going to have to start carrying a roll of toilet paper," I said.

"Hang on, we can make the light," he answered.

# CHAPTER 51

*W*e followed *Freeholder east and south. The* traffic was thinner now, and Dee Lane hung back, trying not to make us even more conspicuous. Either Freeholder wasn't used to checking for tails or he wasn't very good at it. Or he knew we were back there and had his own reasons for leading us on. But I didn't think so. I thought he was a man with something on his mind, and wasn't paying any attention, and told Dee Lane so.

"Maybe, but I'd think antique dealers would be pretty cautious by nature," he answered, then a second later, "He's turning." Dee Lane slowed and we eased up to a park entrance into which Freeholder had disappeared. The small sign at the gated opening said, "Scanlan Park. Closed between sunset and sunrise. Trespassers will be prosecuted." There was a chain that stretched across the gap, but someone had unhooked it and it now lay on the ground across the roadway. A cut padlock lay beside it.

"What do you think, a meeting?" Dee Lane asked.

"Don't know," I answered. Dee Lane turned us into the dark archway. There was no sign of Freeholder. We wound our way slowly through the almost empty park.

"Look at that, Top," Dee Lane said. Under an ornate styled lamppost, a figure stood alongside the road ahead of us, one hand on a jutting hip. She turned and gave us a lipsticked smile as we passed. Sudden recognition left me breathless. Dee Lane had the same reaction. "Oh, Christ. It's a kid," he said.

Around the next turn, we saw another, this one African-American, and dressed up in a frilly white dress with pink bows, like girls wear at confirmation. Beyond her stood another young white girl, this one dressed in a powder blue soccer uniform, hip similarly slung out toward the road.

"How old do you think these girls are?" I asked.

"I don't know," he answered. "Ten, twelve."

"No chance they're just made up to look young?"

"Too short," he answered.

A black Suburban with tinted windows approached us and cruised slowly by. Only its parking lights were on. A few minutes later we passed a silver Toyota Camry pulled over to the side. A tiny girl leaned in the driver's side window. On the bumper of the Camry was a sticker that said "My child is an honor student at Dunworth Elementary." The child turned and held up a stubby hand to shield her eyes from our headlights. The driver turned his head away as we passed. Dee Lane doused the headlights, and we crept by on parking lights only, like the black Chevrolet we'd passed a few minutes before.

"Up ahead, do you think that's him?" Dee Lane used his chin to point forward.

"Maybe." In front of us a hundred yards or so, I saw a large dark car without lights pull over, fifty feet before a yellowish streetlight. A small figure in a white T-shirt and pink skirt walked toward the rear of the car. Dee Lane killed the parking lights and pulled over. "Are you carrying?" I asked. Dee Lane shook his head. "Take this, then," I handed him the SIG. "Come up wide, outside the arc of his mirrors. I'm going to surprise him." From my pocket I pulled a pair of latex gloves and tugged them on. I reached down for the Leatherman, and unfolded the knife.

"What do you want me to do?" Dee Lane said, eyeing the gloves nervously.

"Whatever it takes," I answered. "Are the interior lights going to come on when I open this door?" Dee Lane shook his head. "Good, let's go." The small figure now leaned into the Jaguar's window. A hand came out of the window, and the fingers slid under the tube top. The girl stood patiently, letting the hand explore. After a moment, she stepped back and tugged the top back down.

I left the vehicle and walked quickly across the wet grass strip until I was very close to the bushes that lined the roadway. I moved quickly through the anonymous shadows toward Freeholder and the diminutive hooker. About fifty yards from the back of the vehicle, a gaunt figure stepped out.

Blocking my way stood an emaciated woman wearing a dirty T-shirt and cut-off blue jean shorts. Her limp, filthy hair framed a drug-ravaged face. She held a length of tree limb about two feet long and two inches thick. "Where do you think you're going?" she spat. She raised the limb shoulder-high. Her arms shook with the effort. "This is none of your business." Mother? Sister? Lover? It was impossible to tell her age.

I stepped directly toward her. She drew the limb back, expecting me to stop. Instead I took two quick steps forward. She hesitated. Her face said she'd been around and anyone who's been around knows that a ninety-pound woman never wins a fight with a two-hundred-pound man without the involvement of Colonel Colt. Ask the karate champion from LA who was raped and beaten five years ago by an overweight, middle-aged office worker. She now teaches her students to run and scream.

I raised the sharp point of the Leatherman until it was a half inch away from her left eye. "Don't push it," I whispered. With my free hand, I dug in my jeans pocket and came out with a twenty and a few ones. I threw the money on the ground. "You two get out of here. You don't want any part of this."

She cocked the limb again and stood shaking, fighting the urge to dive for the cash. After a few seconds, she lost the battle, dropped the limb to the ground and sank to her knees, pawing through the wet grass. Twenty feet ahead of me the little girl left the driver's window and walked around the back of the Jaguar toward the passenger door. I stepped past the woman.

I overtook the child just as she reached for the door handle. She opened the door and lifted one foot to step into the car. I grabbed her thin arm and spun her backward. She was weightless, and my adrenaline-powered pull lifted her off her feet and sent her sailing across the grass. She landed, lost her footing on the slick grass, and slipped to one knee.

I stepped quickly into the space where she had been, seated myself in the car, and pulled the door shut. Freeholder, too, had disabled the switch that automatically turns on the interior lights when a door is opened. I leaned back in the warm leather seat. In the glow from the dashboard, Sam Freeholder's excited sweaty face stared straight ahead. Behind me, I heard a high-pitched voice say, "Hey!" Freeholder turned to look.

"Can I sit on your lap, Uncle Bunny?" I said.

Freeholder literally jumped straight up. I smiled my friendliest smile and waved the Leatherman at him like a conductor's baton. His face hardened and his left hand came up quickly from the shadows behind him. In it was a silver-plated short-barreled 22. "Don't move," he said.

"OK," I said.

Freeholder panted and licked his lips. "Put that down." From this perspective the mouth of the 22 barrel, which I knew to be roughly the size of a drinking straw, looked as large as my fist. When someone points a gun at you, the barrel of the gun fills the room. Everything else fades into the unfocused background, and that gun barrel is the only thing you can see. This one quivered, but still stayed pointed in the general vicinity of the tip of my nose. I carefully laid the Leatherman on the floor at my feet.

"Get out of my car," he said.

"I have to tell you, Sam, I thought you might have a gun. That's why my friend Dee Lane is standing behind you with a 9-mil SIG. If he pulls that trigger, it's going to take your head off." Over his shoulder I saw the black leather of Dee Lane's coat just outside the driver's side window. My SIG rested in one massive knuckly hand. Dee Lane bent over at the waist, and his craggy face appeared in the window over Freeholder's shoulder. He wore small John Lennon-style sunglasses and I saw his eyebrows shoot up as he took in Free-holder's pistol.

"Please, Mr. Kiernan," Freeholder smiled a tired smile, "I am old, not senile."

Dee Lane opened his free hand and spread his fingers palm up in a questioning gesture.

"Last chance," I said.

"Get out of my car," he said, "It's *your* last chance."

I nodded to Dee Lane. His face disappeared as he straightened up. A long arm swung the dark pistol back across his body, and slashed downward into the window behind Freeholder's head.

"Easy!" I yelled. The window exploded inward and little pebbles of safety glass flew across the car, bouncing off the dash and covering my lap. Freeholder turned his head at my yell, and the pistol butt caught him right across the eyebrow, slamming his head into the headrest.

But he didn't drop the gun. I heard a loud supersonic snap, saw a small flash of flame, and felt a rush of hot wind immediately under my chin. The window behind me shattered and more pebbles rained down into my lap. A second later, there was another snap and a thump in the roof just above my head. I reached for the gun, pushing it from my face. There was another pop and a thud as a slug hit the leather-covered dash. I held his fist with the gun in it in my hand, and felt the cylinder begin to rotate against my fingertips.

# CHAPTER 52

*I*t's easy to forget that despite Dee Lane's long and accomplished criminal past, he's really not very useful in that sort of situation. Dee Lane's trip is to talk his way out of trouble. For him guns are usually just a prop. So I shouldn't have been surprised that instead of simply tapping lightly on the window, which would have given me a chance to grab Freeholder's gun, he did the one thing almost guaranteed to get me killed—forcing Freeholder into a reflexive action. It would have been funny if it hadn't been for that hot wind I felt just under my chin, and the glass pebbles that now continued to fall out of my clothes, even though I'd brushed myself thoroughly, and already peeled off my T-shirt and shaken it out.

Although it was a warm night, I was cold, the result both of my sweat-soaked T-shirt and the cool night air pouring in through the two missing windows. I turned on the heater in the Jaguar. A button on the console showed a seat with three wavy lines coming out of it, and I punched that, too. Ten minutes later warmth spread across my back and bottom. I followed Dee Lane back to the interstate at a sedate, excessively legal pace. Neither one of us wanted the Jaguar stopped, not with Sam Freeholder tied up on the backseat and a front seat covered with glass and blood.

"This hurts," he said from the back.

We'd used Freeholder's string tie to bind his hands behind his back, and had tied it tightly. "What hurts?"

"Everything. My head. My arms. You could untie me."

"Not going to happen."

"What am I going to do, jump out of the car on I-75? Fight you for the wheel? I'm seventy-four next month. I don't think you have much to worry about."

"Just get comfortable. Traffic's not bad. We'll be back to your store in thirty minutes."

"What then? Are you going to rob me?" he said. "You can't go inside. There are security cameras. Everything is all catalogued and registered anyway."

"I don't have to think about that until we get there."

"How did you find me?"

"Just good luck. We spotted you coming out of Willingham's and decided to see what you were up to."

"It wasn't very lucky for me," Freeholder wheezed bitterly. Ahead Dee Lane turned onto the ramp onto I-75 North. I carefully put on my right blinker, checked all of my mirrors, and edged over.

"You've had your good luck for the night," I answered.

Freeholder groaned and shifted. "How's that?"

"You're lucky Dee Lane didn't kill you."

"You don't understand," he said. I heard a sharp intake of breath.

"Nope, I don't understand. And do me a favor, don't explain it to me."

"What do you want?"

"Nothing," I lied.

"What?"

"Nothing," I repeated. "You don't have anything I want. You don't know anything we don't already know."

"Nonsense," he protested. I heard him scruffle around on the backseat. "This cut is bleeding profusely."

"Cuts in the brow do, but they're not fatal."

"I need to sit up. I don't feel well."

"Forget it."

"What are you going to do with me?" he asked.

"I don't know yet," I answered.

"I can give you the flag," he whimpered. "I can, really."

"No, you can give me the fake, the one you're going to swap for the real one that you're then going to sell to Jo Ann Wilde. You're taking over the deal from your old bunny-buddy Herbert."

"How do you? . . ."

"Because you're a lousy criminal. You're not even a particularly good pervert, letting us follow you all over Atlanta in a car just slightly less conspicuous than a fire engine." My voice sounded loud and shrill in my ears, and I knew I was still hyped up.

"But you don't know who's got the flag," he said. "I can give you that."

"Alstott's got it," I guessed, and listened for the reaction.

There was a gulp, and a pause, then Freeholder laughed tightly. "Very, very good, Mr. Kiernan. You're not the muscle-bound oaf you appear to be, are you? Very good guess, but it's not quite right."

"Who has it then?" I asked.

"I don't feel well, Mr. Kiernan. Really, this is not a ruse. My arms are completely numb and my head feels like it's coming apart."

"Of course you're hurting, you're trussed up like a pig and you just got hit in the head with a pistol."

"Aaach. Please, I have a history of heart trouble. I think I need to get to a hospital. Please. Get me to a hospital, and I will tell you." A very real-sounding gasp came from over my shoulder.

"That's not the way the trade works. Who has the flag?" I wondered how sick he really was. Ahead I saw a billboard for HopeStar Cobb Hospital. The sign said exit at 260, then head west. We passed

I-285. A huge green overhead sign said Windy Hill Road, right lane. "We're just a few minutes from HopeStar. Tell me a name."

"Please." There was a groan and the sound of labored breathing. "Please, I'm dying." I could barely hear him.

Another sign said Exit 260, one half mile. "Give me a name, Sam." I moved over into the right lane. "This is our exit."

"Please."

"Going." I drew out the syllables like an auctioneer.

"So dark."

"Going," I said.

"Have mercy," he gasped. I thought about the hand under the girl's shirt.

"Gone," I said, and stomped on the accelerator. From the corner of my eye I saw the exit zip by and heard another loud gasp from the backseat. Then silence.

# CHAPTER 53

"*W*hat is it, a stroke?" Dee Lane said. We stood beside the Jag, parked in the corner of a small lot two blocks from Freeholder's store. A hedge at our back threw a triangle of black shadow across the area where we stood.

"That's my guess." Freeholder lay on the backseat, eyes wide open and pupils of different sizes, a large bubble of spittle quivering over his mouth. His shirt was soaked in blood from his head wound. Red-brown smears ran across the tan leather and spots dotted the carpeting.

"He tell you who has the flag?"

"Nope," I answered.

"Did you know he was in trouble?"

"He said his head hurt and his arms were numb. But I didn't think we wanted to pull into an ER in a bullet-riddled car and drop off a beat-up old man with ligature marks on his wrists." When Dee Lane had opened the rear door, Freeholder's head had fallen out and his comb-over had flipped down like a daybed. We stared down at the pink top of his bald head.

"Bullshit, Top." Dee Lane said. "You shouldn't lie to your

friends." He threw a long arm across my shoulders. We stood over the old man.

"Who else can I lie to? My enemies will never believe me," I answered.

"*Good* point. Let's put him in the front, pull his pants down, steal his wallet and jewelry and hope it goes as a trick-turned-robbery."

"I wore gloves but the girl touched the car." I raised my hands.

"Don't you worry about someday having to explain to a cop why you carry a pair of latex gloves in your pocket?"

"Not in this day and age."

"I guess not," he agreed.

"It shouldn't take much to wipe it down."

"I'll wipe. If you've got gloves, you can handle the body."

"Deal. I'll pop the trunk. If it's the fake flag, let's take it. It may come in handy," I said. We worked quickly and efficiently. I emptied the wallet of money and cards and threw it on the ground. The pistol, credit cards, jewelry, and a small rock the size of a tennis ball I wrapped in a blue bandanna, which I then tied up into a tight knot. The bundle would end up at the bottom of the Chattahoochee River. I used the remote on the keychain to set the alarm, opened the car door, tossed in the keys, and we walked quickly back to the Testarossa. We could hear the shrieking alarm and blaring horn behind us as we drove away. By nine-thirty we were working our way down Highway 41.

Dee Lane reached inside his jacket and pulled out a cell phone, flipped it open, and scrolled down. Finding the number he wanted, he pressed the "Call" button and held it to his ear. We drove slowly and legally. I pointed to a Wendy's restaurant, and Dee Lane pulled in and parked. I sat and waited on him to finish his call. A chill overtook me and I sat shaking, pressing my hands between my legs to try to warm up.

"Bob John? Dee Lane . . . Not much . . . Took our friend to the big city to kill some time, get his mind off his troubles . . . No, it didn't work, not really. He's about as much fun as a boil . . . Listen, we were driving around in north Atlanta and cut through a place called Scanlan Park. Bob John, there were child prostitutes there . . . Girls . . . Yeah, four or five of them. Maybe ten years old. Freaked both of us out . . . Yeah, I got some plates. Hold on." Dee Lane opened the ashtray and pulled out a scrap of paper. He read the numbers into the phone and described the cars. "OK," he said. "Whatever you can do." He flipped the phone shut.

"What's he going to do?"

"He says he will make some calls. But he said not to expect much."

"Why?"

"Apparently these guys move around. They're open for business for an hour or two, then they shut down. That's why Freeholder never checked his rearview mirror, he was in too big a hurry not to miss the party."

"How do the short eyes know where it's going to be?"

"The creeps and the kids make contact by e-mail, phone trees, stuff like that. It's not likely there will be anyone there when the cops roll in. But he'll try."

"The plates?"

"He says they usually doctor them when they go cruising." It's easy enough to use tape to change a 3 to an 8 and an L to an E on a plate, and if done carefully, almost impossible to spot from more than a foot away.

"If they do grab anyone, they'll remember Freeholder and this car. We could go down for aggravated at a minimum," I said.

Dee Lane turned and looked at me. "I have to be able to sleep."

"Do you want chicken or cheeseburger? My treat," I answered.

# CHAPTER 54

*O*n Friday night, the tattoo convention stayed open until eleven, but the lots began to thin out by the time we arrived, ten thirty, and we had no trouble spotting Styrell's truck. Dee Lane circled the lot, identifying the most likely routes out, and we set up camp behind a mammoth RV a few hundred yards away from Styrell's vehicle. Dee Lane and I sat on his leather coat on the tarmac, our backs against the Ferrari, and finished our Frosties. We could just see the bottom half of Styrell's truck through the space under the large motor home.

Bored, I turned on my cell phone to check messages. The screen said I had two new voice mails. I played them both. The first was a hiya from Amanda from earlier in the day. The second had been left two hours ago by Maggie. She'd spent some time digging on the question I'd asked her, the scoop on Monday's Klan convention. Officially, according to the Web site, this was just another annual konvocation. But she'd also surfed through some Klan chat rooms and picked up a few hints that something special might be in the air.

No one, though, seemed to be quite sure what it was. There was some speculation around Alstott stepping down. Some more around new funding. And one posting suggested a church had made overtures to the group about a merger, which provoked a spirited exchange over separation of church and hate group. Maggie's message asked me if I wanted her to work the phones and try to get more. I called her line and left a message thanking her. On a hunch, I asked her to check out Ben McShane and "Our Redeemer's Church of the Chosen, St. Illa."

"Do you want to take him here?" Dee Lane asked.

"I'd like to, but I can't see how we can get close enough. And there's his posse to worry about. Let's see how it plays."

The lot slowly emptied as we sat there. Several groups walked past us to get to their cars. The guys immediately detoured over to check out Dee Lane's car, but in every case spotted us sitting in the shadows and veered off. By eleven there were only a handful of vehicles left in the huge lot, including a row of shiny Harleys parked on the sidewalk. We began to worry that the RV owner would come out and move the vehicle, or ask us to move away. At eleven-fifteen, three men wearing colors walked out of the shadows and climbed on their bikes. Two I recognized as the ones who'd grabbed me in the convention center. The third was a bearded giant, with arms the size of hams, probably the ex-wrestler who'd choked me into unconsciousness. I pointed them out to Dee Lane.

"Proves evolution is not a one-way street," he said, smiling.

"Maybe, or maybe they're like possums. Nature got them close enough and just stopped trying." They started their bikes, and the deep trademark Harley roars bounced off the side of the convention center and blasted across the almost empty lot. Delighted with the echo effect, they took turns revving their engines, seeing who could make the most noise. Finally satisfied, they peeled out in a neat, fast formation. At the exit, they slowed momentarily, then powered into an ear-splitting left turn.

"Close enough to what?" Dee Lane said. I shrugged, and we both laughed. It felt good. "You want to move in closer now that they're out of the way?"

"He knows the car, remember? There's no cover, unless we hide in the bed of the truck. We'll have to take him somewhere else."

"We're pressing our luck," Dee Lane said.

"I know," I agreed.

At eleven-thirty, a metal door in the rear of the building opened, and Styrell stepped out. He wore a black sleeveless T-shirt, blue jeans and black boots with lots of silver studs on them. Pausing outside the door, he lit up a cigarette. He stood in place for a moment, taking deep, successive hits and blowing blue plumes up into the cone of yellow light overhead. Satiated, he tucked the smoke in a corner of his mouth and sauntered toward the truck. Using the silver chain on his belt, he fished a large set of keys from his pocket. As he reached the truck, he flicked the butt, ground it out with a toe, and lit another. He cranked the truck and pulled away.

"We have got to get a beige Taurus," Dee Lane said, as we rolled across the lot without lights. Ahead of us, he turned left. We pulled up to the gate and watched as the truck drove down three or four lights and turned into a driveway. Dee Lane put on his lights before we pulled out and slowly cruised down the quiet four-lane street. Styrell had turned under a pink, heart-shaped sign that read "Heart-o-Lanta Motel and Bar. Vacancy. Free Movies." Beneath that was a lighted board, and someone had used plastic letters to spell out "Bikers Welcome."

The motel was a two-story cinder-block construction, with two unenclosed metal stairways at either end of the building. A small freestanding office stood just in front of the left stairway. Coke and ice machines stood sentry just beneath the one to the right. Behind the counter in the office we could see a heavy-set bearded man wearing a white dress shirt and a maroon turban. He stared into a small TV perched on the counter while he held a plate up just under his chin and shoveled rice into his mouth. The man didn't take his eyes off the television.

Beyond the office was a small bar, its windows lit up by neon signs.

Most of the signs were for beer, but one said "Chrome and Leather Saloon." Motorcycles filled the lot, the small lawn in front of it, and spilled over into two handicapped spaces in front of the motel office. At the other end of the motel parking lot sat the worn, white trailer that said "Styrell the Stencil." Its tongue was supported by two short pieces of 2 by 4 stacked on top of an overturned black metal pail. As we pulled in, we saw Styrell's back disappear into a second-story room.

Dee Lane eased past the office. The man in the turban looked up, and Dee Lane waved. The man didn't respond, but went back to inhaling his dinner and watching his program. We parked beside Styrell's pickup and made our way up the end stairway. I thumbed back the hammer on the SIG and held it against the side of my leg facing away from the street.

"Any ideas on how to get him to let us in?" Dee Lane whispered to my back.

"Sure," I said, walking up to the door. Using the black metal rail to steady myself, I raised my leg, and kicked as hard as I could, aiming for a place just to the right and above the door handle. A bolt of pain lightning shot up my right leg, and my left almost gave way, but the door flew open, a big hole appearing where the door handle and lock were torn out of the flimsy wood. Styrell stepped out of the bathroom, unfiltered Camel between his lips and his fly still open. He dove for the mattress nearest him.

"Don't do it," I said, limping as fast as I could into the room. I sighted the SIG at the bridge of his nose. "Don't escalate." He knelt on the ugly shag carpet, one hand stuck between the mattress and box springs, deciding. I spoke, "You've taken me twice, bud. It's not going to happen a third time. Unless your hand comes out empty, I'm pulling the trigger." Slowly Styrell pulled his hand from beneath the mattress.

Behind me, I heard Dee Lane say, "Now I get it. *Easy*." It's unusual for Dee Lane to sink to sarcasm. He usually leaves that to me. Across the room, Styrell reached slowly for the cigarette stub between his lips. He raised his eyebrows.

"Yeah, stand up and put the butt in the ashtray. Then lie on the bed, stomach down, and put your hands behind your head. Dee Lane, could you take a look outside and make sure we didn't attract too much attention?"

"You're going to get plenty of attention in about two minutes. I'm supposed to be meeting my club at the bar. I don't show up, they're going to come looking," growled Styrell, twisting the cigarette into an already-full ashtray.

"Good," I said. "Then that gives you about one-hundred-and-twenty seconds to tell me who you sold that flag to, before I cap all four of your sorry asses."

# CHAPTER 55

*S*tyrell laughed, *"Fuck you." He dropped onto the* bed and laced his fingers behind his head. I handed the SIG to Dee Lane, stripped the other bed in the room and pulled off a sheet, which I quickly ripped into long strips. I used the strips to bind his feet, knees, and hands behind his back. I also ran a double sash around his chest and arms and knotted that tightly in back. Picking up a dirty sock off the floor, I rolled it into a ball, stuffed it in his mouth, and secured it with another strip of cloth. Styrell's eyes widened as he tried to puzzle out this development. He wasn't going to because there wasn't a reason, exactly. It was an old interrogation trick—do something unexpected just to throw the subject off balance.

I picked Styrell up by the arms and stood him straight up, bent over, and tossed him over my shoulder in a fireman's carry. "Dee Lane, could you check around outside for us?" The biker couldn't weigh more than a hundred-and-twenty pounds.

"Where are we going?" Dee Lane asked.

"There is a metal ladder next to the stairs. It looks like there's some sort of flat roof. I think we'll talk to Styrell up there." I felt Styrell buck, and I swung around fast so his shoulder and head thumped hard into the doorframe. I was rewarded with a grunt. "Hold still, you dried-up old fart."

Quickly we exited the room and walked to the stairs. I climbed over the railing and grabbed the ladder with one hand. "You don't want to do any more of that wiggling stuff here, Styrell." I stepped off the metal platform onto the ladder and climbed one-handed up the iron rungs.

The roof was flat, surfaced in tar and gravel. A small two-foot-high wall with openings for drainage ran around the entire perimeter. Sitting in the center of the area were a tiny round metal grill with its legs removed and two white plastic lawn chairs. Two bricks in the seat of each chair weighted them down and kept them from blowing off in a strong wind. The bricks weren't needed tonight, because there was not a whisper of a breeze.

"Nice view," said Dee Lane, and it was. Atlanta has so many trees that it's unusual to get sweeping vistas. But from here we could see both the skyline of the city and the twinkling lights of the endless suburbs. The traffic was a red-and-white ribbon on I-20, cutting across the night canvas.

"Beautiful. Let's see how Styrell appreciates it." I dropped Styrell heavily onto the roof, trusting that this was not the sort of establishment where patrons called management about the occasional unexplained bump or thump. Walking over to the back wall, I looked over the edge. Twenty feet below me was a scraggly concrete pad, fissured with weedy strips. A single security light threw a harsh blue white glare that made the weeds look a black green color. Sitting in the center of the pad was what might have once been a small offset printing press, but was now simply a rusting heap of metal.

I pulled the gag from Styrell's mouth and tossed it over the edge. Styrell saw that, and he frowned. "Here's the dealio, Steelio. I'm going to hang you by your feet over the edge. I don't want to hear any bullshit threats and I don't want to hear any lies. If you don't tell me what I want to know by the time my arms get tired, I'm going to let go and you're going to drop straight down, headfirst onto that concrete. It may not kill you, but you're going to get real messed up. Christopher Reeve fucked up. You got me?"

"Fuck you," he said. I slapped him hard across the face.

"Didn't I say none of that?"

"I'm not going to tell you anything," he said. I dragged him feet first to the edge, hoping the little pebbles on the roof were taking the skin off his back and arms. Once more I stood him up. Hands on his shoulders, I backed him up to the edge, dropped my arms to grab his ankles and rammed my shoulder into his gut. He flew off into space, and for a moment I thought I'd lost him, then I felt the weight, and heard his body smack against the wall below.

"Goddamn, that hurt," a gravelly voice said from over the edge. I sat down and adjusted his body so the back of his knees were on top of the wall and I wasn't holding his full weight.

"I told you, don't bother. Just keep your mouth shut until you have something to tell me."

"I'm not going to tell you jack. Go ahead and let go."

"Styrell, Styrell, Styrell. It doesn't have to be that way. What you say here, stays here."

"They'll know."

"Who'll know?"

"Some guys a lot tougher than you, asshole," he said.

"Like who?" I asked. I readjusted my grip, letting my left hand slip off, and grabbing his jeans leg a second later. "Whew, that was close. Had to scratch my nose. Your belt on pretty tight, Styrell?"

"Fucking comedian," came a voice from over the edge. I looked at Dee Lane. His face was contorted, and he stood hands in pockets, shifting from leg to leg. He stared over my head into the distance. Styrell spoke again, "I'm doing you a favor by not telling you who's got the flag. You should be thanking me for it."

"You got your eyes closed, Styrell?"

"Hell no," he said. "Want to hear me spit? You can't spit when you're scared. I got a mouthful. I'm not afraid to die, man. I been closer than this."

"Styrell. You know you haven't been any closer than this. Closer than this is dead. Now just tell us. Who are you afraid of?"

"It's who I'm afraid for, dipshit."

I let go with my right hand for a minute, then took hold again. "Hay fever. This nose is driving me nuts. Sorry about that. I suppose you mean you're afraid for Pam."

"Yes, and I'm not going to create a situation where every time I leave home I have to take her out of school and haul her all over the country. She needs everything to be regular and orderly or she gets real emotional. I'm also not going to have it where when I am at home, I have to patrol the fence line at night with double aught shot. I'd rather fucking die than put that on her."

"I hear you man, but she needs a daddy."

"Aww, ain't you sweet. But you don't need to worry your pretty little head about old Styrell. Just go ahead and drop me if you're going to, pissface. My knees hurt and I'm getting bored with your lame bullshit."

I stood up and moved closer to the wall. "Come on, Styrell, my arms are starting to cramp, here." I carefully put my knees on the small wall, and lowered him another foot or two.

"Same answer as before. Fuck you. Fuck your buddy. Fuck Caron for dropping me in this shit. Fuck states with helmet laws. Fuck the whole damn universe. But I still ain't going to tell you one fucking thing."

"Want me to help pull him up?" Dee Lane whispered.

"I'm going to drop him," I insisted.

"No, you're not," he said, shaking his head.

"Give me one good reason why not," I said.

"If he was going to talk, he'd be telling lies by now," Dee Lane said. "And you know it."

"That wasn't good enough. Try again," I said.

"How about because the stubborn old fool is doing exactly what you and I would do? It's the right thing, and you and I know you're not going to kill someone for that," he said.

"Well, I should kill him for this tattoo," I said.

"Probably, but you won't."

I stepped backward and pulled as hard as I could. Styrell came sailing up over the short wall, plopped down onto the tar roof and bounced. His eyes were squeezed shut and his lips were dry and cracked. "I knew you were lying about looking down, you deceitful old cancer-ridden cup of slime," I said. Styrell opened his eyes and grinned at us.

# CHAPTER 56

"**W**ell, not a total bust. We have a flag, but we still don't know who's got *the* flag," Dee Lane said, as we walked across the parking lot to the office.

"Yes, we do. At least I think we do," I answered.

Dee Lane looked at me, waiting for an answer. When I didn't say any more, he shrugged and said, "So we can go home, now?"

"Nope," I looked at my watch. It said "11:43." "We're going to check in and stay the night."

"In this place?" Dee Lane said. "Are you nuts? Let me treat you to a Holiday Inn."

I pushed opened the glass door into the small office. The plump Sikh behind the counter put one hand beneath the counter. "Yes?" he said. I stepped up to the counter, hands out wide and open. Behind his head a security camera was mounted into a corner, its red light shining dully. I smiled into it and used an eyebrow to point the camera out to Dee Lane. He stepped up and smiled. Pulling out my wallet, I laid a credit card and driver's license on the counter. Dee Lane produced his license. I read off our names loudly. The innkeeper solemnly repeated them back to us. Dee Lane tipped the man twenty dollars to keep an eye on the Ferrari. Fifteen minutes later we had our room, a double twin on the first floor.

"Now what?" Dee Lane said.

"Now you get your reward for helping me break half the laws of Georgia in a single evening, Dee Lane. I'm going to buy you a drink," I said.

"Where?" he asked.

"Somewhere where they'll remember our faces," I said.

"I figured it was something like that," he grumbled. "Why am I doing this? I got no dog in this fight."

"Sure you do, me," I laughed. I jammed both hands in the pockets of my jeans. We weaved our way through the motorcycles. Dee Lane opened the glass door of the Chrome and Leather Saloon. "After you, he grinned.

I stepped over the threshold, and was blasted with a wave of sour, smoky air and right behind it a deafening mix of loud oaths and ZZ Top. We made our way into the edge of the throng, and Dee Lane pulled the door shut behind us. Conversation died away, and the noise level dropped down to a surprisingly quiet ninety decibels of Texas rock and roll. In front of us stood forty or fifty watchful men, most of whom held pool cues or beer bottles. A few women were scattered amongst them. The unisex dress code seemed to be blue jeans, leather vests, piercings, and tattoos.

At the bar, Styrell devoured an unfiltered Camel. A shot glass of brown whiskey and a beer sat in front of him. Surrounding him protectively stood Moustache, Goatee, and Pro Wrestler.

"Howdy," Dee Lane grinned at the crowd.

"You sure you in the right place, fellows?" called the bartender, a woman of fifty or so with bright yellow hair pulled back into a ponytail. Behind her above the bar hung a Confederate flag with the word "Hate" appliquéd onto it. At the pool tables to our left, one tall, thin boy giggled, then stifled it when no one joined him.

"We're looking for Styrell Wooten," Dee Lane said. Styrell

shifted nervously on his stool, and Pro Wrestler took his foot off the rail, turned, and straightened. He had to be almost as tall as Dee Lane, and a hundred pounds heavier. He unbuckled his metal-studded belt and pulled it six inches out of his pants.

Dee Lane reached over and peeled up the sleeve of my T-shirt. He turned my arm to face the crowd. "We wanted to buy *the whole bar* a drink in honor of Styrell the Stencil, the best tattoo artist working in *America* today. I got two hundred-dollar bills, honey, pour until the money runs out." Dee Lane reached in his pocket, pulled out two bills and held them up toward the ceiling. "To *Styrell*." A ragged cheer broke out. Dee Lane moved toward the bar and the crowd parted in front of him like he was Moses and then quickly closed, following him toward the Promised Land.

I stayed planted where I was, staring down Styrell and his friends. Slowly I patted my T-shirt, near the spot where the SIG was tucked into my jeans. I held up two fingers of my left hand in a peace symbol. Styrell stared back, then I saw his mouth move. I lip-read, "What the hell." Moustache leaned over and whispered something to Goatee. Goatee nodded. I waited for them to decide.

Finally, Styrell held up two fingers in a peace symbol, and then a moment later, Pro Wrestler joined him. I nodded and moved wide, away from Dee Lane and his admirers, past Styrell and his crew, and toward a now-vacant spot at the end of the bar. I sat on a stool, leaned back against the wall, and stretched my legs out as far as they would reach in front of me. Stripes of pain ran up and down each leg. Twenty minutes later the bedlam slowed, and I was able to catch the bartender's eye long enough to order two white angels, Truman Capote's drink, equal parts of gin and vodka, served ice cold. I drained the first one, took a sip of the second, and watched the bikers slap Dee Lane on the back. I knew by the end of the evening that he'd be best friends in the whole world with everybody in the place, even Styrell, and I was right.

At three A.M., we stumbled back to our room. Me walking in front and Dee Lane behind, Pro Wrestler tripping and drooling beside him, telling Dee Lane just how close he'd come to being the world heavyweight champion, but how he'd gotten food poisoning the night of his chance at the title. "Hey," he said. "That story that I was afraid of Logan was total bullshit, spread by Neville 'The Smash' Kash." He then tried to explain why Kash would do such a thing. It was a variant on a story I'd heard an hour earlier in the bar, and now, as then, Dee Lane nodded in warm sympathy.

The other two bikers from Styrell's entourage staggered behind us, bouncing off bikes and cars. Styrell brought up the rear, walking very erect and hardly weaving at all, the only sign he was also drunk was his right hand, which he held primly covering his right eye. Through the office window, I saw the Sikh watching us impassively, his face lit by the flickering reflection from the small television set.

# CHAPTER 57

**T**he cell phone woke me around 8:30 A.M. I looked over at the other bed. Dee Lane lay on it facedown wearing nothing but a pair of white shorts. His huge bare feet hung over the end. I groped around on the floor for my jeans, dug around in the pocket, fished out the phone and flipped it open.

"Top," I said. A nasty burp followed the word, and I tried to exhale it away.

"This is John Slocum, Athens-Clarke County Police," the voice said. "Good morning."

"What can I do for you?" I closed my eyes to block out the bright line of sunlight slicing through the gap in the curtains. It didn't work, and I lay back on the pillow and laid a forearm across my eyes. Next to me, Dee Lane made a sound like a chainsaw biting into a log.

"Where are you Mr. Kiernan?"

"I'm in a hotel in Atlanta," I answered. Carefully I opened my eyes and squinted. Our clothes lay scattered around the small room. My SIG sat neatly on top of the television set. There was a chair leaned up against the handle of the door. A Confederate flag with a big brown stain across it was spread out on top of the small bureau. Dee Lane let go with another loud, rumbling snore.

"Did you spend the night there?" Slocum asked.

"Yes," I answered. "We drove over late yesterday afternoon and stayed all night."

"Can you prove it?"

"I think so," I said. "We checked in around midnight, and the clerk might remember us. Wait, there's a security camera in the office, and we should be on the tape. It's the Heart-O-Lanta Motel," I read a phone number off of a little white sticker on the corner of the nightstand between us. "Then we drank in the bar next door until two or three A.M., and the place was full. I'm sure someone saw us."

"We?"

"My friend DeWayne Lane and myself."

There was a considerable silence on the other end of the phone. Finally, he spoke, "Do you know the only thing cops distrust more than no alibi, Mr. Kiernan?"

"No, I'm afraid I don't," I said.

"A perfect alibi," he said. "Make that two perfect alibis."

Another nasty burp rolled up and fought its way out. "Do you want to tell me what this is about?"

"No, I don't," he answered. "But I will. Someone was at it with the red paint again last night."

"Gillie?"

"What did you say, Mr. Kiernan?" His voice quickened.

"Did someone attack Gillie again?"

"No," he said. "Not that."

"What did you think I meant?" I asked.

"Never mind," he said. And then, "Good-bye."

I grinned at the phone a moment, then called Amanda, but got her machine, and felt a twinge of disappointment. After a few minutes, I stood and started the almost impossible task of getting Dee Lane up and going before noon. I could have let him sleep, but I wanted to get back to Athens and see Amanda. I pulled the curtains back to let the blinding sun pour in. He pulled a pillow over his head. I snatched it away and tossed it in a corner, punched the on button on the television and twisted the volume knob up to full blast. Then I bolted for the bathroom, hearing the expected thud of the cowboy boot against the flimsy door behind me. Through the door I heard Dee Lane's curses. Smiling, I laid out a two-story row of toothpaste on my brush and tried to scrub all the enamel off my teeth.

# CHAPTER 58

"*What did you decide about helping me get the* flag back? Are you in or out?" I asked Benny. We sat in my office, our feet up on the desk. We'd already exchanged updates on our respective evenings. What we assumed was the phony Bloody Red Rag was laid out neatly on the small table across the room. I drank a Heineken from a bottle, my third of the morning.

"What help do you need?" he asked. He sipped a can of apple juice. The windows were open and a strong, warm breeze blew in the windows, swirled the papers on the desk, and exited through the door.

"You want to break into a church?"

"I came here to leave my criminal ways behind and now you're asking me if I want to break into a church?" he replied. "Are you serious?"

"Does that mean 'no'?"

"Not necessarily," he answered. "What church?"

"It's called the Church of the Chosen down in St. Illa. Founded by Ben McShane, who died in prison last year. Now it's run by his son Matt. It's ultra-right Christianity. You know, militia training in the woods, funded by armored-car robberies, that sort of stuff. Maggie pulled a stack of articles if you want to read more."

He shook his head. "Why do we want to break in?" The breeze caught a stack of papers and lifted them off the desk. Before I could react, Benny had swung his feet down and reached out with his free hand. He caught four sheets in the air. Replacing them on the desk and putting his apple juice on them to hold them in place, he walked over the wall, and picked up the sheet he'd missed.

"Two plus two equals five," I said.

"That means you think they're involved in the flag thing, but you aren't sure?" he said.

"The church is right next door to Styrell Wooten's property. When we sweated him, he said something about not wanting to have to stay up all night watching his fence line. Add that to the rumors about a church doing some sort of merger with the Klan and Alstott selling the flag, and I think there's a fair chance the Bloody Red Rag is in that compound."

"You think son Matt is going to give the flag to Alstott? For money?"

"I don't know why he'd involve Alstott if it was just money. The newpapers say the church wants to become more respectable. Maybe they're going to merge with the Klan. Maybe the son even gets some sort of big leadership role in the combined entity. What do you think of the idea that the flag could be the church's dowry to the Klan?"

"Two plus two equals a thousand, four-hundred-and-eighty-seven. There are some big leaps in there," Benny answered. "You want to do this tonight?"

"Tomorrow. I'm hoping we can snatch it back before they move it to Atlanta for the konvocation," I answered.

"If it's there," Benny said. "Otherwise, we're wasting our time."

I didn't answer, just finished my beer. I set the bottle on the side of the desk, where I'd see it and remember to take it to the recycling bin when I went to the kitchen to get another. "Is Dee Lane in this?" Benny asked.

"Nope, just us," I said. "He needs to recover from last night."

"But you're up for it?"

"Yep, I'm up for it," I agreed.

"I still have reservations about being involved with the flag. But I suppose invading a compound full of heavily armed neo-Nazis falls within my comfort zone." This was the second time in two days that Benny had attempted a bit of levity. In our years together, that brought the sum total of those attempts over that time to two. And both within the last thirty six hours. I wondered why he was so cheery.

"I don't want you to actually go in. Just cover me," I said.

"We can talk about it on the way. When do we leave?"

"First thing tomorrow," I suggested. "Today I need to take that flag to Pope-Scott and make sure it's not the real thing. It would be pretty embarrassing if we end up doing some sort of swap and give them the real one."

"Very embarrassing. Anything else?" He stood up to leave.

# CHAPTER 59

*W*e left at midmorning on a warm Sunday under gray and overcast skies. A damp Southerly wind blew in our faces, and occasionally a few drops of rain dotted the windshield. We rode with minimal conversation, most of the sounds coming from the brass ensembles on Benny's CDs. We drove in two-hour shifts, each of us napping while the other drove. We were in no hurry, setting the speed control at an inconspicuous four miles per hour over the posted limit, and stopping for a leisurely lunch at a truck stop an hour above Tifton. By late afternoon, we'd reached the always empty streets of St. Illa. I was glad we weren't driving the Ferrari, since I didn't want to have to explain to the police chief why I was back in town.

"You know these guys?" Benny asked, jerking his head to indicate the vehicle stopped next to us at the light.

I looked across him and saw Leeson and Buddy in a jacked-up four-wheel-drive truck. Buddy had lost a few pounds—there were hollows in his cheeks and the skin under his jaw hung loosely. Both of them looked straight ahead, jaws rigid. "Yeah, we've met," I said. Neither would glance in our direction.

"I can tell," Benny answered. I grunted. We turned right as they drove straight ahead. In the back of their pickup, I saw the same hound in his wire cage. He sat splay-legged, a long red tongue hanging out of his mouth. A pair of aluminum crutches was jammed between the side of his pen and the wall of the pickup bed.

"Do you want to go out to the church, now?" Benny asked. "Or wait until dark?"

"Let's drive by now, while we can still see something, and then come back and get a burger. We can head back once it gets dark." I gave him directions.

Benny drove slowly down the long sandy road. We crept by the front of the church compound, but saw little except two rows of chain-link fence, both high, and both topped by razor wire. It's easy enough to get over a fence like that with a ladder and an old piece of thick carpet, but each of the fence posts on the inside row had a thick black rubber bumper on the base, meaning the fence was electrified. We could get through that too, but not without letting someone inside knowing about it. Beyond the fence, a gravel driveway disappeared into a grove of pine trees. We could see no buildings or movement.

We continued along the road and parked in Styrell's driveway. No one responded to our knock. Nor did I expect a response. The house had that nobody-at-home look. I walked around the corner of the house and to the farthest corner of the backyard, close to the tree line, where I stood and unzipped my pants. Through the spindly pine trees, I could just see the side fence separating the two properties. The same high, double chain-link setup ran as far as I could see in the fading light. I zipped up and walked back to the truck and climbed up into the cab.

"Not good," I said.

"How do you plan to get in?" Benny said, backing out smoothly. We rode slowly by the compound again. A white Jeep SUV with tinted windows sat just beyond the second gate facing outward. From the tailpipe trailed a slight downward-pointing plume of gray exhaust. As we passed, the inside gate began to slide sideways. "Do you think they made us?"

I reached out of the window and adjusted the passenger-side mirror so I could see behind us. "We should know about it pretty quick." The Jeep pulled out onto the sandy road and turned right. By the time we turned onto the county road, its grill filled my mirror. Benny sped up a little. The Jeep matched our speed. I opened the glove box and pulled out the SIG, placing it on my lap. I reached into the backseat for the flannel shirt I'd tossed there this morning and pulled it into the front seat, using it to cover the hand holding the gun. Together the two vehicles drove deliberately back to the highway. At the stop sign, the Jeep swung out and pulled up beside us. A tinted window slid smoothly down.

"You guys look lost. Can we help you with something?" The inquiry came from a young, thin man wearing heavy-rimmed glasses. He wore a white short-sleeved shirt and a black tie patterned with red, white, and blue crosses. A shock of thick, dark hair jutted up. He bore a passing resemblance to a young Elvis Costello. His driver leaned forward, peering over the thin man's shoulder.

"We're looking for Styrell. I owe him some money," I said. I rolled up my sleeve and showed off my tattoo. The thin man looked back and forth between my tattoo and Benny.

"I think he's out of town. I haven't seen him for a few days. In fact, I think he might be up in your neck of the woods. Atlanta, maybe." The driver leaned on the steering wheel, both hands crossed across the top. He was a young bull, with thick muscled arms and beefy shoulders. He wore a white satin UKS baseball cap low across his forehead, large sunglasses, and a bushy moustache. It was hard to make out much of his face. He gave us a goofy grin.

"Damn," I said. "I missed him." The man questioning us frowned at my profanity.

"You can give me the money," he said. "I'm Reverend Matt

McShane, the pastor of the church you passed. I'll get it to him when he gets back."

I tried to look uncomfortable. "Oh, that's OK. We're headed back tonight, I'll just try to catch him up there. Thanks for offering. So long." The pastor nodded solemnly, and turned to face forward. The window on the Jeep rose and the SUV pulled out on to the highway ahead of us. A sticker on the bumper read "Body piercing saves souls," and showed a drawing of a hand with a nail through the palm. Benny turned behind it and we followed it into town, exactly five car-lengths back.

"Did you feel the vibes coming off that guy at the wheel?"

"Yeah, he seemed to be a little intense," I answered.

"That's what you feel like when you get wound up," he said.

I couldn't think of a suitable response. "Let's grab something to eat. I think it may be a long night."

# CHAPTER 60

*I*t wasn't a great plan, but it was the best we could do. I lay flat in the soybean field across from the double gate. Even though I wore two pairs of pants, leather gloves, a balaclava, and a denim jacket, I was still cold from the combination of the damp ground and the time I'd spent not moving. I remembered the row of diamondback rattlers hung on the fence a quarter mile away, and thought about the factoid that they are nocturnal hunters. The wind stirred the soybean plants and I wondered what a rattlesnake at night sounded like.

In my right hand I held a piece of rope about three-feet-long, with a six-inch loop spliced in each end. That was what I planned to use to hook over the trailer hitch, or failing that, through a leaf spring of the next vehicle entering the compound. I'd then hang on while it dragged me through the two metal gates. I continually flexed my knees, trying to keep them from stiffening up. I didn't want to stand up to make my move, only to have one of my balky legs pick that moment to go dead and drop me on my face.

It had been almost two hours ago that Benny had driven slowly down the paved road. "What if there are a thousand Aryan Nation militia inside that compound?" he'd asked. I'd shouldered the small backpack with the Beretta SC-70 short-stock assault rifle, Radio Shack walkie-talkie, rope, and nightscope in it and shrugged.

"I don't think it's big enough to house a thousand people," I said. "I pulled the satellite photos. Nothing but a few small buildings. Pole barns and the like."

"That's still big enough. Are you sure about this, Top?"

"I've done it before," I said.

Benny slowed down and pulled gently off onto the shoulder. "According to the GPS, here's your spot. I'll circle around and come in from the other end and wait a half-mile or so up the road. That is if I don't get busted for vagrancy and sentenced to the county farm." Neither of us laughed. I gave him the thumbs up and he pulled over. I stepped out of the truck and he pulled away without looking back.

I'd spent the next hour making my way to this spot, directly across from the main gate of the church, and the second lying prone and still between the short soybean plants. Soon after I'd arrived, the gates had swung open and a white van had come out and driven away toward town. Since then, nothing had passed in or out.

I checked my watch. It read 10:48. Across the fields I saw headlights move along the county road, and then turn and head toward me. I pressed my face into the dirt, and flattened myself among the plants. The headlights came closer, throwing a harsh yellow glare across the top of the field where I lay. As they approached the gate, the van slowed and a signal flashed.

The van turned into the driveway and pulled close to the chain-link gate. I rose and raced in a crouch to the rear of the vehicle, and dropped to my stomach. I heard the gates begin to move. Rolling onto my back, I groped underneath for something to hang my rope on. Attached to the frame, I found a loading eyelet, a squarish tab of metal with a silver-dollar-sized hole in it. Quickly I slipped the rope through and evened the two loops. Scooting on my butt away from the bumper until the ropes were taut, I stretched out behind the van, one hand through either loop. I heard a clink as the first gate reached the fully open position.

I put a little tension on the rope. The pitch on the motor changed as the driver slipped the van into gear. I heard the second gate begin to move. And then a moment later, it too clinked into place. I tested the loops again, hoping for a slow, smooth driver. I also hoped he rode with the windows up, so he didn't hear me dragging behind.

The ropes tightened and a small spray of gravel from a back tire rained across my stomach. I slowly relaxed my arms until they were completely extended. We eased through the narrow openings. The van drove slowly up the driveway about twenty feet and I bumped along behind. Behind me, I heard the two gates grind shut. I released one loop, and felt the rope pull cleanly through the eyelet. I came to a stop and rolled over onto all fours. In front of me, the brake lights of the van went on.

I stared at the lights, waiting, wondering if they'd heard something and were stopping to investigate. Fifteen feet, max, I reckoned to be the distance to the edge of the pine forest. There was a glint in the bottom of the shallow, grassy ditch, and I knew it held water. I rose into a stoop.

Behind me I heard the unmistakable sound of the slide on an automatic rifle, and a quiet voice said, "Don't move. There are four rifles on you. If you move, we will shoot." I saw two red dots on my chest, and assumed that there were two more on my back. The double back doors of the van flew open, and someone shone a powerful flashlight on me. I turned my head to the side to avoid the glare.

"Four rifles and a shotgun," the quiet voice said.

The passenger door on the van opened and closed. Footsteps came around the side of the van. The muscled driver from the afternoon stepped into the light. Without the hat, sunglasses, and false moustache, he looked vaguely familiar. He stepped between me and the back of the van. The bright light behind him threw his face into dark shadow.

The driver spoke. "This is the twenty-first century, mister. We've been watching you with infrared for hours. Did you really think you were going to get into this compound with that old trick?" He sounded happy, almost giddy. As he turned, the light caught his features, and I knew where I'd seen him before. Or to be more accurate, I knew where I'd seen his picture before. On CNN. His name was Walter Caldwell, the Sword of Michael. My knees felt weak as I realized the implications. I'd come here chasing a moldy old flag, and now I'd won the lottery.

"I'm going to pull this backpack off your shoulders and then I'm going to pat you down," said the quiet voice behind me. "Then Major Caldwell's going to drive up the road slowly and you're going to walk behind the van. We're in a staggered offset formation. I'm hoping you know what that means and don't try anything stupid. Reverend McShane wants to speak to you." There was the slightest emphasis on the word "Reverend." I felt the straps of the pack fall away, and a hand searched me. When he'd finished, he reached up and peeled off my balaclava.

I then waited some more while he searched my backpack. There was a sharp intake of breath when he found the Berretta assault minirifle. But he said nothing. The Sword of Michael stood in front of me, shifting from foot to foot and smiling. He looked excited, like a child at a birthday party. Behind me, the voice said, "Major Caldwell?" The bomber didn't move. The man behind me spoke again, "Demolition Mission?" Caldwell nodded happily, turned, and jogged back to the van.

"Please put your hands on top of your head. Now, let's go see the reverend." The truck moved slowly forward, and we walked down the road behind it, through an ess-bend and into a small, well-lit parade ground. We drove to the center. "Stop," said the voice. There was the sound of footsteps as the squad closed up.

I turned in a slow circle. Around me stood four very young men in hunting camouflage, all holding M-16s. The van pulled away, turned, and disappeared between two buildings. Behind them, around the perimeter of the ground, were two large pole barns, a long wooden barracks, and an immense green-metal Butler building with camouflage netting strung above them, a small dark red house with white trim, and, directly across from me, a neat, white, wooden church.

Voices came from the open doors of the metal building to my right. In one pole barn to our left, two helmeted men welded the bucket of a front-end loader attached to a blue Ford tractor. One held a piece of metal with long tongs and the other worked the rod. We could hear the hum of the generator and the hiss of the melting metal. Across the ground, sitting on the steps of the barracks was a young man in a white T-shirt and blue jeans. He was thin, very pale, with tiny eyes above jutting cheekbones and an invisible chin. In his hand was a Bible with numerous small, torn-paper bookmarks jutting unevenly from the top. "He's in the sanctuary," he called out.

# CHAPTER 61

*T**he Reverend Matt McShane sat on the front* of the altar, directly in front of the podium. He whistled softly as he efficiently disassembled and cleaned a 12-gauge Mossberg 590 automatic shotgun, the combat version with the black parkerized barrel, eight-clip magazine, and plastic grip. I sat on the front pew, about six or so feet in front of him, my hands tied together with pink and blue rope of a construction made popular by rock climbers. My fingertips tingled, and I looked down and saw my fingers beginning to swell and redden.

They'd bound my feet together with another piece of rope. I watched the reverend run a brass brush hog down the shotgun bore, withdraw it smoothly and then hold the barrel up to the light and peer into it. Whenever his eyes were averted, I tried to work my ropes looser. I thought I could feel some give in the ones around my ankles. I was on full buzz, so much adrenaline pumping through my system that my stomach ached, and my senses were so acute that McShane's whistling sounded like the shriek of a train.

"My father died in prison. He died for what we believe in. I'm proud of that," he said, breaking the silence. His eyes glanced at the front of my jeans, glanced away, and then glanced back quickly. A pink flush glowed under his jawline.

" 'A thing is not necessarily true because a man dies for it,' Oscar Wilde, 1901," I answered.

The reverend shook his head tiredly, hopped down off the edge of the altar, and stepped directly in front of me. Casually, he whipped the hardwood rod with the brass brush on the end across my face. I turned my head quickly, but still felt the tough wire bristles strip away the skin, leaving a streak of fire across my cheek and nose. "No more of that," he said in a low tone. "My father is off-limits to this discussion. At least from your side of the discussion. And no more references to homosexual perverts." He was panting slightly, and licked his upper lip with a quick, pointed tongue.

He turned and stepped back to the altar, appraising me while he used an oily rag to wipe my skin off the end of the gun brush, which he then unscrewed and replaced precisely in the wooden box that held the cleaning kit. I glanced down at the ropes around my ankles and saw a tiny gap that hadn't been there before. He pulled a small mop from the box, fluffed it with a finger, and attached that to the end of the rod.

"You better let me go. My name is Chinn and I am an agent of the Bureau of Alcohol, Tobacco, Firearms and Explosives."

"No, you're not. No ID. Italian gun. Radio Shack walkie-talkie. You're not ATF. Try again." He had trouble forcing himself to hold my eyes. His gaze kept floating down to my jeans, and I wondered if my fly was open.

"My name is John Slocum, I'm from Atlanta and I'm a bounty hunter."

"How did you find out that Walter was here?"

"I have a Web site. A bartender named Linda sold me the tip for a hundred dollars."

"If you are lying, Walter's going to test out his new theory."

"Which is?" I asked.

"He thinks if you put a live person in a closed-in chamber and explode a sufficiently large charge, that it will erase all identifiable characteristics, even screw up their gene sequences."

"That's insane," I said.

"Sure is," he nodded. "DNA sequences are molecular scale. Unless he plans to bury you in a 55-gallon drum with a thermonuclear device, I don't think he's going to be scrambling your genes." Looking up at me, he smiled, and using the clean back side of his wrist, pushed his glasses up his nose.

"This doesn't bother you?" I asked.

"Why should it bother me? Bombers are insane," he said matter-of-factly. "Walter just wants to blow you to bits and he's worked up this cockamamie theory to try to hide just how sick he is from the rest of us. But we're not fooled. We keep a very close eye on the young Demolition Mission, as he now calls himself."

"I thought he called himself the Sword of Michael?"

"Oh that's just his stage name. He loves to give himself nicknames," the reverend smiled. His teeth shone brightly and I could picture him flossing ten strokes per tooth each night, even the ones in back that are hard to get to. "For a while, he wanted us to call him Boom Boom. Now it's Demolition Mission."

"I'm not much on bombers," I said.

"They are a particularly interesting breed of criminal. I studied criminalistics in college. Down in Gainesville," he explained.

"Too bad," I said, an automatic response when someone tells a Georgia grad that they attended the University of Florida.

"I hate sports, so I don't care about that rivalry stuff. What I was saying," he said with a smile and mock patience, "was that my professors argued that most criminal behavior is learned. A young man gets an opportunity to steal a car, does so, and enjoys it, and then does it again at some point. But without just the right situation and opportunity, he would never have become a car thief. Most thefts, assaults, and even the majority of rapes are situational behaviors."

"But not bombers?"

"Absolutely not bomb makers. Or cat burglars, peeping toms, homosexuals, arsonists, sexual sadists, and murderers. Those are all pathological behaviors, based on natural tendencies. People with those tendencies will create the right set of circumstances to exercise their proclivities. Serial killers sometimes join the military, child rapists the priesthood, arsonists the fire department. Peeping toms become meter readers and cable installers. Do you see what I'm saying? For most criminals, the situation catalyzes the illegal act. For psychopaths, the need for the act creates the situation," he said.

"Your professors said homosexuality was the same as serial murder?" I asked.

"You know very well they did not," he said blandly. "Political correctness and all that. I have supplemented what they taught me with my own research and observations."

"Are you afraid of gays, Reverend?" I asked.

He blushed down to the roots of his dark hair. His eyes tried to hold mine and didn't, inadvertently dropping down. He looked up and waved the cleaning rod ominously, "Enough of that topic."

"OK then, explain to me why a church is harboring a murderer," I said.

"Don't be patronizing." His gaze was level and his smile tight. "Yes, Walter is evil, pure and simple. If he wasn't working for us, he'd be blowing up cosmetics laboratories for PETA or buses in Israel or judges in Colombia. More likely, if he wasn't working for us, he probably would have blown himself up by now. They usually do. But with Walter we have effectively put an end to abortions in the South. Most of the clinics are either closed or going broke. So we have turned evil to good, just as our sweet savior turned water to wine."

"Lucky you."

"Indeed. Bombers are very rare."

"How do you know so much about bombers?" I asked.

"My studies," he said.

"Sounds like fascinating research," I said.

He put down his rod and leaned toward me, locking his eyes on mine. "Do you know serial bombers wear adult diapers while they work? Do you know why? Because they often have a spontaneous ejaculation. During the explosion, and often after, when the emergency vehicles arrive. Anytime there's a bombing the FBI sends the bomb dogs through the crowd sniffing. And they're not smelling for explosive residue. It's in the training manual," he smiled. "I've got a copy."

"Why in the world are you telling me all this?"

He laughed, cupped his hands around one knee, and leaned back. "Why indeed? I'm supposed to be getting information from you, and yet here I am, chatting away like the villain in a James Bond movie."

"So, why are you?"

"Probably because I'm in a mood to talk, and you're a good person to talk to because in thirty minutes or so, Walter's going to pack you in a fifty-five-gallon drum along with one of his devices, bury you under a few loaderfuls of dirt and turn you into red jelly. So it doesn't much matter what I tell you," he said. His eyes dropped down and he smiled a quiet private smile. He pulled the hammer back and removed a small cotton patch.

"Well, I still think I can have some fun before I go."

"What do you mean?" he said absentmindedly, holding the gun close to his face and checking the hammer for stray threads.

"As your boys are stuffing me in that drum, I'm going to tell them that while they were gone, you pulled down my pants and played drink-the-milkshake. See what they think of Reverend McShane, then."

"What did you say?" McShane lifted his eyes.

"I said you don't wear a wedding ring and I think you dream about making love to boys and pray every night for the dreams to go away. I think you envy your daddy, because he got to do in the shower every day what you've been thinking about since you were six years old."

"Stop!" he screamed, his face turning a purple red and the tendons in his neck standing out like steel cables. Bull's eye.

"Why? So we can talk about Walter turning me to red jelly? No thanks, I'm bored with that discussion."

# CHAPTER 62

"*S* *top! Stop it!*" *He put the gun down on the edge of* the stage, and balled up his fists

"I'm so mad I could just cry," I said with a greatly exaggerated lisp. "Go ahead, McFruit, I know you want to stamp your feet."

McShane reached back for the shotgun. He took a quick step toward me. I twisted on the bench bringing my legs up protectively. McShane brought the gun up, grasping it with two hands, one shaking hand on the stock and the other on the freshly polished barrel.

The young reverend took another stiff, angry step forward. Then another, and then his right foot caught on the corner of the altar, sending him into a quick-stepped stumble. To regain his balance, he shoved the shotgun straight out in front of him. I brought both feet up as quickly as I could and kicked at his face. And missed. Instead, my clumsy double-footed kick caught the shotgun at a midpoint between his handholds, and sent it flying upward, cracking into his jaw. His head flew backward.

I rolled off the pew and tried to stand, but unable to balance on my closely tied, almost numb feet, toppled over. McShane stood swaying, his back to me. I squirmed closer to him. Both of his hands slowly dropped and the shotgun leaked from his slack fingers to bounce on the floor and slide under the same pew where I'd been sitting moments before. I drew my legs up and kicked at his knees, and missed again, this time because he was already falling, toppling on a vector to his right and front, hands loose beside him, falling straight and graceful and unimpeded, like one of those tall, thin pine trees on logging day. The top of McShane's head hit the armrest of the pew across the aisle with a satisfying thud, and he landed heavily on the floor, unmoving.

Sometimes, many times, that's what it comes down to: an inch of luck. If one of those bullets had gone an inch to the left in Lima, I'd be dead instead of the woman I'd been paid to rescue. If Vance's knife had been an inch longer, I'd have lost an arm or worse in that bank parking lot. And if McShane's size-twelve shoe hadn't caught the corner of that altar, right now I'd have the barrel of that Mossberg pressed against my throat and black spots appearing in front of my eyes, getting the fate I probably deserved for taking these people too lightly and racing in where a Delta squad in a Bradley fighting vehicle would fear to tread. But instead I was alive and McShane was laying there bleeding. Because his feet were some portion of an inch too long.

I brought my wrists up to my mouth and used my teeth to try to loosen the knot. For a brief moment I thought I felt one of the loops give, but when I moved my hands away to examine it, I could see nothing except a small dark wet spot on the rope. Without tools, I quickly decided, I was unlikely to untie these knots before Walter and the others showed up. I struggled to my feet, and in an unsteady bunny hop made my way past the altar to a brown wooden door set into the far wall. I grasped the handle with my numb fingers and twisted it open.

In the short hallway, were four doors, three of which stood open. I hopped to the first one and stared into a small cluttered office. Most of the room was taken up by an overflowing desk, three chairs, and a computer stand. The wall to my left was dominated by a floor-to-ceiling bookshelf, stuffed with books and papers. On the wall across from it was a huge airbrushed portrait of a severe-looking jowly man. In a ring around his head were various symbols, a cross, a Confederate flag, an automatic rifle. It looked a great deal like the ones that Hamas sends to the families of suicide bombers in Palestine. Underneath it, fastened to the wall with brass screws, were two crossed bayonets, one an antique sharp spike, and the other a Vietnam-era blade.

I hopped to the wall and grabbed the blade by its round base and pulled. The metal slipped from my fingers and I fell backward, landing with a grunt in the space in front of the desk. The bayonets were screwed in too tightly to be pulled out by my numb fingers. I worked my way to my feet, using the desk as leverage, and bunny-hopped around it. The drawers to the desk were locked. Inside the knee-well stood an aluminum Haliburton suitcase of the kind that technicians use to carry tools. I swung it up onto the desk, popped the two clasps, and lifted the lid. Inside was a neatly folded Confederate flag with a big, brown stain on it. I should have been elated, or at least felt a bit of satisfaction knowing that my hunch was right, but I was too focused on getting free before Walter returned. Dropping the lid closed, I hopped back into the hall.

The second door in the hallway opened into a bathroom, and the third into a kitchen. I thumped loudly across the room to the sink. In the top drawer were cloths, birthday candles, an almost-new roll of duct tape, and a box of kitchen matches. A muffled sound came from the front of the church and I froze. There was a shout. Quickly I shoved the top drawer back in and pulled out the second. Inside was a tray with spoons, forks, and knives, and there alongside the plastic tray, a white-handled steak knife. I grabbed it, turned it to point toward me, and sawed the ropes on my wrists frantically.

From the front of the church came the sounds of people running. The pink and blue sheath of the rope parted, and I hacked through the black synthetic material beneath it, and finally into the white cotton core. The rope fell away.

Frantically I slashed at the rope around my ankles. One loop parted and I unwound the remainder. I heard a loud "Beep beep" sound coming from outside the church, and assumed it was some sort of general alarm. There was a sound of boots running in the church, and I imagined the squad systematically searching each pew and behind the altar, laser-scoped M-16s at ready.

Taking three steps to the door of the kitchen, I quickly peeked out into the still empty hall. I stepped across to open the final door, swung it open into the warm night air and threw the hacked rope outside onto the ground. I left that one open, ran back to the kitchen, and stood behind the door. I pulled it back as far as it would go and stood very still.

A few minutes later, there was a sound of running footsteps, shouts, and the soft crunch of boots on the gravel at the base of the outside steps. Through the narrow crack I saw the squad that had captured me race by, accompanied by a man wearing a leather welding apron. A moment later, Walter Caldwell sauntered behind them. He disappeared from my view. I closed my eyes and counted to one-hundred thousand by thousands, then carefully pushed the door away from me.

"Hi," said Walter Caldwell.

# CHAPTER 63

"*H*ide *and seek. You did just what I would have*
done," Walter said. He grinned at me, jaw working as
he chewed his gum furiously. "Let the pursuit pass by,
then double back. Shoot, why would you run out into the woods? You
know that inside fence is hot. Sooner or later you've got to get
through a gate, right?" In his right hand he held a small black,
wooden club, looped to his wrist with a leather thong.

"Is McShane dead?" I asked.

"No," he giggled. "He was already waking up when we came in.
Concussed pretty badly. Didn't know where he was or what happened. But he'll be fine. That thing on your face is probably worse
than what the reverend got."

"Too bad," I said. Walter shrugged, and grinned. His eyes were a
startling Paul Newman-blue.

"Walter, I've enjoyed the chat, but I need to be going now," I said.
I took a small step to my right.

Walter's grin grew even larger and he slid to his left to cut me off.
I could see a fat wad of pink chewing gum rolling around between his
back teeth. He motioned me forward with his left hand. I slid sideways

along the wall in the other direction, not taking my eyes from Walter. He waved the black club in a loose figure eight. One step, two steps, and then I came to a stop, as the outside of my foot bumped into the edge of the counter. With my left hand, I groped along the counter, feeling the outline of a pan, and exploring for the handle.

Walter came in overhanded, a huge sweeping hack intended to finish the fight quickly. It was the move of a bully, and counted on strength and ferocity to overwhelm opposition. His plan didn't account for an opponent that had been in these types of situations before.

I released the pan and dropped to the floor, wedging myself into the corner formed by the cabinet and the wall, and Walter's initial blow clattered against the wood paneling over my head. Walter stepped sideways to improve his angle and tomahawked again with the club. Shielding my head with my left arm, I punched as hard as I could with my free hand into his solar plexus, that bundle of nerves adjacent to the diaphragm. My fist buried into his stomach, and at the same time there was a sharp whacking sound accompanied by a blinding bolt of pain. I felt my left arm go numb.

I grimaced, waiting for a second blow, but Walter froze, digging for breath. I punched again with my right hand. This time, I dispensed with science and tried as hard as I could to drive his testicles up into his throat. He gasped and doubled over, both hands covering his crotch. I scrambled to my feet, reached across my body, and grabbed the cast-iron frying pan I'd felt earlier. I swung it backhanded and smacked Walter across the side of the head. He spun sideways. Raising the pan over my head, I brought it down as hard as I could on top of his head. He flattened into a heap in the center of the floor.

I replaced the pan on the counter and leaned heavily against it, panting. Gently I felt my left forearm. There was a large bump, very tender to the touch. Carefully I pushed against the countertop with my left hand. A shock of pain took my breath away.

"I think you broke it, you asshole," I said to the unconscious Walter. A trickle of blood seeped from the top of his head and dripped onto the white linoleum flooring. "If that's your brains leaking out, good."

It took me almost fifteen minutes to create a makeshift splint for the arm using wooden spoons and duct tape, and used the rest of the roll of duct tape to bind Walter up like a mummy. Finally satisfied, I headed down the hall to the office.

# CHAPTER 64

*I used the phone in the office to call Benny's cell phone.* He answered on the second ring. "Benny," I said. "Very. Bad. Connection. Barely hear," he crackled. "Can you call?"

"I'll try," I said. "But in case I can't, I'll meet you out front in fifteen minutes, exactly. That's 1:45 on the nose. Did you get that?"

"Top," he said, the connection died, and I heard a quick busy signal. I dialed his number again, and this time got a recorded message telling me the subscriber was out of range. I hung up and hoped he'd heard enough to understand. Snapping the Halliburton briefcase shut, I carried it to the back door of the church. I placed it beside the door, edged outside, and crept around the side of the building. The parade ground was empty.

Holding my splinted left arm tight across my body, I quickly walked across the open space to the pole barn. There was no sound except the continued loud beep beep of the alarm. I checked the glowing dial of my watch. It read 1:34.

I climbed up into the seat of the tractor and closed my eyes, cradling my left arm. Mentally, I worked through the necessary steps to ensure Benny and I reached that front gate at exactly and precisely the same second. I hoped again he'd heard enough to understand, and thought of the electronic tripwires that I had triggered and hoped I wasn't leading him into a trap. I felt for the key, started the diesel engine, and pulled a lever mounted beside the seat. The bucket of the front-end loader rose to about four feet off the ground. I slipped the vehicle into gear and released the clutch. I drove slowly, hunched over, my useless left arm resting on my thigh.

Carefully I maneuvered the tractor to the rear of the church, and dropped the bucket to the first step. Holding my arm, I climbed down and clambered around the front end into the building. Caldwell lay unconscious across the linoleum floor. Using my one good arm and one of his ankles, I dragged him across the linoleum and through the two doors. His head bounced across the sill as I pulled him outside. I dropped his legs into the bucket, then stepped over him and down to the ground. Using my thighs and then chest as leverage, I rolled his torso in as well. His lids opened, and his startling blue eyes stared at me. "Hi," I panted, and left him struggling against the duct tape.

Retrieving the flag, I settled in the driver's seat and tucked the thin case behind my legs. I worked the levers until the bucket was at eye level and turned straight up—I didn't want Walter falling out. For a final time, I checked my watch, 1:41. I drove deliberately into the parade ground.

There was a shout, and I looked left and saw the youth in the white T-shirt raising a pistol. I gunned the tractor, and tore down the road toward the front gate. A pistol cracked behind me and I automatically dipped my head, even though by the time you hear it, it's too late to duck.

Just beyond the first bend, the white van sat sideways across the road. I dropped into second gear and swung over into the grassy ditch. Using the van as cover, a single soldier fired four bullet bursts from an M-16 at me. The bullets pinged off the upright bucket and thudded into the radiator. I heard the hiss of a tire and saw one front tire widen and sling partially off the rim. A bullet hit the fan and metal screamed as the off-kilter blades rode against the housing.

I shifted to third and pulled the accelerator lever down. The soldier dove back behind the vehicle, and I flew by the van, weaving back and forth as I fought the effects of the deflated tire. I knelt on the floor of the tractor and steered by looking down at the left front tire and using the edge of the roadway as a guide. Bullets whistled over my head and thudded into the fat rear tires. I wrestled the tractor back up onto the roadway. The rims of shredded tires dug into the gravel roadway as big strips of tire peeled away and fell behind me onto the road bed.

Around the next bend lay the two gates, lit up by the harsh light of a low three-quarter moon. My truck was nowhere in sight. From the forest to my right came a staccato burst of automatic weapon fire, and the other heavy rear tire went flat and the tractor spun to the left. The bucket bounced and I saw Caldwell's feet appear for a moment above the rim. Bullets ricocheted off the cowling of the tractor, sending trails of orange sparks into the night. There was a spray of warm, thick fluid as a bullet cut a hydraulic line in half. I lifted my head and saw the bucket begin a slow-motion drop. I grabbed the appropriate lever and pulled backward, but felt no resistance, and my pull had no effect. The tractor veered left, and I grabbed for the wheel. There was another burst of bullets and I ducked again. I pointed the tractor toward the gates.

The pickup truck slid to a stop just outside the fence. Benny popped up through the driver's side window. He leveled my SIG across the truck's roof and fired toward the woods. The automatic weapon fire slowed for a moment. I lifted my head and aimed the tractor at the center of the electrified first gate. There was a blinding blue flash, a tearing noise, and the inside gate popped off its runners and flattened on the road. The tractor rolled across it, twisting and sliding, and into the gap. The rims screeched and spun on the wire mesh of the gate, metal against metal.

We drove slowly into the second gate, and slammed to a halt. My head bounced off the steering wheel and my left arm slammed against my chest. Scalding reflux rose in my throat. I stood up to look.

The body of the tractor was stuck in the gap between the two fences, but the bucket of the loader had torn a huge gaping rectangular hole in the wire of the outside gate. The bucket now extended beyond the fence and hovered just over the bed of the pickup. I shifted to a lower gear, and released the clutch. There was a clunk, and the diesel engine choked and died. I shoved in the clutch, ground the starter, gave up and hit the lever to dump the bucket, dropping the inert Walter with a wet thud into the bed of the truck. The firing behind me intensified.

"Come on!" screamed Benny. He dumped the clip from the SIG and jammed another in. As he pulled the trigger, a series of orange flashes reflected off the roof of the truck and lit up his face. I held my left arm tight to my body and stood. One side of the steering wheel disintegrated as a tumbling bullet hit the hardened black plastic. I let go of my wounded arm, reached back for the suitcase, climbed over the wheel and onto the hood. My foot slipped, and I fought to regain my balance. I heard the whistle of bullets around me.

"Come on!" Benny repeated. I tightroped to the front of the tractor and dropped to my butt. Something grabbed my right arm and gave it a hard pull, then released. I looked down and saw myself holding only the handle of the briefcase. The silver case itself lay back under the tractor, unscathed except for where a bullet had surgically separated the handle from the aluminum body. I hesitated.

"Leave it. Let's go!" shouted Benny. He dropped back into the cab. I slid down the front of the tractor into the bucket, dove over the front into the bed of the pickup and rolled over Walter.

"Go! Go! Go!" I yelled.

There was a thud as a bullet hit a truck panel. The back end slewed sideways on the loose road surface before the tires found traction, and hurtled us down the dirt road toward safety. Another bullet thudded into the rear of the truck as we raced away.

# CHAPTER 65

*I* *lay there, eyes closed, cradling my left arm, tossed* helplessly back and forth between the wheel well and Walter as Benny bounced up the dirt road and fishtailed onto the pavement. The pain rolled up my arm in electric waves. When we reached the highway, Benny whipped us right and floored it, and we raced away from St. Illa and toward the Florida line.

The turn pushed me against the side of the truck and rolled the mummy-wrapped Walter across the bed and up against me. I felt warm breath on my face and opened my eyes to see Walter's face a few inches from mine. The Sword of Michael glared at me with three eyes, two deep blue irises flanking a single, fearsome yellow eye. I gave an involuntary yelp. Slowly I raised my hand and poked at one blue eye. A contact lens came off onto my fingertip. The lens had slipped sideways, giving him an extra eye and causing me to squeal like a teenager at the forty-fifth sequel to *Nightmare on Elm Street.*

"No wonder you wear those contacts, Walter," I said. I flicked the lens over the side of the truck. Walter glared at me, his face a horror-movie mask created by the strip of gray duct tape across his mouth, his one yellow eye and one deep blue one, and the red-brown stripes across his face where the blood from his head wound had leaked down and dried.

I shoved Walter hard back to his side of the truck, eased myself onto my back and looked up at the bright night sky. I mentally contrasted my holier-than-thou position on gay tolerance with what I'd said to McShane and my theory that we're all bigots underneath, tattooed at birth with the beliefs of our tribe, as Oliver Wendell Senior said. It seemed to me I should feel some guilt at abandoning my principles without the slightest hesitation when threatened with being turned into red jelly. But I didn't. I felt happy. Buzzed. Victorious. No, make that: Alive. I felt alive. And I'd come way closer than I wanted to knowing what it feels like to be dead.

I was in excruciating pain, shivering from the cold and saddled with a raging, all-consuming thirst that swelled up my tongue and made my throat hurt. But, by God, I was *alive* and I felt pure, primitive exultation at my aliveness. I could imagine some distant ancestor feeling the same howling emotional wash after outrunning a sabertoothed cat and returning to the cave carrying the result of the day's hunt, knowing that tonight around the campfire the tribe would tell stories of my bravery and draw my picture on the walls by firelight and I'd get the best piece of the kill and the prettiest girl. I felt not one shred of the civilized-man shame I knew I should feel at cheaply manipulating McShane's latent homosexuality.

As penance for my callousness, I decided to write as big a check as I could afford to the upcoming AIDS ride. But even that didn't feel right. It was a sterile, intellectual decision, devoid of feeling. My savage joy at survival crowded out any other emotions. I grinned and croaked at Walter, "How does it feel to be the new skin on the floor of my cave, asshole?" He glared back at me.

After fifteen minutes or so, we slowed, and Benny pulled into a small picnic area by the side of the road. He drove behind the concrete tables, hidden from the highway, and shut off the engine. A door slammed and a second later he climbed up and over the side of the truck, seating himself on the toolbox. "How is everything back here?"

"My arm is broken, I think," I said. "I'm hurting and maybe in shock." I shivered.

"I've got a kit. I'll get you some codeine. Let's get you up front and into the sleeping bag," he answered.

"Good," I said, teeth chattering.

"Do we need to find a hospital here, or should we head back to Atlanta?"

"Give me a handful of Tylenol 3. I'll be OK. We've got that hearing at eleven."

"It'll be a stretch to make it. Was the flag in the case?" he asked.

"Yeah, I had it in my hands," I said.

"You almost had more than that in your hands," he answered. He knelt on the wheel well, put an arm behind my shoulders and helped me to a sitting position. "We've got to move, Top. The tractor blocking the gate may buy us a few minutes, but we can't count on it."

I struggled to stand. "If you will drop the tailgate, I can sit down and step out," I said.

"Should I call E. J. and Dice and tell them to get out of the school?"

"I'd call and tell them to be ready. But my guess is the church will spend the rest of the night destroying evidence and cleaning the place up. I think it will take them some time to find out who we are and where we live," I slid off the tailgate and stepped onto the pine needle-covered sandy soil. Benny closed the gate behind me.

"Who's that in the truck?"

"That abortion clinic bomber. There's a bounty on his head," I said.

"How much?"

"A lot," I said.

"We can use the money," he answered. We walked around to the passenger-side door. I stumbled and almost fell, and Benny caught my arm. "You're in bad shape."

"I'd be in a lot worse if not for you. For a guy who doesn't believe in firearms, you looked pretty good with that SIG."

He snorted, "I think the best that can be said for my marksmanship is it kept their heads down and disrupted their aim. Stand still a minute while I find the codeine." I waited beside the door while Benny pulled the seat forward and fished out a sleeping bag, a first aid kit, and a bottle of water.

"I didn't intend to put you in this deep," I said. I waved toward the two bullet holes in the side of the truck, both high on the rear-quarter panel.

"It's OK. Eat these." He held out three white pills and when I took them, unscrewed the top from the water bottle and handed it to me.

"Thanks."

"You're welcome."

"I meant for tonight."

"You're welcome," he said in the same tone of voice.

# CHAPTER 66

*I* *left the hospital against advice, meaning that if* any parts fell off they weren't responsible, and gritted my teeth while Benny drove across town at exactly the speed limit, taking no chances that we might get pulled over and have some young officer find the serial killer wrapped in duct tape stuffed in the toolbox of the truck.

I fidgeted, tapped my fingers on the dash, checked my watch umpteen times, and finally jumped out of the still moving truck as he pulled to the front of the courthouse. Afraid I'd nod off during the hearing, I'd refused painkillers in the ER and now every single joint in my body hurt, although the smaller aches and pains were drowned out by the stabbing jolt of pain that shot up from the broken arm with every movement. I cradled the plastic and elastic-strapped cast in my good arm and hobbled as quickly as I could up the long steps and into the building.

The clock out front said I was a half hour late. I felt fuzzy and discombobulated, and a little lost. Rattlesnake had left a voice mail with the logistical details, and now those details floated just below the surface of my consciousness. I fished for a moment but failed to hook it. Frustrated, I looked around for someone to direct me, but the chair inside the door was empty. I heard voices and walked through the metal detector and up the short flight of stairs. Down the hall I saw two overweight women in deputy uniforms with their ears pressed against a thick wooden door. I walked toward them and heard the younger one say, "Go ahead. Open the door. Just a crack."

"Crazy old Judge Manczik? No way, no day. You open the door if you want to hear what she's saying," replied her older colleague. Manczik. That was the name Rattlesnake had left on my voice mail.

"She's letting him have it, I can tell that much."

"He let her have it if she don't shut up. Manczik don't tolerate nothing. That's what them young lawyers say. Nothing."

I said "Excuse me," and they both jumped straight up in the air. The older one gave a small whoop as she spun around and flattened herself against the door, one hand held across her heart.

"Lord, boy, you trying to scare me to death?" she said with a gasp.

"Kiernan v Fourth Federal?" I asked, and reached for the brass handle. Through the wood I heard raised voices, but could not make out what they were saying.

The young one pulled in her lower jaw and bugged her eyes out. "You're going in there?" I nodded. "Here, you're hurt, let me open the door for you." She winked at the older guard and pulled the door as wide open as possible, holding it while I walked through into the din. Inside, Gillie stood up behind the table to the left. No one even glanced at me, every eye in the place on her, including that of the judge, a thin, square-jawed old man with rimless glasses and a perfect part in his short gray hair. His gavel was raised, and fell with a rap just as I entered.

"Order," he shouted. "Order."

Gillie stamped her foot and screamed back, "Listen to me, you senile old fart."

He lifted the gavel and pointed at her, "What did you just say?"

"Will you just listen to me, please? Puh-lease?" she said in a quieter tone.

"You listen to me. You have no standing in these proceedings," the judge said.

"But the defendant, Top Kiernan, isn't here. Shouldn't he be fined?"

"He's the plaintiff, Miss, and he is represented adequately," the judge sighed.

Gillie took a deep breath, "Your honor, I'm sorry. But I've been up most of the night at the police department because the *plaintiff* has been breaking into houses in my neighborhood and terrorizing us. Sweeney's hit my business with eight different lawsuits. I'm a businesswoman. I just want this foreclosure to go through so I can buy this property and expand my business. I need this man stopped."

"You have no standing. I urge you to talk to the Northern District District Attorney's office. Now, be very grateful that I have to this point shown patience which anyone in this courthouse can tell you I do not possess. Now sit down and *shut up!*" He half rose and shouted the last words into the microphone. "And close that door!" Behind me I heard the clack of heels running down the hall and felt the door swing shut.

Gillie looked up at the high ceiling. I couldn't see her face, but I knew what the judge saw. I'd seen her angry before. Hell absolutely has no fury like a Gillie told to shut up. In the temporary quiet, I looked around and saw Rattlesnake to my right. He gave a solemn, concerned look over his shoulder to the judge, then turned away from the bench and gave Gillie a smirk. He stuck out his tongue. She must not have seen him, because she didn't respond, instead simply shifted from one foot to the other and raised a hand.

"Officer, if that woman is not in her seat by the time you reach her, I want her arrested and removed from this courtroom," the judge said. A bulky officer in a brown uniform made his way from a doorway behind the judge and toward Gillie. She stood up straight, and pulled her hands behind her back, folding them.

In a reasonable voice, she said, "Judge, I'm sorry but . . ."

"You may say, 'Yes, your honor,' and that is all you may say. After that if you utter one more word young lady, one more word, I will have you in handcuffs. One loud sigh and you will spend the night in a cell," he said.

She nodded. "Yes, your honor." Her voice was low and soft, contrite, but her hands were balled into fists, the middle finger of each extended straight down. Slowly she unclenched them, and using one to tuck her dark skirt under her, she sat back down in the pew.

# CHAPTER 67

"**W**ho is this?" *the judge said, as I made my way* to the front table and eased into the empty seat between Rattlesnake and a severe-looking young woman in a blue suit and white shirt whom I had never seen before. On the way, I passed Maggie Peterson, Mel Hirschman, and Dee Lane, looking strange and naked without his sunglasses. Sitting across the aisle was Gillie. She glared at me.

"This is my client, Judge Manczik," said Rattlesnake. He bent over and whispered a question to me. I answered him, and Rattlesnake stood and turned back to the judge. "Mr. Kiernan had a bicycling accident this morning. He's just come from Athens General and has documentation to prove it. His lateness does not in any way represent a deliberate act of discourtesy, Your Honor."

"I do not care if he got run over by my wife's Lexus, Mr. Sweeney. My calendar is backed up for weeks and you convinced my clerk to shoehorn this hearing in with the understanding that we would handle it expeditiously. Then your client is late and that young woman," he pointed at Gillie with his gavel, "wastes a quarter of an hour telling me how to do my job, and now your client staggers filthy, with a cast on his arm, and Betadine all over his face. So we have now wasted forty-five minutes with your little circus. Let's settle this, shall we?" The judge flipped through the papers in front of him. We sat quietly while he scanned the document.

There was a small man sitting at the other table in front of Gillie. Greenfell and Nelson were not in attendance. He watched the judge anxiously. After five minutes or so, the judge spoke. "Now despite your excellent and highly creative brief, counselor—kudos to Ms. Pettibone, I'm sure," he nodded to the severe-looking woman who sat at our table, "and despite the fact that I am sorely tempted to find for your client just out of judicial petulance, I am barred from doing so by the annoying constraint that you have no case. This is a legal contract entered into legally by both parties. Your client is in breach and the contract offers clear remedies in case of such a breach. The bank is well within its rights to foreclose and you have failed to demonstrate irreparable harm. Case dismissed." He pounded his gavel. "Five minutes," he said, standing and turning.

Gillie rose and stepped into the aisle toward my table. I saw huge dark circles under her eyes. Maggie stepped out of her aisle and stood in front of her, putting a tiny hand on Gillie's arm. Staring over the top of Maggie's head, Gillie spoke in a low voice, "You went too far this time, Top. I'm going to have the school bulldozed the second I take title and I hope you're there to watch."

"Gillie . . ." said Maggie.

Gillie looked down at Maggie and snarled, "Traitorous little bitch," and shoved her hard. Maggie flew backward into Pettibone, who grabbed her and kept her from falling. Dee Lane stepped between them and put a huge hand on Gillie's arm. She angrily shrugged it off, turned and spike-heeled her way from the room.

Rattlesnake turned and glared at me. In a low hiss, he said, "This judge is as senile as a goose and Petti's argument is so ingenuously complicated even I can't follow it. We might have won if you'd showed up on time looking like a respectable businessman instead of . . ." he paused, groping for words, "instead of a drunk who just got rolled in an alley."

"What did Gillie cause a fuss about?"

"Her prints were on a water bottle filled with red paint found near Nelson's house. Slocum picked her up for questioning. He might charge her."

"Careless of her," I said.

"What really happened to you?" Rattlesnake said.

"I've got the Sword of Michael," I whispered. From the corner of my eye, I saw Dee Lane slip on a pair of silver-framed sunglasses. Mel Hirschman stood, mumbled something, patted my shoulder, and left.

"You've got what?" Sweeney said.

"Who. I've got who. Benny's sitting in a parking garage with that abortion-clinic bomber taped up in the back of the truck."

Ratttlesnake looked around, grabbed me under the arm and said, "Come on, let's get somewhere we can talk."

He led me outside, and looked around for a moment before leading us through the open door of a small room. The woman named Pettibone, Maggie, and Dee Lane followed us into the room. Sweeney pushed the door closed. There was a wastebasket, two chairs, and a table in the room. A large red and white "No Smoking" sign was the sole decoration. I dropped heavily into one of the chairs. Rattlesnake sat on the edge of the table. The other three arranged themselves around the walls of the tiny conference room.

"Are you doped up?" Sweeney asked.

"Not yet. Just a warm beer from the toolbox," I said. I reached into my jeans pocket and pulled out a small brown drug vial. Vainly I tried to get the top of the childproof lock off one-handed, then with my teeth. Finally Rattlesnake reached over, took it from me, wiped it dry on his pants, and opened it. He spilled four out onto the table.

"Percocet?"

"Yes," I said.

"Great," he said, "So tell me again. Who's in the truck?"

"The abortion-clinic bomber. There's a million-dollar reward on his head."

"So this was your plan to raise the money?" he asked.

"No, I planned to borrow it from a guy who sells fried chicken. I ran into the bomber down in St. Illa last night," I said.

Rattlesnake looked dubious. "And now he's in the back of your truck being guarded by the notorious Benny the Blade, who the Atlanta PD still dreams about putting away even though he's been retired for years. Don't tell me any more about any of this unless it's absolutely necessary. Just promise me you are completely, one hundred percent positive it's him and that you haven't kidnapped some insurance salesman who just looks like the guy." He flipped open his pack of cigarettes, offered them around, and when no one accepted, lit one up. Pettibone used her foot to shove the wastebasket over to the table. Sweeney absentmindedly tapped nonexistent ash into the basket.

"Positive," I answered. Dee Lane grinned from ear to ear. Maggie looked slightly confused. Pettibone showed no emotion whatsoever.

"You may still need to borrow the money from your fried-chicken guy. You'll never get the million," Rattlesnake said.

"Why not?" I asked.

"Because this is the government. Instead of cash, you'll get red-tape, bullshit, and tax forms. They'll argue imminent apprehension. You'll be lucky to get fifty thousand six months from now," he said. Pettibone opened her case and laid a yellow pad and a plastic pencil on the table. Sweeney picked the pencil up with his empty hand and tapped the eraser against his teeth. "Unless we can get an auction going."

I said, "Do you know anything about auctions?"

"Of course, I know something about auctions," he lisped. "What do you think a plea bargain is?" I think I genuinely offended him. "Come on, let's go find a quiet place. How many cell phones you got,

Petti? Two? Good. I've got two, too, that should be enough. You," he pointed to Maggie, "are you sure you want to be in this?"

"I wouldn't miss it for the world," she chirped.

"All right, then, let's go," he hissed.

# CHAPTER 68

**W**e drove to the same empty lot where Bob John and I met just before the raid on the school. Benny was waiting for us when we arrived. We parked the other three cars in a circle around the truck, under the generous shade of an oak tree. Rattlesnake set up shop on the hood of his dove gray Mercedes. He borrowed a pad of small green Post-it self-stick notes from Pettibone. On the first he wrote "GBI Task Force." He peeled it off and stuck it onto the hood and placed a phone right above it. He repeated the process three more times, labeling the second phone "APD," the third "Homeland Security," and the final one "ATF."

"What about the FBI?" I asked.

"The FBI, DEA, and most of the Feds are all part of the Homeland Security thing. So is the ATF, officially, but they'll cut a side deal if they can," he answered.

"I don't want to seem stupid," Maggie said. "But why would these guys bid against each other. Aren't they all on the same side?"

"Ho, ho, ho," said Rattlesnake. Even Pettibone smiled. "That's not the way the world works. These guys are competitors. Whoever brings in Caldwell gets fame and riches. Fame in terms of getting prime-time shots on the networks and CNN. Riches means having their appropriation increased in next year's budget. For the agent responsible, we're talking at least one pay grade up, maybe two. And Caldwell is number one on the Top Ten list. I think one of these agencies will find a quarter of a million somewhere."

Rattlesnake looked at each of the four of us in turn. "I suggest I do the talking. Petti, would you get out your pad and something to write with? If you guys want to tell me anything, please write it down. You ready?" We nodded. "OK, then, let's have some fun."

He scrolled down on his PDA and found a number, which he then dialed on the first phone. "Mary, this is Jimmy Sweeney. Is Harold around? Well, could you find him? I think he's going to want to hear this. Sure, I'll hold." He grinned at each of us. "Harold, this is Jimmy. Let me tell you what I've got. The Sword of Michael is ready to surrender." He paused, "Today. But here's the deal: My client, the guy who's bringing him in, is scared shitless. He thinks his militia pals will kill him, and he's probably right." There was a pause, "Hell no, he doesn't want protection. He wants a big pile of money to scram with. Today."

Rattlesnake listened for a moment, then replied, "Well, that's fine, Harold, except he doesn't think if he hangs around, he'll be alive long enough to collect the million-dollar prize. So I'm calling you, Bob John Wynn at the Task Force, Leo over at ATF, and Greg at the APD. Whoever comes up with the most money wins the prize." He held the phone away from his ear and grimaced. "OK, Harold, forget it. I didn't mean to piss you off and I sure as hell don't want you to send me before the ethics committee. I want to do the right thing here, but my client's not in an advice-taking mood. I'm cutting you in on this because we go way back. If you're not interested, that's fine." Sweeney smiled like a pirate as he listened. "OK, then, you're in. Good. This is the real thing Harold. You're not going to regret this. Hey, I've got to call the others. Why don't you go see how much cash you can scrape together, and call me back on this line? Good, I'll be waiting. But not for long, my guy is really jumpy." Rattlesnake repeated the call three more times. He lit a cigarette and walked around in a tight circle in front of the Mercedes.

I said, "Now what?" Dee Lane cleaned his glasses on his shirttail and Benny stared off into the middle distance. Everyone else watched Sweeney expectantly.

"Now, we wait. How long depends on how hungry they are." The second phone rang. Rattlesnake picked it up and said, "Sweeney." He listened, then said, "I don't think that's going to be enough Greg. Why don't you call Harold over at the GBI and you guys pool your resources? The Feds are coming in big on this one. OK? Call me back." He put the phone down and held up two fingers. The ATF telephone rang. Sweeney answered, listened, and said, "OK, Leo, that might do it. Let me see what the others can do." He held up three fingers to us.

The second phone rang. "Sweeney." After a moment, he held up three fingers. "Greg, the ATF has opened with that. I'm not sure you guys are going to be in this one. I'm sorry, you know I hate to see those bastards get him, but I've got to do what's in the best interests of my client." He paused and listened. "We don't need immunity on this one, Greg, my client is as clean as a new white satin sheet. Call if you can do better." The auction lasted another thirty minutes and half dozen phone calls.

At the end there were two bidders left, the ATF and the Homeland Security Task Force. "I'm going to put you guys on speakerphone. Bob John, Leo, can you hear me?" We heard two tinny yesses.

"OK, here's where we're at. You've both bid three-hundred and seventy-five. We're ready to make the exchange within the half hour. Are you both sure you can come up with the cash? We're not handing him over until I've counted it and examined every single bill under a UV light." Leo and Bob John both answered affirmatively. "OK, then gentlemen, go raid your snitch funds, empty your wallets, and shake out the coffee can, because I'm going to listen to one more bid from

292

each of you." Rattlesnake leaned close to the phones and sang the theme from *Final Jeopardy*.

After a pause, Bob John said, "Three ninety."

Then from the other phone, a voice said, "Four-hundred and twelve."

"That's it?" said Rattlesnake.

"Yes," came the answer from both cell phones. I borrowed the pen from Pettibone and wrote a message on the yellow pad. I handed it to Rattlesnake. He looked at it and snickered. "OK, then gentlemen, the winner is Homeland Security." From one phone came a small cheer, and from the other a loud "What the hell!"

"Thank you very much, gentlemen. Bob John, please stay on the line so we can arrange the transfer," the lawyer said. Benny balled up his fist and bumped it against mine. Dee Lane hugged Maggie, the top of her head coming up to the center of his chest.

"Wait," protested the ATF man. "We had the highest bid. You can't do this!"

"I can do whatever my client instructs me to do as long as I do not break the law or violate the ethics of my profession. I can definitely screw you over."

"Jimmy, come on, what's going on here?"

"Leo, do you have an agent named Chinn who works for you?"

"You know we don't answer questions like that," he answered.

"Well, here's the thing, Leo. My client thinks you do. He is a very religious man and feels very strongly about sexual morality. You know me, I don't care if a client sleeps with underage mentally retarded transsexual Chihuahuas, but my client's real strict about these things. And he's heard that Agent Chinn has some sexual habits he doesn't care for."

"What in the hell are you talking about, Sweeney?"

"Leo, I don't know how to put this," Rattlesnake fought to keep from laughing. Benny, Dee Lane, and Maggie looked puzzled. "Leo, the word on the street is that Chinn is a sisterfucker." Even Benny wasn't fast enough to get his hand to his mouth in time to stifle the giggles, and one came out as wet snort. "So long," said Sweeney and hung up.

Rattlesnake turned to us. "Now, we need somebody else to help pull this off. Someone cool enough to deliver this dangerous son of a bitch when I give the OK. None of you guys, because I don't want them closing the loop and figuring out your involvement. Any ideas?"

"Absolutely," I said.

# CHAPTER 69

"**S**o the deal is I wait here with this smelly gentleman in my trunk until Mr. Sweeney calls me, and then I drive up to the front steps of the courthouse and surrender him to the officers there. I don't tell them anything about you guys, just that Mr. Sweeney asked me to do this. You'll give me ten thousand dollars for that?" Today Caron wore pink from the Jackie O-style pillbox hat on her head down to the polish on the nails peeking through her open-toed sandals. Her flirtatious tone fitted her study in pinkness.

"That's it," I said. "You meet Rattlesnake and Pettibone at the bank after you're done and they'll pay you."

Sweeney watched Caron and drooled. In a smooth, warm voice, he asked "Are you sure about this, Ms. Pope-Scott? This is a very dangerous man." He laid one proprietary hand on her forearm, and with the other motioned to Caldwell, who lay in the tiny trunk, its lid held partially closed with a Bungee cord.

"My oh my, Mr. Kiernan, what *ever* do you think I should do if Mr. Caldwell should work his way free from all that duct tape, claw his way through my steel trunk and climb into the car and ravish me?"

I slowed down my already slow drawl, "Why don't you just shoot him right between his little old eyes with your little old thirty-two, darling?"

"Well, that's a *fine* idea, kind sir," she said sweetly, lifting her large, plastic pink handbag and waving it at me. "Although today I brought my Smith & Wesson 1076, so it will be a big old ten-millimeter hole."

"If Sweeney keeps hitting on you, I'd shoot him, too," I said. Dee Lane laughed and Sweeney glared at me. He turned away from Caron and stepped over to me, once more all business.

"OK, Top, here's what's going to happen. Pettibone and I are going to pick up the money, count it . . ."

"Do you really have an UV light?"

"Of course not, but these guys could very well have some counterfeit money laying around and believe me, they're not above trying to pass it off on you. So I put them on notice," he said.

"Just asking," I said.

"As I said, we pick up the money. We're going to take three-hundred and forty-one thousand dollars to the bank. That's three ninety less ten percent for us and ten thousand for Caron. We will negotiate with Greenfell to stop the foreclosure proceedings. You'll probably need to sign a new loan agreement. Petti will call you and help you with that. She'll also be the one who handles any other suits you may wish to bring."

"From your brusque tone, I take it this is good-bye, then," I said.

"You've got your school back," he hissed, shrugging.

"Then you'll be heading back to the courthouse when you're done with the bank?" I asked. Maggie raised her eyebrows.

"Of course," said Rattlesnake. He patted Walter's ankle. "Look at the shape my new client is in. Under the law, bounty hunters are allowed considerable latitude, but the ones who captured Mr. Caldwell, and we'll probably never know who they are, used far too much force. The thugs may have caused him permanent injury. Look at those wounds on his head. They kept him confined for twelve hours with no water and no bathroom privileges. He reeks of urine. Accused terrorist or not, and no one has proven he is, this is America and we do not treat Americans like this," Sweeney said indignantly.

"You're something, Rattler," said Dee Lane.

He shrugged, "Hey, I got to get something out of this deal. A little Larry King can't hurt. Look at the press Mark Geragos is getting. I'm going to put his lucky ass on page two. Let's go, Petti."

# CHAPTER 70

*W*e waited until Caron drove off with Caldwell in the trunk of her Jag. After a brief story conference, Maggie headed back to the school to tell the staff the good news. Benny, Dee Lane, and I smiled at each other. A small black boy on a silver trick bike rode by slowly and eyed us suspiciously. I didn't blame him—three men standing beside a truck and a Ferrari in an empty lot.

Dee Lane looked at me, "I'm hoping this is all over now, and we can go out to the school, put our feet up and drink beer. Sierra Nevada, now that you're rich."

"You can go out to the school, put your feet up, and drink Pale Ale. I'll buy as much as you want and all the apple juice Mr. Culpepper can hold," I said.

"I can see this three-hundred thousand isn't going to last long," said Dee Lane.

"And where are you going?" asked Benny.

"To the klan convocation in Atlanta to steal back the flag," I said.

Dee Lane looked at Benny. "He says it just like it makes perfect sense for a Buddhist like me, a man with two busted knees and a broken arm like him, and an *African-American,* a very *dark-skinned* African-American like you, to walk into a convention center filled with fifty thousand armed white supremacist lunatics and steal a flag. I love the way he doesn't even change inflection. He says it in the same tone of voice he'd use to tell us he needs to stop by the store and pick up some milk for his morning Raisin Bran cereal."

Benny nodded philosophically. "He does have a logic structure all his own. It always seems to be very clear to him, but it often eludes the rest of us."

"Wait guys, I'm not asking for help. In fact, I don't want you guys involved in this," I protested.

"Please," said Dee Lane. "You're so banged up you can't put on a T-shirt without help. And anyway, as destructive as you can be even when under my close supervision, it genuinely scares me to imagine what havoc you might wreak in this situation without me to provide some balance."

'This is a smash and grab, Dee Lane. That's not your sort of thing," I said. "Thanks but no thanks."

He ignored me and looked at Benny. "You know, I think I might just have a plan that might let us do this without getting killed, that is if Benny still has some connections in his old hometown. We don't need much, just a uniform."

"What's the plan?" I asked.

"We can talk on the way. First, we need to head out to the school and get the fake flag. But as payment for my services, you do need to promise me one thing, Top."

"What?"

"Promise me this is it for a while. No more crazy trips to Atlanta or to Bumstead, Georgia. No more home invasions. No more kidnapping serial killers. No more Top-type stuff for at least a week. Instead we just drink some beer, play basketball, listen to Benny play music, chill out for a few days. Deal?" he asked.

I decided not to mention I left in less than a week to go on Morton's errand in Montevideo. "Deal," I said.

"I want in on this deal, too," Benny said.

# CHAPTER 71

*W*e parked our rented beige Taurus in the parking lot of the convention center. At the entrance, an African-American woman wearing an ill-fitting security uniform took Benny's ten-dollar bill and handed him a white ticket to place on the dashboard. She looked at him and at us, and raised a single eyebrow skyward, but said nothing. We drove across the lot and parked away from the rest of the cars, as close as we could to the exit. Judging from the fullness of the lot, it looked to me like the crowd would be closer to five thousand than fifty.

Dee Lane peeled off his windbreaker, revealing badge, white shirt, and tan pants with a maroon stripe down the seam, exactly the same uniform as the woman who'd taken our money at the gate. He climbed out of the car and leaned in Benny's window.

"OK, I've got my cell, and I'll leave it turned on so you can hear. I'm going to try to locate the flag. When I do, I will let you know where it is and what kind of security is involved."

"If you get into trouble, yell, and I'll come in after you," I said.

"I will not. This get-up is actually legit, right Benny?" Dee Lane said.

"Yes, the ArcLight Security company is run by Elbert's brother, ironically," Benny replied.

"So I'll call a cop," said Dee Lane. "If you go charging in there, Top, it could turn into a riot. I know it doesn't bother you, but I think we need to avoid violence when outnumbered fifty thousand to three."

"Violence does seem to find me a lot," I said.

"Violence has your number on speed dial, my friend," said Dee Lane. "OK, I'm gone." Benny and I watched him walk down the parking lane and disappear into the swelling crowd. I turned up the volume on the cell phone speaker. On the frontage road, an Atlanta PD cruiser rode by slowly. A cop wearing shades examined our car closely. Benny slumped in his seat. I climbed out of the car so the cop could get a good look at me, opened the rear door, and acted as if I was unloading something. Satisfied, the cruiser picked up speed and moved off.

I leaned against the side of the car and watched the lot fill with older American cars, shiny new SUVs and minivans. Many had "Heritage not Hate" bumper stickers stuck to the chrome bumpers or rear windows. The vehicles threw long shadows across the half-full lot.

We heard some sort of dull rumble and snatches from the cell phone. "What do you think is going on?" Benny asked.

I shrugged, "Security checkpoint?"

Dee Lane's voice came over the phone. It sounded far away. "I just put you through the X-ray machine, guys. If your ears turn red, swell up, and drop off, it's radiation poisoning. Now I'm headed for the backstage area. So far, lots of security—private, Atlanta PD, guys in white satin baseball caps. I haven't seen Elvis Costello or any of the guys you described to me, but I'll keep an eye out."

A gold Volvo drove carefully down the farthest lane just inside the fence. A large black Ford Navigator crept along behind it. The Volvo angled across the empty spaces toward us. I pointed them out to Benny with a nod, and eased the SIG from the glove box. "Is that the same Volvo you ran into in the bank parking lot?" he asked.

"The very same," I answered. The two cars pulled parallel, facing us. The cars passing on the frontage road now had their lights on. The doors of the Volvo opened and the twins, Lance and Vance got out. Vance wore a plastic neck brace. Alstott and two men in gray turtle-necks and gray pants climbed down from the SUV. I shrugged at Benny, "Speed dial."

We got out of the car. "I know I invited you, but I don't think it was such a good idea to bring this particular friend. What are you doing here?" Alstott asked.

"I've come to get the flag back," I said.

Alstott looked at me. "No."

"No? That's it? No?" I said.

"Why don't you leave now?" Alstott said.

"Go on, Uncle Marcus, let us take care of this," Vance said. "You're needed inside."

"Where's Billy?" I said. Vance pursed his lips. "I thought so," I continued. "He quit your little circus when I whapped him across the face with that antenna. You're a bunch of gutless wonders."

"Mr. Alstott," said one of the men in gray, "you don't need to be here for this."

"You're a horse's ass, Kiernan," said Alstott.

"512-555-6739. There's a club of people-who-think-Top's-a-horse's ass. Gillie Lynfield is the president. Why don't you give her a call and she can send you the membership packet, sign you up for the newsletter, teach you the handshake, you know."

"Is that supposed to be funny?" the older man said.

"Supposed to be, but I've got kind of a weird sense of humor, right Benny?'

"Mr. Alstott?" said the gray man.

"Call me when you're done," Alstott said to Lance and Vance, and turned back to the Navigator. One of the men in gray scrambled to open the door. He closed it behind Alstott and climbed into the passenger seat. The SUV turned and pulled away.

"Well, here we are," said Vance. "Just us."

"Here we are," I agreed. Behind me, from the phone, I heard Dee Lane's voice, and someone else's. It sounded hollow, as if he was in a large room.

"We're going to teach you a little lesson now," Vance said. He reached into his waistband in the small of his back and pulled out his large Bowie knife. A fraction of a second later, Lance pulled out an identical blade. They glinted dully in the twilight of the early evening.

"Go sit down, Top," Benny said quietly. "I'll handle this." I turned and walked back to the hood and sat down. The stream of cars into the lot had slowed, and we were still isolated from the main body of vehicles.

"You stay right here, Kiernan," said Vance. "What do you think you're doing?"

"I think I'm sitting down, like Mr. Culpepper told me to. But the better question is what do you think you're doing, challenging Benny the Blade to a knife fight?"

"I don't feel we are disadvantaged here," laughed Lance.

"Two hamsters in a blender. I'm about to do you a favor. Here it is. Turn around and run as fast as you can." Behind me on the cell phone I heard Dee Lane having a conversation with someone. He laughed. Benny smiled and made a little move and there was the dull glint of a razor in the hand I could see. It was his black "everyday" razor, and I assumed his gaudy Huddie Ledbetter "business" razor was in his other hand.

"He's got a straight razor, Vance," Lance said. He stepped sideways, increasing the angle between him, his brother and Benny. He lowered the blade and stepped closer.

"You'd asked me about how to use a razor, Top. I think you'll find this instructive. These men have used their knives before. You see that underhanded grip? Don't you believe what you see in the movies, the underhand grip offers maximum flexibility and striking speed. It's what the better edgemen use," Benny said. "But their footwork isn't very good." Lance lunged at Benny. He stepped slightly to the side, and his hand moved. Lance stumbled back. As he stood, a thin red line appeared on his forehead and little drops of blood popped out across it. He looked surprised. The blood welled into a sheet and streaked down his face.

From the other side, Vance slashed at Benny. He gave a small flinch and a large slice of Vance's cheek peeled away like an avalanche. Blood spurted from the open red hole above the flap of skin and fat.

"What are their names? Lance and Vance?" Benny said dreamily, slowly walking toward Vance, one foot carefully in front of the other, "Lance and Vance. Stop jabbing with your arms so much. It's footwork, like dancing. Sure, hand speed is important, but with a blade you need to be close." Vance poked at Benny, who turned slightly to let the blade go by and drew another red line from the edge of Vance's scalp to his chin. "Especially with a razor because you have no point. That limits your choice of moves. Closeness gives you the cut, and if you position it right, deprives your opponent of an angle."

I saw the other brother tuck his blade under his arm and wipe his palms, then regrip the knife. Lance spun it into a reverse grip and raised it over his head. He gave a Tarzan yell and charged Benny, who stepped sideways and as Lance passed, lifted his razor to the blond man's arm. The knife clattered onto the tarmac and Lance grabbed his wrist. Blood pumped from between his fingers.

I sat on the hood of the car and watched. Despite myself I felt sympathy for the brothers, the same impotent sympathy you feel for the doomed wildebeest calf on the Nature Channel. Benny spoke in a voice that sounded like warm ice, "I'm not going to kill you. But I will disfigure you, cut enough tendons that you'll never dress or feed yourself again, maybe even castrate you. Every time you come at me, I'm going to hurt you. Anytime you want to stop, you just drop your knife and walk away, and I'll let you go."

"To hell with you," said Vance, lunging again. Benny stepped sideways, tapped the knife away with his hip, and used both hands to draw an X across Vance's face.

"OK, then, let's keep going. I have nowhere I have to be," Benny smiled. A chill ran down my spine and I attributed it to the cool night air.

"Vance," gasped Lance from the kneeling position where he held his bloody wrist. "Vance, get me to the hospital. Please."

"But . . ."

"Vance, come on, please," he said. Vance used his forearm to wipe the blood away from his eyes. "Vance," pleaded Lance. Vance looked at Benny once more, then edged over and tugged Lance to his feet.

"The knife," said Benny. Vance looked back at him, then pulled his arm back and threw the knife over the fence behind us. I heard it land in the bushes. Vance helped Lance into the car, staggered around to the other side and joined his brother. He used something from the seat to mop the blood from his eyes so he could see well enough to drive. He held it to his forehead as they drove away.

Benny carefully set the razors on the ground, and using two fingers, tugged a white handkerchief from his pocket. Except for Lance's and Vance's blood on his hands, I could see no wounds and not a speck of blood on him. He wiped his hands carefully, then began cleaning the razors.

"I see why you quit," I said. "That's very intense."

Benny stood and walked over to me. He thrust out his arm and said, "No, this is why I quit." I looked at the arm. "Take my pulse," he said.

After a minute, I said, "Forty-two."

"That's why I quit," he said, and returned to his razors.

# CHAPTER 72

*T*he phone crackled and Dee Lane's hollow bass voice said, "Top?" I held the set up to my ear and thumbed down the volume, "Everything OK?"

"Better than OK. Everything is fantastic. Absolutely *fan-tas-tic*," Dee Lane rumbled. His voice dropped to a loud whisper, "I found it, man, I found the Bloody Red Rag."

"Where?"

"We have to move fast. Come on. Bring the fake."

Benny stood and raised one eyebrow in a question. I gave him a thumbs-up. He returned the gesture, then used that hand to fold the black razor, which he then slipped into his right rear pocket. He knelt again and began cleaning the other razor, the one with the pearl handle and the rhinestones, the one he claimed had once belonged to Huddie Ledbetter. I moved to the backseat of the car, pulled out the backpack and slung it over my shoulder. I gave Benny a small salute and headed through the lot toward the convention center.

"I'm on my way," I said.

"I can see you. I'm standing at this big window that looks out over the lot," he answered. I looked up and saw him, a two-inch-high figure, waving an arm. Dee Lane continued, "Here's what's happening. You guessed right. The reverend is going to present the flag to Marcus Alstott and Alstott is going to designate McShane as the honorary assistant grand dragon in-waiting or something. Or maybe McShane gets designated first and then he gives Alstott the flag. Anyway, it's scheduled for seven-thirty exactly, and this thing is running like a Swiss train, so I'd say we have . . ." He paused, then said, "Twenty-six minutes."

"So where's the flag?"

"Inside an aluminum case in a green room behind the stage. There are two thick bullet-stopper types dressed in gray outside the door. McShane's baby brother Brett is inside babysitting the flag. I talked to him a little and he seems to be a nice kid, a little lost now that his father's . . ."

For a microsecond, I thought about that "nice kid" shooting at me back in St. Illa. "Dee Lane, hold it a minute, could you?" I approached the glass doors. Just inside was what looked like the security station at an airport, two metal detectors, two X-ray machines, a half dozen security guards, and two Atlanta PD officers wearing Kevlar vests and helmets with plastic visors. Pushing open the doors, I joined the short line of latecomers.

"Left at the top of the escalator," Dee Lane said.

"I've got metal in my knee braces, it's going to set off the machine," I told the guard.

"Wouldn't make no difference, we have to wand you and use the sniffer anyway because of that cast," he answered, motioning me over to a rubber mat. I stood on the two footprints stenciled on the black rubber and extended my arms while he waved the wand over me. "Could you roll up your pants please so I could see the knee braces?" he asked and I did. After he finished, while I rolled my pant legs down, one of the guards at the X-ray machine picked up the backpack and brought it over. "Don't want to forget this," she said, and set it down beside a plastic and metal chair. I thanked her while I unbuckled my belt and turned it inside out so the first guard could inspect it.

"That it?" I said.

"No, sir, we need to scope your cast," he said. I peeked at my watch, twelve minutes. He swabbed the edge of the cast with a small cotton patch and handed it to the guard at the sniffer machine. That guard took the sample, and handed my guard a long white plastic tube, which he slipped inside the cast. He hit a thumb switch and a glow came through the plaster. The guard saw my expression and explained, "It's new. It lets the fellow at that machine see what's inside there." I didn't want to think too carefully about where else that tube might have been.

"Could you move it around a little?" I asked. "These things itch like crazy." The guard smiled.

"Up the escalator and to the right," he said when he'd finished with me. "Thank you," I said, and rode the escalator to the top, walked five or so steps forward and turned left, moving briskly along a large open concourse. Ahead I saw Dee Lane standing beside the glass. He motioned me to "hurry up" with his hand.

"Where are they holding the flag?" I asked as I walked up.

"It's down there," he motioned behind him where the corridor disappeared around a bend.

"OK, here's the plan," I said. "I'll cause a distraction and draw off the guards. Your description of the guys at the doors sounds like Alstott's bodyguards. If it is, I think there's a good chance they'll recognize me and come after me. When they do, you do the swap and get out of here. I'll keep them busy," I said. I handed him the backpack.

Dee Lane looked at me incredulously. "Don't you ever have any plans that don't involve Blue Cross/Blue Shield? What happens when they catch you?"

"I don't know. Something."

Dee Lane looked at me without speaking. "So, you got anything better?" I asked. The helmeted head of one of the APD from the security checkpoint appeared at the top of the escalator. He looked both ways then did a double take as he saw me talking to Dee Lane. Stepping off the escalator, he turned and stood straddle-legged, watching us.

Dee Lane raised his arm and said to me loudly, "No, sir. It's that way." Under his voice he whispered, "Leave the backpack and go. Keep the phone on." He shoved me in the back with one hand. "Go."

The policeman reached one hand up to the radio that was fastened with Velcro to the strap of his vest and held it close to his mouth. I walked toward him. He released the radio and watched me approach. The reflective lenses of his glasses followed me as I walked by toward the front of the convention center. There was a long row of doors to my left. The center set was open, and I heard an amplified voice followed by applause. Behind me, I felt the policeman staring at my back. I attached a microphone and earpiece to the telephone, cranked the volume up, dropped it into my shirt pocket, and entered the cavernous auditorium.

In my ear, I heard Dee Lane say, "Hi, fellows. I need to finish up in there. Thanks."

Alstott stood on a large brightly lit stage. Two small Plexiglass shields on long thin stands stood between him and the audience. The shields appeared clear, but I knew his speech was being scrolled onto them from a teleprompter. Projected onto the wall behind him were photographs of families, U.S. flags, eagles, farms, workers, and in the center, a photo of a massive burning cross with the Klan logo beside it. The floor of the darkened auditorium was full. Another few thousand were clumped across the first thirty or forty rows of seats.

I stepped sideways and leaned back against the wall. Alstott said something about return to decency. There was thunderous applause, and a smattering of people jumped to their feet and cheered. A cameraman on the edge of the stage dashed out and knelt, aiming his shoulder cam at Alstott. His gopher fed wire out to him.

In my ear, I heard Dee Lane say, "I'm back. Forgot to do the goddam cans. I don't get them and I'll get chewed out when this is over." I heard a voice answer him, but couldn't make out any words. "Sorry, Brett," said Dee Lane, "I didn't mean to swear. It just came out."

I checked my watch. "Six minutes," I whispered into the phone mike. I heard a grunt.

On the stage, Alstott said something about the values from a better time. The montage behind him was replaced with a live camera feed. His giant face beamed out over the crowd. There was another round of thunderous applause, and this time I noticed that some of it came from over my head. I looked up and saw a huge set of speakers hanging in the rafters. Leaving nothing to chance, they were piping sound in. The policeman who'd watched me come in didn't even look in my direction, just walked down the steps halfway and settled into an empty seat.

"So you're going to get to go on the stage, man? I never done nothing like that. I'm afraid I'd piss myself. Hey, Brett, what happens if you do need to go, man, and you just turn around and go back or what?" There was a pause, and then Dee Lane said, "I don't know, Brett, I got this list of stuff I have to do. I mean I don't mind watching the case while you pee and all, but . . ." There was another pause, then Dee Lane said, "OK, I'll stand here until you get back. But hurry, OK?" I heard a door close, and Dee Lane mumbled, "I hope you're taking notes, Kiernan."

"Three minutes," I answered. "Do you have to pick it?" There was no answer. Onstage, a huge portrait of Stonewall Jackson flashed up on the screen. Alstott turned and pointed to the portrait, and said something about courage and nobility. Everyone on the floor stood and clapped. The sound rose. "Dee Lane?" I asked. There was no answer. "Two minutes," I said. The policeman below me stood, cupped his hands around his mouth and yelled out, "Yee hiiiii."

A huge Confederate flag appeared on the screen behind Alstott. The Reverend Matt McShane walked onstage, one minute early. Behind him walked Brett, a gleaming Halliburton case in his left hand. Alstott turned and applauded. On the side of the stage another man faced the audience and waved everyone up, but he didn't need to, they were already on their feet. Alstott shook McShane's hand and ushered him to the microphone. The spotlights illuminating the stage were joined by strobes and rotating red and blue flashing lights. The noise level rose. People climbed onto their seats and stomped. On the floor, near the stage one man wearing red war paint and a green kilt beat a large drum. McShane leaned into the microphone. He appeared to be speaking, but I couldn't make anything out over the din.

"Dee Lane?" I shouted into the mike.

"What?" he shouted back. I turned to find him standing beside me, grinning like a wolf. He waved the black backpack at me. "I hate to drag you away from the show, but this would be a real good time for us to get the hell out of Dodge," he yelled. I grinned back, and shouldered the backpack. As we walked out, over my shoulder I heard a rising, rhythmic chant, "Heritage, not hate. Heritage, not hate."

# CHAPTER 73

*O**n the ride home, Benny was even quieter than* usual. While I drove, Dee Lane peeled off the white uniform shirt and pulled on a black T-shirt and his black leather jacket. In the worst falsetto ever attempted by a natural bass, he sang along to the radio, "I'll be there." I looked the other way while he shucked off the uniform pants and wiggled into his black jeans. In the mirror, I could see Benny staring quietly out of the window.

It took us two hours to negotiate traffic and get back to Athens. When we arrived, we stopped in Sluts and Mullets in the Normaltown neighborhood and bought a round in celebration—a Bushmill's for me, a Sierra Nevada for Dee Lane, and a glass of club soda for Benny the Blade. Dee Lane called out greetings across the room. Someone sent us a round, and Dee Lane raised his glass in thanks to a table of Latinos wearing dirty coveralls. A heavy-set man with a ponytail solemnly raised his glass in acknowledgment.

Benny and I left Dee Lane sitting at the bar, listening to the bartender shakily explain how yesterday he'd blown his big audition for an upcoming play being staged by the theater department at the university. I slapped Dee Lane on his leather-clad shoulder and said

"Good night." He waved a farewell without taking his sympathetic eyes off the distraught bartender.

We arrived home just after eleven, shot baskets for another hour, and then went to bed. As I lay in the dark, looking up at the moonlit banners in the ceiling, I thought to check my messages. There was only one, from Amanda, saying we need to talk. Despite the lateness, I called her back. I got her machine, which when I thought about it was fine, since I didn't feel like talking. I did like hearing her voice, though, and the recorded "Hi, this is Amanda, leave a message" sufficed.

I suppose that's why when the telephone rang five hours later, I answered it with, "Amanda?" I thought I'd only been asleep a few minutes and she was calling me back. Instead I heard Gillie's harsh laugh.

"Not Amanda," she said.

"Gillie," I answered.

"Yes, it's Gillie," she said. There was an uncharacteristic slur in her voice. I waited for her to say something. "You got me good with the water bottle. I should know better than to get tricky with Top Kiernan and his band of Merry Men. You got me real good with that one."

"Gillie, have you been drinking?"

"Two glasses of wine. But I haven't been sleeping much either, so I probably sound like hell," she answered. I didn't answer.

"George left me. Took the kids and moved into the basement of his sister's house. He says he wants a divorce."

"I'm sorry to hear that, Gillie," I said.

"You shouldn't have let me seduce you. That's what got me started screwing around on good old George. Now I've got nothing. That makes it your fault, you know."

I lay there silently. I heard a loud slurp and she spoke again. "You're not going to discuss that, are you? Let's change the subject. How's business, Top?" she laughed. "Although you probably don't know, do you? Well, let me tell you how Polymath's business is. It's just great thank you very much. Maggie's taken a dozen customers from me. She's a real firecracker, boy. I should have offered her more so she would have come with me. Four of the researchers I stole from you quit me today, starting back at Polymath on Monday."

"Really just two glasses of wine?"

"Two big glasses," she slurred.

"How much trouble are you in with Slocum?"

"None. Jeff Nelson told him he wouldn't press charges, so they dropped it. But Jeff won't take my calls. His wife left him, too, and he blames me. I blame you. Who do you blame, Top?"

"It will sort itself out, Gillie," I said.

"Who cares? I really screwed up, Top, I really did."

"You have to move on, Gillie," I answered.

There was a long silence, followed by the clink of a glass against the mouthpiece and a slurping sound. "Hey, Top, if AWS doesn't make it, any chance I can come back? Get a fresh start? You have to admit I was good at the job, right?"

I thought for a moment. I'd loved Gillie, some, and she'd loved me, some, and there was always the unspoken "if" between us. If George. If this, if that. Then I remembered Harlan Q. Winslow, the obnoxious researcher who wouldn't have ended up floating in the river with cigarette burns all over his body if Gillie hadn't stolen money that belonged to Raoul Menes. "No way, Gillie." She started crying and I hung up. I lay awake for a long time after the phone hit the cradle.

# CHAPTER 74

*I* *took the flag back to Pope-Scott the next day. Just* like the first time I'd met him, I parked in the lot behind the antebellum mansion, crunched my way around to the front door. Caron gave me a hug and a kiss on the cheek, then carefully searched me. She was cheerful and chatty, but didn't mention the errand with Walter. I didn't either. Today Caron was dressed in lilac. She led me back to Pope-Scott's office.

"Morning, Top," he said, looking up from the floor where he was packing a box of books. He wore a comfortable-looking work shirt and loose-fitting blue jeans in which he looked ill-at-ease and uncomfortable. He stood, dusted nonexistent dust from his knees and moved to shake my hand. "We're starting to get ready for the move."

"Are you well enough to be doing that?" I asked.

"I can work for an hour or so, then I have to rest forever," he said, motioning to the two chairs we'd sat in the first day. "Here, sit down. Give me an excuse to stop. Can I get you something to drink?" I asked for coffee and before he could relay the request, Caron called "fine" from the other room. He smiled and opened his hands.

"I saw on TV where some church gave the flag to the Knights of the South. I guess you're here to tell me it's time to call in the lawyers," he said. Before I could answer, he held up a hand to stop me, "Don't apologize Top. I can see how banged up you are. I can only guess, knowing the crowd Styrell runs with, how you got that way. Now, I want you to keep the ten thousand. You earned it."

"Here's the real flag," I said, lifting a backpack onto the corner of the desk. "The church gave the Knights the fake you examined day before yesterday."

He looked dumbfounded. "But the news said——"

"Why don't you just examine the flag, Professor?" Caron came in, put down the tray, smiled and left, never looking at the backpack, although since she'd searched me outside, she already knew what was inside. With trembling hands, he took out the flag from the bag and unfolded it onto his lap.

"Would you get me the magnifying glass from the desk drawer, Top? Do you mind?" he asked.

I rose and retrieved the large round glass and handed it to him, then sat and drank coffee for fifteen minutes while he scrutinized the flag through the glass. He looked up, "I suppose I need to write you a rather large check."

"Ten thousand, the rest of what we agreed on," I said, refilling my cup. There were four Oreo cookies on a small plate on the tray. I took one and popped it into my mouth. It jutted against my cheek.

"But what about the money Caron received from Styrell?" he protested.

"If you want to, write a check to Our Redeemer's Church of the Chosen in St. Illa, but understand that they'll use it to buy C-4 to blow up abortion clinics. If I was you, I'd just add the money you got from Styrell to the down payment on the new house. What will an extra hundred thousand buy you in California real estate, a shingle?" I smiled.

But he wasn't looking at me, he was gazing out the window. I watched as the eye nearest me, then the other, teared up and overflowed.

Two wet lines ran down his face and dripped from his chin, forming wet spots on the blue of the shirt. He motioned toward the doorway, and I rose and closed it. "Thank you," he said in a husky, choked voice.

"You OK?" I asked.

"I don't know. To be honest, I didn't think you'd get it back. I didn't expect to really have to sell it." He turned and stared at me. "I'm struggling here."

"I think it's the right thing," I said.

"So why do I feel like I'm running away, Top, just quitting and running away?"

"You are quitting and running away. What's your point?" I answered.

"What do you mean?"

"You've got yourself in a bad situation and you're running away. So what?"

"Part of being a man is facing your problems, not running from them," he said.

"The way I see it is none of us run away often enough. The whole world would be better off just moving on," I said.

"Do you think that holds for you? Should you move on?"

"Especially for me," I said.

"And will you?"

"Will I what? Move on? No, probably not. But then you don't want to be me," I said. "Some days I don't want to be me."

He nodded carefully, then spoke, "Caron's pregnant. Did I tell you that? No, I couldn't, we just found out yesterday."

"Congratulations."

"I'm scared. I know how to be the iconoclastic historian and I even know how to be the literary l'enfant terrible. But I'm not sure I know how to be an untenured instructor at a mediocre school. I know I don't know how to be a father."

"You will be whatever it is you resolve to be," I quoted.

"Did Stonewall Jackson really say that like the books say, or are you going to tell me it was Lord Chesterfield or Ben Franklin?" Jay asked. I smiled and shrugged.

## CHAPTER 75

The parking lot in front of the school was full when I returned. Amanda's car sat in the drive and I pulled the truck up beside it. I found her in my office winding a string around my blue spinner. "You been waiting long?" I asked, leaning over and giving her a kiss.

"Not really." She wore a man's T-shirt over loose-fitting drawstring pants. I bent down and kissed her again, longer this time. "Mmmm, that's nice," she said.

"I'm beat," I said, and eased myself onto the corner of the desk. She handed me the blue top, and I rewound it quickly and tossed it across the room. It landed in a clear space on the floor, bounced twice, and settled into a perfect spin.

"You're beat up," she said. "Is all this stuff done now? You've got the school back. You found Jay's flag. I suppose Gillie's going to keep calling you in the middle of the night."

"I don't think so," I said.

"I do," she answered.

"You said you wanted to talk?"

"I do," she said.

"Do you need something to drink?" I asked. The top was starting to wobble.

"Sure, what do you say we get a bottle of water and head down to the auditorium. We can talk there," she said.

"Why there?"

"Because that's where I fell in love with you, when you stood on that stage in your underwear showing me those terrible scars on your knees."

"It's never, ever good when you get a message that says someone wants to talk. Do you want to tell me what we're talking about?" I asked.

"Nope," she said, shaking her head from side to side in that little girl way of hers. I went down to the kitchen to get a bottle of water. On the way, I looked in Classroom 1. It was empty and I wondered where everyone was. I came back to find her standing at the corner waiting on me.

Amanda and I walked slowly down the hall toward the auditorium. "I think Benny told me he was going to lock it up. We may be out of luck," I said.

"Maybe," she said. But when we got there, the lock and chain were gone from the double doors, although the canvas still hung inside, blocking the windows. I pulled opened the doors, and parted the canvas. Amanda stepped inside, and I joined her.

I couldn't take it all in. Part of me saw the staff, the Driggers family, Benny, Dee Lane, and Bob John. Part of me noticed the tall, thin young man with the long, long hair and translucent vegetarian skin. Part of me saw Amanda's beaming face, tongue stuck between her teeth as she pulled my hand, dragging me deeper into the room. But for the most part, I could only see the mural—as it must have looked the day it was painted seventy years ago, with living, vibrant colors.

"Who?" I stuttered.

"Painted it?" asked Amanda. "The skinny guy. His name is Elihu

Goode, grandson of the woman who painted it originally. A team from his commune actually, but he led the work. Some of the background's not quite finished yet."

"No, who?" I asked.

"Whose idea? Mine. But Dee Lane, Bob John, and Morton chipped in to pay for it." She tugged me by the hand down the center aisle. Someone started clapping. It sounded like it was coming through cotton. More applause came. She led me to the steps of the stage. I sat down heavily, not taking my eyes off the mural. In the background, Benny softly played his Buzz Funk song.

I heard Bob John say, "I think he likes it, Elihu." I couldn't take my eyes off the wall long enough to acknowledge the artist.

Amanda leaned over and softly whispered in my ear, "And we still need to talk."

# ACKNOWLEDGMENTS
# AND DISCLAIMERS

*I* *vaguely recall a story from Hotchner's biography of* Hemingway. Late in Hemingway's career he sends a fifty-five thousand-word article to one of the big magazines. They send back a letter saying it is wonderful, but they only contracted for thirty-three thousand words and don't have space for a piece of that size. After three months of work, Hemingway returns a fifty-four thousand, nine-hundred and ninety-seven-word article with a note that says, "Have cut it to the bone. Will not stand another word removed." I greatly envy his absolute confidence in every word. Unfortunately, I don't have it. Yet. So I rely on a small network of friends, editors, and my agent to slog through early drafts and help me understand what is good and what needs work.

Therefore, great thanks to Phil Grant, Christopher Ainsley, Liz Upsall, Mike Hill, and Rachel Hill for reading early drafts and offering useful guidance. Thanks to Nanscy Neiman-Legette and Otto Penzler for their careful editing. Retired judges Pete and Joan Marrosso and appeal lawyer Kristen Brown reviewed the book to make sure there were no glaring misstatements about the legal process. Dr. Abby Adams of Northwestern Hospital did a similar chore on the medical side. Norm Plaistowe corrected numerous Ferrari details and provided useful comments overall.

I did a fair bit of research for this book. Thanks to Phil Weiss, one of the world's leading experts on Civil War collectibles, for helping me understand the antique flag market. I also found useful discussions on www.confederateflags.org and in an article by David Sansing in Mississippi History Now, available online at www.mshistory.k12.ms.us. I learned the basics of abortion clinic bombing from www.religioustolerance.org, and on tops at John Sandstrum's Web site, www.sandstrum.com. (Curiously enough, John is a librarian who collects tops, but he assures me the resemblance between him and Top ends there.)

Among the books I mined for quotes are: *The Oxford Dictionary of Quotations,* edited by Elizabeth Knowles (Oxford, 1999); *The Great Quotations,* compiled by George Seldes (Pocket, 1971); *Respectfully Quoted,* edited by Suzy Platt (Library of Congress, 1989); *Noteworthy Quotes,* edited by Joel Kurtzman (Strategy & Business, 1998); *The 2548 Best Things Anybody Ever Said,* Robert Byrne (Galahad, 1996); and *Stonewall Jackson's Book of Maxims,* edited by James I. Robertson, Jr. (Cumberland House, 2002) In an amazon.com review of the Robertson book, an anonymous reviewer pointed out that Stonewall often borrowed quotes from Ben Franklin. I thought this was interesting enough that I worked it into the plot, and wished I could give him or her credit.

Finally, as always, thanks to the folks who provided encouragement along the way, including my friends who critiqued my drafts, my agent Philip Spitzer, Otto and Nanscy, Wendie Carr at Carroll & Graf, Steve Silver, Joyce Knauff, and bookstore folks like Judy Duhl, Mystery Mike, Sheldon McArthur, Moni Draper, and Richard Katz. This is, by necessity, only a small subset of the many others who have encouraged me to keep at it and I appreciate all of you.

Thanks to my neighbor Jim Sweeney for loaning me his name. For the record, he is nothing like Rattlesnake. Even though I think it should be obvious, all of the events, places, bars, motels, people, phone numbers, Web sites, and anything else of that sort in this book are fiction and bear no resemblance to real people, places, and businesses.